The Dragon Variation

ANTHONY GLYN

 Simon and Schuster • New York

The sonnet by Edna St. Vincent Millay on pages 270 and 271 is Sonnet XLII from "Fatal Interview," *Collected Poems,* Harper & Row. Copyright © 1931, 1958 by Edna St. Vincent Millay and Norma Millay Ellis. By permission of Norma Millay Ellis.

The lines on page 280 are from "Unchained Melody" by Alex North and Hy Zaret. Copyright © 1955 Frank Music Corp. Used by permission.

Contents

Author's Note

This book, despite the title, is a novel and not a treatise on chess, of which there are thousands available on all aspects of the game. However, I have tried to get the details right, and I would like to thank International Master Harry Golombek, o.b.e. (Chess Correspondent of *The Times*), Mrs. William Gresser (U.S. Ladies' Chess Champion), Lieutenant-Colonel E. B. Edmondson (Executive Director, U.S. Chess Federation) and Mrs. Richard Shaw (who doesn't even know the moves) for reading the book in typescript and making helpful technical suggestions. This, of course, does not make them responsible for anything I have written.

The games quoted have (except in one case) all been taken or adapted from recently published games, and experts may amuse themselves by trying to identify the real players and the occasions where the games were played. I have also introduced many living players under their own names. But the principal characters are not intended to be portraits of any living persons and, unlike their games, they have been wholly invented by myself.

ISFAHAN

The midday sun poured down on to the Maidan-Shah, the Royal Square of Isfahan. Round the square were biscuit-coloured walls, the little dark shops that sold souvenirs and fly-blown sweets. Inside the square were pools and fountains and roses. Opposite were the slender pillars of the Ali-Qapu pavilion; behind was the cream dome of the Lutfullah Mosque; to the right was the entrance of the Souk; to the left the great blue dome of the Shah Mosque. It was the most romantic place on earth.

Moraine Oppenheimer took a deep breath. She took off her sunglasses, sucked the end, screwed up her eyes against the glare, and let the air out in another sigh.

Mrs. Oppenheimer said, "Oh, the sun shines bright on Mrs. Oppenheimer. And on her daughter. They wash their feet in soda water. Canada Dry Club Soda." She glanced up at her tall willowy daughter. "Poem, dear. By Edna St. Vincent Millay."

Moraine flew up in arms. "I'm sure Edna never wrote that."

"But it's a famous poem."

"Well, all I know, Mommy, is that Edna never wrote that. I've read every poem she ever wrote and she never wrote anything about Canada Dry. It must have been some other poet," she added. She looked down at her small blue-haired mother. "Yes, that's it," she said kindly, "I guess it was some other poet."

"Is there any other poet?"

Moraine worked this out for a few seconds. The tone of voice gave her a clue; she was being teased. Yes, that must be it. Why must Mommy keep on teasing her, even here, among the domes and the roses and the nightingales? And why could she never spot it in time? She sighed and straightened up, looked round her, riveted her mind on romance and beauty.

"Can't you just feel it round your toes? Ice-cold. Bubbling. Tickling slightly."

"Feel what?"

"Canada Dry Club Soda. What we're talking about."

Moraine pointed with her glasses at the pavilion. "That's where the Shah sat and watched the polo. Then he'd present the cup to the winners and off they'd all go and have marvellous nights of revelry on the bridges of Isfahan. I wish I could've been there!"

"Why didn't he play himself? Was he too fat? Was he the one we saw the picture of, with the great beer belly?"

"It couldn't have been beer, Mommy, he was a Moslem."

"Well, candy then. Why didn't he get on a pony and play too? I read in a magazine that Prince Philip plays polo four days a week, and he's quite slim."

Moraine put on her glasses again and turned away. She looked at the blue portico of the Shah Mosque, reflected in the pool.

"Mommy, just look at the way it angles back. I mean, the main entrance faces square on to the square, and then the mosque goes back at an angle so as you're facing east towards Mecca."

"I'd have thought Mecca was west from here."

"Just look at those blues together." The cobalt sky, the turquoise dome, the ultramarine portico. Moraine took her glasses off again. "If only Walt were here, he could take a marvellous colour movie of that."

"Except that it doesn't move."

Moraine suddenly looked at her small gold Omega wristwatch.

"Help! I'd forgotten the call to prayer. I just can't miss that. Here, of all places. I just wish I knew what time they do it."

"An hour before sunrise, the man said."

"No, I'm sure they do it again about now."

She went across to a boy who was standing by the pool, watching her. "Excuse me, but do you speak English?"

Instantly about thirty children sprung from nowhere crowded round her. "Hello miss, hello miss, hello miss, hello miss."

"Excuse me, but does anyone know when they do the call to prayer here?"

"Hello miss, hello miss, hello, hello miss."

She said very slowly, "What time the man on the tower, I mean the minaret, the priest I mean, I forget what you call him."

"Hello miss, hello miss." The boy, the original watching boy, said something incomprehensible.

"What? I mean, please say that again."

The boy said it again, slowly and clearly. "Church-chill."

"Oh no, not him."

"Hello miss, hello miss."

Moraine came back to her mother. "It's no use, they don't really speak English." She looked round her. "Look at that woman in the black veil. Isn't she fantastic! I wonder if she speaks any English."

"I doubt it."

The woman held her black veil between her teeth, showing her nose and her upper lip as well as her eyes. She knelt by the edge of the road, washing clothes in the meagre unattractive drain. Her veil flopped messily in the drain too. It was a picturesque though impractical way of laundering. Moraine moved towards her.

An old man came by on his hands and knees. He wore his shoes on his hands, as he had no feet. He was romantic too. He paused on his long arduous journey and spat heavily into the drain just upstream of the laundress. She went on washing unconcernedly.

Moraine turned on her heel and came back to her mother.

Mrs. Oppenheimer said, "As you don't seem to be communicating very successfully, I suggest we move into the shade. This sun is hotter than Dallas."

They crossed the empty road to the Lutfullah Mosque, and turned right into the arcade which ran behind the shops. It was a gloomy tunnel, lit fitfully by skylights. It echoed to the sound of hammering, silversmiths, tinsmiths, carpenters, all banging away. Moraine gasped with excitement.

A hot desert wind blew along the tunnel like a train, stinging their faces with sand. They turned away, eyes screwed up, coughing, hands over their faces, but the hammering never stopped for a moment. Then, suddenly, the wind died and the sand settled.

"How romantic!" murmured Mrs. Oppenheimer. "A hot wind from Samarkand."

"Samarkand!"

They turned right, back into the square, passing a small souvenir shop. A young man was painting a miniature scene on a small bone plaque. A pot-bellied shah was reclining on cushions and carpets in a pavilion, while a diaphanously veiled maiden knelt before him, offering him a cup. In the middle distance was the Shah Mosque.

"Oh, look at that, isn't he doing it beautifully. I wonder how much it is."

"Picture of you, dear, after you've become a white slave. Why don't you buy it and give it to Carl for Christmas? Make him jealous."

Moraine scowled. She couldn't buy it now. Mrs. Oppenheimer said, "It might teach him to behave more romantically. A book of verse, a glass of wine, and thou. Part of a poem by Edna St. Vincent Millay."

"No, that isn't Edna, that's Omar Khay . . ." Moraine managed just not to finish the sentence.

On the steps of the Shah Mosque, Mrs. Oppenheimer suddenly saw something which made her forget her hot feet, her crossness. She bounded forward like a spaniel, heading for two young men who were sitting on a stone bench, their heads bowed over some unseen object. But she could tell from their positions that it was a chess-board.

Moraine trailed her, barely glancing at the game, and turned to look at the great portico. It was incredible! Never had she seen such blue, such a riot of patterns. Lettering, was it, bits of the Koran probably. And the two turquoise minarets against the sky! "Oh, Mommy, do come on! It'll shut soon."

"You go on, dear. I'm busy."

"But aren't you even coming inside?"

"I've checked two mosques already this morning, and that's

enough." One of the young men stood up and Mrs. Oppenheimer promptly sat down in his place.

"But, Mommy, this is the Blue Mosque, the one we've come to see." The girl's cry was despairing, everyone was watching her.

"They're all blue."

"No, they aren't." She pointed across the square at the Lutfullah Mosque. "That one's cream."

"It's blue inside."

"But I can't just go in by myself."

"Why not? Think how romantic it would be to be kidnapped in the middle of the Blue Mosque and sold into slavery. You'd dine out on it for years."

Their dialogue was screeched across the forecourt, while others present, Moslems and sightseers, listened in awe. Mrs. Oppenheimer wondered how many of them spoke English.

"But, Mommy, you can't just sit there and play chess, I mean, with everyone watching."

"I think I can," she said firmly. "You run away and check your mosque."

Moraine went into the blue shadow, and paid her five rials. Was she the only person in the world, she wondered, who wasn't crazy about chess? She and Daddy, and that was about the lot. Mommy was really impossible. Even here, with so much else to do and see. To come all this way and then settle in to play chess with a casual pick-up. Kind of crazy. Then she saw the courtyards and the colonnades, the riot of patterns, above all the deep soothing blue, and she put chess out of her mind. She abandoned herself to the exotic East and the flame of Islam.

She waved away a guide. Guides always took away all the romance. She glanced shyly at a group of men, facing the distant prayer-niche, Mecca, at various stages of their complicated obeisances, or else taking off their trousers, which seemed to be a necessary preliminary. She wanted to gaze and gaze, and also she didn't want to stare, so she walked along the arcade, gazing at the foliated patterns, sucking the end of her dark glasses. She almost tripped over an old man, lying on the ground, fast asleep. He had bare feet and a long white beard, and she looked at him fondly.

She emerged into the white sunlight of the great court. Above

13

her was the dome, like a vast turquoise onion, covered in gaudy patterns; round it was the wide stripe of ultramarine and the white Arabic lettering. On either side were the minarets with their balconies like thimbles. Moraine took a deep breath. It must be the most beautiful place in the world, the holiest, the most perfect, it had to be, and she was seeing it with her own eyes. She must find out more about Moslems. Maybe she'd take instruction, convert, become one, come and live here in Isfahan, then this would be her mosque, she'd come here every day. Though wait, wasn't it true that Moslem women weren't allowed in mosques unless they were tourists? She looked round. There were no black-veiled figures in sight; only men putting their foreheads on the ground, taking their trousers on and off, washing in the pool.

She walked across to the edge of the winter prayer-hall, and leant against the wall. She put her cheek against the cool smooth tile, feeling it with her face, her fingers, rubbing her breasts against it, wondering if she were committing some sort of sacrilege. It was perfect. Almost perfect. If Carl were beside her now, touching her too, saying something, well it would most likely be something like, "Honey, I feel like a Coke and you look like one." She smiled happily, purring. Then they'd go back to the hotel, for a long hot afternoon in bed, stroking. If only she were here with Carl and not with her crazy old mommy.

She pulled away from the wall and sighed. She knew perfectly well what Carl would be doing if he were in Isfahan right now. No doubt at all. He'd be sitting on the steps of the Mosque like her mother, playing chess.

The sun had moved from the stone seats that flanked the steps, but Mrs. Oppenheimer could still feel the warmth in her behind, through the silk dress and the nylon underwear. Distantly her mind registered that she must move before the stone cooled and it became bad for piles. Her weight was on her right hand on the seat beside her, the wrist bent back. Her left hand set up the pieces on the board, and she noticed that it was shaking. She felt like a chain-smoker lighting the first cigarette of the day, or an alcoholic gulping the first Scotch. It was nearly three months since she had last touched a chess-piece in combat.

14

"Would you like a game?" she remembered to ask.

There was no answer. She looked for the first time at her opponent. He was young, about twenty she guessed, though it was difficult to be sure with these Middle Easterners. He had a long straight nose, and thick black eyebrows, very good-looking. He wore a striped cotton shirt, torn and badly darned, and very grubby round the neck; a pair of unpressed dark-blue pinstripe trousers, and his bare feet were pushed into a cracked pair of brogues, treading down the heels. The fingers, with which he was setting up the pieces, had black-rimmed fingernails.

"Do you speak English?" she asked.

He looked up at her from the board. "Hello, miss," he said unsmiling.

"Hello," she said, rather at a loss.

They finished setting up the pieces. At least he knew how to do that correctly: the Queen was on the right square. "Will you have white or black?" she asked.

As he made no answer, she fished in her purse and found a quarter. She flipped it on to the back of her left hand, and covered it with the right. The boy looked at her uncomprehendingly. She took away the right hand and looked at the coin. "You get white," she said, putting away the quarter and turning the board round.

"American?" he said at last.

She nodded.

He held up one brown finger. "Do-lar, do-lar, do-lar."

"What?"

"Do-lar."

She got the point. "Oh, you want to play for money. Oh, all right." She looked again in her purse and found a dollar. She put it on the seat between them. "Right? If you win, you keep it, if I win I get it back. Nice and fair, you can't lose either way. Okay?" She smiled coldly at him.

He nodded gravely. "Okay miss."

She felt excited and queasy. She was badly out of practice. Then she told herself not to be silly. This was just any boy from the bazaar on the look-out for a fast buck. He probably didn't even know the rules correctly, while she had been No. 2 in the U.S. Ladies' Championship four times, and that was against some pretty tough competition.

Two boys were standing watching them, her opponent's ex-opponent and another. She was quite accustomed to playing in front of a crowd, but all the same she waved them back and concentrated on the board. It was a cheap pocket cardboard board, sagging in the middle. The white and the black squares were merely different shades of grey, and the same could be said of the pieces. As she looked, the dirty fingernails moved forward the White King's Pawn.

Mrs. Oppenheimer suddenly felt that this was one of the crucial games of her life. Silly, she said to herself, when did you ever feel any different at the start of a game? All the same, she looked again in her purse and found her ball-point and her Pan-American ticket wallet. She tore it back, folded it inside out, and wrote "White 1. P–K4" at the top of the blank sheet.

"What's your name?" she asked.

The boy didn't answer. He just went on staring at the board.

She thought, well why not the Sicilian Defence? It was all nonsense, of course. He almost certainly didn't know any proper openings. Still, it was her favourite defence to the King's Pawn opening, and she felt an instinct to use it now. She moved her Queen's Bishop's Pawn forward. The piece stuck in the hole and all the pieces wobbled.

The boy instantly, and without looking up, brought out his King's Knight. Mrs. Oppenheimer wrote it down, thinking automatically. It was merely a choice between moving out her Queen's Knight or her Queen's Pawn. And which variation of the Sicilian was she intending to use? The Dragon, the Paulsen, the Scheveningen, the Taimanov? Perhaps the Dragon, not that it mattered much. She moved out the Queen's Knight to Bishop 3.

The boy replied instantly with Pawn to Bishop 3, instead of the usual Pawn to Queen 4. Mrs. Oppenheimer relaxed. So he didn't know any openings, and anyway he played much too fast. It was a virtual pushover. She wrote down the score so far, and then moved out her other Knight.

Incredibly the boy advanced his Pawn to King 5. This was ludicrous. She moved her Knight out of danger to Queen 4, and the boy played Pawn to Queen 4, the move he should have played two moves earlier. She took the Queen's Pawn with her Bishop's Pawn and was promptly retaken by his Bishop's Pawn. Well, at least he knew the moves correctly. She moved out her Queen's Pawn.

He quickly took it with his King's Pawn. Mrs. Oppenheimer felt a twinge of regret that she hadn't already moved out her King's Pawn, which would have allowed her to retake with her Bishop. There was obviously no question of retaking with the King's Pawn, and leaving it isolated, so she recaptured with the Queen herself. A little early to bring out the Queen, but maybe it didn't matter.

The boy brought out his other Knight, she at once took it with her Knight, and was retaken by the Pawn. She moved at last her King's Pawn forward to King 3. They both moved out their Bishops, his to Queen 3, hers to King 2. He moved his Queen to Bishop 2 on the same diagonal as the Bishop, strongly attacking Black's Rook's Pawn, and Mrs. Oppenheimer moved it out of the way to Rook 3. They both castled, and she noted with relief that he castled correctly, moving the King before the Rook. The sight of his fingernails once again distracted her from strategy, and she put them firmly out of her mind.

He now moved his Queen's Rook's Pawn forward to Rook 4, to prepare the way for his Bishop on Rook 3. Mrs. Oppenheimer decided to fianchetto her white-square Bishop and moved her Queen's Knight's Pawn to Knight 3. He brought his Queen to King 2, on to the open file, and she countered by moving her King's Rook to the same file. He advanced his Knight to King 5. Mrs. Oppenheimer took stock.

The game was pretty even, and this was in itself a tribute to the boy's skill. They had both lost a Knight and two Pawns. His position was rather more open than hers, but she commanded the black diagonals and she hadn't got an isolated Pawn. His last move was attacking, his Knight a threat, but the attack was as yet unsupported. She decided to complete the fianchetto of her Bishop, and played Bishop to Knight 2, defending her Knight and commanding the long white diagonal.

Immediately, without pause for reflection, the boy played Knight takes Pawn. Mrs. Oppenheimer sat up straight, all the alarm bells ringing. In her mind's eye she saw the printed scoresheet, "N x P!!," shriek-mark, shriek-mark. Sacrificing his Knight! Was this something she should have foreseen? Indeed it was!

Dare she reject the sacrifice? Could she counter-sacrifice her own Knight? She stayed motionless for ten minutes or more. The two watchers, bored, wandered away. The ants crawled slowly over the dollar bill. Her pulse thumped, sweat ran down her back. She hadn't been in a position like this for years. She looked up at the boy. He wasn't even looking at the board. He was looking at the dollar, without any expression on his face.

She decided at last that she must accept the sacrifice. She took the Knight with her King. Immediately he played, as she expected, Queen to Rook 5, check. She hesitated whether to move her King to Bishop 1 or back to Knight 1. On Bishop 1 it would allow him to make a second sacrifice; he seemed to be the sort of player that liked sacrifices. He could take her Rook's Pawn with his Bishop. If she accepted this second sacrifice she could see mate coming in a few moves. If she refused it, playing Bishop to Bishop 3, he would simply have won a Pawn. If she moved her Queen to Queen 4, he could play Bishop takes Knight's Pawn shriek-mark! Another Pawn gone, another sacrifice which she would be forced to accept, a terrific attack.

She played her King back to Knight 1, and, keeping up the attack, he played Queen to Knight 6. She moved on her King's Pawn to King 4 to clear the rank for her Queen, and he continued with Queen to Rook 7, check. There it was, the White Queen on the seventh rank, protected by the Bishop, alongside her King, check. Humiliating.

She moved her King back again to Bishop 2 and relentlessly he played his Bishop to Bishop 4, check. There was nothing for it, the Black King was driven forward again to Bishop 3. Effortlessly he played Pawn to Bishop 4, a quiet move with a terrible threat: Bishop's Pawn takes Pawn, double-checkmate. Without much hope she played Pawn takes Queen's Pawn, getting her own Pawn out of the way. He continued with Pawn to Knight 4. It was hopeless; the continuation was simple and forced. He would play Pawn to Knight 5, check, Pawn takes Pawn, Pawn takes Pawn double check, King to King 4, Queen to Bishop 5, mate. No escape.

With a wan smile she held out her hand in surrender. She suddenly did not want to shake his dirty hand. Did Persians use paper in the john, she wondered, or were they like Indians? Instead she picked up the dollar, shook the ants off it, and handed it to him. He took it, examined it carefully to see if it was a forgery, and then folded it and put it away in his trouser pocket.

Mrs. Oppenheimer seethed with mortification and fury. She, four times United States Ladies' No. 2, who was on first-name terms with practically every first-class player outside Russia—or even inside; who knew *Modern Chess Openings* almost by heart, mowed down by a dirty, probably illiterate boy casually picked up outside a mosque, mowed down in twenty-two moves. Twenty-two moves.

Of course she hadn't been concentrating properly. She was tired from sightseeing. She was uncomfortable, her right hand, which she had been leaning on, had gone to sleep. And his wretched cheap little set, the black and white squares worn to different shades of grey, and the Bishops indistinguishable from Pawns. She looked in her purse and found her own new magnetic set. She began to set it up. The boy snatched it, turning it on its side, upside down, fascinated by its magnetism. Firmly she took it back. Little things please little minds, she thought censoriously.

"American?" the boy asked, pointing at the set.

"No, French."

She gave herself the white pieces this time. She would open, and what's more she would open with the Queen's Pawn. She would play the Queen's Gambit, and she was ready to bet he didn't know it.

The boy held up his finger. "Do-lar."

"Oh, all right." She found another dollar bill and laid it on the seat beside them. Where was she, Queen's Pawn opening, Queen's Gambit, probably Queen's Gambit Accepted. She knew her way through that all right.

Above them the hoarse voice of the muezzin crackled through the Tannoy, calling the faithful to prayer. Mrs. Oppenheimer glanced up at the minaret above them and frowned.

Moraine heard the call as she sat on the edge of the pool in the middle of the courtyard. She looked up entranced, wondering which minaret it came from. Then she remembered that they would soon be clearing the mosque of unbelievers, and she mustn't dawdle if she wanted to see the rest of it. This time tomorrow they would be on their way to Shiraz.

She passed through an archway into a little garden full of roses and mulberry trees. Roses in Isfahan! A quotation hovered in the back of her mind, something about buried Caesar bleeding. She couldn't ask Mommy to quote it, although she'd undoubtedly know it, because she'd only tease her about Edna St. Vincent Millay. The mulberry trees were shaking in the sunlight. Two boys were concealed in them, shaking down the mulberries into the thick white dust. A boy jumped down, scooped up a handful of dust and mulberries, and with an unexpected gesture of chivalry offered them to Moraine.

"American miss?" he said.

"Yes," she said. "Thank you very much." She looked at the fruit in the palm of her hand. Mulberries from the court of the Blue Mosque! They lay like white maggots. She hesitated between the thrill of romance and the fear of amoebic dysentery. Finally she ate them.

As she walked away, swallowing devotedly, she banged into a young man with a book in his hand.

"I'm sorry," she said. Then she noticed that the arcade was full of young men walking up and down, mouthing, books in their hands. It was like seeing a group of drama students learning their lines. "Are you learning that by heart?" she asked.

He showed her the book, but of course she couldn't read the Arab script.

"Holy book," he explained.

"Oh, the Koran. You're learning the Koran by heart? The whole Koran? That's what you're all doing? God!"

He bowed. He had a thin beard. "Happiness, miss. I learn English three years. English miss?"

"No, American. Thank you so much, I musn't disturb you." She spoke in a low devout voice and moved away. All round her the young men were pacing up and down, mouthing. Twenty, thirty of them, all learning the whole Koran by heart. Just imagine! Supposing they made her learn the whole Bible by heart in college.

Mrs. Oppenheimer was being made aware, not for the first time, that knowing the openings by heart was not enough. Even with her own magnetic board, even with her determination not to underrate her opponent, she had lost three further games and was in the process of losing the fifth. She had lost a Queen's Gambit Accepted, a Sicilian Defence Dragon Variation, an English Opening and now she was losing a French Defence Winawer Variation. Of course, it was silly calling them by their proper names, as they were playing them in the most irregular fashion. The boy simply didn't know the regular openings, he was making them up as he went along. This should have given Mrs. Oppenheimer an initial advantage, and indeed she sometimes thought that it did. But the advantage always slipped away from her in the middle-game. She wasn't feeling so annoyed now, more awestruck.

"Pardon me, madam," said a voice at her ear. "My name is Ghassabiyan. I am an authorised money-changer. Can I render assistance?"

She waved him away crossly. Her King was being driven into the middle of the board, her Rook was under attack, her Pawns broken up. She considered for another few minutes and then she resigned. She handed over the dollar bill, and looked around for the money-changer.

"You! What did you say your name was?"

"Ghassabiyan, madam." He produced some illegible cards and showed them to her.

"Are you Armenian?"

"Yes, madam. I was born in Isfahan."

"Well, will you change this note for me?" She found a five-dollar bill in her purse. "Five single dollars. Not rials, dollars."

He took the point at once. He pulled a shabby leather wallet out of his trouser pocket, and produced four dollar bills and two quarters.

"What's this? You're fifty cents short."

"My commission," he said, bowing. "Authorised commission." He flourished the dog-eared card again.

She hesitated, on the verge of kicking up a fuss. "Right, well, you earn your commission then. Will you ask this boy what his name is? Where he lives, how old he is, what he does, when he learnt chess? Has he any relations? Does he go to school?"

There was a conversation between the Armenian and the boy, laconic on the boy's side. Ghassabiyan said, "His name is Jaafar.

His family comes from a village far away from here, but he lives here in Isfahan with his sister. He has seventeen brothers and sisters. He is nineteen. He does not remember when he first learnt to play. He wants to become a shoe-cleaning boy in a big hotel."

"A shoe-shine boy! What a waste! Will you tell him that I want to move to that café there. It's pretty uncomfortable here. It's easier to play at a table."

There was another altercation, this time, it seemed, rather a heated one. The boy Jaafar spoke at some length.

Ghassabiyan said, "Yes, he says he will play with you at that bar. But he wants to play for more money. He wishes to double the stakes. You understand, one dollar the first game, two the next, four the next, eight the next and so on, doubling each time, you understand?"

Mrs. Oppenheimer said, "I understand all right. But I'm not falling for that one. It's a pretty well-known catch. In a few games we'd be playing for ten grand. Tell him we'll go on playing for a dollar a game, but I'll buy him a drink."

Moraine looked into the pool and wondered if it were holy water. On the far side of the pool a young man, a Koran-learner no doubt, was washing in the pool, his feet, his legs, higher than that. She looked away. Was there something special about washing here, she wondered, was it part of praying? Or was it simply that there was nowhere to wash at home? She sat on the stone rim and dangled her fingers in the water. Then she dried them on her handkerchief and walked forward to the prayer-niche under the big blue dome.

This was the holy of holies. It was a kind of privilege being allowed to see it, especially for her, a woman. She felt herself encased in deep blue tiles, stroked with foliated patterns. Above her the blue dome soared up, shiny, intricate, glorious. It was like being inside an expensive elaborate Worcester tea-cup. A holy tea-cup, kind of a chalice. She jumped as a series of sharp bangs went off immediately behind her.

The young man who had been washing his legs was standing behind her, clapping. He grinned as she turned round, and shouted strange words without consonants. Then he gestured at the courtyard behind them. Finally she understood. He was demonstrating the acoustics.

"Oh, please don't," she said sadly. "Oh, do go away."

He grinned and clapped again.

Outside in the Maidan-Shah, in the café which was apparently called Pepsi—no other name was visible—the boy Jaafar drank tea out of the saucer, scorning to use the cup. Mrs. Oppenheimer wiped the rim of the Canada Dry bottle with her handkerchief, and swallowed some of the contents; neither glass nor straw was provided by the management, a middle-aged Iranian who sat at an adjoining table, smoking a hubble-bubble, sipping tea from a saucer and contemplating the sky. He did not glance at Mrs. Oppenheimer.

Jaafar set up the chess-pieces again and picked up the board, tilting it this way and that, holding it upside down, shaking it to make the pieces drop off. None of them did. Mrs. Oppenheimer watched him. The magic of magnetism, the wonders of modern science! He could throw off a Rook sacrifice, win a complicated game apparently without thinking. But it was the marvels of simple magnetism that held his interest. And it wasn't as if electronics had not reached Isfahan. There was a transistor on inside the café, pouring out Iranian music, a single unaccompanied male voice, wailing away without a second's pause. Non-stop unaccompanied flamenco, only worse.

Mrs. Oppenheimer suppressed a burp from the Club Soda, watching Jaafar's face, his fingers shaking the little board, his fingernails. What was his I.Q.? His mental age? A simple child. Yet game after game he outmanœuvred her in the most involved positions. Deliberately she was complicating the games, but he remained unworried. He still played his moves immediately after her without a second's pause for thought. And she had been No. 2 in the U.S. Ladies'.

Firmly she took the board from him and turned it up the right way, ready for a new game. She searched in her purse for a dollar, and found it empty. She pulled out an album of First National City Bank travellers cheques. Immediately Ghassabiyan was beside her.

"Perhaps I can render assistance, madam?"

"Can you change a travellers cheque for me? Into rials?"

The cheque was for $100. The Armenian's eyes popped.

"Of course yes, madam. I come back in five minutes."

His shadow disappeared, Moraine's rose up.

"Oh, there you are, Mommy! I thought maybe they'd sold you into slavery. God, it's hot!"

Mrs. Oppenheimer barely glanced at her daughter. "Back safely. How was the mosque?"

"Great. Simply great. It's so blue, and all those patterns."

The proprietor hooked up the mouthpiece of his hubble-bubble, went to the ice-box and, without an order, brought Moraine a bottle of Canada Dry.

Mrs. Oppenheimer said, "Better wipe the rim, dear."

"And you'd never guess, there are dozens of boys, hundreds, walking up and down, all learning the Koran by heart. It's fabulous, that's what they're doing, would you believe that?"

"And you'd never guess, would you, that this boy is a chess genius. He's a natural. I think maybe he's the greatest combinative player since Tal. Maybe he's even greater."

"Isn't that great! Isfahan's just got everything, hasn't it." She took a long swallow of Canada Dry. Her mother looked at her with little pleasure.

"It's not a question of having everything. It's a question of one chess genius, that's all."

"Well, he's pretty good-looking, anyway. He looks just like the Shah."

"All Persians look just like the Shah," Mrs. Oppenheimer said. "It's his brain I'm interested in, not his eyebrows."

"Are you sure he doesn't understand English?" asked Moraine.

The Armenian reappeared and obsequiously poured thousands of rials into Mrs. Oppenheimer's hand. She didn't count them.

"Tell Jaafar," she commanded, "no more dollars. From now on we play fifty rials a game."

"Oh, Mommy, you're not going to play any more! It's lunchtime and I'm hungry."

"Then go and have lunch, dear. Fill thy belly with an ancient dish, as dear Edna put it."

"Mommy . . ."

"There's a taxi line over there. Don't wait for me, I'm not hungry."

"But, Mommy, are you going to sit here and play chess the whole afternoon? You can't, you just can't!"

"I shall refresh myself from the cool pure springs of the St. Lawrence river." She took another gulp of soda water. "Leave me alone, I can't think if you keep pestering me."

She moved her King's Pawn forward. He advanced his King's Pawn too. So it was going to be some variation of the Ruy Lopez. One of her favourite openings. She felt confident he wouldn't ever have heard of the Marshall Attack. She'd keep the game wide open, test him in free-ranging open positions. Her palms were damp with excitement, her heart pounded. Moraine went quietly away.

When the muezzin called the faithful to prayer once again the shadows of Ali-Qapu were low across the square. The dome of the Lutfullah Mosque was golden in the sunset. The whole square was now crowded with young men walking up and down mouthing the Koran. Mrs. Oppenheimer sighed and stretched her legs. She was stiff, the metal chair was hard on her thin thighs. She had lost nine dollars and over three thousand rials, about seventy games. Not one game had she won. Twice she had thought she had a draw, once by a repetition of moves and once in a totally deadlocked position, and each time he had smoothly and apparently effortlessly broken through with a beautiful combination. The boy was undeniably a genius; ignorant, dirty, illiterate, not over-polite, but, in this one subject at least, a genius. He was already in the world class. He could probably win the Zonal or even the Interzonal now. Teach him the openings, give him a greater grasp of positional play, of strategy, and he could be World Champion. And she could get him there.

He was putting up the pieces for another fifty rials, but she shook her head. "Enough, *assez, bastante.*" She was exhausted, her head ached, her eyes had dust in them, she felt hollow and sick, her legs ached where she had been screwing up her toes in deep thought. The board had been too small, the light too bright, the heat too great. She had drunk too much Canada Dry. She had played too many games. But what was any of that compared with her discovery? She felt like Columbus.

She pulled out her travellers cheques again. Immediately Ghassabiyan was at her side. He had had a six-hour hovering wait since she had last needed him, but he wasn't tired.

"Can I render service, madam?"

"Yes, tell him that I have much enjoyed our games today, and that I think he is a very promising player. Ask him if he will come to my hotel tomorrow morning and we will play some more games."

She doubted if the whole of this was translated. The boy answered very briefly.

"He says he agrees, but tomorrow he wishes to play for one hundred rials a game."

She nodded. She signed a travellers cheque and gave it to the Armenian. "Tell him to get himself some new clothes. A good suit, shirt, tie, shoes. Something suitable for big hotels. And tell him to take a bath. Do you have public baths here?"

"Yes, madam."

"Well, tell him to get himself cleaned up and come to the Hotel Isfahan at ten o'clock tomorrow morning. And after that I take him to Teheran, and then to New York," she added casually, throwing away the line.

The boy took the news impassively. Ghassabiyan said, "I will arrange everything. I give a better exchange rate than the hotel."

Mrs. Oppenheimer took a taxi back to the hotel, showered and changed her girdle. She took two aspirins and went down to the bar.

"Canada Dry, I suppose," she said resignedly. "Can you put some Scotch in it for me? I'm not a Moslem."

The bartender smiled. "Nor am I." She stopped him putting in ice. Not ice, not in Isfahan. She was just starting her second when Moraine arrived, fresh and lovely.

"Hello, Mommy. I've had a marvellous time. I had a sleep, and then I went and looked at the Chehel-Sotoon."

"The what?"

"It's that pavilion in the garden, the one the man said was the most poetic building in the world."

"And was it?"

"It was beautiful, really. All those pillars reflected in the pool. They used to have huge banquets there, going on literally for days, and thousands of dancing girls, and they'd cover all the lawns with beautiful Persian carpets, and all the pools with rose petals."

"Wasn't that rather a waste of the garden?"

Moraine ordered a Pepsi. "How did your games go? Did you win?"

"No, I did not. We played about seventy games . . ."

"Seventy! You mean that?"

"And he won every one. Quite easily. And I wasn't playing that badly either. I bet Jacqueline Piatigorsky couldn't take a game off that boy. Or Gisela Gresser. Or that Russian girl. He's a genius, that boy."

"Here in Isfahan?"

"Why not here? It was once the capital of Persia, so you say. And the Persians invented chess."

"I thought it was the Chinese."

"Persians, dear. Rook is a Persian word. It means wind or spirit."

"Sol says it means a chariot. But Carl says it's a castle."

"Carl would."

They had dinner in the garden. The menu was vaguely Swiss. The air was sweet with the night-scented stock. Moraine took a deep breath.

"Just smell that!" she said ecstatically.

"Quite like Massachusetts," remarked Mrs. Oppenheimer. "Oh to be in New England, now that summer stock is there. Edna always had a word for it, didn't she?"

The whisky had revived her, her exhaustion had gone away. She ordered some more, and her daughter chose doogh, a mixture of yoghurt and mineral water.

"After a Pepsi," commented Mrs. Oppenheimer.

On the other side of the garden a local dinner party was assembling; young married couples, the men in dark suits, the women in simple black frocks. The women sat on one side of the table, the men on the other. A bottle of Canada Dry was put before each guest. Nobody spoke.

Mrs. Oppenheimer said, "That's how you'll be when you marry your sheikh, dear. Don't get the idea that you'll kneel before him on silk carpets, offering him pomegranate juice in goblets. You'll come here to dinner, wearing a little black frock, and you'll sit with all the other wives, and you won't say a word the whole evening."

A voice behind her said, "It's worth coming here. I just hate Teheran, just hate it. The whole of Texas seems to be there. It's just oil, oil, oil all day long."

Mrs. Oppenheimer pushed away the consommé julienne and said, "I gave him a hundred dollars."

"Gave who?"

"Jaafar, of course. My genius. I told him to take a bath and get himself some clothes. I only hope they do have public baths."

"Oh yes, they do!" Moraine enthused. "They're called hammams or something, there's one in the Souk, it's hundreds of years old and all heated by just one candle. Would you believe it, just one candle, it reflects in some way. I read about it."

"So long as it works I don't mind if they use electricity. I can't take him into the Teheran Hilton looking like that."

"Filthy, wasn't he," agreed Moraine. "And you had to touch the same pieces as he did. Ugh! Hilton," she added after a pause, "are we taking him there?"

"Yes, tomorrow evening. I've had the desk clerk reserve us three seats on the afternoon flight."

"Tomorrow!" Moraine wailed. "But we're going to Shiraz tomorrow!"

"Not any more. I've cancelled our reservation."

"But Shiraz! We must see Shiraz."

"I'm sure it'll be just the same as here."

"But the roses. It's the City of Roses!"

Mrs. Oppenheimer looked coolly at her daughter. Soppy girl, mental age about fourteen. And not even a virgin.

"This place is full of roses. And there are even more back home."

"But I can't go there alone."

"Indeed you can't."

"And Persepolis, what about Persepolis?" wailing again.

"Maybe Daddy'll take you next year."

"He won't! He'd never do that. It's just not his bag."

"Well, it's not my bag either. I do have to contact the American consul in Teheran straight away about a visa for Jaafar. Maybe I should call him from here. No, it's too late, it'll have to wait till we get to Teheran. But we haven't any time to lose. Jaafar is nineteen already. Bobby Fischer was American Champion at sixteen, Carl was Western Champion and won Bled when he was seventeen. And Jaafar doesn't even know the openings yet. We'll get him back to New York as fast as we can, find him an apartment. Or, better still, have him stay with us, then I can keep an eye on him."

"Oh no, Mommy, not that dirty boy! In our apartment! You just can't! What would everyone say?"

Mrs. Oppenheimer waved that away. "I'll have him taught to speak English and to read and write. And I'll hire Al or Sol or Sammy to come and teach him the openings and study positional play with him. That's enough, we don't want to fill him up with a lot of Latin or history. I'll make him the new Sultan Khan," she ended breathlessly.

"Sultan who?"

"Sultan Khan. Never heard of him? He wasn't a sultan or a khan, he was just an Indian slave. He couldn't even read or write. Anyway his maharajah brought him to England and he became British Champion. I'll make Jaafar American Champion."

"But he isn't even American."

"Well, he can take out citizenship, can't he? I'll have Daddy talk to Dean. In the meanwhile he can win the Open Championship. I know! Moraine, listen, I've just had a really brilliant idea." She took a swallow of Scotch while Moraine waited. "I'll stage a match between him and Bobby or Carl. Twenty-four games. In New York. Or maybe somewhere like Miami. I'll give a really big prize, something that'll get the headlines. Five thousand dollars for the winner. Make it a great event like the Piatigorsky Cup." She sat back and looked at Moraine. "Isn't that a great idea? Do you think Carl would do it for five thousand dollars?"

Moraine said nothing. It wasn't a question that needed an answer.

"I know, you shall marry the winner. Five grand and my daughter for the winner. That ought to make the headlines. It's just the sort of thing those old shahs would have done."

Moraine began to cry.

After dinner Moraine went down to see the bridges of Isfahan by moonlight.

"If you're not back by midnight I'll have the whole U.S. Air Force looking for you."

Mrs. Oppenheimer went to the desk and sent off two cables, one to the Teheran Hilton booking three single rooms, and one to her husband in Abadan telling him of her change of plan. She had a deep urge to cable somebody else, to confide in somebody about her wonderful day, her wonderful discovery. But whom? No use telling either Walter or the Hilton about Jaafar. Carl? He wouldn't be bothered to read the cable. Mrs. Piatigorsky, perhaps. Possibly Gisela Gresser. Or Sol or Al or Larry, any of them. Or Paul. Of course, Paul, the obvious one, he'd understand, he'd sympathise, it might be a useful piece of advance publicity too.

Where would he be now? She took out her chess-players' calendar and looked up the congresses. At the moment it was Bled, Yugoslavia. He'd be sure to be there. So would most of the others, come to that. Where would Paul be staying in Bled? Was it called the Hotel Toplice? Or would it be safer just to send it to the congress?

"I want to send a long cable to Bled, Yugoslavia," she said to the night-clerk. She'd tell Paul all about it, send a full score of Jaafar's best game, get him excited. "A long cable, sixty or seventy words. A lot of it will be in code, at least it'll seem like a code to you."

"Yes, madam," said the night-clerk, looking apprehensive.

"I'll go and draft it."

She must choose his best game, one which really would impress Paul. Maybe that first Sicilian. Or that Exchange Variation Lopez. Or that Centre-Counter Gambit. She'd have to see.

She went up to her bedroom and got her set of full size chess-pieces; she always played better with full size pieces. She also got out her copy of *Modern Chess Openings,* that heavy volume which she was never without, no matter how overweight her baggage was. She put on some more lipstick and came down to the lounge. She always analysed better when there were other people in the room.

The lounge was carpeted, like the stairs, in opulent Persian carpets. Everything was, in Isfahan, even the settees you sat on. The Iranian dinner party had melted away into the night, but the Teheran-hating quartet sat nearby, telling each other about Beirut. Through the open door came the wail of Arab music from the night-clerk's transistor. A boy sat at the piano, picking out "A Hard Day's Night" with one finger. Mrs. Oppenheimer pulled the tiled chess-table towards her and set up the pieces. She didn't want another drink, her pulse was fast enough already.

She got out the scores of her games with Jaafar, scribbled on the inside of her Pan-American wallet, all over the tickets themselves, on the back of her First National City travellers cheques, on her vaccination certificate, in her diary. She opened *Modern Chess Openings* with trembling fingers.

The Morra Gambit! Of course. That was where she had gone wrong in the very first game. She hadn't played through the Morra Gambit for a long time, she had simply forgotten the book version. She started to play through it now, to see where she had gone wrong, and where he had gone right. Not, of course, that he knew the book version any better than she did, or knew even that it was the Morra Gambit.

A shadow loomed over her, tall, willowy.

"Back already?"

"I had to make the taxi wait. I didn't dare pay him off in case I didn't get another one down there."

"And how were the nights of revelry?"

"Oh, beautiful! The bridges are covered with these little alcoves where they used to recline on carpets and have parties and dance. I found some students picnicking in one. They invited me to join them."

"How nice of them. What did you eat, nightingales' tongues?"

"They had some rice with them, a bowl of rice."

"Risotto?"

"No, just rice. And some plates."

"Oh good. And what did you drink? Canada Dry?"

"We didn't drink anything. But one of the boys did imitations of the Beatles. He was great, we laughed like anything."

"It sounds really swinging. Isn't that the word?"

"And I've booked the same taxi to take me early tomorrow

to see the Shaking Minarets and the Fire Temple. I must see them before we go. Would you like to come too?"

"Not tomorrow morning. I'll be busy. But you go, have a good time."

"Well, I'm going to bed," said Moraine. "I'm sleepy. Good night, Mommy, don't sit up all night playing chess."

"Good night, dear."

They kissed formally, left cheekbone to left cheekbone, kissing towards each other's left ears. Mrs. Oppenheimer didn't watch her daughter out of the room. Her mind was already on the consequences of Pawn to Bishop 3 on Move 3.

She was still sitting there at half past nine the next morning. Whether she had been to bed in the meantime nobody knew, not even the night-clerk, as he had slept peacefully through the night. The pieces were still set out on the board, *Modern Chess Openings* open on the settee beside her. But she didn't consult the book. She didn't move the pieces. For once she wasn't thinking about chess. She was palpitating like a young girl waiting for her lover. Every few seconds her eyes went to the door, through which he would soon walk; with a flashy new suit, glossy hair, reeking of cologne, his bare heels already treading down the backs of his new suède shoes.

BLED

Paul swam slowly on his back towards the Grand Hotel Toplice. The water, which had a summer-lake smell, was warm and cold in patches, which was irritating. It kept drawing attention to itself. It was impossible to forget the water when the next stroke might take him into a cold bracing shock. The Wörthersee was more homogeneous, more uniformly tepid so that you could relax and forget swimming and look at the mountains and dream the nostalgic Austrian dream. Or Zell, uniformly cold and bracing so that you emerged snorting with self-admiration and appetite for lunch. He would write a book someday about the world's lakes, the big and the small, the hot and the cold, the historic and the boring, the pretty and the industrial. *Michigan to Bled* he'd call it, one extreme to the other. No, the second lake should begin with an M too. Maggiore perhaps, or what was the name of that one in Egypt Durrell kept writing about? Was it Mareotis? Not that it mattered, as he hadn't been there, not yet. Loch Maree. Or one of those thousands of Finnish lakes must begin with an M. It was like one of those pencil and paper games you play at Christmas, all the lakes you can think of beginning with M in one minute starting now.

He discovered that all his limbs were at the moment in tepid water and gingerly he began to tread water. There was no doubt this was one of the prettiest lakes of them all, in a rather banal and obvious way. That little island with the white church and the red spire exactly like a child's toy. You rowed out to it, landed and climbed the steps and sat under the big chestnut tree in the little square at the top by the church which might look like a toy from here but was gratifyingly Baroque inside, and drank a glass of beer and thought what a perfect setting it would make for a folk opera; perhaps *The Bartered Bride* or *Schwanda the Bagpiper* or what was the name of that awful one he'd seen at the Ljubljana Festival last time he was here? Could it be *Hero from Outer Space*?

The sun had gone in. Yet another thunderstorm was building up over the Julian Alps. This must be one of the stormiest parts of Europe. The lake was steel-coloured and polished in the breathless calm. It would be pouring in a few hours' time, and that would cause more cold patches in the water. Across the lake was the public bathing beach with its bright huts. In front someone was kicking his heels, splashing everybody within range.

Frowning with disapproval, Paul swivelled round with his hands till he was facing Bled itself. Strange to think that such a quiet remote little resort should be so historic. This was one of the great names in the history of chess. Here Alekhine had swept all before him. Here so many great players had played great or, sometimes, lamentable games. Fischer, Tal, Chaimovitz, Larsen, Toklovsky, Ivkov. It was like looking at Marathon or Waterloo.

No, not quite. Those had been once and for all battles, but these continued, year after year, congress after congress. It was more like—yes, that was it—a bull-ring. A great bull-ring. Madrid, say, or Pamplona. All that skill and resolution and sense of timing and—why not?—genius, poured out in the same place, season after season. An idea came to him—he'd write a book about it. Not the usual technical book, *The Elements of the End-Game,* but something deeper, wider-ranging, more philosophical. He'd become the Hemingway of chess, he'd write a *Mate in the Afternoon.* No, that wouldn't do as a title, and anyway grandmasters were rarely mated. They resigned a long time before, when their position became hopeless. But it would do as a working title.

He'd follow up the analogy with bullfighting. Both were forms of a death-cult, formal, ritual killings. Kill the bull, kill the king. But there was a twist to chess. The ambition of a humble pawn was to reach the last rank and be promoted not to a king but to a queen who would then attack the king. A weird variation of the Oedipus legend, the deep-down urge in everybody to be a woman, to be a king-killer and not a king. There'd be a Freudian chapter, of course, in *Mate in the Afternoon*. That would surprise his friends who didn't know he knew any psychology.

A chilly current drifted across him and he swam for the shore. The big old-fashioned hotel, green with creeper, reminded him of the large lunch ahead, the excellent Riesling. Really, life was very pleasant, as long as the thunderstorms held off. He looked round in case any of the rest of the congress were swimming too. But of course they weren't. No competitor would take time off to go swimming. The thought would never even occur. They'd be sitting in the hotel lounge playing lightning chess. Or, even more likely, sitting on the edge of their beds, staring at their pocket boards, analysing. Studying the latest theories from the world's tournaments, playing through their prospective opponents' most recent games, trying out new ideas. Paul felt a guilty twinge of relief that he personally was out of the race. He'd made his own niche in the game, he was read, published, respected. The celebrated author, the friend of all the masters, the man who saw everything and knew everything. A cultured man whose horizons were wider than the chess-board. He climbed up the steps and stood dripping on the warm concrete, towelling the body of the cultured all-rounder, the thoughtful psychologist, the man who understood the art of living.

In his bedroom he changed into a dark-blue linen suit. This was his hot weather congress suit. He had worn it in Los Angeles and Havana. It was getting a little shabby, smooth on the seat, baggy at the knees. He'd have to get a new one if he were to maintain his successful *homme-de-lettres* greying-above-the-temples appearance in front of people who saw him so often. He'd better get it before he went to Barcelona. He half closed his eyes and shook his head interestingly. Clothes were always a problem. Unlike Grand Hotels or airline tickets they couldn't be charged to expenses.

He tied his dark-blue and white-spotted bow tie. He had adopted it as his insignia after reading an article about Ian Fleming who had had the same idea. It was literary, distinguished and he always wore it at chess congresses, meetings of the International P.E.N., English Centre, and for lunching at the Savile Club. He checked his profile in the mirror, fingered back the hair over his ears and went down the stairs to the lobby.

There were a lot of letters in his pigeon-hole behind the desk. This was good news. A large mail was a reassurance of success, of distinction, of existence even. The worst thing in the world would be to get no letters day after day; to be alone and derelict in some small seaside hotel, waiting for the postman to come in case there might be a letter from his grand-daughter—not that he had a grand-daughter.

The boy who deputised for the concierge at lunchtime tried to give him a small thin letter from the wrong box. Paul pointed and insisted on his own mail. The boy put the correct pile down in front of him; on top of it, alarmingly, was the blue envelope of a cable, and cables were always bad news.

To cover his alarm he said severely to the boy, "Has this been here long? You should have brought it to me immediately."

The boy muttered something incomprehensible in Slovene. Paul turned away, the letters in one hand, the cable like a red-hot coal in the other. It must be from his editor; who else would cable him here? The editor must be cancelling his assignment, bored with paying three weeks' hotel expenses to cover a congress where the only British participant was obviously finishing last, ordering him to return immediately to London. By this time tomorrow night Paul might be back in his two-room flat in Kensington, eating charcuterie in his tiny kitchen.

He walked into the lounge, where the white lake-water light was making patterns on the ceiling. Beside him was a long brown table strewn with newspapers, British, German, Italian, Swiss. Among them was a copy of the *Post,* three weeks old, a Thursday edition. Ignoring the front page, he put down the hateful cable and turned at once to page eighteen, his chess column, and read it through once again. Yes, it was a nice piece of writing, neat, pointed, amusing. He had taken for his theme that you shouldn't always believe what you are told. For instance every junior knows that you should never give up two Rooks in return for your opponent's Queen; that two Rooks are far stronger than a single Queen in the end-game. And then last summer in Santa Monica Fischer going right against the book had given up his two Rooks for Portisch's Queen, and had won brilliantly a few moves later.

Paul had concluded his article: "Those who have puzzled over the eternal conundrum of what happens when an irresistible force meets an immovable object should take note of Fischer's solution. The irresistible force moves to the rear of the immovable object and attacks it from the rear. Fischer's move Q–K6 breaks Portisch's resistance and wins the game."

Paul smiled at the beauty of it and at the neat way he had described it. But all the same it had been a waste of material to use two good points, the don't-believe-what-you're-told and the irresistible force in the same article. He could have kept one for a later column. Then he reassured himself. He could use the point again elsewhere. One of the good things about writing for five different papers was that you could use the same material more than once. There were other advantages too.

He looked round the lounge for one of the grandmasters. He'd like to show him the article, translate it if necessary, suggest laughingly that he'd get his name in next week's *Post* too if he played brilliantly that afternoon. But there were no grandmasters in the lounge. They were all probably still sitting on the edges of their beds, analysing games.

He picked up the dread cable and walked across to the big windows. The hotel kept a couple of chess-boards lying out on the tables for the amusement of visitors, grandmasters or rabbits alike. But one board was not in use and at the other only two small fair-haired boys were playing. Paul glanced instinctively at their game in case they were infant prodigies, but it seemed they were not.

"Why don't you take his Queen?" he asked. And then, getting no reply, *"Warum nehmst du nicht seine Königin?"*

He suddenly realised that the blue envelope was unusually heavy. It must be a very long cable. In which case it was most unlikely to come from his editor. He sat down gracefully and tore it open.

It was indeed long; four pages and seemed to be the complete score of a chess game. He turned to the last line: MATE HOWBOUT THAT LOVE JOANN. He laughed and relaxed. Dear Joann Oppenheimer, of course he should have realised it would be from her. She was always bombarding him with cables from remote places giving him details of her latest win. Of course it could never have been from his paper, he had got in a fuss about nothing. He would still be here tomorrow night, eating a Toplice Platte or stuffed paprika and meditating on the good things of life. He snapped his fingers at the waiter and ordered an ice-cold Slivovitz.

While he sipped it he looked at the rest of his mail which had been forwarded from London. A note from his bank acknowledging a cheque for fifteen guineas which had been credited to his account and, Paul calculated, would just about put him back in the black. A letter from his publishers thanking him for returning the corrected proofs of *Asymmetrical Defences,* and saying that they were hoping after all to publish on the 25th September as provisionally scheduled, and had he any special ideas for promotion and publicity? They were interested to hear that he was planning a book unconnected with chess and looked forward to reading it when it was ready, though they did not think *Sixty-Four Squares* was a very attractive title.

Paul frowned. Of course he had no special ideas for publicising *Asymmetrical Defences.* It was a companion volume to his earlier *Symmetrical Defences,* and would go the same way. Why did they trouble him with such silly routine questions as if he were a sexy teenager publishing his first novel. And of course *Sixty-Four Squares* was an excellent title: it was intriguing, it suggested chess and travel. And anyway the book would be a series of mood pieces written round the great squares of the world: Concorde, Washington, Red, San Marco, Sloane, Catalunia, Castle, Odeon, Charlotte and so on all the way to number sixty-four. It was a brilliant idea, demonstrating how he could be an expert on travel as well as chess. The grandmasters, who never even noticed which city they were in, would read it and be amazed.

He looked at the other letters. Four had been forwarded by the *Post.* Readers in Ealing, Macclesfield, Birmingham and Torquay were writing, with varying degrees of smugness, to point out that in his article two weeks ago Black's fourth move N–R3 should surely have been N–B3, as otherwise Black's eleventh move N–Q2 would be impossible. Paul sighed. Of course it was a misprint, and not his fault either. He'd noticed it with horror the following morning and had immediately checked his own typescript. It was the printer's fault, and not his; and now every single reader of his column was going to write to him and point it out. Anyway, whoever heard of playing N–R3 on the fourth move of the Ruy Lopez?

He threw them aside wearily and picked up the other letter. It had been forwarded not by the *Post* but by his publishers, so it might just be a fan-letter. Paul opened it with more enthusiasm. Fan-letters were important to him, evidence of existence, even of success; they were the equivalent to him of a win over the board. This particular one was long, handwritten in joined script, on cheap lined writing paper, from someone called Robin Jackson, in Manchester. Skimming down the first page his eye caught the title of one of his books, *The Early Middle-Game*. Yes, it could count as a fan-letter. He'd answer it in due course. He always answered his fan-letters, recommending his fan to buy his new book which would be specially interesting to him. He put the letter in his pocket, finished his Slivovitz, and went down to lunch.

The head waiter had decided that the storm was not imminent and had laid lunch on the terrace beside the lake under the thick canopy of chestnut leaves. The terrace was already crowded with lunching tourists, mostly British and German. Paul looked round for any chess-players, but the only one in sight was Grandmaster Dietrich, chewing his way through the set lunch and reading *Der Schachtpraktiker*. Paul went across to him and said, *"Guten Tag."* The German jumped to his feet and shook hands with great formality, nodding but not smiling. He sat down again immediately and went on eating and reading.

Paul wandered on to his table. It was always rather a mystery about the others, why they didn't eat in the hotel. Some of the players, especially the Yugoslav players, preferred cevapcici and raw onions in the buffet across the road. Others liked to sleep late, after sitting up half the night analysing, and then have brunch of ham buns and yoghurt and coffee, also in the buffet. The others presumably ate, if they ate at all, on trays in their bedrooms.

He sat down at his table and waved away the set lunch. Instead he ordered Russian eggs and truite au bleu and a bottle of Laski Riesling. As he sipped the cold mock-hock, he studied the view yet again. One of those strange boats which looked like something out of a Guardi picture, halfway between a gondola and the Doge's barge. After a sunny morning on the island, the rower was bringing his passengers back to their trout, a little late for lunch but still in time to avoid a wetting. The wake spread out like op art on the glassy lake.

One of the nice things about chess was that it was always played in beautiful places. Unnecessarily beautiful or interesting. Grandmasters were hardly likely to take time off to go sightseeing or visit the opera or put their heads inside San Marco or the Rijksmuseum. But it was nice for the correspondents. Just supposing he had been a mining correspondent, trudging from coalfield to coalfield. He put the distressing thought behind him, finished a second glass of Riesling and pulled Mrs. Oppenheimer's cable out of his pocket. He read:

PAUL BUTLER GRAND HOTEL TOPLICE BLED YUGOSLAVIA EYEVE FOUND YOUNG ISFAHAN BOY COMPLETE NATURAL GENIUS FILTHY CANNOT READ OR WRITE KNOWS NO OPENINGS ALL DONE BY PURE INSTINCT BUT TOTAL GENIUS REPEAT GENIUS STOP WITH TRAINING AND SUBSTANTIAL BACKING PROBABLY FUTURE WORLD CHAMPION BRINGING HIM NEWYORK SOONEST CUMME STOP PLEASE ASK CHAIMOVITZ IF WILLING TO UNDERTAKE BOYS TRAINING AND FEE REQUIRED STOP TRY THIS FOR SIZE WHITE OPPENHEIMER BLACK BOY JAAFAR ONE PAWN KING FOUR PAWN KING FOUR TWO KNIGHT KINGS BISHOP THREE KNIGHT QUEENS BISHOP THREE THREE BISHOP BISHOP FOUR KNIGHT BISHOP THREE FOUR KNIGHT KNIGHT FIVE BISHOP BISHOP FOUR SHRIEKMARK FIVE KNIGHT TAKES PAWN BISHOP TAKES PAWN CHECK SIX KING BISHOP ONE OF COURSE QUEEN KING TWO SEVEN KNIGHT TAKES ROOK PAWN QUEEN FOUR EIGHT PAWN TAKES PAWN KNIGHT QUEEN FIVE NINE PAWN KINGS ROOK THREE BISHOP KNIGHT SIX SHRIEKMARK TEN PAWN BISHOP THREE KNIGHT BISHOP FOUR ELEVEN QUEEN ROOK FOUR CHECK BISHOP QUEEN TWO TWELVE BISHOP KNIGHT FIVE QUEEN BISHOP FOUR THIRTEEN BISHOP TAKES BISHOP CHECK KNIGHT TAKES BISHOP FOUR-

TEEN KING KING TWO QUEEN TAKES QUEENS PAWN SHRIEK-
MARK FIFTEEN ROOK KNIGHT ONE PAWN KING FIVE SIXTEEN
PAWN QUEEN FOUR PAWN TAKES PAWN ENPASSANT CHECK
SEVENTEEN KING QUEEN ONE BISHOP BISHOP SEVEN EIGHT-
EEN ROOK BISHOP ONE QUEEN TAKES KNIGHTS PAWN NINE-
TEEN ROOK TAKES BISHOP QUEEN KNIGHT EIGHT CHECK SHRIEK-
MARK TWENTY KING QUEEN TWO QUEEN TAKES ROOK CHECK
TWENTYONE KING TAKES PAWN BLACK CASTLES TWENTY-
TWO QUEEN KINGS BISHOP FOUR KNIGHT KING FOUR DOUBLE
CHECK TWENTYTHREE KING KING FOUR KNIGHT KNIGHT SIX
CHECK TWENTYFOUR KING TAKES KNIGHT QUEEN BISHOP
FOUR CHECK TWENTYFIVE KING KING SIX QUEEN QUEEN FOUR
CHECK TWENTYSIX KING KING SEVEN QUEEN QUEEN TWO
MATE HOWBOUT THAT LOVE JOANN

Paul looked up and smiled. Dear romantic Joann! Trust her
to find a boy genius and of course it would have to be in Isfahan
and he would have to be dirty and illiterate—not that he seemed
to be that untutored. He seemed to know the moves all right,
even the en passant move. It was a real joke. Dear Joann always
going on about how soppy and romantic her daughter was, and
here was she the soppiest of the lot.

He read the game through again and this time everything van-
ished from his mind except an imaginary chess-board. He had
always had the trick of being able to read a game without a board
in front of him. Indeed it was one of the things that had first
shown him that he had a good future in the world of chess. He
might have become famous as a blindfold player, if he hadn't
had other interests.

When he had finished it, he smiled again. A delightful game,
exciting and spectacular. That Knight fork accepted, those sacrifices declined and finally Black, down in material, forcing the
White King to march forward to the seventh rank and his doom.
It was like something out of a past age, the sort of game Morphy
or Anderssen might have played, but it wouldn't do nowadays.
It was like going to hear the newest Britten opera and finding he
had written it in the style of Wagner. These spectacular finishes
were no longer possible at a time when grandmasters resigned
at the prospect of losing a Pawn. The boy obviously had some
talent, but how would he cope with modern positional play, how

would he defend himself against the strategic steamrollers of Botvinnik or Chaimovitz or Mischchov? Bobby Fischer or Carl Sandbach would cut him to ribbons.

Still he mustn't be unkind. It would be fun for everybody, fun for Joann, fun for the boy himself and probably cash for Sol Chaimovitz. And if by any chance something did come of it, he would be in on the ground floor, he would have a scoop. He would send her an encouraging answer.

He cut himself a large helping of Bel Paese and poured out some more wine. Then, feeling happy, he read his fan-letter from Robin Jackson. It started discouragingly. The boy disagreed with some analysis in *The Early Middle-Game*. "Surely," he wrote, "P—KR4 is fully answered by B—K3 because then . . ." Oh Lord, thought Paul, these clever young men, always having to show off. "And if KN–Q2, then N–N5, P x P, N–Q6 ch, K–K2 etc. Or if P x P, O–O, then 10 N–B3, N–KB3 etc."

Paul sighed and turned over two more pages, filled with similar analysis. I suppose he's got to send it to someone, he thought, but why pick on me? Hasn't he got any chums?

The boy started in on himself. He was at Lady Wynyard's Grammar School, a sixth-former, getting ready for his "A" levels. Paul could just imagine him, tall, lamp-post thin, with glasses, just growing out of his spots. He was hoping to go to either Manchester or Liverpool University—"but my dad says I shall never get in if I spend so much time on chess. *I* tell *him* that's *lèse majesté* against the game of Kings! Or perhaps nowadays we should say the game of Pawns!" Typical thought Paul, facetious and long-winded. He turned over again. Robin Jackson had helped found his school chess club and chess ladder last year, wasn't it incredible there hadn't even been a board in the school before, wasn't it tragic there was so little interest in schools these days, no wonder there were no British grandmasters. But now they'd got a new master who had played for Lancashire ("lower board only!") and between them they were trying to get the school chess club off the ground. They hoped to go in for the *Sunday Times* competition next year, but he wasn't too hopeful as they literally hadn't anyone who even knew the openings except for yours truly!

"I am hoping (!) to play in the next Blackpool Congress, unless prevented by family etc. and that you will be covering same for your papers. I'd like to show you something I've written, and I've got a new idea about the answer to P–KR4 in the Sicilian I'd like to discuss with you."

Paul put down the letter in cold fury. These cocky teenagers always wanting him to see some analysis they had done. Let them become grandmasters first before they began theorising and laying down the law on what was sound and what was inexact. There was another page to read, but he put it back in its envelope and threw the whole thing into the lake. It flicked through the air like a bird, spinning over and over, across the table, the balustrade, the green edge of the water, wheeling to the left, falling with a faint but invisible plop on to the surface below. The other guests looked at him with disapproval.

Immediately Paul was sorry. He should have sent young Robin Jackson a picture postcard of Bled Castle, thanking him for his interesting letter and urging him to buy a copy of *Asymmetrical Defences*. He'd have to keep a wary eye out at Blackpool, though, or he'd be pestered to death.

There was a last glass of Riesling in the bottle and he drank it with his coffee, rejecting rather nobly the thought of a glass of Slivovitz. It didn't do to get too sleepy these hot afternoons. The terrace was emptying, the tourists were moving on to Dubrovnik or Ljubljana. Grandmaster Dietrich had gone and none of the others had come. Paul heaved himself to his feet, contented with wine and chestnut leaves, and strolled up to the lounge. There in lonely splendour sat Grandmaster Boghossian, hunched over a chess-board on which a complicated position had been set up. It was the same board the two boys had been using before lunch. Paul went over and shook hands with him.

"Not coming down to the games today?"

"Later." Boghossian spoke English, and nine other languages, perfectly. "When I have solved this little problem."

"Who are you playing?"

"I am not sure. Matanovic, I think."

This casualness was careful. It was only the technical problem that mattered, not the opponent or the occasion. Boghossian liked to arrive late for his games. He liked to sit on in his hotel while his clock in the congress hall down the road ticked away the precious minutes of his playing time. He would arrive after ten or fifteen minutes, calm, courteous, unhurried, master of the situation. It was his punctual opponent who often became rattled; who started to think about time in the first few minutes of the session when he ought to be thinking about the development of his pieces.

By the concierge's desk Mischchov was standing, holding a bulky envelope. Paul went and shook hands with him too, Mischchov changing the envelope to his left hand. He said "Good day" in Russian, but he didn't smile. As Paul knew only a few words of Russian, no further communication was possible. The concierge came up, and Mischchov went with him into an inner room.

This also was routine. Every afternoon, before going down to the games, one or other of the Soviet players would go into the inner room with the concierge and lock the big envelope up in the hotel safe, obtaining a receipt. When they returned in the evening, they would take delivery of it again, and smuggle it upstairs to their bedroom. Nobody knew what was inside the envelope, so top secret, classified, for Soviet eyes alone. Carl Sandbach said he guessed it was the scores of the recently finished Moscow tournament, which had not yet been published. Paul thought it was the report of the recent study group which had been working for three weeks in Riga on a depth analysis of the Sicilian Defence. Either way, the information would give the Russians a temporary, slight but definite advantage. As if they needed any advantage, Paul thought.

Paul went to get his umbrella. Never mind the secret sessions in Riga, it would be raining before the end of the session, and he didn't want his linen suit soaked and shrunk on the way back. Then he strolled down the road through the thundery afternoon to the handsome Congress Hall beside the lake. Unlike Boghossian he liked to be early, to get the feel of the round, to chat to the players and perhaps pick up some gossip which would be useful in an article. He liked to see the openings too; it was sometimes not easy to reconstruct them from a complicated middle-game. That's all any reader cares about nowadays, he thought; which opening, which variation, which line and never what happened later on, who won, what was the score. You put the name of the

44

opening, a glamorous romantic name (not that anyone would notice that), in capital letters at the head of the score and all your readers played through the opening, the first twenty moves, analysing carefully, arguing furiously. Then they would scrap the game and start another. All these bright schoolboys, like Robin whatshisname, who knew the Slav Defence or the King's Indian Defence by heart, and never looked at an end-game. It was just the opposite of the British Army, he reflected, which always lost every battle till the last. Perhaps that explained the long series of British successes in war, and failures in chess. It was a point, perhaps he would write an article about it, it would fill one of his weekly columns.

In the meantime he had learnt his lesson. And as he was bound to please his readers he must report the openings carefully, by name, with established variations and experimental innovations. After that he could relax, go and have a beer, make his notes, wait for the resignations and draws to emerge. Unless one or two of the games should have an unexpectedly exciting finish: a mating attack, a Queen sacrifice, a time scramble; that could be news. But the end-games, forty or fifty moves distant and played off in an adjournment session some other time, they could be skipped. Those games of eighty or a hundred moves, with bare boards and Kings moving one square at a time to attack or threaten Pawns, who would ever have the patience to play them through?

The Congress Hall was a new building facing the lake through a carefully contrived vista of lawns and trees. Paul walked up the steps, through the glass doors into the big hall, and at once he felt the thrill of expectancy, the queasy suspense before a big sporting event. The ten boards were set out, five on either side of the hall, behind protecting ropes, each table with its clock, its score-pads, cards showing the names of the players, small flags showing their nationalities and the big beautiful pieces on their starting ranks, as regular and satisfying as a line of guardsmen. Above the platform at the end, behind the umpire's desk, was a big blue banner with an incomprehensible slogan out of which Paul could only recognise the word SAH.

There were some twenty spectators standing in the main body of the hall, or sitting on small hard chairs. They were all Yugoslav, probably, Paul guessed, waiters off duty. Tourists rarely found their way here. Paul went up to the other journalists and greeted them in their separate huddle: one German, two Yugoslavs and one Hungarian. Then, regarding himself as privileged, he stepped over the ropes and moved round the tables shaking hands with the players. It was important to be noticed, to make the scene.

The players were standing by their tables, shaking hands with each other, taking off their coats because the hall was hot, looking for their ball-points, polishing their glasses, none of them speaking, their minds far away from small talk. Relaxed tension, he thought, screwing themselves up for their monumental five-hour ordeal. Two of the players, Haslund and Marovic, were already seated, staring at the boards on which no move had as yet been played.

Shaking hands with Sol Chaimovitz, Paul was tempted to tell him of Mrs. Oppenheimer's offer. He liked to be the bearer of good tidings, indeed of any tidings. It was, he told himself, his function as a professional communicator of news. But he bit it back, this was not the moment. Chaimovitz was thinking about his opening, he wouldn't take it in, the story would go off at half-cock. He'd do it that night, show him the cable, get his terms.

Paul moved on to the last table and shook hands with George Wheaton, the representative of Great Britain. Paul was grateful to him; it was difficult to persuade an editor to send him to cover a congress if there was no British player there. All the same Paul wished a stronger player had been invited. Wheaton had been a good player in his time. He had had a long series of successes at British congresses and had always done respectably in foreign tournaments. But that was ten or fifteen years ago. He must be nearly sixty now. He was too old to have the stamina, let alone the resilience, for a congress of this size and strength. He stood there beside his Union Jack, tall, grey-haired, shaggy, in baggy and worn tweeds, the picture of sad defeat.

"I'm keeping my fingers crossed for you," Paul said brightly. "It's a big chance today."

Wheaton smiled lugubriously and said nothing.

Paul said, "Good game for you to win."

Wheaton, at the moment bottom of the tournament, was to play Mischchov, who was half a point ahead of anybody else.

An easy game for Mischchov, everyone thought, which should help him increase his lead.

Wheaton said, "With Black?" Black, starting behind White, is supposed to have the harder task. Grandmasters, playing with the black pieces, are usually happy to get a draw.

Paul joked cheerfully, "Why not? Will you play the Dragon?"

Some fifteen years ago at Hastings Wheaton had won a famous game against Vokhorov with the Dragon Variation of the Sicilian Defence. If he could repeat it today, it would indeed be a famous victory. More than that, it would be a scoop for Paul. There was no other British journalist present; Golombek was in South Africa, Barden and Alexander were otherwise engaged, B. H. Wood was busy editing his magazine. Paul would telephone the news through tonight, the full score. They'd give him a whole column for that, possibly a mention on the front page, BRITISH PLAYER BEATS RUSSIAN EXPERT.

Wheaton shook his head slowly. "Mischchov knows too much about the Dragon. He has studied it carefully."

"But it would give you a psychological advantage. He'll remember what happened to Vokhorov at Hastings. He knows that game as well as you do."

"Too well. The Dragon is too dangerous. There are too many good lines against it."

Mischchov came up at this point, shook hands with Wheaton and once again with Paul, said not a word, sat down behind the white pieces, glanced at his Soviet flag, checked his clock to see that it was correctly set and still stopped, and stared at his pieces. Wheaton looked at Paul, shrugged, and sat down behind the black pieces. Paul resisted the temptation to say "Good luck!" Chess was not a game of luck.

The position was clear enough to everyone in the room. Wheaton had given up hope of ever winning another game in an international tournament. He was hoping to draw, this game and every other, with White as well as Black. That was no way to come first in the tournament, but a half-point from each drawn game should give him a respectable final score and a place somewhere in the lower half of the table, high enough to keep his flag flying. As long as he did not finish bottom, there was a chance he would be invited to play at Palma or Beverwijk or Havana.

But at the moment he was bottom, the result of having lost his first two games. He could not afford to risk losing another.

Paul could guess his plan. He would try to play a good drawing line, defend stoutly, block the open files, exchange off Queens as soon as possible, and offer a draw on the thirtieth move. It would be a dull game to watch, a dull game to describe to the *Post* readers. Paul drafted a sentence in his mind: "The veteran British expert George Wheaton scored a notable success in drawing with the ex-World Champion Nikolai Mischchov." And indeed it would be a notable achievement. Paul doubted if he himself could hold Mischchov or any other player in the room to a draw.

At half past two the umpire, a senior Yugoslav grandmaster, looked at his watch and decided to start the day's play, five gruelling hours, after which the unfinished games would be adjourned till the following morning. The time control was set at Move 40: each player would have to play at least forty moves in the two and a half hours allowed to him, or lose on time. The double clocks stood on each table, the real masters of the game, their faces like owls' eyes staring across the boards. Each clock was set at the notional time of half past three. The crux for any slow player would come as the hands on his own clock approached the fatal (though still notional) time of six o'clock. That would probably occur shortly before seven o'clock real time.

There was no ceremony about the start. The umpire moved along the tables, pressing the button each time on the top of Black's clock, which started White's clock ticking. The players sat down, without even glancing at each other. Most of the players made their first moves immediately. But two players, Haslund and Belic, remained motionless, staring at the board, apparently unable to decide which Pawn (or Knight) to move. Since they had presumably decided on their opening hours, if not weeks, before, there were psychological reasons for this: a reluctance to commit themselves or to start a long hard game, a pause to collect their thoughts or rub up their memories, or a wish to show their opponents that they at least were impervious to the time factor. Then finally they too moved. The session had begun.

Only one chair was still empty, Boghossian's. He was still at the hotel, studying some problem, preparing like a bride his late entry. His clock ticked the minutes away. The two flags on the table were French and American. Boghossian, the wandering Armenian, who changed his country every other year, was apparently playing this tournament under French colours. His opponent was not after all Matanovic, but, as he had no doubt known all along, the young Californian Grandmaster, Carl Sandbach. Carl sat alone at the table, his long legs crossed nonchalantly, staring at the United States flag without necessarily seeing it. He was chewing the top of his left thumb. Then he pulled a black Knight out of his pocket, a souvenir from some other set or game, and started fiddling with it, turning it over and over between the thumb and middle finger of his right hand. Rubbing his mascot, thought Paul. Nerves! Boghossian's trick was having some effect, though whether it was worth the lost ten or fifteen minutes was questionable.

A hush had settled over the room. The only identifiable sounds were the ticking of the ten clocks. The spectators and journalists moved softly, watching the openings. The players themselves sat motionless, staring at the board, lost in thought. Suddenly a hand would move out, slide a Pawn forward, move straight to press the clock button, pick up the ball-point and write down the move on the pad and return to propping its owner's chin. When the opponent moved it would pick up the ball-point, write down the opponent's move and return to the chin.

The masters were moving relatively fast now, a move every fifteen or thirty seconds. There was no point in wasting precious minutes on openings they knew by heart. The moment to pause and reflect would come after ten moves, or perhaps fifteen, or even in some openings like the Ruy Lopez after twenty moves, when the players would move away from their prepared lines of play, and embark on agonising and irrevocable experiment.

Paul watched the Mischchov-Wheaton game first, since that was the one he had been sent to cover. Mischchov opened with the King's Pawn, and Wheaton replied with his King's Pawn, thus refusing the Sicilian Defence in any of its variations, Dragon or otherwise, and opting for the Ruy Lopez. It only remained to be seen if he would play the Marshall Attack on Move 8, the fashionable move at the moment for those wanting a draw. Paul waited till Move 9, and then wrote "Ruy Lopez, Marshall" on his notes.

Then he moved softly round the room on his crêpe-soled suède shoes, noting the openings in his note-book. It was the usual lot: Ruy Lopez, Sicilian Defence, French Defence, King's Indian Defence, Nimzo-Indian Defence, Modern Benoni, Queen's Gambit Accepted. There wasn't much variety these days. Almost alone Grandmaster Larsen of Denmark was prepared to try Reti's Opening or Alekhine's Defence and Larsen wasn't playing today.

Thinking these thoughts, Paul paused baffled before the game Belic-Dietrich. Dietrich was playing an extraordinary defence. He seemed to be trying to keep all his pieces on the back rank, but on different squares from their original starting squares, whilst moving as few Pawns as possible in the process. At least it was unusual, though it did not seem to be a strong attacking opening. But then Grandmaster Dietrich was a noticeably defensive player, preferring to draw wherever possible. The game between him and Wheaton, still to be played, should be a real yawner. Paul watched for several minutes, until Dietrich played N–K1, and then wrote the words "Irregular Hippopotamus" in his notebook.

At this moment Grandmaster Boghossian finally arrived. He strolled in without haste, nodded to Paul and the other journalists, pausing to study the games of the other tables as he passed, finally reaching his own. He shook hands with Carl Sandbach who rose politely, but said not a word either in greeting or in apology for his lateness. He sat slowly down, glanced at his clock which then showed ten to four, took out his ball-point and slowly wrote the date, the place, his name and Carl's on top of his score-pad. Then he sat back, folded his arms, and considered the lines of unmoved pieces. Three minutes later he finally made his first move, his Queen's Pawn. Carl replied immediately with his King's Knight. The speed of his move was like a silent scream. Calm yourself, boy, thought Paul, relax, take it easy, he's twenty minutes behind you on the clock. Everyone, including Carl and Paul knew what Boghossian's next move would be, but he still took three minutes to make it: P–QB4. Paul watched the game until he was sure it was a King's Indian Defence, and then moved on. It was going to be a long hard struggle.

Two hours later the hall wasn't quite so silent. Some more spectators had arrived, local boys, and were muttering among themselves. The players stretched their legs between moves, by walking round the hall, looking at the other games. They never spoke, either to their opponents or to anyone else. Carl relieved his tension by striding rapidly to the furthest table, as if he had an urgent message to deliver to Wheaton or Mischchov, throwing a hasty but probably unseeing glance at the game, and striding back to his own, glancing briefly to see if Boghossian had moved, and then striding away again.

Paul studied the position. Exactly the same position, he recalled, had occurred in the tenth game of the World Championship match between Petrosian and Spassky, and also in the 1965 U.S. Championship in the game Reshevsky v. Chaimovitz. Both players of course knew this as well as Paul. Finally Boghossian played, like Petrosian and Reshevsky, Bishop takes Pawn. Carl threw himself on his chair, hunched forward, his arms on his knees, his fingers rubbing his private black Knight, as if they wished to polish it smooth. Carl had the choice of playing Bishop takes Bishop, like Spassky, or N–K4, like Chaimovitz, or of discovering some new and untested move. He considered the move for twenty-eight minutes before finally playing, in one quick jerk, N–K4. Good boy, thought Paul, agreeing with him. He kept his black square Bishop in play and prevented the opening of his King's Knight's file, which would probably, though not certainly, be to his ultimate advantage. But he was now behind Boghossian on the clock.

Paul sighed. The agonies of modern positional play. What would Joann Oppenheimer's poor little illiterate Persian boy do in this sort of company?

Wheaton was holding Mischchov well, though he was taking too long over his moves. Dietrich and Belic were involved in a complicated struggle for the control of White's Queen 4 square. Portisch v. Matanovic was another dour struggle, Portisch bringing some pressure to bear on the King's side of the board, and Matanovic trying to get some counter-play in the centre. Both players on Table No. 4 had disappeared and Paul wondered if they had agreed a draw; but then one of the players returned, presumably from the lavatory, noted down the move made in his absence, and started once more to think. Chaimovitz seemed completely stuck. He had been thinking about his next move now for forty minutes and had still not moved. It was getting very hot in the hall.

The only game which showed any signs of reaching a climax was Haslund *v*. Tal. Tal, with the black pieces and having used an hour less time than Haslund, had managed to mount a strong King's side attack and Haslund seemed likely to lose a Pawn. But it was Haslund, blond and heavy, who seemed unmoved. Tal, the "brilliant Jew," was standing by the table, chain-smoking nervously.

Paul glanced round the hall. The signs of strain were beginning to show, the nervous tics, the grinding teeth, the twitching cheek muscles, the scowls at any spectator who spoke louder than a whisper. Twenty players, he thought, fifteen or sixteen of them undisputed geniuses, the rest with considerable talent. It wasn't every day that you could find such a gathering of the brilliant and the learned and the dedicated in the same room. The total I.Q. of those assembled today, including those watching, umpiring and reporting, must be astronomical.

It was fascinating too to watch a genius in action, to see him in the act of thinking; not having just had a bright idea, or being about to have one, but actually thinking before your eyes, pulling out the grand design to order by the clock. The only comparative experience was watching a great pianist play a concerto; and then you could never be sure how much of that impassivity or half-closed eyes or concentration on the infinite was involuntary or showmanship. Rubinstein, for instance, playing a Brahms concerto, waiting for his entry, holding his lapels, swaying from side to side on his stool, his eyes raised and half-closed, as he listened to the orchestra. Or Karajan conducting with his eyes shut. Were they totally absorbed in the music, oblivious to the impression they might be making on the audience? Were you watching the rapt genius, or the performer making a calculated effect, or both at once?

But there was no doubt about Sol Chaimovitz, another genius, swaying back and forth on his chair, his blue cotton shirt soaked with sweat, staring at the board in an agony of indecision, his thoughts five, ten, even fifteen moves ahead, knowing that if he decided wrong his opponent Marovic would pounce without mercy. Or was there an element of showmanship in all that suffering too, was there always an element of showmanship in everything?

Chaimovitz finally retreated his Knight; he had a mannerism of pressing his pieces on to the board as if it were a question of suction. He pressed the button with a casual jab and looked up into Paul's eyes. The eyes didn't focus with recognition. Chaimovitz's mind was still far away.

Paul felt the sweat on the back of his neck and mopped with a handkerchief. Time for a breath of fresh air, he thought. On the terrace outside the hall the air was as hot and stuffy as inside. He stood under the plastic shelter watching the storm coming up. The sky and the lake were leaden, the leaves were motionless. Dark rags of cloud were drifting towards Bled. The Julian Alps were hidden, lit every few seconds by the glow of lightning inside the cloud. Half an hour perhaps before the rain, time for some beer.

He walked down the steps and along the street to the Blegas beer garden. This was a very different atmosphere from the Congress Hall, relaxed, cheerful. Parties of young people, tourists as well as Yugoslavs, sat at iron tables under the chestnuts, drinking beer or coffee. A brass band on a platform played a selection of tunes from *White Horse Inn*. Some rather restrained dancing was going on in front of the band. Paul took his coat off, sat down and ordered a bottle of Triglav beer.

It came, tepid and fizzy. Paul pulled out his notes and took stock of the situation. Here he was, sitting and relaxing in a Slovene beer-garden, while the rest of them sweated it out inside there for another three hours. There was a good deal to be said for being on the side-lines, for being a professional voyeur. He might not be a world champion or a grandmaster or even a national hero, but he was well known in the world of international chess, very well known in the British world. Thousands of enthusiasts read his columns every week, quoted his opinions and his bon mots. He made as much money as most good players, even the lucky ones. He travelled free to the most attractive places in the world. And in the middle of a thundery afternoon he could take time off to drink beer, instead of giving himself blood-pressure in front of a chess-board. Tonight he would mingle with them all on equal terms, discussing their games, telling them where they had gone wrong. They'd be polite and friendly, hoping for a favourable mention in his report. He'd drink Slivovitz, telephone London, cable Iran, all on expenses. Yes, whoever won or lost their games inside, it was he who always emerged the winner.

Pity about Wheaton, though. Pity the British hadn't sent a really strong player, who could make him a good story. But who? Wheaton was by any standards a skilled and experienced player, and he was doing well against such a tremendous opponent. But he was hardly a young genius ripe for hero-worshipping. Young talent, young geniuses, that was what British chess needed.

He ordered another bottle of beer and slid into his favourite day-dream. A National Chess Foundation would be started, financed by the Arts Council or the Ministry of Technology or the Duke of Edinburgh's Award scheme (was chess an art or a science or a sport? The endlessly debated question). Anyway, the foundation would be established and he, Paul, would be appointed director. Who better? He would insist on ample funds, so that his chosen colts might be freed from all financial worries. They could study chess twelve hours a day like young hopeful pianists, and not have to bother with anything else. They wouldn't have to be schoolmasters or journalists or computer programmers as well. They'd be whole-time professionals. He'd say, "If you give me a free hand, Prime Minister, I promise you that within five years we'll have a grandmaster. In ten years we'll have five or more. In twenty years we'll have a strong contender for the World Championship. We'll show the Russians and the Americans that we are as intelligent a nation as any other." And the Prime Minister would say, "I'll leave it to you, Mr. Butler, you obviously know how to do it. The country will be very grate . . ."

A heavy plop of rain fell on the table. Within half a minute it was pouring. The band gurgled into silence, the dancers and the coffee-drinkers ran for shelter. Paul put up his umbrella, and went on sipping his beer at the table. The others looked at him goggling, the typical picture of the eccentric Englishman abroad.

When he got back to the Congress Hall the change in the atmosphere was startling. A large number of shop assistants and clerks had arrived after work to see the last hour and a half of the session. Several of the games were over. Portisch and Matanovic had agreed a draw. Dietrich and Belic seemed to be playing surprisingly fast, without touching their ball-points. Paul looked at Dietrich's score-pad and saw that they too had agreed a draw and were now playing a friendly game. Paul noted it down, in routine wonderment. Why not get the hell out of this hot and stuffy hall if their game was over? Or, if they wanted to go on playing chess, why agree a draw?

Paul supposed it was automatic. Both players were glad to finish with the strain of the serious game. It was a difficult and complicated position, and both Dietrich and Belic would be satisfied with the half-point of a draw. But then, the game safely over, the sight of the board and pieces had proved irresistible. They had begun unthinkingly to play a new game, a rapid-transit game in jest, though it was a pretty solemn jest. As Paul watched, Dietrich shrugged in resignation, pushed the pieces with the palm of his hand into the middle of the board and then began to set them up, in preparation for a fresh game. They would go on until the hall caretaker turned them out.

Paul made his way to the Haslund-Tal game, peering with difficulty through the crowd that surrounded that table. It was evident that the *coup de grâce* was being administered. Tal had duly won Haslund's Pawn and was now sacrificing his Rook to move one of the Pawns protecting Haslund's King out of the way. Haslund made a noise like "Pah!" and took the Rook. Immediately Tal moved his Queen right across the board to the back rank, sacrificing that too. The way was now clear for a mating attack by Tal's remaining Rook and Knight. Haslund said "Pah!" again, and then suddenly smiled and held out his hand in resignation. They shook hands and there was a burst of clapping from the spectators, immediately shushed by the umpire. Paul shook hands with Tal, congratulating him on his win.

"A beautiful combination," he said.

Tal grinned like a monkey. Paul wrote down the combination in his notebook; it would be studied and admired all over the world.

The German journalist said in Paul's ear, "Now Mischchov will have to win or Tal will be level with him."

Poor old George Wheaton, thought Paul.

At half past six the hall was crowded with spectators and Paul found it difficult to move from one side to another. The umpire shushed continually. Nobody was sitting down any more, and anyway there weren't enough chairs. The place steamed with the smell of damp clothes drying. This was the last hour of the session, the terrible fifth hour that sorted out the boys from the men. Wheaton was white with exhaustion. He had taken off his tweed coat long before and hung it over the back of his chair. He was swaying gently from side to side like a man in pain, and his lips moved as if he were whistling softly. Paul wondered if he would live through till the end of the day.

But he was still holding Mischchov. They were level in material; each player had, apart from the King, a Bishop, Knight and two Pawns. The Rooks had been exchanged off, like the Queens, half an hour before. There would be no beautiful combinations in this game, no sacrifices. This was a dour positional battle of attrition, full of deep threats and pressures. But it wasn't an exciting game to watch.

Two other games were still unfinished. Chaimovitz was also feeling the strain. His shirt was now blue-black with sweat all over. He was hunched over the board, as if he were very short-sighted, and he no longer remembered to ash his cigarette into the ashtray. The ash fell into the top of the Rook on his K1 square, and he didn't bother to shake it off. In contrast, his opponent Marovic looked relatively spruce and calm; perhaps he was reassured by being on his home territory in front of his fellow-countrymen. This was another strategic battle. Paul judged Chaimovitz, with his more actively placed Bishops, to have the slight advantage.

The interest centred on the Boghossian-Sandbach game, where it was clear that Carl was in time trouble. He had been getting further and further behind the clock, perhaps lulled subconsciously by the thought of Boghossian's late start. Boghossian, on the other hand, had played much faster. Despite losing twenty minutes at the start, he had now over half an hour in hand. His clock showed twenty past five, while Carl's showed two minutes to six. The minute hand was already beginning to push up the red flag on the clock face; it would fall on the stroke of six o'clock, and before then he had to make eleven moves.

He seemed suddenly to wake to his danger. He put his mascot Knight down on the table, and began to move fast, jerking the pieces across the board, pressing the clock button, scribbling down the move, running his hand through his hair while Boghossian played. Boghossian, who was in no time trouble, began to play fast too, to keep up the pressure, to give Carl no time for reflection between moves.

For a while Paul thought Carl was going to make it. His flag was still up, and he had got to Move 36. Only four more moves to go. But on his next move, under extreme pressure, he blundered. He moved a Pawn, and immediately threw up his hands in despair. Boghossian could check him on his next move, and when the King moved, could fork his Rook and Knight on the following move. Carl was bound to lose a piece. He waited for Boghossian to show that he too had seen it, to check him, and then he resigned. The two players shook hands very briefly, there was another burst of applause and shushing. Boghossian pulled his long nose contentedly, wrote up his score-sheet and, moving calmly as always, went to give it to the umpire. Carl's clock flag had now fallen, but it didn't matter any more. The game was over.

Carl moved the pieces back to where they had been before he blundered, and found the move he ought to have made. Then he sat back, crossed his long Californian legs, picked up his black Knight and started rubbing it again.

"I guess I ought to have hung on to it," he said softly. Then he caught sight of Boghossian's back across the hall. He said, louder, "That Frog swindler! That goddam Frog cheat!"

Paul didn't see that Boghossian could justifiably be called a Frog. He had played last year as a Swiss, and two years before as an Egyptian.

"And why don't these shitting Commies get themselves some air-conditioning!" Carl shouted.

Paul held up his hands in shocked distaste. The umpire looked round and shushed.

Carl said to Paul, this time softly, "Well, I guess there'll be another day. You wait, you just wait."

"Sure to be," said Paul. He patted the boy friendlily on the arm. He could sympathise with him. And anyway he might be Joann Oppenheimer's son-in-law at some future date.

Carl nodded at him, stood up, towering above Paul. He put the black Knight in his pocket, and loped out of the hall into the rain.

It was a quarter past seven, fifteen minutes till the end of the session. Paul went back to the Mischchov-Wheaton game. Wheaton was still holding on, but in the last half-hour his position had slightly deteriorated. There had been no question of a mistake, much less of a blunder in time trouble, a dramatic sacrifice or a beautiful combination. But with each move Mischchov had achieved a tiny positional advantage, move by move almost negligible, but adding up over ten moves into a definite advantage. Wheaton had obviously hoped to exchange off the Knights, leaving the two players with Bishops of opposite colour, the safest road to a draw, a game which even Mischchov would find almost impossible to win. But Mischchov had outmanœuvred him, had contrived to exchange Knight for Bishop, leaving Wheaton with a lone Knight, and himself with a white-square Bishop. Neither was sufficient to force checkmate, and everything clearly depended on the chances of queening a Pawn. Both players had still two Pawns. Theoretically they were dead level in material.

Wheaton had caught up with his time problem. He made his fortieth move with a minute in hand. He now had an hour on his clock before the next time control on the fifty-sixth move, and that would come in the adjournment session the following day. As it was now half past seven, the present session was over. The umpire came up and handed out the envelopes. Mischchov finished writing up his score-sheet, put his ball-point primly back in his pocket, and got stiffly up. Without nodding at either his opponent or Paul, he went to watch the Chaimovitz-Marovic position. The spectators and the other players began to drift away from the hall. The noise level rose sharply.

Wheaton had now one last move to make, his sealed move. With his clock ticking and his opponent absent he had to decide on his next move. He could take as long as he liked, bearing in mind that his clock was ticking away the seconds till the next time control. When he had decided his move he would not make it on the board but instead write it secretly and irrevocably on his score-sheet, stop his clock, place the score sheet in the envelope and seal it, and hand it to the umpire. At the start of the adjournment session the umpire would open the envelope and make the sealed move himself, starting Mischchov's clock at the same time. It was the established procedure for avoiding giving one player the advantage of considering his next move all night.

All the same, the sealed move was a great pitfall. It was astonishing how many even games had been irretrievably lost on the sealed move. There was something about the atmosphere perhaps, the noise of the departing crowd, the fatigue after a five-hour session, the unconscious feeling that the caretaker was trying to close the hall round you, the thought that you were going to have all night to repent at leisure of the move you were making now, which caused many great players to blunder on the sealed move.

Paul, standing behind Mischchov's empty chair, smiled encouragingly at Wheaton. Wheaton looked back at him with blank unseeing eyes. He was swaying to and fro and the flesh seemed to hang from his cheeks in bags. He took a deep breath, seeming to summon up once more his last reserves of strength, scraping the barrel once again. He covered his face with his hands, put his elbows on the table and thought, thought, thought.

Paul considered his adjournment position, and wrote it down in Forsyth notation in his notebook: 16; B 2 k 1 p 2; 8; 5 P K p; 3 n 4; 6 P 1; 8. Possibly Wheaton had the advantage of pieces; a Knight could by manoeuvring in the end be brought to attack any square, whereas Mischchov's Bishop was confined to the white squares. But on the other hand Mischchov's Pawns were on adjoining files and could support each other, while Wheaton's were separated by a file. And Mischchov's King was more actively placed among the Pawns, defending his own and attacking Black's, while Wheaton's was remote from the battle. The white King was threatening to take the black Rook's Pawn and simultaneously the white Bishop was attacking the black Knight. It was going to be a difficult game for Wheaton to save.

Obviously Wheaton was going to have to move his Knight. N–B4 or N–N5, attacking the Bishop in return, seemed possible. N–B7 check would merely lose a Pawn. Perhaps there was something to be said for N–K8, attacking the Pawn on N2. Paul was glad once more that he was not Wheaton.

He went to look at the position where Chaimovitz was considering his own sealed move. This was a complicated game which was obviously going to continue for many moves yet, before a probable eventual draw. He thought a little sadly of his telephone call tonight to London; there wasn't much to report despite all the struggle and effort; they mightn't even put it in at all. The lone British player adjourned in a losing position against the great Mischchov; another game adjourned, six others drawn. He'd do his best with Tal's beautiful sacrifice and Carl Sandbach's blunder, but there was no British player involved. A thought struck him. Perhaps an interview with Mischchov might brighten the piece.

He hurried across the now empty hall, through the swing doors to the terrace. Mischchov was standing, gloomily looking at the rain and beside him was the Soviet citizen who seemed to be his friend and interpreter. Paul asked if Grandmaster Mischchov would answer a few questions. The two Russians smiled courteously and warily.

"Do you think you will win your game against Wheaton?"

The friend spoke impassively to Mischchov in Russian, who replied equally impassively. "Grandmaster Mischchov says that either he will win or Mr. Wheaton will win, or it will be a draw."

Well, he should have expected that. He tried again.

"What do you think of Wheaton as a player?"

The reply came back from the friend. "Grandmaster Mischchov is always glad to play against masters from the Western capitalist countries as well as Soviet masters."

Ah well! Paul asked, "Will you be coming to play in Britain again soon?"

"Grandmaster Mischchov says it is many years since he first played against the players of England at an English congress." Paul waited in case there might be more to come. Then, when nothing emerged, he tried a different line.

"Do you think you will regain the World Championship next year?"

This question provoked quite a conversation between Mischchov and his friend. Finally the friend said:

"Grandmaster Mischchov says that either he will regain the World Championship or some other player will gain it or the present World Champion will retain it."

That was that. Paul said, "Thank you, Grandmaster. *Spaseebo.*" He shook hands once again with both of them, and watched them as they put on raincoats and trudged out into the downpour. It was always a discouraging business interviewing Mischchov and this dialogue hadn't helped his piece much. Though, on second thoughts, perhaps he might do something with it. "The Soviet former World Champion Nikolai Mischchov, who is in many people's opinion still the greatest living player, gave me the rare honour of an exclusive interview after today's play finished. He went out of his way to praise British chess players, and in particular the British expert George Wheaton, against whom he is playing a needle game, now adjourned at a tense stage. The Soviet Grandmaster also hinted that the next World Champion might be a new and still unknown player." Perhaps he could draft a paragraph on those lines.

He went back into the hall. Except for an old woman in the background, and two boys who were setting up the pieces on the other tables, Wheaton and the umpire were alone. Wheaton's clock now stood at twenty past six. It was, of course, vital to get the sealed move right, but twenty minutes on one move was too long. Unless he was careful he would be in time trouble tomorrow. Paul began to think hungrily of dinner: thoughts wafted through his head, kalbsrisotto, stuffed paprika, Serbian moussaka, more Riesling, or perhaps that red wine which was a local Chianti. Slivovitz. It had been a long hot day and he felt he deserved a good dinner.

He walked to the door and then turned back yet again. He had better wait for Wheaton. The old boy mightn't have brought his umbrella with him. Paul couldn't risk his getting soaked on the way back to the hotel. If he became ill, pleurisy, pneumonia, bronchitis, he would have to withdraw from the tournament. Then Paul might be recalled to London.

After another ten minutes Wheaton finally wrote his move on his score-sheet and stopped his clock. It said almost half past six. He sealed the score-sheet in the envelope and handed it to the umpire, who put it in his pocket. The umpire shook hands with them both, and said, "Ten o'clock tomorrow morning." He said it in German and Paul translated to Wheaton, who nodded without speaking. Paul thought, Three hours of this end-game against Mischchov tomorrow morning, a break for lunch and then five hours of a new game against someone else. Poor old Wheaton, glad I'm not him.

"You're playing Boghossian tomorrow, aren't you? Or is it Sandbach?"

Wheaton shook his head dully. Paul shepherded him gently out of the hall. On the steps he stopped and said. "Oh, it's raining." They were his first words for many hours. "I haven't brought my umbrella."

"Shelter under mine."

The single umbrella barely sheltered them both and Paul felt his right shoulder getting wet, but he bore it bravely.

"Pretty good game you played today," he remarked brightly. "I hope you're feeling pleased with yourself."

Wheaton said nothing. He was beyond words.

"Holding Mischchov is quite a job for anyone. I'll give you a good puff in my piece tonight."

Wheaton glanced at him, but made no comment.

They had some shelter from the plopping trees beside the lake, but they were fully exposed on the street by the Park Hotel and the shops. Paul wished Wheaton would walk faster. In one of the shop windows was a big scoreboard of the tournament, with today's finished games already marked up. Tiresomely Wheaton stopped to look at it.

"Let's go to dinner," Paul suggested. "You'll feel better with a good dinner inside you."

"I couldn't eat anything. Perhaps if they could bring me a cup of tea and some biscuits."

"That all you want? What about some trout?"

Wheaton's voice was very low. "I couldn't digest it."

Paul left him in the hotel lobby and went straight in to dinner, as it was already half past eight. Over a big, slow and strongly spiced dinner he wrote his piece for the *Post*. He boiled the whole day's play into two terse paragraphs, concentrating on Wheaton's heroic defence and disposing of Tal and Sandbach in one single sentence, but he brought in his interview with Mischchov. Our chess correspondent is always at the heart of things.

After dinner he booked a telephone call to London and wandered into the lounge. Most of the chess masters were sitting there, playing quick informal games against each other. Paul looked at them with amusement. Five gruelling hours this afternoon, and now they were going to continue playing all night. It's like a drug, like smoking, like gambling, like drinking, he thought, they just cannot stop.

Mischchov and his friend were absent; they were presumably in their bedrooms analysing the adjourned game. Wheaton was presumably doing the same in some solitary corner. But all the others were here. Four of them, Tal, Belic, Haslund and a Yugoslav, were playing chess doubles, like tennis doubles, the confusions and misunderstandings causing wild amusement. The two Americans, Sandbach and Chaimovitz, were playing five-minute chess: they had produced a chess clock and set both sets of hands at five minutes before the hour; they then played as fast as they could, and the player whose flag fell first was the loser. It was the most tiring of all the light-hearted versions of chess, and terribly bad for the clock, which got bashed in the scramble.

Other players were playing normal, though rather quick, chess. They asked Paul to come and join the fun, but he smilingly declined. He was, he explained, awaiting a call to London, and in the meantime had to draft his piece for tomorrow's *Post*. He had, he refrained from explaining, played his last game of chess several years ago and he had an awful feeling that his game was no longer up to the required standard. To play now, and play stupidly, even informally, might damage his international reputation. Things got around. He consoled himself with Slivovitz.

The sight of Chaimovitz, a tall hunched figure, playing five-minute chess puzzled him. He would have supposed him to have been occupied in analysing his adjourned game. Perhaps he was tired of that game, even though he couldn't stop playing chess. Paul remembered Mrs. Oppenheimer's cable and showed it to Chaimovitz between games.

Chaimovitz groaned. "Shit! What's she up to now?"

He set up the pieces and began to play through the game in the cable, commenting volubly. Carl contributed comments and variations. The others drifted across to watch and discuss it.

"Well, that's it, folks," said Chaimovitz. "The first game by the next World Champion, right?"

There were suitable sniggers.

Haslund said, "When was this game played? In 1800? Perhaps during a performance at the opera."

Dietrich said, "I do not think he would have won that game against me."

"Oh, give the kid a break," said Carl from the seniority of his twenty-one years. "I don't reckon that game's too bad, even granted the opposition wasn't too strong. I guess that kid's no drop-out."

Chaimovitz waved his hands over the board. "Okay, okay. The kid's a genius, right? He's going to win the World Championship one day, right? But he can't speak English. He can't read or write, he doesn't wash. Right? Right! He doesn't know who the hell Ruy Lopez is. So she hires me to tell him all about it. I've got to teach this snot-nosed kid the Lopez. *And* the Sicilian. *And* the Queen's Gambit Declined. *And* all the rest of them. And it's no use just throwing *M.C.O.* at him and telling him to get on with it, because he can't read or write." He looked up at Paul. "Do I have to teach him to read and write too? Do I have to teach him to wash?"

"She doesn't say anything about that. I suppose she'll hire someone else for that."

"And just how do you teach the Queen's Gambit Declined to someone who doesn't speak English? With gestures?" He made an obscene gesture with his finger. "Right? Tell her I'll do it for —for—for five hundred dollars a week. Think she'll ride that?"

Carl said, "There's plenty more where that comes from."

"Yeah. Okay, tell her I'll do it for five hundred bucks a week. Right? And free Scotch." He looked up at Carl. "And a free poke at her beautiful daughter every night."

"Cut that out!" said Carl in a low voice. "Just cut that out!"

"Okay, okay, just a figure of speech. Tell her five hundred bucks. And the kid's got to take a shower before each lesson."

"I'll send the cable," said Paul, moving away rather thankfully. His call to London came through at half past eleven and he had the experience, more glamorous in the telling than in the act, of dictating his report over a bad line to someone on the sports desk who wasn't the least interested in chess. He consoled himself with some more Slivovitz.

At one in the morning half the players were still in the lounge, though all the tourists had gone to bed. The night porter moved round, turning out lights, straightening tables. Finally he suggested that, as the lounge was now being closed, the masters might continue their games in the card-room which had been reserved for the masters' use. The masters ignored this.

Paul, however, decided it was time for bed. The bar was now shut, which was probably as well, as his ears were singing with wine and Slivovitz. He glanced into the card-room, where the lights were still on. A lone grey figure was sitting there: Wheaton. He had a cheap cardboard chess-board on his knees, and a cheap set of pieces. On the table was an empty tea-cup and an empty pot of yoghurt. He must have been there all the evening, Paul realised.

Wheaton was banging the pieces down on his board, picking them up and then banging them down again, in frenzy. He's gone mad, was Paul's first thought. Something's snapped.

But he stopped when Paul came in, starting guiltily, but not saying anything. Paul said:

"Still at it?"

Wheaton said nothing.

"Found the road to the draw?"

"I think so. I *think* so. But it will seem different over the board tomorrow."

"Well, it sounds as if you've done all you can. What about calling it a day?"

"Could you possibly tell me the time?"

"Ten past one."

"So late? I hadn't noticed. Yes, perhaps it is time to go to bed. I'm afraid I shall not sleep, but it's restful even to lie down, isn't it."

"You ought to sleep. You've got a long day tomorrow. Oh, by the way, this is what I telephoned through to London tonight."

He pulled out a piece of paper and handed it to Wheaton, who read it slowly.

"Thank you. You are very kind."

"I was glad to see the British representative"—he stumbled a little over the word—"keeping the flag flying so well."

"I only hope I can still keep it flying tomorrow," Wheaton said sadly.

At this moment, the door opened and Mischchov and his friend came in. They walked quickly over to Wheaton and shook hands with him, and then with Paul.

The friend said, "Former World Champion Mischchov says that if your adjournment move is h3, he offers a draw."

"h3?" Paul translated the algebraic move into descriptive notation. "P–R6?" He made the move on the board and looked enquiringly at Wheaton.

Wheaton nodded slowly. He pulled his copy of the score-sheet out of his pocket and handed it to Mischchov. He looked at it and passed it to his friend, who showed it to Paul, who confirmed the move.

"Pawn to Rook 6," said Paul. "h3."

Wheaton said, "Good. Draw agreed then."

Mischchov said *"Neechya"* and shook hands with Wheaton again. The friend shook hands with Wheaton. Both Russians shook hands with Paul again, and then trooped out of the room.

"Well, you've made it," said Paul. "Congratulations!"

Wheaton just looked at him.

"I thought you were going to have to move your Knight. Pawn to Rook 6, that's a pretty subtle move. Let's see, if he takes your Knight now, you play Pawn on and then Queen it, and his own Pawn protects the queening square from his Bishop. So he doesn't take your Knight at all or he loses. Instead he plays Pawn to Knight 3, getting his Pawn out of the way. Then what do you play? Pawn on?"

Wheaton nodded.

Paul moved the pieces on the board. "All right, Pawn to Rook 7, he plays what? Bishop to Knight 7, attacking the queening square, Pawn on and Queens, Bishop takes Queen. Then what?"

Wheaton moved his Knight to Bishop 7.

Paul said, "Check, forking King and Bishop. You win his Bishop, though I don't think you'd win the game. So he doesn't play Pawn to Knight 3, he answers your sealed move with Pawn takes Pawn." He put the pieces back on their original squares and made the new move.

Wheaton sighed, and then played Knight takes Pawn.

"Sacrificing your Knight? That's bold at this stage of the game. And you're meant to be a cautious player. All right, he accepts

66

your sacrifice, otherwise he loses his second Pawn, and then he can't win because he can't force mate with King and Bishop alone. So he plays King takes Knight. Then what?"

Wheaton played King to King 2.

"Yes," said Paul thoughtfully, "yes."

Wheaton said in a low, slow voice, "That's what I've been worrying about all the evening. I don't think he can ever queen his Rook's Pawn. His Bishop can't control the queening square."

"Cunning." The queening square was black, and the Bishop could only move on the white squares. "Can't he make it with King and Pawn alone?"

"I don't think so," Wheaton said. "It's difficult to be sure, especially against someone like Mischchov, but I don't think so. I think it's a drawn position."

"Mischchov obviously thinks so too," said Paul, punching Wheaton playfully on the arm. "You crafty old devil! And there was I thinking you were going to lose."

Wheaton smiled wanly.

"It's too bad of Mischchov to get round to it so late. If he'd agreed the draw earlier, I could have got all this into my report. I could have made quite a thing of it. I'd have given you a good puff. I'd have sent through the full score. I know!" He looked at his watch. It said half past one. "Why don't I ring London again now. There shouldn't be such a delay at this hour."

Moving briskly and dramatically, as if he were about to send through the first news of an assassination or a man on the moon, he reached the lobby. There was only one light on, and the night porter was dozing behind the desk. The excitement dwindled. Paul felt defeated—defeated by the lateness of the hour and too much Slivovitz, defeated by the thought of making the night porter book a call to London, defeated by the prospect of reading out, probably shouting, a forty-one move game, move by move, to someone on the sports desk who didn't know what it all meant and had never heard of either Wheaton or Mischchov and couldn't care less about chess anyway.

It could wait till tomorrow. The great news that Wheaton had managed to draw with the ex-World Champion could wait till tomorrow. It would be something to say.

TEHERAN

The air-conditioning in the Hunt Bar had been turned up to its
highest, and Mrs. Oppenheimer shivered slightly. She gazed at
the fountain splashing in the middle of the room with distaste.
They just want me to feel chilly, she thought. She pulled her blue
mink stole closer round her shoulders—she had chosen it because
it exactly matched her hair—and read Paul's cable again.

MRS OPPENHEIMER HILTON HOTEL TEHERAN
YOU MARVELLOUS TALENT SCOUT STOP ALL GRANDMASTERS
HERE INTERESTED YOUR DISCOVERY AND WANT TO PLAY HIM STOP
MISCHCHOV THINKS NEXT WORLD CHAMPION MAY BE UNKNOWN
GENIUS SO WHY NOT YOUR BOY STOP CHAIMOVITZ AGREES COACH
HIM FOR FIVE HUNDRED DOLLARS WEEKLY LOVE PAUL

She read it through a third time. It was a heart-warming cable.
They all agreed with her. Even Mischchov thought the boy might
be the next World Champion, and Mischchov didn't usually say
things like that.

She put the cable back in her purse and smiled as her long-
legged daughter came up.

"You weren't in your room, so I came on down."

"I was beside the pool." Moraine sat down. "How's my suntan coming on?"

She lifted her silk stole to show her upper arm. Mrs. Oppenheimer looked at her golden smiling face.

"Did you swim?"

"Just one length, Mommy, it was so cold! How can that pool be cold with that sun on it day after day?"

"I expect Mr. Hilton has it specially chilled to be more refreshing."

Moraine nodded. "Would you believe that? Well, I just wish he wouldn't." She rubbed her forearm through the stole and then nibbled a potato chip.

"Bad for your figure," said Mrs. Oppenheimer. "What news of the infant prodigy?"

"He's at the pool too," said Moraine, putting the uneaten part of the chip in the ashtray. "He's still there."

"But he doesn't need to worry over his suntan."

"No, he's under an umbrella. Oh, Mommy, it's the funniest thing. He's gotten himself a pair of bathing trunks and a big flashy wristwatch, and he sits there hour after hour just looking at his watch. He doesn't do anything else."

"I expect he's really thinking about chess all the time."

"I don't think so. I guess he's just thinking about his watch. I don't suppose he's ever had one before."

"Was it going?"

"I didn't get near enough to find out."

"Did you talk to him?"

"I did not! He doesn't speak English. And anyway I kept the far side of the pool. He may have leprosy or something."

"Leprosy is so romantic, dear."

Moraine grimaced. As the waiter came up, Mrs. Oppenheimer asked, "What would you like to drink?"

"Could I have one of those love-potion things they give you as a courtesy drink when you arrive. Gol-something."

"The sweetest drink in the world," Mrs. Oppenheimer said drily.

"Two golnars?"

"One golnar. And I should like a vodka and tonic on the rocks. And I'd like some caviar."

"Oh yes, I'd like some too. I'm hungry."

"Love-potions *and* caviar? Do you think they'd go well together?"

"I expect they've been having them together here since the beginning of time. The caviar comes from the Caspian just up the road. I expect Xerxes often had them together. Or Darius."

"Darius was a man of great taste." She fished in her purse again and brought out the cable. "Look, I've had an answer from Paul."

She passed the cable over, and Moraine read it impassively.

Mrs. Oppenheimer said, "You see, they all think he's a genius, even Mischchov. He doesn't usually say things like that."

"He doesn't usually say anything at all. Five hundred dollars, are you going to pay that?"

"Why not? It'll be worth every cent. Sol's a good teacher."

"Is Sol also going to teach him not to tread down the backs of his shoes? Oh, he'll look so funny on Fifth Avenue like that."

"I shall teach him about his shoes," Mrs. Oppenheimer said firmly. She put the cable back in her purse.

The waiter brought the caviar and the drinks. The vodka and tonic was in a long glass, the golnar in a silver goblet. Mrs. Oppenheimer said, "And would you ask the bartender Azizyan to come over here when he's not too busy."

Moraine held her drink like a chalice, peering into it and sniffing. "They say it's made from the secret recipe of Shah Jehan."

"Then how does Mr. Hilton know it?"

"Oh, you just want to crab everything." She looked up defiantly at her mother. "Why shouldn't Shah Jehan's favourite wine steward have passed the recipe to his son and so on generation after generation. Why shouldn't the bartender here be a descendant of his wine steward?"

"I wonder if Shah Jehan had an Armenian wine steward. Was he a very amorous man?"

Moraine said, "I'd just love to know what's in it. But I don't suppose they'll ever tell me."

"Maybe it's something indecent." Moraine looked up sharply. "They usually put ground-up rhinoceros horns into aphrodisiacs." Mrs. Oppenheimer gestured at the murals of hunting scenes. "I expect sabre-toothed tigers would do here. Sex symbols, dear," she added.

"But there aren't any sabre-toothed tigers here any more!" Moraine said hopelessly. "Anyway."

They ate their caviar in silence until Azizyan the bartender came up. "Good morning, ladies."

Moraine looked up brightly. "Maybe he can tell us. Please, what's in these golnar drinks? Or aren't you allowed to tell us?"

Azizyan smiled toothily at her. "Vodka, cherry brandy, pomegranate juice and orange. Specialty of the house."

Moraine drooped. Mrs. Oppenheimer said, "Not so very special, after all." Moraine came back bravely with "Pomegranates are special. I mean, they don't offer you iced pomegranate juice in Schrafft's, do they?"

Mrs. Oppenheimer was fishing once again in her purse. She pulled out a green ten-dollar bill and laid it carefully on the table in front of her. She was becoming accustomed to the routine.

Azizyan scooped it up in a smooth movement and bowed. "Thank you, madam."

She said quietly, "Any word yet from your wife's brother's cousin?"

His head stayed bowed over the table and he spoke even lower. "He is my wife's brother's cousin's wife's brother. My wife's brother's cousin works in a bank."

"Well, never mind that. Any news?"

"My wife's brother's cousin's wife's brother says it is very difficult for an Iranian to leave Iran. He has to have a passport."

"Naturally."

"Also a birth certificate."

"My friend already has one of those. I've seen it. It has enough place for his whole family tree."

"Good. For a passport they will need to see that, and also to ask many questions."

"What sort of questions?"

"Such as why does he want to go, how long will he be there, how will he live, when will he come back. All kinds of questions."

"Well, I think we can answer all those."

"My wife's brother's cousin's wife's brother says it is best if he asks to go as a student for one year."

"That's fine. He's going to be a student. He's a brilliant boy and he's going to study under the greatest masters of his art. After a year, we can think again."

"It is also difficult to get an entry visa into America."

Mrs. Oppenheimer swept that one aside. "I can fix that. I'm

sponsoring him. In fact I'm seeing the Ambassador this after-noon."

Azizyan nodded gravely. "A passport costs two hundred and fifty dollars."

She stared at him. "Two hundred and fifty? But you said twenty-five two days ago."

He gestured deprecatingly. "I fear I was in error. Forgive me. My wife's brother's cousin's wife's brother says it is two hundred and fifty dollars for everybody. It takes two months to get."

"Two months! But I can't wait two months. We're in a hurry."

"There are many questions to be asked. Many enquiries to be made."

"Like hell there are! I have to wait here for two months while the application sits on some clerk's desk." She controlled herself. "Can't we hustle it?"

Azizyan glanced over his shoulder and spoke even lower. "It can be obtained quicker with priority."

"How do we get priority?"

He gestured hopelessly. "It is a question of having friends, the right friends in the right department. It will be expensive. It will cost more than than two hundred and fifty dollars."

"How much more?"

He gesticulated meaninglessly. "I will ask my wife's brother's cousin's wife's brother. But you understand. There must be enough friends, important friends."

Mrs. Oppenheimer looked him straight in the eye. "You tell him to go ahead. I'll finance him. But I'd like the passport by the middle of next week. I want to leave for the States then, with my friend."

He bowed even lower. "I shall tell him." His eyes flickered over the mink stole and on to Moraine's Saint-Laurent dress. "I am glad you like our golnars."

"Oh yes. Oh, I remember something I wanted to ask you." Moraine seemed to wake from a dream. "That chocolate they put beside your bed each night, stuck on to that pink bit of paper saying good night. What is it?"

He flattened his hands hospitably. "Just a good-night kiss from Mr. Hilton."

"Oh, isn't that just sweet. I was afraid it was a tranquilliser, or something."

"Just candy. Thank you, ladies," he said, withdrawing backwards.

Mrs. Oppenheimer had missed the part about the chocolate. She was staring at the fountain.

"I'll fix it," she said softly. "I'll fix it by the middle of next week, if I have to see the Shah himself."

"Mommy, the Shah's in France, so's Farah. I saw it in the paper. It called them the Sovereigns. Isn't that funny?"

"Well, I'll see the Crown Prince then."

"He's only six. There was a picture of him too. He looked a sweet little boy. Big dark eyes."

"If necessary I'll see the Shah's wife's brother's cousin's wife's brother. That should fix it." She hunted in her purse and produced her travellers cheques, the covers scribbled over with chess scores. She counted them fast. "Hell, I'm running short of cash. I doubt there's enough to finance this operation. Who'd have thought I'd need so much in Iran?"

"I've got about two hundred left," said Moraine.

"That won't be enough. I wonder if there's anywhere I can cash a cheque here. I know there isn't an American Express, I wonder if there's a First National City Bank. I'll ask the Ambassador this afternoon."

Moraine said, "Daddy'll have plenty when he gets here."

"All the same, I can't stick around here for two months. It would mean missing the Manhattan Tournament."

Moraine finished her golnar. "I could stay here two months," she said dreamily. "I could stay here for ever." Her mother cocked a sharp eye at her, but she didn't notice. "We could go back to Isfahan again. And we could go on to Shiraz and see the Rose Gardens. And Persepolis. Cyrus the Great, Alexander the Great. And Tabriz with all those beautiful silk carpets. And the nomad tribesmen galloping from place to place on their white ponies. Cherry blossom by the Caspian."

"Sham, at this time of year," Mrs. Oppenheimer commented.

They lunched informally in the coffee shop off shrimp curry which was sweet with raisins and very hot. Mrs. Oppenheimer finished with *paloudeh* which was a lemon sherbet with crisp wheat on top. Moraine ordered *jelly* which turned out to be fresh strawberries. Neither woman spoke very much. Moraine stared out of the big windows at the brown mountains. Sometimes she looked at the oriental lanterns overhead which, according to the handout, had come from fabled Isfahan. Mrs. Oppenheimer saw nothing, her mind far away in New York.

They separated after lunch. Moraine returned to the pool and Mrs. Oppenheimer went to her room to leave her stole before venturing into the hot city. In the elevators was gentle Muzak, and in the passage a notice which likened her to "a potentate in cosy opulence." She let herself into her cool room and put her stole carefully away in the closet. Then she stepped out on to the balcony.

The dry heat and the glare hit her. She put on her sunglasses and checked the distant city. There wasn't much to be seen from here, just a brown dusty haze several miles away. Her eyes dropped to the blue pool a dizzy drop below her. Round it a battery of sprinklers were just succeeding in keeping a patch of emerald lawn in the desert. She couldn't see Moraine. The girl was probably changing into her bathing-suit in the cabana. But under a yellow umbrella she could detect in the black shadow a slim brown figure wearing black trunks. His legs were crossed and his head was bent. He seemed to be staring at his left wrist. Mrs. Oppenheimer nodded approvingly. He was still there, he hadn't run away.

She went down to the lobby and took a Hilltop taxi into the city. When she returned, she was hot and only moderately cheerful. She had been half an hour late for her interview. Her taxi had been blocked by a flock of sheep being driven calmly by a shepherd boy down the middle of the Avenue Pahlevi. The Ambassador himself had been friendly, but rather distracted. He had talked of friends in Washington and Paris. He hadn't seemed too interested in the thought of a chess prodigy, but he promised to have a word with his Consul-General, who was away sick this week. She could have funds cabled from New York to any bank here without difficulty. If she was going to be here the week after next, he would send her an invitation to a cocktail party he was giving.

When she returned to her room in the Hilton, her first act was to go on to the balcony and look down. But there was nobody there now. She ordered iced coffee from Room Service and took a shower while it came. She changed into a silk dress from Michèle Morgan's boutique and sat on the purple divan, sipping her coffee. On the low white table with its sad flowers was her copy of *Modern Chess Openings*. She flipped it open and began to re-read the Sicilian Defence.

There was a sharp knocking on her door. She got up and let in Moraine, flustered and shiny and angry.

"Mommy, the most awful thing's happened. That Jaafar, ugh!"

"What's happened? Is he all right?"

"Oh, he's all right. He's just insulted me, that's all."

Mrs. Oppenheimer sighed and led her daugter into the room. "What did he do? Push you into the pool?"

"No, we weren't near each other at the pool. It was just now, he came to my room. When I saw who it was, I should have slammed the door in his face. I wish I had now."

"You let him in?"

"Yes. He had his chess-board with a position all set up and he kept saying something I couldn't understand. I thought maybe he had some problem troubling him, but I told him I was no expert. He put the board down on the table and began fiddling with the pieces. Then he suddenly jumped up and put his arms round me and tried to kiss me. Ugh! I could have died."

"Suddenly overcome by your beauty, I suppose. Though, if he'd been watching you all day half-naked beside the pool . . ."

"Mommy, he was trying to rape me!"

Mrs. Oppenheimer gazed calmly at her daughter. "Did he succeed?"

"He did not. That filthy boy, I'd fight him till I was dead first."

"Persians are supposed to be great lovers," Mrs. Oppenheimer remarked. "What's the name of that book? Is it *The Perfumed Garden?* You might have learnt a great deal from him. And then you could have passed it on to Carl, and then you'd have had a much happier love-life."

"Oh, Mommy, don't talk like that. It's not a joke. He was stinking of cologne," she added irrelevantly.

"How did you get rid of him?"

"Oh, I kicked and fought and then I threw him out. Well, when he saw it wasn't on, he just bowed and picked up the chess-set and went quietly out. I chained the door after him."

"Did you hurt him?"

"No, I don't think so. Only his ego. I wish I had."

"Egos are important to chess-players," Mrs. Oppenheimer

mused. "It's possible he simply misunderstood the situation, thought he'd been hired to be your lover."

"Yugh!" said Moraine.

"Or perhaps he thought you were trying to attract him when you were at the pool. I don't suppose he's ever seen a girl in a bikini before."

"I wasn't the only one."

"All right," she said wearily. "I'll tell him to lay off you. I'll warn him that he's to concentrate on chess and not pester you or he won't get that Cadillac. I wonder how you say that in Iranian."

"And if he's moving into our apartment, I'm moving out, that's for sure."

"We haven't got him to New York yet. Let's drop it for the moment. Let's go somewhere jolly for dinner. I need cheering up."

"Oh yes, let's."

"Shall we dine graciously here in the Persian Room and watch the belly-dancing? Or shall we go out and try The Shoppe? That's supposed to be fun."

"Oh, let's stay here. The Shoppe sounds so British."

"Right. We'll meet for a love-potion in the bar. I think I'll have a little rest now."

The telephone rang beside the bed. Moraine answered it.

"Mommy, it's for you."

Mrs. Oppenheimer sat down on the edge of the bed and picked up the receiver.

"Hallo! Hallo! Hallo, Joann?" A man's voice.

"Walter! How nice! Where are you? Are you in Teheran?"

"No, I'm still in Abadan."

"But your voice sounds so near. You might be in the next room."

"No, I'm still in Abadan. It's just a good line. I expect the U.S. put it in."

"When are you arriving?"

"That's what I'm calling about. Joann, listen, Joann, there's something I want to talk about."

"Yes."

"Joann, there's something I want to say to you."

"People usually want to say something when they call long distance."

"What?"

"Go ahead, Walter, I'm listening."

"Joann, you remember that night in Beirut. At dinner. You remember what we talked about?"

Mrs. Oppenheimer's hands went damp, and she thought she was going to retch. She took a deep breath.

"I remember, honey. You were mad with Moraine for eating those little bits of raw liver."

"No, not that night. The other night when we dined alone in the Phoenicia. You remember what we talked about?"

"Yes, I remember."

"Well, I want to go ahead. I want to go ahead with the settlement."

"I thought we agreed to let it ride for the moment. Why the sudden change of plan?"

"It isn't easy to explain."

"Debbie find herself knocked up?"

"What?"

"I asked you, dear, if your secretary was pregnant."

"No, of course not. Well, yes, she thinks maybe she is."

"What a lovely surprise for her."

"Joann, please, don't let's make this harder than we need for either of us."

"Debbie's such a sweet girl. She'll make a lovely little mother."

"At least she doesn't sit up all night playing chess."

There was a hard little silence.

"Hallo! Hallo, Joann, are you there?"

"I'm here, honey."

"Sorry, Joann, I didn't mean to say that. It just sort of slipped out. I'm sorry."

"I doubt she could even learn the moves."

"Joann, I'm sorry about all this. I know it's a shock to you. But let's try and make it easy for everyone, shall we?"

"And how do we do that?"

"I'm not coming to Teheran. Debbie and I are flying tomorrow to Cairo. We'll fly direct to New York T.W.A. I want you and Moraine to fly direct Pan Am. Then we won't risk travelling on the same plane."

"Oh, I don't think those big jets often crash. And anyway Moraine's quite old enough to . . ."

"I wasn't thinking about crashes. I just don't want you and

Debbie to find yourselves sitting in adjacent seats."

"Why not? I might be able to give her some tips about her condition. Where to get her maternity clothes. The most swinging ones are said to be in London."

"Joann, please let's take this easy. When I get to New York I won't go to the apartment. I'll move into the St. Regis."

"You'll be comfortable there. Have you reserved a room? New York's pretty full just now."

"When you arrive, first thing I want you to call Henry. I'll cable ahead to warn him and get him moving on the settlement."

"Walter, you keep using the wrong word. It's called a divorce, not a settlement."

Moraine interrupted. "Divorce! Mommy, what's he saying?" Mrs. Oppenheimer looked away.

"Yes, well both. I want to get him moving on both. Joann, I'm sincerely sorry about all this, but I think we both want it in our hearts."

"You'll need to get moving fast. To Mexico. What's the name of that place across from El Paso? No, wait a minute, you don't need to go to Mexico any more. They have quickie divorces in Nevada now. You don't have to wait six weeks any more and the hotels are better than in Mexico. I don't have to come too, do I?"

"I'll check, but I don't think so. Joann, I'd like to say I really appreciate the way you're co-operating over this."

"It doesn't have to be Reno. Las Vegas is just as good and you'd have more fun there. And it's so convenient, you can get your marriage licence in the same courthouse you get your divorce, and it's open all day and night, seven days a week. You'll have to produce your passport or something to show you're over twenty-one. But Debbie need only produce her driving licence to show she's over eighteen. I suppose she is over eighteen?"

"Joann, please . . ."

"And then you can go right on and be married in one of those sweet little wedding chapels along the Strip. You remember them? The Hitching Post Wedding Chapel or the Wee Kirk o' the Heather Wedding Chapel or the Silver Bells Wedding Chapel or the Sweethearts Wedding Chapel or the Roses Chapel. Oh, I've forgotten all their names. The Sunset Wedding Chapel. No, maybe that wouldn't be right at your age. They're all open twenty-four hours a day, and they guarantee to get a minister or judge there within five minutes. You'd rather have a minister, wouldn't you, honey? I mean, you'd like the blessing of the Church on your union."

"Joann, this is a long-distance call."

"I've got it! You remember those two nice boys, what were their names? Pete and Buster, that's right. They were both ministers, each had ordained the other. So they're always there all day and night. And they provide everything, flowers, corsages, soft music, candlelight, validated free parking, a room to freshen up in first, photographs, baby-sitter. No, I guess you won't need a baby-sitter. Would you like Moraine to come and be a bridesmaid?"

"Oh no, Mommy, no!"

"And for only seven dollars fifty extra you can have a recording of the ceremony. You play it through on your anniversaries, and thrill again to hear yourselves making your vows. What was its name, was it the Romeo and Juliet Wedding Chapel with the balcony in neon over the door?"

"Please, Joann, listen . . ."

"It would be so romantic to be married at night. And so convenient too. You have a good dinner at the Sands or the Desert Inn or the Thunderbird, and then you go and watch the Topless Watusis or listen to Sinatra until you're feeling nice and sexy. And then you go along to the chapel and freshen up and become man and wife. And afterwards there's no need to rush straight to bed, you go back to your hotel and play craps as long as you like. You've always liked craps, haven't you, honey, you said it gave you the best chance of winning. You'd like to have a good big win on your wedding night. You can go on playing right through the night until Debbie has to go upstairs for her morning sickness."

Tiresomely a tear trickled down her cheek. She brushed it away impatiently.

"Are you through yet, Joann? This is a long-distance call."

"I'm only trying to be helpful, dear. Make sure you and Debbie have a really lovely honeymoon."

"The most helpful thing you can do is to go straight back to New York and call Henry. Can you fly tomorrow, or the day after?"

"Not so soon. I've got some things to see to here first."

"Oh, cut the sightseeing. You must have seen enough mosques by now."

"It's not sightseeing. It's just something I've got to arrange before I leave."

"What sort of thing?"

"Something important to me. I'm telling the First National City Bank to send me five thousand dollars here."

"We can arrange all that with Henry."

"It's nothing to do with Henry. I need five thousand here, and I have to wait till it comes. I'll cable the First National City and tell them to send it here. I'm telling them to sell some of my I.B.M. or Xerox."

"Joann, I'd strongly advise against selling either of those stocks at the present time. Glamour stocks are moving right ahead."

"Well, some of my American Telephone, then."

"I'd advise against selling that too. The whole market is set to reach a new high for the year."

"I have to sell something. I need the money here. Or maybe I could borrow it."

"What do you need five thousand dollars for?"

"Oh, expenses."

"But you can charge your hotel to your card. You do still have your Carte Blanche Hers card?"

"Yes, I think so."

"And you can charge your excess baggage on Pan Am to it too. That only leaves tipping and things like that. Don't you have any travellers cheques left?"

"A few."

"Then I don't see what you want five thousand dollars for?"

"Oh, forget it, Walter," Mrs. Oppenheimer said wearily. "I'll just wait here till it arrives from New York."

There was a moment's silence. "If it will speed things up, I can have the office here cable you the money."

"Well, thanks, Walter."

"I'll have the money sent to the Omran Bank, the branch in the Hilton. It should be there tomorrow. We can make the adjustment later. Now in return will you get back to New York as quick as you can? By the end of next week, when you've bought your carpets or gold chessmen or whatever it is you're buying."

"I'll do my best."

"Okay, thanks. I'll get in touch with you in New York. Give my love to Moraine. 'Bye."

She was crying now from both eyes. So was Moraine.

"I suppose that's the last time I'll ever hear his voice," said Mrs. Oppenheimer, putting down the receiver.

"Oh, Mommy! Oh, Mommy! Does he really mean it, about the divorce, I mean?"

"Seems so. Oh, that stupid Debbie, why couldn't she look after herself. I wouldn't have minded his going on seeing her. He could have gone to her apartment nights when I was at the Manhattan Chess Club."

"Oh, Mommy!"

Mother and daughter, weeping hard, sat on the edge of the bed. They hugged each other and said nothing coherent. Their tears ran down their cheeks, over their jawbones and down their necks into their dresses. They mopped wanly with the corners of the mauve counterpane.

Mrs. Oppenheimer said, "I don't think I feel like the Persian Room tonight. I think I'll have Room Service send me up something here. Will you be all right?"

"I'll stay with you, Mommy."

Mrs. Oppenheimer squeezed her. "That's lovely of you. But I think I'd rather be by myself."

"Okay. I understand. I think I'll go and read some poetry. Mommy, do you remember what Edna St. Vincent Millay wrote about things like this, I mean the deserted wife?"

"Yes, I do. She said, 'Laugh and the world laughs with you, weep and you weep alone.' "

"Mommy, that wasn't Edna, that was Ella Wheeler Wilcox."

"Please leave me alone."

When Moraine had gone Mrs. Oppenheimer had a real cry, sprawled on the mauve bed. Then she got up resolutely, went to the bathroom, bathed her face and fixed it. Then she emerged and called Room Service, ordering a large Scotch and soda on the rocks and a double portion of scrambled eggs. Then she went out on the balcony.

It was dark now and the desert night was growing cool. The

distant view of Teheran looked better now, a giant arrow of twinkling lights. Everywhere was the loud whirr of a million crickets. A strong smell of diesel oil drifted up to her. She felt a great wish to throw herself over into the Persian night, so positive in its sound and its scent and its thickness. But she steadied herself and instead looked down at the pool below her. There was nothing to be seen, the pool area was in darkness. If he were still sitting there, he would be sitting in the dark. Perhaps his watch was luminous.

When her supper came, she drank the whisky slowly, but with her first mouthful of the scrambled egg she knew that she couldn't swallow it. She spat it out in the bathroom. Then there was a knock at the door.

She opened it cautiously. Before it was open, she knew who it was by the stench of cologne. She thought of closing it again as she couldn't stand the thought of a visitor. But her hand opened the door all the same. At least there was someone who needed her.

He was standing just outside, grave and brown, in a dark suit and white shirt. In his hand was a small chess-board with some pieces on it."

"What's the matter? Are you stuck on some problem?"

He came in and put the board down on the table. She looked over his shoulder at the position. It was absurd, the two Kings were only two squares apart. White had an overwhelming advantage in material. The pieces might have been set up at random.

He looked at her and then began moving the pieces, crazily, without purpose.

"What on earth . . . ?"

He suddenly put his arms round her and tried to kiss her, rather clumsily. She stiffened, thinking fast: Oh, of course, I should have expected this, it's the same trick he tried on Moraine, I would have guessed it if I hadn't been so deadened, oh that cologne, he must use a whole bottle every hour, he's bigger than me, I'm so small.

She pushed herself clear and got the table between them.

"Don't you try that," she said in a hoarse voice she hardly recognised. "Don't you ever try that again or I'll call the bell captain and have you thrown out. Right? Next time you pester my daughter or me I'll have you back in your slum in Isfahan by the next plane, whether you're a chess genius or no. You don't understand a word I'm saying, do you, but I guess you get the point. You're not that dumb."

He looked at her gravely. Then his eyes dropped to the chess-board.

"Now you listen to me! Let's get this clear. I'm not hiring you to be my lover, or my daughter's either. My husband wants to divorce me after twenty-five years of marriage and marry a girl the same age as my daughter. All right, if that's what he wants, I don't want to keep him. But I'm not going round hiring gigolos. I'm not that desperate yet. And my daughter's got a lover already. He's a chess genius too, but he's a six-foot Californian and I sincerely advise you not to tangle with him. Right?"

He had apparently got the point, because he picked up the chess-board again. She held him with her vehemence.

"Now let's get this straight. I'm backing you because I think you're a genius. So does Mischchov, the ex-World Champion. I don't expect you've ever heard of him, but he's still one of the greatest players in the world, so he should know. He's seen the score of one of your games against me, I cabled it to him, and he thinks you may easily be the next World Champion. You realise what that means, don't you? You'd be famous, one of the all-time greats, you'd be talked about and quoted for ever. But it's not enough to be a genius. You have to have backing too. Well, I'm providing that. But that's not enough either, you have to work hard too. It's like a top-class pianist or violinist. They're geniuses too, but they still have to practise eight hours a day. Or take chess, take Bobby Fischer or Carl Sandbach. They're both at the top of the tree, but they still spend six or eight hours a day studying chess, even when they're not playing. They wouldn't stay long at the top otherwise. Listen, I'm hiring you a really good coach, he's a first-class player, I'm paying him five hundred dollars a week to teach you the openings, the middle-game, the end-game. They're all different. You have to play through every important game that's been played in the last two hundred years. You have to learn most of them by heart. You have to be able to glance at a position and say this position occurred in Vokhorov *v.* Szabo, Zürich 1963, when Vokhorov played this, and again in Boghossian *v.* Larsen, Santa Monica 1967, when Boghossian played that. If somebody mentions, say, the Capablanca-Alekhine match for the World Championship in 1927 you have to be able to set up the position where Capablanca first went wrong, without look-- ing at the book, and show where he went wrong. You have to be able to play through any game you've ever played without looking it up in your notes. You have to have total recall. If your mem- ory isn't that good, we'll have to train it with special courses. Right, Grandmaster Chaimovitz will teach you the background and the technique. But on top of that you have to produce fresh ideas, new moves, new situations. That's where you and your genius come in. You find a new move, your technique tells you that it's sound, and then you win. That's the way to the top, boy, there's no other way of getting there. Know everything there is to be known and then add some more. You won't get to the top by gigoloing round rich American women. You haven't under- stood a single word of this, have you?" she added.

He stood and watched her impassively. Then he pointed at the chess-board and gestured enquiringly at her.

"No, I don't want a game now. That's not what I'm saying at all. Look, I'll make it easier for you. I'll give you the simple car- rot and stick. If you win the U.S. Open I'll buy you a gold Rolex watch with a gold bracelet." She pointed at her wrist; he glanced at his own watch. "If you win the match I'm planning for you, you'll get the prize. Probably five thousand dollars." She rubbed her thumb against her middle finger, the international deaf-and- dumb for money. "If you win the World Championship I'll buy you a Cadillac too." She turned an imaginary steering wheel in the air. "Or you can go back to being a slum kid in Isfahan." She pointed at the door. "You choose."

He took the gesture as a sign of dismissal and turned to the door.

"And don't use so much cologne, they'll think you're a fairy. And don't tread down the heels of your shoes, you look like a waiter in the coffee shop."

He bowed slightly and was gone. She pressed the button in the door handle, locking it. She stumbled back to the divan, and dropped on to it. She felt enormously weary and her head ached. God, why did I have to do that? she thought. Why did he have to do it? Why did Walter have to do it? Why is everyone always in a false position? Why does nobody ever understand?

She needed a drink, but her glass was empty. She could call

Room Service, but the thought of anyone else coming to her room was unbearable. She looked with distaste at the Goodnight Kiss on the bedside table, and fetched a glass of iced water from the bathroom.

She sat down again on the divan and sipped the water, trying to find an answer, a pattern, a grain of comfort. On the coffee-table was her travelling magnetic chess-set, the one on which Jaafar had first shown her his genius. While she thought gloomily about Jaafar and Walter and Debbie, her hands set up the pieces in the starting position. She felt a sudden urge to see just what Boghossian had played in Boghossian *v.* Larsen, Santa Monica 1967.

She went to her half-unpacked suitcase and found the tournament book of the Piatigorsky Cup games. She found the game and made the first move, P–K4. Larsen had answered with N–KB3, and Boghossian had advanced his Pawn to K5. Alekhine's Defence. She played the game through, concentrating on the strategic positioning, the concealed long-range threats, the leaps of imagination when a player would become aware of a hidden weakness or a secret threat and would transform the game in one unforeseen move.

Then she played through Dietrich *v.* Fischer and Toklovsky *v.* Portisch. This was the true comforter, better than Scotch or sex or sleeping pills. Beyond the hard edge of the chess-board, beyond the sixty-four black and white squares, nothing existed. The world was confined within two simple dimensions. The pieces were beautiful, their moves clear and unvarying. And within the simple geometric patterns lay hidden a world of exciting subtlety, of endless complexity and of irresistible beauty.

Dietrich *v.* Boghossian. Toklovsky *v.* Fischer. Larsen *v.* Portisch. The siren voices led her on, move after move, page after page, magic cavern after magic cavern, a world of Knights and Queens and Castles. This was her world, her true world, where she and her friends came as often as they could, where they were really themselves. The other world outside was well lost.

She had forgotten her broken marriage, her simple daughter, her venial protégé, forgotten her headache and the cold scrambled eggs on the table, forgotten that it was now four o'clock in the morning.

BLACKPOOL

Paul encountered the Prime Minister on the steps of the Imperial Hotel. The Prime Minister was leaving Blackpool, flushed with the success of his eloquent and rousing speech to his party in the Empress Ballroom of the Winter Gardens. Paul politely stood aside. Then, seizing the moment, he moved in again.

"Excuse me, Prime Minister, I'm from the *Daily Post*. Are you satisfied with your party conference this year?"

The Prime Minister checked, his private secretary and his detective almost knocking into him. "Thank you," he said in his usual friendly way, "thank you."

Paul asked, "How do you feel about this new threat to your leadership?" He was referring to the group of six influential men who had not spent a great deal of time clapping in the Winter Gardens but had been noticed sitting frequently in a corner of the residents' lounge, sitting round a table covered with typewritten quarto sheets and gin and tonics.

The Prime Minister seemed to see Paul for the first time. He nodded thoughtfully. "Let's put it this way," he said. "Perhaps history does or does not repeat itself. Or perhaps not. We shall see. Let us have confidence in the future."

He smiled warmly at Paul and climbed into his waiting car. His private secretary climbed in beside him, his detective got in beside the chauffeur. The car drove off to the airport. Paul walked up the steps, wondering how to present his exclusive interview to his paper.

George Wheaton, just behind him, caught him up and remarked, "I didn't know you'd become a political journalist."

"A good journalist can cover anything. It's only a question of being at the right place at the right time."

"I thought you prided yourself on being an author rather than a journalist."

Paul glanced at him, but made no answer.

They walked into the hotel and turned right into the long carpeted corridor. At the end they turned left at the lit neon sign BALLROOM.

The ballroom was full of people. Coconut matting had been laid on the dancing part of the room, the shiny square of parquet. A grey northern light filtered through thick clouds and the skylights overhead. The girders supporting the glass roof were encrusted with swags of plaster flowers. Below was a riot of plaster dolphins and cherubs on swings. At the end, on the stage, was an Ionic temple, with masks in the middle of the column heads. The velveteen curtains were drawn back to reveal an imitation brick wall. In front of this was the bar, from which, in due course, tea and coffee would be dispensed to the players. Along the north wall of the ballroom, partly obscuring the large and rather unsuitable murals of skiing scenes, were big scoreboards, covered in talc. In front of them harassed grey-haired women checked in the competitors, handed out programmes and dealt with complaints.

In the middle of the ballroom stood the host and sponsor of the congress, Mr. Pearson. Paul and George Wheaton greeted him.

"It's good to see you both again," he said, shaking hands very hard. "Did you have a good journey up here?"

"Fine," said Paul. "I just had a word with the Prime Minister on the steps here."

Mr. Pearson was unimpressed. "Prime Minister? Who's he?" He turned to Wheaton. "And how d'you like being back in the North, eh?"

"I always enjoy myself in Blackpool."

"I bet you do. And it isn't only the chess, eh?" He nudged at Wheaton, missing him. "Now admit it, don't you feel twice the man up in the North?"

"Certainly the air here is most invigorating."

"See?" Mr. Pearson turned to Paul. "There's no place like Lancashire. Now you tell your readers we've got ten grandmasters from across the water here, and a hundred and ten North Country lads and lasses to play them. All this and Reginald Dixon too."

"A hundred and ten?"

"Yes. And every one born in the North. Nobody from the South is allowed in, except him." He pointed at Wheaton.

"I was born the right side of the Trent. My parents moved South when I was two."

"I know, bloody Hendon. Still, you're a North Countryman at heart. And you've played your best games here in Blackpool. Now admit it."

Wheaton blinked. "Well, yes, I have had some good tournament results here."

"It's the air. And the fact that you're a North Countryman. No Southerners admitted in here, unless they're writing for the papers." He grinned at Paul.

"Oh come! I've been here so often I'm almost an honorary Lancastrian by now," said Paul.

"Hark at him! Any day now he'll be playing at Old Trafford."

He nudged Grandmaster Dietrich, who was standing beside him. Dietrich, baffled, said, *"Bitte?"*

Paul kept to the subject. "Ten grandmasters?"

"Yes. Dietrich here. Toklovsky, Mischchov, Sandbach, Haslund, oh, they're all in the programme. Every one of our lads gets at least one game against a grandmaster."

"What happens," asked Wheaton, "if the grandmasters get drawn against each other?"

Mr. Pearson roared with laughter. "They don't, lad, they don't! We fiddle it. They haven't come here to play each other. They play each other all the year round. Besides, they think they'll get easier games against our lads. That's where they're wrong, eh?"

He nudged Dietrich again, who said, "Yes, yes."

"How do you get them to come? Even Hastings doesn't produce a line-up like this."

Mr. Pearson glowered. "Hastings? Where's that?" He lowered

88

his voice and spoke in a deafening whisper. "I'll tell you the answer, lad. Brass. Just brass. Pay out the brass and they'll come all right. Look at it their way. Ten days in this grand hotel by the sea, lovely air, all the beer they can drink. Blackpool Rock. The best entertainers in the country, Reginald Dixon, Dickie Henderson, even the Prime Minister this year. All expenses paid. Lots of prizes, five hundred for the winner. I've got a list this long of grandmasters wanting to be invited here. Isn't that right?"

He nudged Grandmaster Dietrich, who said, "I am heartily thankful for the comfort and friendship."

"That's it, lad, that's it. Comfort and friendship, that's the motto of this congress. A good time had by all, yours truly included. I've got a new idea this year. We're not just starting with Round 1. We're kicking off with a simul. Four simuls to be exact. The two Russkies, Herr Dietrich here and young Carl Sandbach are each taking on twenty-four of our lads and lasses. Here this afternoon. That should get things moving, don't you think? Warm things up a bit." He looked at Wheaton. "I don't suppose you'll be in on that. You wouldn't want to play Herr Dietrich in a simul, would you?"

Wheaton smiled wanly and said, "Herr Dietrich and I usually play each other one against one."

"Well, you get an afternoon off, then. You can go and roll up your trousers and paddle in the sea. Or you can go on the North Pier and find out at last what the butler really saw. I bet you've always wanted to know, eh?" He roared with laughter.

Dietrich looked puzzled and said, *"Bitte?"*

Paul tried to explain. *"Herr Pearson sagt dass Herr Wheaton wunscht was der Herr Ober gesehen hat wissen."*

"Der Herr Ober? Hier?"

"Well, so long as a good time is had by all . . . And so long as all my prizes stay in the North Country . . . It's good to see you all here again."

He moved away genially to talk to Grandmasters Portisch and Sandbach who were standing together. Paul left Wheaton with Dietrich and moved off to talk to Haslund and B. H. Wood who were standing by the scoreboards, looking at the draw.

He remarked, "Rather a novel idea, four simuls simultaneously."

Wood commented, "I'll think about it for Eastbourne."

Haslund said, "Why doesn't he ask Toklovsky to play a hundred of them all at once? Then they could all say they had played the World Champion."

"Or Toklovsky and Mischchov could play it in tandem, playing alternate moves."

"We don't want to make it too easy for the lads and lasses."

A hand clutched Paul's sleeve. He turned, annoyed.

"Mr. Butler? I'm Robin Jackson. I wrote to you a few weeks ago. About some variations in your book *The Early Middle-Game*. I sent you some analysis I had done."

Paul looked at him, recalling nothing. The boy was about seven feet tall, with thick glasses and protruding ears. His tweed sleeves didn't cover his knobbly wrists; his grey flannel trousers didn't cover his ankles with their brown woollen socks. He was wearing an op-art tie. Paul had never seen him before.

Robin Jackson said, "I've got all your books at home, I've read them all. But I didn't agree with what you wrote about P–KR4. I thought that was fully answered by B–K3."

The penny dropped. "Of course, yes, I remember. Didn't you get my answer? I wrote back, disagreeing with you."

"No, I don't think so."

"Your letter was forwarded to me in Yugoslavia. I was covering the Bled tournament. I wrote you a long answer."

"I never got it."

Paul shook his head. "These Yugoslav posts. I suppose it was just lost. Never mind, I agreed with a lot of what you said. Not everything, but a lot of it. Are you playing in the congress?"

It wasn't a very intelligent question, but it served to change the subject.

"Yes, I'm playing in the simul this afternoon. And I'm drawn against Mischchov tomorrow."

"Are you indeed! Nothing like starting off with a bang."

"I know. I'm going to have to sit up all night, analysing Mischchov's recent games." He pulled a sheaf of papers out of his pocket. "This is the analysis I've done on the Sicilian. I said I'd show it to you when we met."

Paul glanced and quailed. "I'd like to look at it later on. Put it in an envelope and give it to the hall porter. I'm staying here. He'll put it in my pigeon-hole. Do you know Mr. Haslund? And I expect you know Mr. Wood."

"Only by name," said the boy. "I subscribe to *Chess*, I'm one of your readers."

Paul extricated himself from the group with a practised cocktail-party manœuvre. He slid out of the side door of the ballroom, along the corridor. He turned right into the main corridor. Fifty yards further on he turned left into *l'aperitif* bar and sat on one of the green high stools at the bar. He greeted the barman.

"Well, back again in Blackpool. And I think I'll start with my usual."

"Back again to see us," said the barman, playing for time. "Let me see, it's a . . ." He scratched his head.

"Vodka martini, very dry, on the rocks with lemon peel."

"That's it, sir. I just couldn't remember if it was gin or vodka you preferred. Vodka martini coming up." He busied himself with the glass shaker. Paul ate a stuffed olive.

"So you've come back to see us in Blackpool."

"I'm covering the chess congress for the *Daily Post*."

"Ah, the chess," said the barman, seeing daylight at last. He pushed the drink across at Paul.

"I had a word with the Prime Minister on my way in."

"Aye, he's been here. We've had them all this year, Tories, Labour, Liberals, the lot."

"And now you've got the chess congress. Which d'you like best, the chess-players or the politicians?"

The barman lowered his voice. "Well, sir, the politicians spend a lot more money and they tip well, some of them do. The chess-players don't spend much money, except for some like you, sir. But they're much quieter. They may sit up all night in the lounge playing chess, but they don't make any trouble, not even the Russians. It's not like the politicians."

"They make trouble?"

"Talk about trouble. Always wanting their rooms changed because some bloke's got a better room than what they have. I say, give me the chess-players any day."

"I'm glad to hear it." Paul slid half a crown across the table. "When I've finished this I'll have another martini."

"Thank you, sir. And I hope you win."

Paul sipped the cold dry drink and looked round the bar. There were only two others present, a couple at a table by the window. Neither looked like a chess-player. Piped music floated through the room. Paul looked through the windows at the grey sky, at the lit alcoves behind the bar, the pictures of Paris on the walls. It was really very pleasant here. Not perhaps the most glamorous of his assignments, but certainly the nicest.

He ate another stuffed olive.

George Wheaton was not staying in the hotel. Like the other British competitors he was paying his own expenses and he was staying at the Glendale Private Hotel, where he always stayed, a hundred yards along the promenade. He slipped out of the Imperial by the side-door. A fresh wind from Ireland blew in his face. The tide was right out and the far distant sea was brown like the sand. A tram clattered by on its way to Princess Parade and the Tower. Wheaton waited till it had gone by, and then he crossed the road to the railings. He took ten long deep breaths of the cool wind. There was no doubt about it, he did feel better up here, there was something about the Blackpool air. Perhaps he'd have a really good congress this year. He felt young and fit.

In the Glendale Mrs. Beckington was waiting for him.

"Ready for your dinner, Mr. Wheaton? It's my hot-pot."

"I'll look forward to that. I'm hungry today."

"Aye, everybody has a good appetite up these parts."

In the dining-room he had a wall-table, pressed against the flowered wallpaper. He usually had this table, though one year he had been the other side. In front of him the tablecloth was brilliantly white. On it were the regulation bottles of tomato ketchup and Lea and Perrins, and a cut-glass vase containing paper table napkins.

He took out his wallet and counted the five-pound notes. Not quite as many as he had hoped. But then, of course, he had already paid the return fare from London. He would have to be very careful. Mrs. Beckington had raised her prices since last year and he hadn't liked to ask Janet for any more. Indeed, what she had already given was a lot for a schoolteacher to save from her salary. Wheaton regarded it as a loan rather than as a gift. If he won a prize this year he would pay her back, for last year as well as this.

Janet had never come to Blackpool. No point, she thought, in doubling the hotel expenses. That was one of the snags about Blackpool. Despite the generosity of Mr. Pearson, it was only the prize-winners and the foreign masters who made anything out of it.

Mr. Pearson had put it clearly. "Aye, I have to pay these foreign grandmasters to come up here, it's the brass that brings them, that and the prizes. But for the rest of us North Country lads it's a grand holiday by the sea. All the fun of the fair. Look at this fine ballroom, all those chess-boards and pieces. Over sixty clocks, all in fine working order. All this and Reginald Dixon too." It was his favourite way of ending a comment on his congress.

It was different abroad, Wheaton reflected. There he was the visiting master, with his expenses paid. If he were invited to Beverwijk he'd try to save something from his expenses to give to Janet. But the invitation hadn't yet arrived. Perhaps it wouldn't come this year, perhaps they were waiting to see how he did here. Expenses or no, he felt Blackpool was his home tournament. It would be a sad day when he was no longer able to come.

He brushed away the dismal thoughts. Everything seemed to be going well this year, he felt well and alert. He was drawn against Toklovsky in the first round, the toughest chess assignment in the world. Quite a compliment; he didn't imagine for a moment that the two names had come out of the hat together by chance. It wouldn't be one of those terrible first-round upsets with well-known players falling to unknown youngsters from Liverpool. Nobody could blame him if he failed to beat the World Champion, especially as he had the black pieces. And if he should win, or even draw, they'd be sure to ask him to Beverwijk, perhaps to Mar del Plata.

He came back out of the dream of far-away cities and interzonals. He'd send a postcard to Janet this afternoon. He always sent her one on the first day of Blackpool. A picture of the Promenade or the Tower Ballroom or Stanley Park.

"Here you are, love, Ma Beckington's special hot-pot."

She ladled it on to his plate. It was mostly potato and gravy with a good deal of onion and rather less meat. She crowned the heap with long slivers of red cabbage.

"Excellent, as always," he commented politely.

She stood back and looked him up and down.

"Don't look to me as you've had a decent meal since the last time you had it." She winked at him. "I'll keep seconds for you in the kitchen."

The others in the dining-room were looking at him. He said, "Ah, you don't get it this way down South."

"I bet you don't, love."

He drank some water and applied himself to the hot-pot. So much onion always gave him indigestion, but that didn't matter so much today, as he hadn't got a game this afternoon. He shook some Lea and Perrins on to the heap to try to mask the onion.

The first mouthful took him straight back to Blackpool, to chess and Pearson and the Imperial Ballroom far more completely than seeing them all again had done. He stared out at the scudding clouds and thought. He would like to win against Toklovsky, but it didn't seem very probable. There was no need to stick his neck out too far. In the circumstances a draw would be almost as good. If Toklovsky opened with the King's Pawn, he'd turn it into a Ruy Lopez; play the Marshall Attack and wait for Toklovsky to overreach himself. After Bled he knew his way through the Marshall blindfold. And if Toklovsky opened with the Queen's Pawn or Queen's Bishop's Pawn, he'd play the King's Indian Defence, close the game down and bide his time. He hadn't studied the Modern Benoni Defence in sufficient depth to be sure of it against the World Champion, but he knew his way through the King's Indian and in particular through Toklovsky's favourite variations of the Defence.

He looked round at the other guests. In the window was a family: father, mother and tall gangling son of about seventeen. The boy was obviously a chess-player too. He was laboriously explaining to his parents about simuls. There were often other chess-players in the hotel. Mrs. Beckington supported the congress and paid for a small advertisement in the congress programme, stating that chess-players were specially catered for. This meant that there was a board and set of pieces in the drawer of the dresser in the lounge.

Against the other wall was a mother and daughter; the mother was prim with glasses and a floral cotton frock and cardigan. The girl looked bright and youthful in a bouffant hair-do, tartan trousers and a yellow sweater. Neither spoke to the other.

Wheaton returned to his hot-pot. When Mrs. Beckington pressed seconds on him he accepted. He never liked a big meal before an important game, but today he had a free afternoon. He might as well gather the rose-buds. Afterwards he ate tinned pears and drank a second glass of water. In between mouthfuls he stared out of the window and thought about the King's Indian and the Modern Benoni and the Sicilian. The Scheveningen Variation wasn't much seen nowadays; possibly Toklovsky wouldn't have prepared any good lines against it. But it would mean studying the variation all afternoon and night and even then he might not be sure of it over the board. It would be safer to stick to the ones he knew.

After dinner the guests gathered in the lounge for a few cups of tea. This was often a social occasion, though Wheaton normally preferred to keep himself to himself. But the boy and the girl had made friends, and their parents, the ice broken, were talking about Millicent Martin at the Winter Gardens. The boy was showing the girl some books.

"But it's in Greek!"

"No, Russian."

"Coo, can you read Russian?"

"Only a few words here and there. But I can follow the scores."

"Ooh, you must be brainy. What's this one?"

"That's in German. And this one's in Spanish. It's the Mar del Plata Congress last year."

"And you can read all that?"

"Oh, it's not so hard. The scores are the same in any language. You only have to know the notation, algebraic notation. It's not the same as the one we use here in England, that's the Descriptive Notation. But it's just as easy to learn, in fact I think it's easier. It's used all over the continent. And, of course, you have to learn the cyrillic script too for the Russian."

She gazed at him in awe. "Ooh, you must be clever. I mean, to do all this as well as chess. My uncle taught me the moves one holidays. But I forgot them soon after."

"This is a book of Toklovsky's best games. I'm playing him this afternoon. He's World Champion," he added, making the point.

It took a few seconds to sink in. "You mean he's the champion of the whole world?"

"Yes. He won the title two years ago from Mischchov. He's going to have to defend it again next year."

"Ooh! And he's a Russian?"

"Yes, from Moscow."

"And you're playing against him?" The point was hard to take.

"Yes. With twenty-three others. He's playing twenty-four of us at once. It's a simul, simultaneous display. But tomorrow I'm playing Mischchov, just him against poor little me. He was World Champion before Toklovsky," he reminded her. "Personally I think he'll win it back next year."

"And he's a Russian too?"

"Very much so. From Leningrad. This is a book of all his recent games. I've got to go over it tonight, and look up all his pet openings and moves."

He handed her the book. She looked at the Russian characters in awe. Her mouth was wide open, but then it usually was as she suffered from adenoids.

"And you've got to learn all this by tonight?"

"Just look it over. I know most of it already. I've been preparing for this game for months. I was just hoping I'd be drawn against him."

The girl turned to her mother. "Mum, do you hear that? Robin's playing the Russian champion at chess this afternoon."

"The World Champion," he corrected her. "The Soviet champion is Vokhorov, he isn't here this year."

The point was too subtle to be comprehended by anyone else in the room except George Wheaton and he decided not to intervene.

"Your boy must be really brainy."

Mr. Jackson lit his pipe very slowly. "Aye, he's a bright boy. Got seven 'O' levels and he's taking two 'A's next year. We're hoping he'll go to university." He felt proud. Then he added, "But he'd sooner be a chess champion. He's daft about chess."

"Oh yes, you've got to be really clever to play chess. My brother-in-law, Val's uncle, he likes a game of chess, though he isn't really what you'd call good, not a champion I mean. But he's a clever man all right, he's a master printer."

Robin said hesitantly, "Val . . ."

She looked up eagerly from Mischchov's recent game.

96

"Would you like to come and watch the game this afternoon?"

"Ooh, can I? I mean, is it allowed?"

"Of course, it's public like a football match. Just come up to the Imperial, the side door, pay your bob at the ballroom entrance, and you're in. There'll be lots of others watching us."

Val turned. "Mum, can I go to the chess this afternoon instead of Bingo?"

"Are you sure?"

Mr. Jackson sucked at his pipe and said, "The girl doesn't know what she's in for. Four hours standing watching a game of chess, one move every five minutes."

"Oh, Mum, can't I? I never win at Bingo, I only ever lose."

"Will you be all right?"

Robin said chivalrously, "I'll look after her. I'll take her up and bring her back afterwards."

"And, Val, don't forget to be back here for your tea at six. We've got tickets for Dickie Henderson tonight." She turned to the Jacksons. "He's on at the North Pier. We always go to see him."

Mrs. Jackson said, "We watch his show on TV. But we don't think a lot of it."

"Oh, Val really loves it. She laughed herself properly sick over it one night."

"Oh, Mum!"

"I'll introduce you to Toklovsky if I can."

Val's mouth opened even wider. "But whatever would I say to him?"

George Wheaton finished his third cup of tea, heaved himself out of the chintz armchair, nodded at the others, and went out. Young love, hero-worship, admiration, he thought wryly. He was a far better-known player than that boy; he had drawn against Mischchov at Bled only a few weeks ago, he had declined to play in a simul this afternoon, he was drawn against Toklovsky tomorrow afternoon. But he would get no hero-worship, no admiration. It was age that counted, not brains. Then he remembered Janet. Not exactly young love, not by many years; not hero-worship, it had never been that. But admiration certainly, respect, affection. She'd never really understood the game, but she had seen that it meant a great deal to him, and she was resigned.

There had been that uncomfortable night at Bognor when he wasn't doing too well, and she' had suggested that he could take a job and keep on with the chess as a hobby. He hadn't argued with her, he had just looked at her with silent misery. The next day he had won a brilliant game against Belic, and she had immediately gone to the opposite extreme and seen him as a future World Champion. He smiled sadly. That was all a long time ago. Now she simply kissed him goodbye, hoped he'd have a good tournament and forked out the five-pound notes. If he could win one of Mr. Pearson's lavish prizes, he would pay her back. If he could beat Toklovsky tomorrow. Perhaps this was a crucial tournament for him, a turning-point, the beginning of his Indian summer. He felt fit and confident, he was playing better than for some time, look at Bled. Perhaps it would be a mistake to be too defensive tomorrow.

He went out into the cool Lancashire afternoon and bought her a postcard of the Promenade and the Tower. Then he struck inland, looking for a supermarket. It took him some time to find one, a Safeway, and he bought a small jar of Devonshire honey. Then he went back to the Glendale, put the honey in his bedroom and wrote the postcard to Janet. He told her that he was feeling fine and was drawn against Toklovsky in the first round and what could be a better way of starting than that. He gave it to Mrs. Beckington to post with the other postcards of the Tower. Then, not knowing what else to do in Blackpool on a summer afternoon, he went up to the Imperial to watch the simuls.

Inside the ballroom the tables were arranged in four hollow oblongs. The ninety-six Lancashire players sat round the outside of the oblongs, studying their games, heads buried in their hands, score-pads and cups of tea beside them. There were, however, no clocks; they were not needed in this sort of display. Behind them stood the spectators, or sat, if they could find chairs, with the correspondents, the hangers-on, those players like Wheaton who had opted out. Inside the oblong, alone, was the Grandmaster giving the display, imprisoned inside the twenty-four tables, the twenty-four chess-boards, the twenty-four players, seven hundred and sixty-eight pieces, each one of which had to be considered and remembered. The oblongs were complete. Should a grandmaster have to interrupt his display on the demands of nature, a table would have to be pushed aside to let him out.

A boxer in the ring, perhaps; but his opponents were all outside the ropes. A panther pacing round and round his cage. Perhaps the best analogy was one Paul Butler had used in his weekly article in *The Statistician:* a doctor doing his rounds, pausing at the next bed, noting the change, making a decision, nodding at the patient, and moving on to the next bed, round and round the ward clock-wise for four hours or more.

Wheaton nodded at Mr. Pearson who was standing just inside the door talking to B. H. Wood. Mr. Pearson said, "Aye, lad, I thought you wouldn't keep away. You ought to be playing." Across the room he could see Paul sitting on a table, swinging his legs, not looking at the games, but talking intently in a low voice to Harry Golombek of *The Times,* who was stooped over him. There was a quiet buzz of conversation in the ballroom, more than would be found on a normal playing day.

George Wheaton went to look at the games. The boy Robin, who was also staying in the Glendale, was hunched over his board, pressing his glasses against the bridge of his nose, but otherwise free of mannerisms. The girl Val was on a chair behind him, from which her view of his board was blocked by his shoulder. This probably did not bother her. She was gazing at Robin, at Toklovsky, at the whole room, with wonder, her mouth wide open, occasionally patting her back-combed hair nervously. Toklovsky himself, a thick bald man in a thick dark suit, seemed to be playing in a great hurry. There was sweat on his forehead, though it was hardly hot in the room.

Toklovsky, like the three other grandmasters, had the white pieces in every game. It was an advantage given him to mitigate the handicaps of playing simultaneously. He had clearly opened with the King's Pawn, and Robin was playing the French Defence against it. Wheaton watched Toklovsky move round the games to Robin's table. In front of his eyes Robin played the move he had already decided on: Pawn takes Pawn. Toklovsky considered for about five seconds and then played his Queen to Knight 4, moving on as he did so to the next game.

Wheaton raised his eyebrows slightly. Queen to Knight 4 was often played at this stage but he never felt happy about bringing out his Queen so early in the game. It was, he felt, too ambitious, too soon, it opened up too many chancy possibilities. He had tried it once or twice and done badly. But equally he knew that it was theoretically sound, and psychologically a good line for the World Champion to play against a schoolboy. Nobody could feel safe at the moment when the World Champion's Queen was loosed into battle against him. Wheaton resolved, if Toklovsky opened tomorrow with the King's Pawn, not to play the French Defence. It was not a lucky defence for him.

He moved on to look at Mischchov's games. These were very solid and correct. In the next oblong Carl Sandbach's height was telling against him. He was six foot three and had to stoop over each board each move. Over perhaps a thousand moves he would play in the next four hours this was bound to tire him. Dietrich was in the oblong at the end of the room, nearest to the Ionic tea-bar. He seemed to be playing rather slowly. His simul was clearly going to last a long time. Wheaton climbed the steps into the temple and ordered a cup of tea.

Two hours later the position was much clearer. Dietrich's games were all bogged down in complicated middle-game positions, though in most of them Wheaton saw that he had a decisive advantage. Carl Sandbach, on the other hand, was playing fast, and despite the stooping, dazzlingly. He had already finished off five games. His toughest opponent seemed to be a grey-haired lady whose nose twitched continually while she thought. Carl stopped before her board, considered the blocked position for a few seconds and said, "Would you agree a draw, ma'am?"

"Certainly not!"

Carl caught Wheaton's eye and shrugged. The grey-haired ladies were the terror of grandmasters giving simuls; there were about twenty of them playing today. Dedicated, tough, tireless, scholarly, often unable to do justice to their keenness and knowledge in the ordinary games, they were determined to do well in the simuls. Wheaton would have unhesitatingly agreed a draw in that position.

Mischchov was wearing down his opponents remorselessly. He had already won three games and drawn another. But it was Toklovsky that Wheaton was studying most closely, and it was clear that Toklovsky was playing very badly indeed. He seemed, despite his anxiety and hurry, to be playing lethargically, with occasional wild moves. He had already resigned three games and agreed a draw in two more. His game against Robin Jackson was still going, but he was on the defensive. Robin was slouched over the table, his head in his hands, his elbows wide apart. Val was still behind him, gaping at the scene; she must either be terribly in love, thought Wheaton, or have nowhere else to go.

"The humbling of the mighty," said a voice beside him.

Wheaton turned. The speaker was a very thin man with a bony nose. Wheaton had beaten him here two years ago in a Queen's Gambit Accepted. The Queens had come off on the twelfth move and Wheaton had established a good Knight on King 5. He had created a passed Pawn on his King's Knight 6, and after that it had only been a question of technique, though the man had struggled on into an adjourned and one-sided end-game. He couldn't remember the man's name.

Wheaton said, "Toklovsky seems to be in a lot of trouble."

"He's in a bad patch. He's been very uneven since he became World Champion."

"It's such a strain becoming World Champion. They often go through a period of reaction afterwards."

"This period of reaction's gone on about two years. It's time he came out of it."

Wheaton commented, "I hope he doesn't come out of it before tomorrow. I'm playing him in the first round."

"I know you are. I think you're in for an easy point."

Wheaton gave a small grimace. "You can never be sure with these Russians. Is your game over?" he added. What was the man's name? Harvey? Harold? Haddock?

"You bet! I was mowed down by Sandbach. Pseudo-Tarrasch. He's really brilliant, that boy." He paused, and when Wheaton said nothing, he went on, "I mean, he doesn't have to be specially brilliant to beat me. But he makes it look so easy. He's mowing down all the others in the same style."

"I drew with him last month in Yugoslavia," said Wheaton firmly. What was the man's name? Hammond, Lower Board for Lancashire? Schoolmaster? Something to do with Nuclear Disarmament?

"I know. I played the game through. You were very solid."

"Thank you."

The man pointed at Robin's back. "What do you think of my boy?"

"Your boy?"

"He's at the school where I teach. Lady Wynyard's, Didsbury."

Wheaton nodded, as if he had heard of it.

"I'm his form master. Believe it or not, he didn't even know the moves three years ago. I was the first to teach him them. He helped me form the school chess club, and I made him captain of it. He's as keen as anything, he's really helped me build it up. I'm planning to enter for the *Sunday Times* competition next year. It'll be the first time for Lady Wynyard."

"Splendid."

"He's really keen, young Jackson. And I think he's a natural."

"He's certainly keen. He's staying in the same hotel as me. He seems to spend all his time studying the Russians' games."

"That's it. That's how to win, isn't it? He's practically got the World Champion in zugzwang."

Toklovsky arrived before Robin's board at that moment and waited for Robin to move. Robin, lost in thought, didn't notice for a moment; then he held up his hand and said, "Would you mind passing this round?" Toklovsky shrugged and moved on.

Wheaton frowned. This was extreme bad manners. The boy had all the time Toklovsky was playing the other boards to decide on his next move. To ask him then to pass without playing, to request double the time for his next move, was unfair on the Grandmaster, and also slowed down the whole display.

"You ought to tell him not to pass in a simul."

The schoolmaster said, "If he keeps up the pressure, I think he ought to win. That'll be something for the school. I mean, it's quite something to beat the World Champion even in a simul. He's got Mischchov tomorrow, and I don't expect him to win that."

"Baptism by fire," said Wheaton thinly. He nodded at the man, and at Val, and strolled round the other boards. He wanted to see the other games. It was Toklovsky he was interested in, not young Robin Jackson.

Toklovsky resigned another game, agreed two draws and mopped his brow yet again. The man was clearly harassed, uneasy and tired. Wheaton was not sorry to see him tiring himself with this simul today. No doubt next year the Soviet players would insist on keeping their simuls till after the tournament proper was over.

Half an hour later there was a small crowd behind Robin: Wheaton, the schoolmaster, Paul, B. H. Wood, Golombek, dozens of players whose games were over, all breathing down Val's neck. The position was indeed virtual zugzwang. For some moves Toklovsky had been moving his King from Knight 1 to Bishop 1 and back again the next move. It was the only piece he could move without losing immediately. And now Robin had brought up his Bishop to end even that tiny manœuvre. Toklovsky considered the position for some ten seconds. Then he pushed the pieces into the centre of the board and held out his hand.

"Zugzwang," he said. "I congratulate you." His English (and German) was good. He shook hands briefly and moved on to the next game.

A hum of conversation broke out among the spectators.

"A classic zugzwang. D'you remember Nimzowitsch v. Saemisch?"

"Or Alekhine v. Nimzowitsch?"

"Or Botvinnik v. Bronstein?"

"But this is only in a simul. It's not in the same class."

Robin stood up, glowing with triumph. So did Val.

"Does that mean you've won?"

"Yes. He's resigned."

"You've checkmated him?"

"Not exactly. But I'd got him in zugzwang and so he was bound to lose. So he resigned rather than waste time by playing on."

"And you've won, I mean as if like you'd really checkmated him?"

"Yes. It's a clear-cut win to me."

"Oo-er!" She glanced at her wristwatch. "Oops! I'm going to be late for tea. Mum'll be furious, I must run. Thanks for letting me watch. 'Bye!"

She slipped away, patting her hair. Robin didn't watch her go. His hand was being shaken by a number of people.

"Well, what do you think of my boy?" said a man to Paul.

"Not bad for a junior," Paul said warily. "He's your son?"

"Lord, no! I'm his form-master at Lady Wynyard's, Didsbury. I taught him to play the game, I taught him the moves, even. He's been helping me run the school chess club. Believe it or not, there wasn't even a chess-board in the school three years ago. And now look where we've got to!"

"Quite a success story!"

"By the way, my name's Hammond. I play here every year. I used to play for Lancashire."

"Yes, of course," Paul said politely. "I've often seen you here."

"Anyway, I'm putting our school into the *Sunday Times* competition next year, and, of course, young Jackson here will captain the team. I don't think we should do too badly, we've got one or two other promising players besides him. And then I thought I might put him in for the Northern Junior after that."

"Why not the International Students Championships this winter?" Wheaton put in.

"Oh, I hardly think he's ready for that yet. We ought to give him a bit more practice first. Some of these young internationals are pretty tough."

"Still, if he can get Toklovsky into zugzwang . . ."

"Only in a simul," said Hammond firmly. "That's not quite the same thing, is it? Anyway, Toklovsky's never been strong in simuls. He's not a Flohr."

A boy said, "Playing like he is today, he couldn't even beat my little sister."

Paul said sharply, "Steady! You don't become World Champion if you're a complete rabbit." The boy subsided. Paul said to Hammond, "I still think your pupil could be a candidate for the British team this winter."

"Eventually, of course. But *I* still think it would be a pity to spoil him by sending him abroad too soon."

Robin was standing, listening to this discussion of his future. Paul caught his eye, winked, and said, "I'd say better too soon than too late."

Hammond said, "We'll have to see how he does in the rest of his games here. Then we can think again. After all, it's only three years since he learnt the moves. We don't want to rush him."

Robin said, "Butanovic is younger than me and he's World Junior Champion. You bet he'll be playing at Munich this winter."

Hammond said, "These Slavs mature much younger than us Anglo-Saxons." He patted Robin's arm. "Take it easy, boy, you've got plenty of time. Oh, and go to bed early tonight. You've had a good game today, but the real test is coming tomorrow."

Paul and Wheaton slipped away from the group. Wheaton said sadly, "He's still too young. I'm too old. It's very difficult to be the right age."

Paul tapped Wheaton on the arm. "You're not too old, he's not too young. Don't pay any attention to that Hammond man, there are too many like him and they are absolute millstones round people's necks. They're so scared of spoiling young players that they keep them playing school chess, club chess, small tournaments, Lancashire Junior, things like that, until they are no good for anything else. The only way to beat these boys like Butanovic is to start playing them in the cradle."

"I'm surprised the boy was allowed to play here this year."

"Ah well, the schools like to keep in with old man Pearson. Who do you think pays for all their boards and clocks? Look, George, don't run away, let's have a drink after this. I've got an idea I'd like to talk about. But I've got to get the scores here first."

The simuls were drawing to a close. Sandbach would have finished first, but for the grey-haired lady with the twitching nose. They were into a Rook and Bishop-of-opposite-colours endgame, and it was still completely drawn.

"Are you sure you wouldn't like to agree a draw, ma'am?" he asked for the third time.

"No, let's play it out."

Carl sighed. He leaned over an empty table, lifted a chair across and sat down opposite her. "Okay," he said wearily, "if that's the way you want it."

Toklovsky and Mischchov finished soon afterwards. Dietrich's games went on for a further half-hour, but in the end they too were over. He had lost none, drawn eight and won sixteen. Sandbach had lost one, drawn three and won nineteen, with one still unfinished. Mischchov had the impressive score of three drawn, none lost and twenty-one won. Only Toklovsky had the shame of a negative result, six lost, eight drawn and only ten won. Paul got the names of all the winners, and also of the lady still battling on against Sandbach, a Miss Davies from Bootle.

"All right, let's go," he said to Wheaton.

In the doorway they said goodbye to Pearson.

"Well, a good time had by all," he said, patting them both on their shoulders. "All except the poor World Champion. Still, that's fun for our North Country lads. And lasses too. Have you seen her?" He pointed at Miss Davies. "She'll go on till she drops. That's Lancashire for you Southerners. Are you going to give us a good write-up in your paper, eh?"

Paul said, "Yes, I've got the scores. I'll telephone them through tonight. It's an original idea, starting with a simultaneous. A sort of simultaneous squared."

Pearson roared with laughter and punched Paul on the elbow.

"You tell them that, lad. That's how we kick off in the North, that's how we make the party go. They'll all be copying us next year, Hastings, Bognor, Eastbourne, all those Southern congresses."

Wheaton observed, "I wonder how much the grandmasters like it. I'd have thought it was a tiring way to start a big tournament."

"They love it. Big crowd, lots of limelight, everyone watching them. And they love playing chess, just keep them playing chess and they're happy. That's my recipe for success." He waved at the almost empty ballroom. "All this and Reginald Dixon too. What a life, eh!"

He punched them both again, and they crept out. He called after Wheaton, "You go to bed early tonight, lad. Don't you go staying up till all hours playing Bingo. We're expecting great things from you tomorrow."

As they walked down the passage to the side door, Paul said, "He's so Lancashire he makes you wonder if he wasn't born in London."

"Oh, I think he's from these parts. He might have been born the other side of the Mersey in Cheshire, but that really counts as North now. He's certainly Liverpool now, Pearson's Pools."

"I know. He makes his money from gambling and uses it to finance chess. He takes from chance and gives to skill. I suppose that makes him feel much happier."

"It's nice for us. I don't play the pools myself."

Wheaton had expected to be taken for the drink to one of the Imperial's bars, *l'aperitif* or the Oregon. With luck they might go to the lounge and have some tea. But Paul led him out of the hotel.

"Let's go down to the Tower. There's something I want to show you."

The clouds were low and scudding. The brown sea had advanced across a lot of sand since they last looked. A few drops of rain spattered at them from across the Irish Sea. They crossed the road and waited for a tram. Paul pointed along the Promenade.

"Is that your hotel?"

"Yes. The Glendale. I always stay there. Mrs. Beckington always makes me very comfortable. Though I'm afraid she's put her prices up this year."

"So has the Imperial," said Paul. Not that it mattered to him.

The tram took them along the Promenade and Princess Parade. They passed holiday-makers in tweed coats and grey flannels, and floral cotton frocks and cardigans, with collapsible prams. They passed jewellers selling engagement rings, and sweet shops selling Blackpool Rock, and stationers selling funny postcards of fat women with enormous behinds, and counters of oysters and mussels and shrimps, and the North Pier, where even now Val's mother was laughing herself sick at Dickie Henderson falling flat on his back. As they got off the tram, Paul pointed upwards.

"There! Lancashire's answer to the Eiffel Tower."

"Do you know, this is my fourteenth Blackpool Congress and this is the first time I've ever been in here."

"Well, you've got an experience coming."

They paid and went in, Wheaton feeling sad at parting with four and sixpence for something so unnecessary. The uniformed commissionaire said, "The olde-tyme dance doesn't start till eight. There's just the organ recital and the menagerie."

"That's fine," said Paul. "We aren't wanting to dance."

He led the way into the entrance hall and up the majestic Romanesque stairs. "Verona, I think," he murmured, "or possibly Padua." The wheezy sound of music came to them.

At the top of the stairs he turned left and led Wheaton into the Tower Ballroom.

"You've never seen this before?"

"Never. It's amazing."

"It's the finest example of British rococo. The Empress Ballroom in the Winter Gardens is more baroque, but this is pure rococo."

It was a huge room, far bigger than the Imperial Ballroom. There were two tiers of balconies bulging like royal boxes, and the place was solid with red plush and gilt carving and chandeliers and robed golden goddesses. The ceiling was painted, clouds and nymphs, and along the frieze were the names of such great composers as Wagner and Balfe suitably garlanded with laurel wreaths. Over the proscenium arch were three golden goddesses and beneath them the inscription BID ME DISCOURSE I WILL ENCHANT THINE EAR.

On the stage, a hundred yards or more from where Paul and Wheaton were standing, Reginald Dixon was playing a selection of tunes from *The Gondoliers* on the Wurlitzer. He was taking a fantastic amount of exercise, bouncing about, handling simultaneously several keyboards, a hundred stops, a full range of pedals. He was bathed in crimson light. Beside him on the stage, in a silver spotlight, was a piano-type instrument linked electrically to the Wurlitzer. Its keys moved with the Wurlitzer's and the audience could thus admire the astonishing nimbleness of the maestro's fingers. Behind was a romantic backcloth of Positano at sunset.

Paul pushed Wheaton into a chair. "The great Reginald Dixon," he murmured.

"Oh, that's who he is. I've heard Pearson talk about him all these years, but I never knew who he was talking about."

"He's the maestro of the Wurlitzer. The Thalben-Ball, the André Marchal." Wheaton looked baffled but said nothing. "Now you can say you've heard him. It's like having heard Liszt or Paganini." Seeing that he was not carrying Wheaton with him, he added, "Or having seen Capablanca."

"I have seen Capablanca. I played against him."

Paul nodded and waved his hands in acknowledgment.

"It was a Queen's Gambit Declined. We drew."

Paul said simply, "Nottingham 1936. I know the game well. One of your greatest. But I'm talking about legends, legendary people. Most people have only heard about Capablanca. You actually drew with him. A cousin of their great-aunt by marriage once heard Paderewski or Caruso or Kreisler. It's a big status symbol. You've actually heard and seen Reginald Dixon. It's just as legendary, with a touch of Abu Simbel about it too."

Wheaton felt himself becoming utterly lost in this conversation. "Egypt?" he ventured.

"Doomed to be lost and gone for ever. Anyone who's seen it before the destruction has a slight advantage over someone who's missed it. It's the same with the Wurlitzer. I don't expect they'll ever build another. You are witnessing the end of an art-form. Like those sonatas for musical glasses they kept writing in the eighteenth century. Supposing they had never made another piano after Liszt, and you had actually heard Liszt. Wouldn't that give you a lift up?"

Wheaton nodded slowly. Then he said, "I think it might make me rather sad. And rather boring."

There was a burst of applause as Reginald Dixon finished on a huge, deafening, jangling C Major chord. He turned round, picked up his hand microphone and thanked the audience for their appreciation. Now, for his older and younger listeners, he announced, he would play a medley of melodies old and new. He turned round, now bathed in orange light, and began to play a tune from *South Pacific*.

Wheaton said, "Is this why we came?"

A woman beyond him said fiercely, "Sssshh!"

Paul, undismayed, said, "No, we're going upstairs for that. But I thought you'd like to see this famous ballroom and hear the great maestro. Enlarge your experience, widen your horizons. Come upstairs and I'll show you what we came for."

The woman scowled and they tiptoed out across the miles of parquet. Back on crimson carpet Paul remarked, "I'm writing about this in my book. I've got a chapter on Blackpool. It's not about chess at all, it's a travel book about all the places where chess is played."

"I remember. You told me about it in Bled. *The City of Squares.*"

"No, no, that's another book. *Sixty-four Squares,*" Paul corrected him.

"I didn't know there were any squares in Blackpool."

"There's Talbot Square just outside. Queen's Square a few yards further back. Oxford Square at the end of Park Road." Paul was impressively expert. "Personally I think Princess Parade counts as a square. I shall say so."

"Won't there be any chess in it?"

"Only by the way. It'll be a travel book. My publishers are very excited about it. After all, my work takes me round the world, to places most people only ever hear about."

Wheaton smiled wanly. Paul said, "Let's go upstairs."

He led the way up the wide Romanesque staircase into the oriental bar. From Augsburg, from Verona they moved into old Pekin, all pagodas and temples. A strong zoo smell hit them from the menagerie next door. Wheaton looked round him in bewilderment. "I've never been here before," he repeated.

Paul took him into the bar. "What'll you have?"

"Oh, yes, thank you, yes, I think I'll just have a plain tonic water, if you don't mind."

"Nothing stronger?"

"Oh no, I hardly think so. Not today."

Paul ordered two tonic waters from the barman. "And please put a large vodka and some ice and a slice of lemon into mine." He propped himself backwards on the bar and looked at Wheaton. "Well?"

"There must be a zoo near here. It smells like a zoo."

"Never mind about zoos, lions and tigers. Concentrate on dragons. Look above you. Three beautiful dragons."

They looked up and Wheaton saw them, three large wooden painted dragons, flashing eyes, red tongues, curly tails.

"You rub up against them, George. They'll bring you good luck."

It was of course only a figure of speech. The dragons were a good fifteen feet above the floor.

Wheaton said, "We don't think too much of dragons in England. Our patron saint became famous for killing one."

"He was just an ignorant Macedonian mercenary. In China dragons are symbols of luck and power and prosperity."

Wheaton looked at them and thought. He commented, "But we're not in China. Whatever the local decorator may think," he added drily.

"But chess came from China. It came with its dragons."

"I thought it came from Persia."

"Plenty of dragons in Persia too. Look at their designs."

Wheaton took his tonic water, said "Cheers!" and sipped it. Paul didn't say "Cheers!" but he took a big gulp.

Wheaton said finally, "You mean you want me to play the Dragon against Toklovsky tomorrow."

"Why not? You scored a famous win with it against Vokhorov a few years ago. Why not complete the double?"

"It's a dangerous opening. There are so many good lines against it. I think the Najdorf or Taimanov variations are sounder."

"Possibly. But the Dragon would give you a big psychological advantage. Toklovsky will remember your game against Vokhorov."

"He has made a great study of the Dragon. He knows a lot about it."

"So do you. You must know as much about it as anyone. If it's a good enough opening for Botvinnik and Reshevsky, you needn't be afraid of it."

Wheaton stared into his glass and sighed. "Toklovsky isn't playing very well just now," he said at last.

"He certainly is not! When the World Champion scores a negative result against schoolboys and middle-aged ladies, there's something wrong."

"He has been playing very erratically since he won the World Championship two years ago. I suppose it's reaction. It's so tough to get to the top nowadays, there are bound to be some after-effects."

"Yes, just so. He's in political trouble too. This is the first time he has been allowed abroad for over a year. It's Mischchov who has been clocking up the mileage."

"What's Toklovsky done wrong?"

Paul sipped and shrugged. "Oh, maybe one of these complicated crimes that only Russians commit. Capitalist revisionism. Reactionary deviationism. Currency offences. Taking part in the propaganda war. Perhaps simply not winning enough games. Anyway, George, I think you've got a nice whole point waiting to be picked up tomorrow. It's a good thing to start a big tournament with a win. And Toklovsky still is World Champion whatever his current form may be. I'll give you a good write-up if you win," he added. "You'd like to be on the front page, wouldn't you?"

Wheaton gave one of his wan smiles, and looked up at the three dragons in the air above him. After a while he said, "It's a difficult opening."

"Difficult if you're playing for a draw. But it's a good winning line, especially if your opponent is rattled."

Wheaton glanced at him and remarked, "Well, I expect you'll get a good story out of it, whatever happens."

Paul winced and felt cross. He had brought Wheaton here to be inspired, not to make snide remarks about the great profession of journalism. He had finished his drink and wanted another. Wheaton clearly wasn't going to buy him a double vodka and tonic. If he bought it here, he would have to pay cash, while he could charge it if he had it in the hotel.

He said, "I expect I'll get a story. After all, I'm a professional like you, different profession that's all. But I'd like the story to be about you. I really would, please believe that." He let a watery gaze rest on Wheaton's profile, and then he too looked up at the dragons. The barman looked at the two of them strangely. Were they religious, or something? Was the bar a bloody church?

"Come on," said Paul, "let's go to our fish and chips. I've got to phone the paper."

Wheaton left most of his tonic water in the glass, and together they went down the great staircase. It did not occur to either of them to look round the menagerie, but the sound of the Wurlitzer came to them. Reginald Dixon was playing "I could have danced all night" on a stop which sounded like clanking chains. Outside a fine rain had cleared the Promenade. They dodged across the road and took refuge in the shelter. In the tram, Wheaton said, "Well, thank you for showing me that. It's most unusual, most unusual." He glanced at his watch. "Dear me, it's later than I thought. I hope Mrs. Beckington has kept her kettle on the hob. She usually has a cup of tea with me when I come in."

"No fish and chips?"

"I don't find I can digest a heavy meal in the evening. Just as well because it's usually too late by the time I come in from the games." As they passed Butlin's Metropole, he remarked out of the blue, "I can't play the Dragon if Toklovsky opens with the Queen's Pawn. It's some time since he last played a King's Pawn opening."

"He'll play one tomorrow. And do you know why? Because it's the official opening of the congress. Today's fun and games were just a foretaste. And the first move on the World Champion's board is going to be made by the Mayor of Blackpool. He's bound to move the King's Pawn, it's the only move he knows. Anyway I'll prompt him."

Wheaton gave one of his wan smiles and got off the tram. Paul continued one more stop to his huge red-brick palace by the sea. He went into the ballroom. Only one game was still in progress, Carl against Miss Davies. Carl was fidgeting with his personal black Knight, but otherwise he looked rather bored. He was sitting sideways on his chair, his legs crossed. Miss Davies, twitching and dogged, sat squarely to the table. They were on move sixty-two. The Rooks had come off, and it was now an end-game of Kings, Pawns, and Bishops of opposite colour. But Carl had a passed Pawn, which might in the end prove decisive, if he could be bothered to play it through to the end.

Paul went into *l'aperitif* bar and over a large and very dry vodka martini wrote his report for the *Post*. It was pretty easy to write, Mr. Pearson's original way of starting his tournament, four simultaneous simultaneous displays, the World Champion's negative result, Mischchov's solid performance, the beautiful zugzwang inflicted on the World Champion by seventeen-year-old Robin Jackson from Wythenshawe, Manchester, Miss Davies from Bootle and her indefatigable performance against Carl Sandbach from Los Angeles, all that and Reginald Dixon too. A fairly light-hearted mood piece; the serious reporting would come tomorrow. He took a second piece of paper and wrote a short political piece ("The Prime Minister told your correspondent that he was not worried by the current rumours of threats to his leadership and expressed confidence in the future"). He then went and telephoned them both through to London.

As he dictated his mood piece to the sports desk, he felt a familiar resentment that his words were being taken down by a young man primarily interested in football and golf. Chess was an art, and his pieces ought to be printed on the arts page along with the concerts and the art exhibitions. He ought to be speaking now to the literary editor, and not to this lout who said, "Have we got to put all that in? It's a bit long, isn't it?" Paul stiffly asked to be transferred to the news editor and read out his piece on the Prime Minister. The young man at the far end (who was he?) thanked him and rang him off. Feeling rather ruffled, Paul went back to the bar, had another vodka martini, ate several stuffed olives, and relaxed in a comfortable armchair with the frosted drink, the Utrillo reproductions and the soft piped music. This was more than he would be getting if he were actually in Fleet Street at the moment. The prospect of lobster à l'américaine and a bottle of Pouilly Fuissé in the Louis XVI Room next door became quite pleasing.

Wheaton, on the other hand, supped on Typhoo tea and several digestive biscuits, which he ate alone in the lounge. He ate fast, taking the tray out himself to Mrs. Beckington, and apologising once more for being late. Then he went up to his room with its view looking towards the backs of the houses in Holmfield Road. He turned on the light, took a number of books and magazines out of his suitcase and, sitting on the edge of his bed, began to read them. Beside him on the pillow was his folding chess-board.

The books were *Modern Chess Openings* (of course!), Paul Butler's *The King's Pawn Openings,* and Leonard Barden's *The Sicilian Defence*. He also found three recent numbers of *Chess* which had been largely devoted to the latest analysis of the Dragon Variation. He read and sighed. It seemed that the latest complication was the Yugoslav Attack. So many new names, so many new variations. This was, formally, the Yugoslav Attack against the Dragon Variation of the Sicilian Defence to the King's Pawn opening. So many clever young men, so many patient and thoughtful players working the thing out, following out the opening lines till the fifteenth or, in this case, the twentieth move. The variations, the ramifications at this stage assumed geometrical proportions, infinite possibilities, and every one had to be studied in advance. So much new analysis was being done every day in study groups in Tbilisi and clubs in New York and back bedrooms in Belgrade. It was useless to think that any player, in this modern world and on the international level, could hope to win by brilliance alone. How could any player, even a genius, find over the board, with his clock ticking, the best line, the soundest answer to a move which his opponent, a man of almost equal brilliance, had already spent many hours analysing? Even

Capablanca, as he himself had admitted towards the end of his life, would be forced to do some homework nowadays.

The Dragon had been under suspicion for some time. The journalistic phrase, "The Sicilian Dragon is a sickly beast," was still quoted in articles. Dr. Euwe, the Dutch ex-World Champion, had stated in his recent *Archives* (which Wheaton had not got with him) that the Dragon failed against White's Yugoslav Attack, which was based on White playing his King's Rook's Pawn to the fourth and then the fifth rank, coupled with castling Queen's side. However even more recent analysis had swung the opposite way and had considered that Black had excellent chances with the Dragon, even against the Yugoslav Attack.

Wheaton read: "9 B–QB4. With this move the strategy of both sides becomes clear. White will castle Queen's side and launch a storming attack on the opposite wing involving the moves P–KR4–R5, B–R6 and if necessary P–KN4. Black's counterplay stems from the occupation of the half-open QB file. At the right moment Black will invariably sacrifice the exchange on his QB6 square, in order to break the force of White's onslaught. It must be remembered that an end-game where Black has one Pawn for the exchange and White has doubled QB Pawns usually means equality for the second player. If in addition White has weakened his King's side Pawn structure with P–KN4, then Black has decidedly the better chances."

The point was reinforced by games from Olympiads and tournaments in Krakow, Vrnjacka Banja and Bognor Regis. Feeling very old, Wheaton played the games through on his folding board.

By eleven o'clock he knew that he could do no more. Analysis was vital, but so was sleep. It was always difficult to sleep the night before a big tournament, before a game with a grandmaster. It was important to forget that he had not done enough analysis, that nobody ever had; that there always came a moment when it was pointless to play through one more game, Levy *v.* Suarez or Savon *v.* Shtain. There was always one more game to be played through till the dawn came over the houses in Holmfield Road.

Relaxation was important too and some twenty years ago he had flirted briefly with Yoga. But it had been embarrassing to do some of those exercises in front of Janet, and they took up so much time, time which he considered would be better spent in analysis. He had abandoned it after a few months and put the book away between *Alekhine's Best Games* and *The Middle-Game Book II*. Though he took out the other two books continually, *A First Guide to Yoga* remained thereafter unopened.

But some things stayed: a dislike for stimulants, a need for periods of quiet and contemplation, and this, his eve-of-congress procedure. First he sat on the edge of his bed, his hands relaxed on his knees, his head erect, his eyes closed. He concentrated on golden light, beautiful golden sunlight flooding down in bars, not lighting anything in particular, but illuminating itself. He did this for what he thought was ten minutes, but which was usually about three by his watch. Then he changed into pyjamas, unpacked a stainless-steel tea-spoon from his case, and carefully spooned out four tea-spoons of the honey he had bought in the supermarket that afternoon into his tooth-glass. He filled up the tooth-glass with tepid water and stirred until the honey was dissolved. Then he unpacked a thin orange rubber tube from his suitcase and, looking furtively about him, he went along the dark passage carrying the tube and the tooth-glass.

The position he was forced to adopt was practised but degrading; this was rather satisfying, humiliation before purification. The sweet-sour discomfort of the nozzle, the essence inside him, brought back like the tunes of yesteryear other congresses in Bognor, Hastings, Bled, Beverwijk, other hotels, other lavatories. Here too, though he had skipped this part the last two years. It was three years since he had last knelt on this particular piece of cold white tiling, fumbling with the pyjama cord, the orange tube in the other hand, the vaseline on the seat beside him, the shining sculptured bowl, the fragrance of Jeyes. It was at moments like these that he returned to his earthly origins and was rejuvenated.

Fulfilled, but emptied. Soiled, but cleansed. He returned proudly to his bedroom, and did not look furtively round him. He washed the tube in the basin and dried it and put it back in his suitcase, with the vaseline. He screwed the top back on the pot of honey and put it in the waste-paper basket; it would be unthinkable to eat the rest of it for breakfast, though Mrs. Beckington herself might well do so. After all these years she would have become accustomed to finding partly consumed jars of honey in the waste-paper basket of the second floor back. Wheaton cleaned his teeth and climbed into the firm narrow bed. The sheets were smooth with much ironing, he stretched luxuriously, relaxation stole over him, golden light, the seven stages of the soul, bars of golden light, Krishna, fountains, golden fountains in a pool with water-lilies, reflecting seven temples, each one higher than the last, Vishnu and the seven water-lilies, the golden reflections shimmering in the pool, beside the water-lilies, the seven temples weaving in the golden light. He was deeply asleep, untroubled by dragons.

When he had finished his lobster, Paul ordered angels on horseback, black grapes, black coffee, Remy Martin and a Romeo y Julieta cigar. He was the last to leave the Louis XVI Room, but he had not been wasting his time. While he dined, he had drafted in his mind his piece for the *East Anglian News,* which he would telephone through tomorrow morning, and his regular article for *New Princess.* His next article for *Chess World* was also pending, but it would have to wait till some serious games had been played; no game played in a simul would count for serious analysis. But simuls were perfect for *New Princess.*

When he had first suggested a chess column, the editor had been sceptical. But he had given her figures, the amazing number of dedicated women chess-players, Miss Davies of Bootle and her thousands of sisters under the skin. They often bought a woman's magazine for the cooking and knitting, and, though they might have denied this, the romance. But, faced with a considerable choice, Miss Davies might change to the magazine which had a chess column too. The editor had taken the point rapidly, but she had begged him not to make it too technical, to remember Nurse Jenny who barely knew the moves, as well as Miss Davies and her club friends.

Paul had felt this was a challenge, and was pleased with the way he had solved the problem. Sometimes he would write a learned and technical piece for Miss Davies, and another week he would concoct a fey little fantasy about kings in their castles and sly bishops and prancing knights. But in the main he thought it best to write about the glamour of brains and brilliance, the romance of genius. Everyone, Nurse Jenny as well as Miss Davies, could understand and enjoy his descriptions of the personalities, the incidents, the colourful episodes: little Sammy Reshevsky playing Edward Lasker without a board in a taxi, Koltanowski playing his simuls blindfold, Sultan Khan the Indian slave, Bobby Fischer playing in the Havana tournament by telex, Carl Sandbach winning the U.S. Open aged fifteen, Najdorf announcing mate hours before anyone else could possibly have foreseen it, Morphy playing the Duke of Brunswick at the opera, Capablanca, William Winter, Pillsbury—though the editor had decided that the last two were not suitable for the readers of *New Princess*.

Today's four simul simuls were ideal for his purpose, four grandmasters taking on ninety-six opponents at once, the four musketeers defying the Cardinal's men, Dirk Bogarde playing a piano concerto against the ranged might of the London Symphony Orchestra. Alternatively there was tall young Robin Jackson getting the great Russian into zugzwang, a Jack-the-Giant-Killer, David-and-Goliath story, and Nurse Jenny would love a word like zugzwang. Halfway through the lobster he decided to make two articles of it. He would give Miss Davies later a tough piece on double exchange sacrifices to make up.

Smoking his cigar, he walked down the interminable corridor. The ballroom was in darkness; Miss Davies's game against Carl Sandbach was evidently over. He looked into the residents' lounge, but there was nobody there that he knew. Then he went into the writing-room; being a hotel designed for conferences, the management had provided typewriters and Paul puffed and clattered away at his three pieces. He put the two *New Princess* pieces into an envelope and gave them to the night telephone operator to be franked. It didn't matter in which order the magazine printed them.

Then feeling satisfied with his evening and his productivity he went along the eighty-five yards of passage to the main lounge. There was piped music here too, but the huge room buzzed to the sounds of chess. About thirty chess-players sat in a group in one corner playing each other on folding boards, laughing, joking, drinking beer. In the opposite corner a large group of sanitary engineers, who were also having a conference

118

in the hotel, told funny stories about sewage disposal, drank beer and glared at the chess-players.

Paul explained to the waiter that he was a hotel resident and ordered a pint of Double Diamond. He wandered across to the chess-players. Carl Sandbach, who had still not played enough chess that day, was playing a friendly against Dietrich.

Paul asked him, "What happened in your game with Miss Davies?"

Carl moved, his head down, his hand on the Bishop. He said, "I won. Well, I hope to Christ I could win against her. But she went on till I had actually queened that Pawn." He looked up at Paul. "Would you believe eighty-two moves?"

"Eighty-two?" Paul sat down.

"Right! Somebody ought to tell these British dames to give in when they're beat."

Mr. Pearson, who seemed to be the host of the gathering, waved expansively and said, "Fight on, lads, till the whistle blows. Do you know who said that?"

"Barrie," said Paul promptly.

"And lasses too. Never forget you may always score the equalising goal in the last half-minute."

Carl growled, "Maybe that works for ball games. It's not the same for chess."

"Why, don't you like playing chess?" Paul asked disingenuously.

During the dialogue Carl and Dietrich had continued playing, fast five-minute chess punctuated by pause for thought. Carl suddenly gestured helplessly in resignation, and began to set the pieces up for a new game. Dietrich opened with the Queen's Pawn and they rattled through the first eight moves of the Nimzo-Indian Defence in a few seconds. Then Carl paused for thought.

Dietrich looked up and said, in German, "Do you remember the simultaneous display of Hansgeorg Stuck here? It went on for seven hours."

"I remember well."

"Three games of more than seventy moves. One game of ninety moves. All against ladies with grey hair."

Paul laughed and said, "Poor Hansgeorg. He was never the same player afterwards. What has happened to him nowadays?"

Carl moved and glanced at Paul with some irritation. He did not speak German. Dietrich moved and said, "Did you not hear? He has given up chess. His wife made him. She said she would leave him, with the children, if he did not. Poor Hansgeorg, chess was his life. His wife is a hard woman."

"Ursula. Yes, I have met her. She is very beautiful."

"Beauty, yes, and money too. Poor Hansgeorg!"

"What does he do now?"

"He lives in Stuttgart. I think he is learning to be a lawyer. But I do not know for sure. I do not see him now, just a Christmas card. His wife does not like him to see his old chess friends. He is now to be only a husband and father."

"Speak English, lads, so we can know who you're talking about," said Pearson.

Paul said, "We were talking about Stuck. His wife made him give up chess."

"I know. I invited him here three years ago and he didn't even answer. Some of these wives are bloody terrors. We wouldn't stand for that in Lancashire, would we?"

The remark was addressed to the gathering, but it produced only grunts. Everybody else's head was well down over the games, sitting in low chairs, leaning forward uncomfortably. Dietrich resigned his game to Carl and they set up the pieces again. He opened once more with the Queen's Pawn and once again they rattled through the opening eight moves of the Nimzo-Indian Defence. Paul sat back in his chair and drank some of his beer. It had been a long and tiring day, and there was more to come tomorrow. He'd stay up another half an hour with this lot, not longer.

He looked round the group, Pearson, the grandmasters and about twenty keen young North Countrymen. Paul noticed the boy Robin Jameson or Jackson playing against his schoolmaster, Harvey or Hammond. The boy caught his eye and smiled.

"Getting in some practice before tomorrow."

"Sleep's important too," said Paul severely.

"It's all right, I'm going home after this lot."

Paul thought of telling him that he had just written a romantic piece about him for the readers of *New Princess*. Jackson his name was, not Jameson, Jackson the giant-killer. But he decided against it. It would be seven or eight weeks before the *Princess* piece came out, and he didn't want the boy to become too familiar. He still had the makings of a prize bore. Anyway he'd see his name tomorrow in the *Daily Post* as one of today's winners, and that should be enough for him.

He noticed his neighbour playing on a small shabby pocket board and remarked to him, "Do you know Keres's story about when he was asked to play on a board like that at a simul?"

The man played a move, it took two hands, one to hold down the board, the other to pull the piece out. He said vaguely, "Keres?"

"Yes, Paul Keres. It was a pretty scruffy board, even worse than yours. You could hardly tell the white squares from the black, and all the pieces were grey. Anyway Paul complained and said he couldn't possibly play on a board like that. And do you know what the man answered?"

The man made another move laboriously, glanced at Paul, and said, "No? What?"

"Well, the man was quite old and he just said, 'Well, it was good enough for Grandmaster Reti to play on. And he was playing blindfold.'"

Paul sat back smiling, expecting appreciation. The man said, "Well, if it's blindfold chess, it doesn't really matter what the board's like, does it?"

Paul decided he hadn't really been listening. Pearson, however, had. He leaned forward and said, "Blindfold chess! That gives me an idea. I think we'll kick off next year with four blindfold simuls. That would make a good story for you, eh?"

"Excellent!" said Paul, thinking of *New Princess*. The blind swordsman, the blind pianist, the blind chess-player. It would be a knock-out for Nurse Jenny.

"And if these lads won't do it"—Pearson gestured at the assembled grandmasters—"I know some that will. I bet Reshevsky would do it for me. Or Boghossian. Or Paul Keres himself, for that matter."

"I'd do it," said Carl Sandbach. "I wouldn't mind playing blindfold. At least I wouldn't know it was one of these grey-haired British dames who meant to go on playing all night."

"Right, lad," said Pearson, "you're on for next year. I'll get together twenty-four, or more if you like, of our greyest-haired lasses and you shall play them all in a blindfold simul."

"It's a deal," Carl growled, not looking up, playing Rook to Bishop 8 check. Dietrich answered Rook takes Rook. Carl played Bishop takes Rook.

Pearson said, "What about that, Mr. Butler? Would that make a story for you?"

"Ye-es. But it would be better if he played twenty-four beauty queens. Miss Blackpool, Miss Morecambe, Miss St. Annes, Miss Widnes, girls like that. I'd get a photographer up for that."

"Twenty-four beauty queens, and I'm to play chess against them blindfold. Jeez, what do you think I am!" He played Pawn to Rook 6. Paul sniggered.

There had been a subtle change in the lounge's atmosphere. Drinking his bitter, Paul realised that the piped music, Reditone, had been turned off. The waiter came up and said, "Excuse me, gentlemen, but we are closing this lounge now. But the residents' lounge is still open and the night porter will look after your orders." He picked up some glasses and went away.

"Well, that's it, lads," said Pearson, heaving himself to his feet. "Drink up, play up and shut up."

The party came to an end in a gulping of beer, a banging of pieces, a sudden hubbub. They trooped out into the passage.

"Where is this residents' lounge?" Carl asked.

"Other end of the passage. Eighty-three yards from here."

"What a way to build a hotel!"

In the hall the group split up. The grandmasters went on to the residents' lounge.

"They'll go on till four in the morning," said Pearson, who was speeding the non-residents on their way. "Tire themselves out, make it easier for you lads tomorrow. What a life, eh?"

Paul slipped away, into the lift, up to the first floor, along the vast passage, past the stained-glass window, to his room. The Reditone had been turned off in the lift too. It was time he was in bed.

The non-residents shrugged into their raincoats, said good night to Pearson, and straggled out on to the Promenade.

Mr. Hammond said to Robin, "I'm going the other way. Well, good night, try and get a good night's sleep. Tomorrow could be a big day for you, one of the biggest days of your life. It isn't every day that a boy like you gets the chance to play someone like Mischchov. Anyway, good luck."

"Thank you, sir," said Robin.

Apart from them the Promenade was deserted. It was raining hard, and the illuminations danced and swung, reflecting in the wet road, outlining the Tower, an improbable dazzle of colour and light. Robin gripped the wet railings and stared out at the distant sea. Mr. Hammond was right, tomorrow would probably be one of the most important days of his life. He had already decided that, if Mischchov opened with the King's Pawn, he would play the Caro-Kann. But if he opened with the Queen's Pawn, as was more likely, he was still undecided whether to play the King's Indian or the Modern Benoni. He wished that girl Val was beside him, he could tell her about the problem, put his arm round her. She would look up at him, her lips parted, while he told her about the positional advantages of the King's Indian. Perhaps he would kiss her. But Val had been in bed hours ago

Suddenly all the illuminations went out, and he was left alone with the street lamps and the rain and the sea.

It was still raining the following morning when the maid brought Paul's early-morning tea. He sipped it and stared at the spattered window. There was something to be said for holding congresses only in southern resorts. Santa Monica was ideal. The players themselves would never notice, but it was jolly for the correspondents who could swim and get themselves youthful and becoming suntans. But then his mind went back to chess, and while he bathed and dressed he drafted in his mind his article for *The Statistician*.

Downstairs he bought a copy of today's *Daily Post*. He glanced at the headline (TIME TO CLOSE OUR RANKS, CALLS PREMIER), and took the paper unopened along to the dining-room. He ordered porridge, scrambled eggs and bacon, toast, marmalade and coffee. Then he changed his mind, called back the waitress and said he would like kipper fillets as well before the eggs and bacon. It was part of the inclusive breakfast and there was no point in missing anything. It wasn't as if kippers were fattening. He thought of changing his mind and having orange juice instead of porridge, but the waitress had already disappeared into the kitchens. Anyway the orange juice would probably be tinned.

He opened the *Post* and turned immediately to the sports page. As he had feared, his piece was tucked away under the golf. And it had been cut to ribbons; just the scores of the simuls and the names of those who had won. His mood piece, his evocation of Blackpool, had all gone. He felt discouraged; it was hardly worth bothering to write well for a sports editor like that. Then he remembered that he could use the whole thing in *Sixty-four Squares*. He had the copy and it would hardly need any alteration, only the elimination of the chess part. An evocation of Blackpool on a rainy September evening.

He turned to the political news and read it carefully, but he could find no account of his exclusive interview with the Prime Minister. Had that been crowded out too? A phrase in the leading article comforted him: "Doggedly though the Prime Minister may trumpet his confidence in the future, it is difficult not to feel considerable anxiety about several points." Yes, obviously the leader-writer had read his piece, though he did not acknowledge it. Still, it counted.

Feeling better, he wiped his mouth and left the dining-room. In the hall he looked at all the magazines in case the new copies of *The Statistician* or *New Princess* might be in. But there were only last week's, which he had already seen. He went on to the residents' lounge in case Carl Sandbach and Dietrich were still playing chess, but the place was empty, cleaned, ready for a new day. The grandmasters were evidently snatching a few hours' sleep before they started again. Then he went into the equally empty writing-room and typed out his article for *The Statistician*.

This was not a romantic piece. It was firmly statistical. One hundred and twenty players assembled, of whom ten were invited foreign grandmasters and the rest more or less from the North Country; a big open tournament on the Swiss system, but arranged, so it is said, so that the grandmasters never played each other ("I haven't brought these foreign masters here to play yet more grandmaster draws against each other," the congress's generous sponsor Mr. William Pearson said to your correspondent). This was unique in that the winner or winners would have won by playing every game against a weaker opponent, and in theory all ten grandmasters should tie first. One of the attractions of the tournament was that the prizes were not divided in this event, and every winner would receive the full prize. In practice experience had shown that things did not work out so simply. There were often surprises. Far from playing eleven easy games and one simultaneous display, the masters often found themselves playing surprisingly tough games against the young, or less young, giant-killers of the North, for whom the congress provided such invaluable experience. Further, as the figures for recent international congresses had shown, grandmasters liked to draw two out of three games played, and they were not always conditioned to playing every game for a win against opponents who would only agree a draw reluctantly and at the bitter end. So though it was probable that N. Mischchov (U.S.S.R.) and C. Sandbach (U.S.A.) would be among the winners, many reversals were possible during the next two weeks.

He read it through several times, liking it more and more each time, sealed it and gave it to the girl on the switchboard to frank. Then he went back to his room, which the maid had done specially early. He got out his books and papers, and began to work on Chapter 4 of his current book, *The Queen's Pawn Openings.* How hard I work, he thought, not for the first time. All these players who think they do all the work while I collect all the perks, if they would only understand how much work I do. They have only got to be chess masters; I've got to be a chess expert *and* an author *and* a journalist. And if I do eat and drink a certain amount, why not? A high-powered car needs more fuel, and higher grade fuel at that, than a Mini. That was a good analogy, he must remember it for future occasions.

He had a slight headache this morning, it was that article for *The Statistician,* it had taken a lot out of him. He bent his head and his mind to yet further study of the weaknesses of the Queen's Indian Defence. In an hour and a half it would be time for the first martini of the day in *l'aperitif* bar.

At two o'clock the Mayor of Blackpool, wearing his mayoral chain, climbed the steps of the Ionic temple in the ballroom, and made a speech. He welcomed everyone to Britain's Holiday Town and hoped they would get time off from chess for a bit of Bingo too. This was received in stony silence. Then he paid tribute to

Mr. William Pearson, which was applauded; he remarked that Mr. Pearson was using his gains from luck to reward brains, which raised a titter. He told a story about the doorman at the Empress Ballroom who had told the politicians arriving for their conference, that it was olde-tyme dancing that afternoon, and not politics. This also raised a gentle laugh. He specially welcomed the foreign visitors, reading out their names from a typed list, stumbling over the pronunciation.

Then he descended the steps, bear-led by Pearson, Paul hovering at his elbow. He was led to Board No. 1, A. Toklovsky *v.* G. Wheaton, shook hands with both, said, "Well, I hope you lads have a proper scrap," and, prompted by Paul, moved White's King's Pawn. He advanced it one square to K3. He held the position while the photographers snapped and flashed, then released the Pawn, looked up and bellowed, "I now declare this congress open."

Pearson called out, "Will all players with the white pieces please start their clocks—now!"

The mayoral party moved on to the other boards; the mayor would spend another ten minutes or so here before going to his next engagement. Stewards moved round the hall, making sure that all the clocks had been started. Toklovsky gazed in consternation at the move which had been made for him, caught Wheaton's eye, shrugged, said *"J'adoube,"* moved his Pawn on to K4, and pressed his button.

Wheaton nodded in agreement, though he had had a secret hope that Toklovsky would take the whole move back and open with the Queen's Pawn, thus avoiding the dilemma in Wheaton's mind. Last night he had confidently decided on the Dragon, but this morning he had weakened. Why stick his neck out, why not play the Ruy Lopez and the Marshall and hope for a draw? After all, a draw against the World Champion was a creditable achievement, and he was sure Toklovsky, in his present bad patch, would be only too happy to agree a draw somewhere between Move 30 and Move 40. And if he could draw every game in the congress, he would get five and a half points, which was quite respectable with the additional credit he would get for being unbeaten. What more could a man of his age and seniority hope for? It was not likely that he could hope to become an international master now, still less a grandmaster. And he was already one of the country's greats, a player who still often represented his country abroad, and who was worthy still to open this congress with a game against the World Champion. What more did he want?

He had wrestled with the choice all morning in his bedroom, all through dinner, while that egregious boy with glasses had been showing off to the girl at the next table, telling her all about Mischchov and Toklovsky and Petrosian and Ruy Lopez and half-closed openings and asymmetrical defences and all the rest of it. The girl had seemed extraordinarily patient and well mannered. Later he decided that she was just plain infatuated with the boy, his genius, his brilliance and knowledge, with the extraordinary new world she was being sucked into. Janet had never been overwhelmed like that. She had respected chess, she had admired his achievements, but she had never looked at him like that, mouth open, goggle-eyed. Janet had never been infatuated by anything. He felt misused and old.

He had picked at his liver and bacon and onions and chips. He hadn't dared eat onions a second day running. How he wished Mrs. Beckington had never heard of onions. Or cloves either, when he came on to the apple pie. He should have asked her if, as it was a special game for him, she would put on fish pie as a special favour for him. But he couldn't bring himself to ask for favours from her. He'd had a little Cheshire cheese and biscuits—he hadn't felt hungry—and thought about the Dragon.

It was such a complicated defence, a theoretical jungle someone had called it. And the advantage it gave Black was marginal and arguable. But nobody could say that the Ruy Lopez, even with the Marshall Attack, gave safety to Black. Bobby Fischer liked to play the Lopez with White and he was a player who liked to win. On the other hand strong defensive players like Botvinnik and Reshevsky played the Dragon. He had wrestled with the problem all through lunch, through the mayor's speech, through these opening seconds.

His clock was now ticking. Twenty years ago he would have (and had) played the Dragon and got away with it, but now what did it matter? He moved to play the Lopez and be safe, to move his King's Pawn, P–K4. But at the last moment, his finger and thumb an inch away from the Pawn, he hesitated, and flinched. A flash-bulb went off in his face.

He relaxed and sat back, let them get their photographs over;

he was glad of the breather, even though his clock was ticking. Toklovsky nodded sympathetically at him. Paul almost danced with anxiety.

When they had finished taking World Champion A. Toklovsky from Moscow (leaning forward, touching his Pawn once again) playing British expert George Wheaton of Hendon (though born in Durham), they moved on to take ex-World Champion N. Mischchov of Leningrad playing Robin Jackson of Lady Wynyard's Grammar School, Didsbury, Manchester. They asked Val, who was, of course, standing by the table to squat down so that they could get her pretty face and bouffant hair into the picture too ("seen here with a friend and admirer"). Then they moved on to take Grandmaster F. Dietrich from West Germany who was playing a student from Newcastle University.

Wheaton put his head in his hands and tried to think it out again. Botvinnik playing White in the Lopez had beaten Wade, no less, and Botvinnik had been World Champion three times. On the other hand, Larsen had lost playing Black with the Dragon, to Ivkov, whom he usually beat. Toklovsky was looking at him in some surprise. Players usually decided on their opening move before coming into the hall.

Clearing his mind, Wheaton glanced up, straight into the smiling pretty face of Val. She had turned round, and was looking at him.

"You're staying in the same hotel as us, aren't you?" she remarked. "I hope you win too."

"Ssshh!" hissed Paul harshly.

The girl realised her gaffe, and put her hand over her mouth, blushing. But Wheaton had been charmed. He smiled at her, said "Thank you," and, not giving the matter another second's thought, played his Queen's Bishop's Pawn, to QB4. Paul sighed audibly with relief. At least it was the Sicilian Defence, his advice might not have been spoken in vain. He watched closely while Toklovsky and Wheaton rattled through the opening moves:

1	P–K4	P–QB4
2	N–KB3	P–Q3
3	P–Q4	P x P
4	N x P	N–KB3
5	N–QB3	P–KN3

He had waited in some anxiety for Black's fifth move. It was necessary for Black to move a Pawn at this point, and the Pawn chosen decreed the variation of the Sicilian selected, Paulsen, Scheveningen, Najdorf or Taimanov or, as in this case, the Dragon. Black would next fianchetto his black-square Bishop, develop it on his KN2 square "round the corner," intending in due course to control the long diagonal. He wrote down "Sicilian Dragon" in his notebook, and trotted off to look at the other games, not even bothering to nod at Wheaton. All going well, the man ought to have it in the bag now.

Toklovsky thought for eight minutes before playing his next move: 6 B–K2. Wheaton thought for ten minutes in reply. So Toklovsky was not playing the Yugoslav Attack after all. If he had been, he would have played P–B3 in preparation for castling Queen's side and advancing his King's Rook's Pawn. It seemed that Toklovsky was hoping to play the more orthodox version. A safer version! Wheaton felt a surge of confidence, coupled with a slight feeling of annoyance that he should have spent so many hours yesterday studying the Yugoslav Attack. When he finally played his Bishop to Knight 2, 6 . . . B–N2, the key move of the Dragon, two spectators glanced at each other and shrugged, surprised that the old boy should have apparently taken so long to decide on a move which was both obvious and already prepared. In fact Wheaton's mind had been several moves ahead, rethinking his entire strategy. But time, all the same, was passing.

On the seventh move both players castled King's side, and on the eighth move Toklovsky played B–KN5, a wild and unforeseen move at this stage. Wheaton considered it carefully and decided to ignore it for the moment, preferring to develop his other Knight to B3 in orthodox fashion. Toklovsky spent some time on his next move, swaying back and forth, chewing imaginary chewing gum. Finally he played his white-square Bishop to N5, attacking Wheaton's Knight and leaving both his Bishops advanced and exposed. Wheaton decided on a strong freeing move and played his Queen to N3. Toklovsky retreated his other Bishop to K3, a wasted move back to defend his Knight. Wheaton decided to drive the other Bishop away with P–QR3, and Toklovsky retreated it to K2, the square to which it ought to have moved in the first place.

There was no doubt Toklovsky was playing extraordinary and erratic chess. He had already moved one Bishop three times, and the other twice, losing tempos each time, tempos he could not afford. This was no way for a World Champion to play, even against a humbler talent. Wheaton toyed with the idea of playing Q x NP, and swiftly rejected it. He mustn't become wild too. It was possible he was going to have the good win he had promised himself, and which Paul had almost promised him. But he must play very, very carefully. He mustn't make any mistakes. He buried his head in his hands.

On the next board Robin Jackson found himself playing black in a King's Gambit Declined. It was not an opening that he had prepared for, and he had some trouble in summoning the moves from the back of his memory. But something else was guiding him today, a feeling of buoyant confidence, an intimation that this was one of the crucial days of his life, past or to come; it was a sense of occasion, the photographers, the new board bought in honour of the event, the shiny pieces, the blacks so black, the whites so ivory yellow, the world's strongest living player across the board from him, thick and square and unsmiling, the girl in her yellow jeans perched alongside, watching the game as if she understood it, watching him and admiring him. He had nothing to lose; he was expected to lose to Mischchov. If by any chance he could draw, that would indeed be an achievement. And if he could win, if Mischchov should make a mistake, a small strategic miscalculation, and he could take advantage of it, if he could bring off the double, Toklovsky yesterday, Mischchov today, if if if.

Paul noted down the opening with some surprise and moved on to look at Board No. 3, Carl Sandbach against Miss Lewis of Leeds. As he had first caught sight of the grey grizzled head he had exclaimed involuntarily, "Oh no! Not again!"

She had said coolly, "I beg your pardon?"

As they shook hands, he had said, "I beg yours, ma'am. I just meant that I played a game yesterday against a British lady like you, and the game went on for eighty-two moves. I was really tired afterwards."

Miss Lewis, writing up her score-sheet, remarked without looking up, "Let's hope this one goes on for a hundred moves."

"Boy!" Sandbach murmured, sitting down, scratching his head.

She opened with her Queen's Bishop's Pawn, and he replied quickly with his King's Knight. He seemed in a hurry, to want to get on with it, and she was brisk and knowledgeable. Passing by a few minutes later, Paul glanced at the positions and at the score-sheets. He wrote down in his notebook: "English Opening, Gruenfeld Defence."

Miss Davies herself was playing Mr. Hammond, the schoolmaster from Didsbury, somewhere in the middle of the hall. Paul wandered round, noting down points from the games of the better known players, and the more interesting points from the games of the unknown players. Then he returned to Board No. 1.

It required the eye of faith, and romantic faith at that, to see the shape of a dragon in Black's Pawn position, but that was what you were meant to see. Perhaps he might write a piece about dragons for *New Princess,* following on earlier ones about Castles and Queens and Knights. But he had to be careful about such fantasies; somebody would love to write and tell him that it wasn't really called that because it looked like a dragon (what do dragons look like?) but after some place probably called Dragonavica in Serbia where it was first played. He had once written a piece explaining that the Castle, that dynamic and mobile piece so unlike a real castle, should be always called a Rook, which was nothing to do with a bird but came from the old Persian word *rukh* meaning a spirit or wind or chariot. It was pleasant talking about such unknown, picturesque and ambiguous tongues. And then some professor (what was he doing reading *New Princess* anyway?) had written to say that, on the contrary, *rukh* was the ancient Persian for a tower or castle, and, worse still, *New Princess* had printed it. Still he should be safe with dragons.

He caught Wheaton's eye and nodded approvingly. The old boy was playing soundly and well. So far, so good. Paul went off to sit down and chat to the other correspondents.

The long afternoon uncoiled slowly. The daylight coming through the skylights faded and the lights were turned on. Val brought Robin cups of tea, paying for them herself. As he sipped he noticed her for the first time for an hour.

"You're a real Hebe," he remarked.

This sounded nice, though she didn't understand it. She smiled at him, glad to be of help. But she wished that he would say something to her, just thank you or hullo, but she supposed he wasn't allowed to speak to anyone while he was playing in case they helped him. Her helping him! She gave a little giggle.

She was noting their habits. The formidable Russian beside her stayed solid in his chair, rooted like a tree, not fidgeting or smoking or biting his nails or drinking tea—not that anyone brought him any; Val didn't feel that her generosity need go that far. But every three-quarters of an hour or so, he would get up abruptly and clump out of the hall, returning a few minutes later, having presumably answered the needs of nature. She thought of the war-cry of her football-fan uncle when he had taken her to watch Everton: "Roll up yer Footee Echo!" Roll up yer Chessee Echo! She giggled again, and Robin glared at her.

The other Russian on the other side of her, the little one, was wearing much too thick a suit and was drenched in sweat, which he mopped continually with a grubby handkerchief. Between moves he prowled round the hall like a cat. That's it, she thought, a cat feeling the heat, not that it was so hot ever in Blackpool, was it, specially not today when it was raining. The old Englishman he was playing, the one with the grey hair, liked to stand behind his own chair, his bony fingers gripping the back of his chair, staring at the game, swallowing. Then he would move and look at the game from behind his opponent's chair, swallowing. She supposed he had indigestion. Then he would sit down, and bury his head in his hands, deep in thought. She supposed he must be super brainy.

The tall American on the other side—and Ooo-er! wasn't he gorgeous, so tall and lean like a film-star in a Western, though her boy friend Robin was almost as tall, but he was more sort of scholarly, the clever boy who knew all the answers in a film about American colleges—anyway the American would stride rapidly round the tables, glancing at all the other games, my! he must be clever to take it all in so quickly. And that blond German beyond him—ugh! she couldn't bear blond men—who strutted about with his hands in the small of his back and his nose in the air. And that grey-haired lady in the dark blue floral frock like her mum, who never left the table for any purpose, and wrote pages of notes when she wasn't actually playing, and didn't seem to have any needs of nature, not even a Chessee Echo—Val suppressed a giggle. She was a bit like Miss Thomas at school. Val didn't like her.

She looked up at her own boy friend, standing beside the table, staring at his game from the side, pressing his glasses against the bridge of his nose. Perhaps the shanks were too long and they slid forward when his head was bent. She tried to read his expression: was he doing well, how was it going, was he happy? She looked at the board and counted the pieces: eleven white, eleven black, all square. So far, so good. But she hadn't realised these things went on so long. Her uncle's games (the one who played chess, not the one who watched Everton) were always over in half an hour. Think of going on playing one game for five hours! Ooops! she couldn't ever do that. She went and got him some more tea. It was the only way she could think of to help.

By half past six many of the games were over. Sandbach had succeeded in beating Miss Lewis in thirty-four moves. Dietrich had also won. Miss Davies was still locked indecisively with Mr. Hammond, but many of the less distinguished games were over, the boards deserted, set up ready for tomorrow's games, the scores marked up in chinagraph on the scoreboards. Most of the players went to watch the games of the two Russians, which were, after all, the major attraction of the tournament. Val felt the breath of half Lancashire on the back of her neck.

Both games were interesting, apart from the international angle. For one thing, both English players were behind on the clock. Unless they speeded up their play in the next hour, they would both be in time trouble. But there was no doubt that Robin was holding Mischchov well. He was level in material and had succeeded in getting his Queen's Rook through to the seventh rank. On the other hand Mischchov's Rook dominated the open King's file.

"I think he should get a draw out of it," commented the Newcastle student in a low voice.

Wheaton was doing even better. There was no doubt that Toklovsky was playing very wildly. He had sacrificed a Pawn in the early middle-game, without any advantage. And he had now sacrificed the exchange as well, again to little purpose.

"Sad to see a great player off form like this," said Pearson to Paul. "But I'll be glad to see old George get a point from him."

Paul agreed. "He's got it pretty well in the bag. But I hope he clinches it soon. He tends to get very tired in the last hour."

"Don't you fret, lad. I bet old Toklovsky'll resign within the next few minutes."

But Toklovsky did not resign, not even when he lost a further Pawn. He wasn't prowling about any more, just sitting and mopping his brow and staring at his sad position. He had left King, Queen, both Bishops and three Pawns, adjacent in front of his King, which was still on N1 after castling several hours earlier. Wheaton, on the other hand, had King, Queen, Rook, Knight and five Pawns. He was the equivalent of four Pawns up, and two of his Pawns were passed Pawns, one of them on the fifth rank, only three moves from the queening square. His Queen had penetrated to the eighth rank and was pinning Toklovsky's white-square Bishop. Carl Sandbach leaned over, glanced at the game, caught Paul's eye and nodded happily. He was no ally of any Russian.

Wheaton, however, sat with his head in his hands, apparently lost in thought or gloom. He was oblivious of the excited low-voiced crowd murmuring round him, of the fact that his clock flag was up and that he had still three more moves to make before the time control. Only the twitching muscle in his right cheek showed the tension.

Toklovsky's hands were also visible and being watched, both on the table, the left one holding the damp handkerchief, the right one clenched. All the eyes were on the right one, waiting for the moment when it would rise up and offer the resignation handshake.

"He'll resign next move."

"Bet he waits till the time control. Old Wheaton's pushed for time."

"He's only got three moves to make. He can make them all in a couple of seconds. Any of them will win."

Paul was dancing with anxiety. He wanted to scream, "Play something, man, anything. Don't lose on time! You've got a won game, practically any move will clinch it. Move something!"

To calm himself, he reminded himself that this exciting moment would make a good article for one of his papers, the *Post* or the *East Anglian News,* or even *The Statistician.* And of course he would deal with it in depth in *Chess World.* He scribbled down the position in Forsyth notation: "5rk1; 5p1p; p3nQp1; 8; 3p2P1; 7P; 3B1P2; 1q3BK1."

Finally Wheaton moved, deliberately, calmly, with all the time in the world. He played P–Q6, advancing his passed Pawn one step nearer the queening square, threatened by the white Bishop but defended by the black Queen. A simple aggressive move. He pressed the button stopping his clock, wrote the move down on his score-pad, and buried his head once more in his hands.

It took several seconds for the intimations of disaster to dawn on the spectators. Toklovsky saw it first, made a little grimace, and played B–QB3, moving his Bishop on to the long diagonal in support of his Queen. The following move he would play his Queen into the corner, Q–R8, mate, and there was nothing Wheaton could do to prevent it.

A long slow gasp went up from the crowd gathered round, as they took it in. With a won game, faced with several moves which would have forced Toklovsky's immediate resignation, Wheaton had found the one move which lost immediately and irretrievably. He had thought too long, or too little; he had followed his instinct or he had rejected it; how to follow the workings of a man's mind at these moments of crisis and disaster?

"Pity about that," said someone, shrugging it off. "Old Wheaton could have used that point."

"Lucky for Toklovsky, though. Saved him from being sent to the salt mines when he gets back to Russia."

Paul could have cried. The win of the year, which he had plotted and planned so subtly, had been dashed from his grasp in the moment of victory. The dragon had turned round and bitten the hand that was feeding it. Wait a minute, perhaps he could make something out of that; the tricky unreliable dragon, though you could hardly blame the opening for a blunder made on the thirty-eighth move. British expert's tragic error. World Champion's first win for three months, snatches victory in time scramble, though you could hardly call Wheaton's deliberate move a scramble. The strain of the fifth hour when you're over fifty. The ups and downs of chess, the hammer strokes of fate, count no man happy until the other chap has actually resigned.

Yes, maybe he could make something out of it, save something from the wreck.

Wheaton, however, seemed to notice nothing of the perturbation round him. Head still in hands, he seemed to be considering his next move with all the time and all the chances in the world. The tip of his flag hung on the tip of the minute hand, a millimetre of metal holding it up. The crowd watched his right hand against his twitching cheek, waiting to see it come out in the resignation handshake, the wan smile, the silent nod. But the hand stayed still on the cheek. In a lost game it was discourteous not to resign, to prefer to lose on time. But Wheaton seemed oblivious to such niceties. Toklovsky mopped his forehead.

The flag fell, the minute hand moved on into the next hour. Toklovsky looked pointedly at the clock, then at Wheaton, and at the clock again. He caught Paul's eye and shrugged again. Then he signed his scoresheet and tore it off the pad, mopped his brow once more, looked again at Wheaton, and staggered to his feet, and pushed his way through the crowd to the scoreboards. Nobody congratulated him. The crowd moved on to watch the end of the Mischchov-Jackson game, Paul with them. Wheaton simply went on staring at the board, as if he had still another move to make. His cheek, however, was no longer twitching.

Meanwhile on Board No. 2, things were not looking quite so good for Robin Jackson. He had lost a Pawn which was enough to give a decisive advantage to a player of Mischchov's calibre. He might hold it for a while in the end-game which lay ahead, but the end was no longer in doubt. He looked at his flag which had begun to rise, threw a quick glance to see if Val were still there, and pressed his glasses back on to his nose. Pity! It was daft to have ever imagined that he could beat someone like Mischchov. But it would have been nice to have won just this game. Mr. Hammond would have been so pleased, Val would have been impressed. Toklovsky yesterday, Mischchov today. Still, there it was.

The news of Toklovsky's win filtered through to them. Mischchov nodded impassively, Robin felt a stab of satisfaction. So he wasn't the only one to lose to a Russian grandmaster. If an experienced old so-and-so like Wheaton could lose to an out-of-form Toklovsky, there was no disgrace in his losing to the most formidable living player. All the same! He concentrated on his next move. Q–N3 threatening Q x P mate would fail to White's P–N3. Anyway it was Mischchov to move.

Just what Mischchov's ideas were at this stage nobody could guess. He remained solid, enigmatic, giving nothing away. Yet he did give away a good deal, and Paul, later, in a masterly article in *The Statistician* speculated on his mental processes at this stage. Was he too becoming tired in the fifth hour? He was a man of fifty, with a lifetime of chess behind him. From time to time there were bound to be momentary, though not necessarily fatal, aberrations. Or was it impatience? The out-of-form Toklovsky on the next board had just notched up a win. It was high time he won too. He was an ex-World Champion, a grandmaster, playing with the white pieces, a Pawn to the good, and he was being held up too long by an unknown and inexperienced boy. Or was it a calculated risk? He saw the flaw in his plan and hoped that his opponent would not, that he could hustle Robin into a lost position and resignation. Nobody ever knew, and Mischchov himself never explained anything. But he began to play like a man who has almost won and has a train to catch. He had over half an hour left on his clock, but he moved as decisively as a player whose flag is hanging.

R–K8 check! He drove his Rook down the open file to the end rank, checking. Robin had foreseen this and had prepared a bolt hole for his King, K–R2. The King was now safe "round the corner," behind Robin's Rook. Mischchov immediately played R–Q6. On this square, protected by the Queen's Pawn, the Rook was attacking Robin's Queen, driving it off the rank. Paul did not note the position, but later he reconstructed it for the benefit of his readers: "8; 1bp3rk; 1p1pRq2; 3P1p1p; 1PP2P2; 3Q4; r1N3PP; 5RK1."

It was like a punch in the solar plexus when Robin understood the significance of the move, two seconds after Mischchov had made it. He broke out in a sweat, his heart hammered in his throat at about a hundred and twenty to the minute, he felt sick with excitement. Was it possible? His hands shook and he put them under the table. He gave a slight retch. Another moment and he would be actually sick over the board, or over Val's yellow jeans. Or perhaps he would faint. The room was swimming round him.

He mastered his nausea, took a deep breath, and studied the combination which had dawned on him. His flag was hanging but he resolutely ignored it. He had only a minute or so left, but he mustn't let himself be bothered by that. Was the combination possible against a player like Mischchov? Was it sound? Rubbing the wet palms of his hands on his knees, he tried to think it through.

The crowd were tense too. Few, if any, understood the possibilities of the situation, but they were all acutely aware of Robin's clock, the hanging flag, and three moves still to make. Even Val, when it was pointed out to her, understood that Robin's survival was a matter of seconds.

Finally Robin moved. His hand was shaking so much he almost knocked the pieces over. He took Mischchov's Rook with his Queen, Q x R, stopped his clock and tried to write the move on his score-pad. But his hand was uncontrollable and would only make an illegible squiggle.

The reaction was delayed a few seconds, and of course many could not see the board clearly from where they were. Then there was a gasp. A Queen sacrifice! Young Jackson sacrificing his Queen against Mischchov. There was a buzz as people pointed it out to each other.

Mischchov alone was calm and unexcited. He folded his arms and considered the position for half a minute without signs of emotion. Then he accepted the sacrifice, Pawn takes Queen, P x Q. It would have been unthinkable to let his Rook go for nothing, even against Robin. Robin, his hand still trembling, played immediately Rook takes Pawn check, R x P ch. In taking Robin's Queen, Mischchov had moved his Pawn off the long diagonal, and Robin's well-placed Bishop now protected the Rook.

Mischchov played the move he was forced to make, his King into the corner, K–R1. Robin moved his Rook, taking Mischchov's Knight, bringing his other Rook into play and exposing Mischchov's King to discovered check from the Bishop, R x N dis ch. Mischchov considered the position for another fifteen seconds, and then he held out his hand in resignation.

Robin shook it briefly with his sweaty hand. Mischchov impassively wrote up the score-sheet, signed it and without a word shouldered his way through the crowd. Robin rose too, pressing his glasses on to his nose, stunned and shaken. People were banging his back, trying to shake his hand, congratulating him.

"Super, lad, super. That was a fine combination."

"Talk about turning the tables."

"You don't often see a game end with a bang like that."

"And against Mischchov too. Fancy him falling into a trap like that."

"Ssshh! Please remember that other games are still going on."

"That Queen sacrifice, wasn't that beautiful. Like a Mozart aria." That, of course, was Paul.

"Toklovsky yesterday, Mischchov today. Not bad for a young un."

"Mischchov isn't the player he used to be. I bet he wouldn't have fallen for that ten years ago."

Val was standing too. "You've won? You mean you've won?"

"Yes. He resigned."

"You checkmated him?"

"No, but I was going to bloody soon, if he hadn't resigned."

"Oh, Robin! And now you're the World Champion." She glowed with pride. A trickle of sweat ran down his cheek. Of course, beating the ex-World Champion in one game didn't make him World Champion. He'd explain the system to her later.

"Not yet," he said. "But give it time." He grinned at her, glorying in the triumph of the moment and glad that she was there to see it.

"I told you we'd got a good lad there."

Paul looked round and saw Mr. Hammond, the schoolmaster. "Beautiful combination."

"I wouldn't be surprised if he won the Lancashire Junior."

"Never mind the Lancashire Junior. I'll see he gets that trip to Munich."

"Oh, I hardly think he's ready for an international tournament yet. We don't want to push him too fast. I don't think he's ready for an international yet. It's only three years since I taught him the moves."

"Isn't this an international tournament?" Paul freed himself from the man. He was trying to think. Poor old Wheaton throws away a won game against Toklovsky, but young Jackson brings off a sensational win against Mischchov. The old order changeth, yielding place to new. The king is dead, long live the king. Clichés crowded into his mind.

"Ssshh, quiet, please! Games are still in progress."

He'd get the front page with this. And he'd make that dreary sports editor print the full game with annotations. He'd telephone the score through now. He'd get a photographer up, they'd need pictures of the boy. Studious, intense, not bad-looking really. He'd write him up in all his papers. He could do a nice piece about Jackson the Giant-Killer for *New Princess,* the young romantic hero, the boy with brains, the Queen sacrifice. And, of course, chess was an art form, not a dreary sport like golf or boxing. That combination was pure beauty. He was right, it was like a Mozart aria. Or the slow movement of the D minor piano concerto. He'd need a photo for *New Princess* too.

"Hey, how about that, eh?" Pearson was banging his back. "What a day, eh? All these upsets. Sensational, eh?" He looked down at Wheaton, still hunched over his board, and banged him on the back. "Hey, old George, how d'you come to make a move like that, eh?"

Wheaton made no move or answer.

"Never mind, all in the day's work, eh. I expect you'll get your revenge tomorrow." He grinned happily at Paul. "What a day, eh? Upsets all along the line. Plenty for your rags, eh? I hope you'll tell them all about this."

"I'll put phone calls through now."

"That's it, lad. Give us a good spread. All this and Reginald Dixon too!"

He moved off, shaking hands and banging shoulders. Paul decided he wouldn't only phone the *Post* and the *East Anglian News,* he'd ring the others too and alert them. No, he'd have to leave *The Statistician* and *New Princess* till the morning, they'd have gone home by now. But he'd phone the editor of *Chess World* at his home number and tell him, talk to him about Munich. And—yes!—he'd send a cable to Joann Oppenheimer telling her of his discovery: FOUND RIVAL FOR YOUR BOY GENIUS STOP JUST BEATEN MISCHCHOV WITH BEAUTIFUL QUEEN SACRIFICE STOP SUGGEST HE PLAYS YOUR BOY MUNICH LOVE PAUL. Well, why not? Perhaps he'd cable the full score through to her. No, he'd have to phone the full score through to that half-witted boy on the sports desk, and once was enough. She'd see the full score soon enough.

Robin Jackson had handed his score in and was standing by

the scoreboards with Val, smiling shyly, accepting congratulations. Nice-looking boy, he might go far if he was handled right. The first British grandmaster since Staunton. After all, Toklovsky yesterday, Mischchov today. Not bad for a schoolboy.

He went up and congratulated Robin. "Nice win, very nice win. That was a pretty Queen sacrifice."

"Thank you," said Robin, smiling happily at Paul and Val. He had stopped shaking and his pulse was normal again. He felt as if he could fly.

"I'd like to borrow your score-sheet. I want to phone it through to the *Daily Post*. I want them to print it in full."

"Charmed, I'm sure." He recovered the sheet from the lady behind the desk and gave it to Paul.

"The *Post!* Oh, Robin!" Val breathed.

"And afterwards I want to have a word with you. I've got an idea for your next big tournament which may appeal to you."

Mr. Hammond had appeared from nowhere. "If it's Munich, I don't think he's ready for that yet."

Paul looked at the thin little man with the bony nose. Laying down the law to me, he thought, and he can't even beat Miss Davies. He ignored him.

"So I'll just ring the *Post* and then we'll have a natter." He smiled at Val. "Keep him happy, don't let him run away while I'm on the phone."

"Oh no!"

He walked purposefully away, busy and important. In the doorway he paused and looked back, making sure that Robin was waiting. They were still there, the tall boy, the girl with her open mouth and bouffant hair, the thin man talking to them earnestly. He won't get anywhere tonight trying to keep the boy back, he's on top of the world. Then he saw George Wheaton still sitting at his table, alone, ignored, his head in his hands, still studying his lost position.

Poor old George, he thought, he should have won that game. Oh well, he'd had his share of successes in his day and you can't go on for ever. It was Paul's job to discover new talent, to encourage youth and promise. The old order changeth, yielding place to new. No, perhaps he shouldn't use that in his piece. Tennyson was not a good man to quote these days, even on the sports page.

LAS VEGAS

Walter Oppenheimer came out of the elevator and turned left into the casino. Like all of the other hotels along the Strip, this one was planned so that, wherever you wanted to go, you had to cross the casino. The temptation would be there to put a few nickels or quarters into a slot machine, to pull out a ten- or twenty-dollar bill and see how the luck was holding at craps or blackjack. This casino was called Caesar's Forum and it was more sumptuous than most, the atmosphere more quietly luxurious. The slot machines seemed less noisy, the craps dealers didn't bawl, the carpets were softer. It was like being in a big black tent. Above was blackness with occasional lights and mirrors and, for all anyone knew, hidden television cameras. The seams of the tent were marked by fringes of lit glass like necklaces. It was early in the day for heavy gambling, but three of the roulette tables, six of the blackjack and three of the craps tables were in action. Caesar's Forum, like every other casino in Las Vegas, ceased not by day nor night.

Walter Oppenheimer didn't pause to check his luck. He crossed between the blackjack and the craps and went up to the front desk.

"Hi, Beverley," he said to the girl in Roman uniform.

"Hello, there, Mr. Oppenheimer. Still with us?"

"Sure. And likely to be for a long time yet."

"Glad to hear it. Have a good day."

This was the arrangement. The hotel, as a courtesy service, would give evidence at his divorce, that he had been resident in Nevada for six weeks and was entitled to a divorce under state law. In return, he had to have a room in the hotel and check with the front desk every twenty-four hours. What he did in between times, where he went, they implied, was none of their business, but they must see him at least once every twenty-four hours. After all, they could hardly ask their girl to commit perjury, could they? Walter Oppenheimer understood the position perfectly. They didn't want him taking a room here and then going back to New York. They wanted him here in the hotel, spending money, gambling, being a real Nevada resident.

He went on to the mail desk and asked for letters. There was nothing for his room number.

"Would you check under my name too. O. Oppenheimer."

"I don't think so," said the girl. "I checked it yesterday." She flipped through a heap. "No, nothing for you."

He smiled at the girl. "Thank you. I'll ask again tomorrow."

"You're welcome!"

He felt an internal need and crossed the casino once again to the rest-rooms, to the Caesars; the ladies' door was marked Cleopatras. Debbie would probably be still in their bathroom upstairs. As he sat on Caesar's throne, he brooded gloomily on life. He had now been here two weeks and he didn't have a single letter from the New York office. His new secretary—what was her name? Dorothy?—had promised to send everything on to him. He'd either send back the answers to her to type out or else dictate to the hotel stenographer. But nothing had arrived, not a letter, not a phone call, nothing.

He felt neglected, frustrated, though a little better physically. He had woken with a headache, the result of a late night, too many cigarettes, too much bourbon. He strolled out of the Caesars, past Cleopatra's Boutique and the Bacchanal, to the swimming pool. The sun beat down on his head, as it had in Abadan; he seemed destined to spend his life in hot deserts. The glare brought his headache back and he wished his sun-glasses weren't upstairs. A pool-boy fixed him up a bed under an umbrella, and covered it with towels, and he tipped the boy. He closed his eyes.

Then he opened them and looked at the girls. One of the good things about Caesar's Palace was that there seemed to be more beautiful girls, and equally scantily dressed whether they were working or hotel guests, than anywhere else in the States outside a Playboy Club. Several of them were lying on air beds with tiger-skin stripes in the pool. They hung on to the rope which divided the shallow end from the deep, lined up like moored yachts. Anyone who let go was blown into the shallow end by the desert wind.

He had suggested to Debbie that she should lie on the tiger-skin air bed too and get herself a suntan. But she refused to get into a bathing-suit, even though he had assured her that there was nothing to see yet. Instead she spent the day dressing and undressing, having her hair done, her face done, outfitting herself from head to toe in "Cleopatra's," gambling. She had developed a taste for roulette, even though her beginner's luck had barely lasted twenty-four hours.

He indulged her. She was enjoying being a rich girl at last, and he played along. He hadn't realised that such things would give her so much pleasure, and was a little surprised. But the expenses were certainly mounting. The room was thirty dollars a day, and then there were the meals, the drinks, the shows, her new bags and shoes, the gambling, the air fares, the car hire, the tipping line. And he hadn't yet started paying alimony to Joann. Another apartment in New York, Debbie's hospital, another kid to put through college. Holy smoke, I'm going to be ruined! he thought. And he was going to be here for another month. Marooned in a Roman courtyard in the middle of a desert, cut off from the outside world. He looked round at the pediments and pilasters and rotundas with annoyance.

It would be fine for Moraine, he thought. She'd like to spend her whole life in a place like this, lying beside the pool, rubbing more and more Sea and Ski into herself until she was solid with the stuff. But he was different. He didn't like being in a vacuum. He lay back and closed his eyes and tried to relax and listen to the Muzak. But every few seconds the sound was interrupted by a voice calling Mr. George Visconti or Mr. Grant Floorman to the telephone, and each time Walter Oppenheimer started, as if the call had really been for him.

Maybe he should have brought a book with him. He'd bought the top fiction best-seller at Kennedy two weeks ago, but he hadn't so far finished page three, hadn't had the opportunity or the mind for it. He'd read today's *Las Vegas Sun* over breakfast, the world news, the news Stateside, Wall Street. Nothing much seemed to have happened. The *Wall Street Journal* wouldn't be in till later. The *Los Angeles Times* might be in by now, but would there be anything in that which wasn't already in the *Las Vegas Sun*? He'd already read this week's *Time* magazine. He might go to the news-stand and get *Newsweek* or *Playboy*. Or maybe something like *Seventeen* and try to relate to these young girls.

The Muzak hummed quietly a tune called "Vaya Con Dios." He recognised it, Moraine had a record of it back home. It broke off in the middle. "Telephone call for Mr. George Visconti."

Whoever wanted Mr. Visconti was holding on a long time. Or else it was someone else calling? He felt an irresistible urge to get things moving, to call Dorothy in New York and find out why the hell he wasn't getting any mail. The Finance Board was due to meet this week or next, and he had that report in, the one about Abadan. He was determined to be there when it was discussed. They were going to let him know the day and he would fly back specially. No trouble in making the round trip to New York and back in twenty-four hours. But he ought to reserve space on the airline soon.

He got up and walked across the blinding concrete to the pool-side telephone. It was white and housed in a little kennel like a miniature Roman temple. He gave his room number and asked for a long-distance call to New York. It came through very quickly. He asked for his extension, but there was no answer. Dorothy wasn't there. He asked to be transferred to Mr. Norstrand's office, but there was no answer there either. "Maybe he's at lunch," the switchboard girl said helpfully.

"Okay, I'll call again later." He checked his watch. It said half after ten. "It's this goddam time difference," he said aloud.

"It's all the same time here," said a girl's voice.

He looked up and saw a beautiful Centurionette before him, dressed in a mini-tunic and sandals. Most of her breasts and all of her legs were visible. She was carrying a tray. She went on, "And it sounds like it's time for another drink."

"I haven't had the first one yet."

"Shall I bring them both at once?"

"Isn't it a little early?"

"It's never too early for a pick-me-up. How about a bullshot?"

He squinted at her through the glare. She was very pretty.

"Okay. But not a bullshot. A Bloody Mary on the rocks, just one." He grinned at her. Women, he remembered, usually found him attractive, still. "And can you raise me a pair of sun-glasses?"

She laughed. "After this you won't need sun-glasses."

She turned and walked away and he watched her back and legs with pleasure. Debbie's legs were just as good as that. And, of course, she wasn't necessarily attracted by him, she was just getting him a drink, doing her job. He felt an urge for Debbie again. She could come and join him at the pool, even though she wouldn't wear a bathing-suit. Make the scene, show the world that he had an attractive girl. Wife, he corrected himself. She could bring his sun-glasses too.

He picked up the telephone and called his room. But there was no answer. Debbie had gone out, probably to Cleopatra's Beauty Salon. He was continually surprised that that short blonde hair needed so much doing, that young snub-nosed face needed so much beauticare. He went back to his umbrella and when his Bloody Mary came he tipped the girl a dollar for her good company.

He would leave it an hour and then call again. It would be half after two by then in New York. He'd talk to Bill Norstrand, find out about the Finance Board and the meeting and his report, discover what was going on. Bill was his best friend, a colleague in the office. All the same, he must be careful. Three times now he had called Bill and each time he'd been out; probably correctly, but Bill had never called him back. He mustn't call New York too often, sound anxious or insecure. But he hadn't given his name just now. Once more would be all right.

In the meantime he might as well use the time since he couldn't relax. He could take some exercise, swim, keep himself young and active. He gulped down his drink, waved at the Centurionette and went into the cool dark hotel, up in the elevator to the eleventh floor. On the door-knob was a parchment notice CAESAR COMMANDS PREPARE THIS CHAMBER WITH DESPATCH. Debbie had no doubt put it there when she went out.

However, inside the maid had not yet got around to the room, though the breakfast had been cleared away. He looked at the two huge and still tumbled beds, both of them big enough for a Roman orgy. He thought back a little nostalgically to the narrow bed on Twenty-Third Street. When he was on top of her he could still put his hands on the carpet either side of the bed.

The television had been left on, but he only watched the gasoline commercial for a few seconds. He went to the window and looked through the concrete lattice-work which covered the tower like something in Saudi-Arabia. He couldn't get out on to the balcony "for security reasons," and also no doubt because the hotel didn't want him treading on the neon tubes. One broken tube would spoil the whole appearance of the tower by night. But the air-conditioning was working well and it was cool in the room. Soon he wouldn't even want a swim.

Beyond the lattice-work it was hot and dusty. In the distance was the spectacular backdrop of mountains, but nearer it was just a bare gritty plateau with a few roads, a few low buildings. Below him the hotel forecourt, the Garden of the Gods, did its best. The fountains played, the precious grass was green, the statues were careful replicas of classical or Renaissance masterpieces, the cypresses had been imported from Italy—though some of them had given up the battle against the Nevada climate and had brownly died. The great signs, the flashing glory of Las Vegas, were not switched on; how could they compete with the sun here? Against the spectacular setting the town could do nothing for itself. It simply disappeared.

Walter Oppenheimer had not wanted to come here. After that last terrible long-distance call with Joann, he had told himself that Las Vegas was the last place on earth he would come for his divorce. His first inclination had been for a normal New York divorce while he occupied himself with his work and the rearrangement of his private life. But Henry had been doubtful. The New York State divorce laws were just being changed. The judges, though they had new powers to grant divorces, also were able to order at their discretion a trial reconciliation for the estranged couple, or marriage counsellors, or even psychiatric treatment. It might be all right, or it might take a year or two. It depended on the judge.

Debbie had been keen on a Mexican divorce, a quickie in Mexico City followed by a honeymoon in Acapulco. But again Henry had been against it. The validity of Mexican divorces was extremely uncertain under the new laws of New York. They would have to be tested in court cases, which might not take place for several years. He reminded them of what happened to some couples who had married after a Mexican mail-order divorce, before these were ruled to be invalid: the man found he was still legally married to his ex-wife while the new wife was an unmarried mother. Debbie had grimaced. Henry had recommended Nevada.

Joann's rumour that there now were quickie divorces in Nevada too was apparently unfounded; the law hadn't yet been changed. But Henry had just laughed and asked what was wrong with six weeks in Nevada, and anyway it would give him time to work out the settlement. Walter Oppenheimer, in a last effort to avoid Las Vegas, had suggested Reno. But the hotels were better here, and the air connections, if he should need to fly back to New York, were better, and there was theoretically more to do in their leisure hours—more casinos to gamble in, more swimming pools to swim in, more golf courses to play on, more bars to drink in, more identical singers to listen to, more TV stations to watch. Anyway Debbie had wanted Las Vegas. So here he was stuck in this oasis for six whole weeks, and everybody else thought it the biggest joke in the world.

He changed into white trunks (chosen by Debbie to set off his suntan, such as it was) and a blue shirt and sneakers. He brushed his hair, threw a towel round his shoulders to show the hotel why he was wearing trunks, and went back to the pool. He dived in and swam twenty or thirty times across the deep end till he felt better, and paused to say hello to a pretty dark girl on an air bed. Then he climbed out, dried his face, ordered another Bloody Mary from the Centurionette, and called New York from the little Roman temple. If Dorothy isn't back from lunch yet, he thought, I'll call Mrs. Anderson and have her fired. He checked the time on his Omega Seamaster. It would be just a quarter of three in New York.

There was still no reply from his office. Red-faced with annoyance, he had the call transferred to Mrs. Anderson.

"Why, Mr. Oppenheimer, how are you? Are you calling from Las Vegas?"

"Yeah, I'm still here."

She was overcome with laughter. "And I bet you're having a lovely time. Is the sun shining there?"

"It sure is."

That was funnier than ever. "And here we are in New York, and it's pouring rain and there seems to be a strike of cab drivers or something. And there you are lying in the sun. We're all just mad with envy."

"Well, maybe . . ."

"Don't tell me! Let me guess. You're calling me from the poolside phone, and you're still wet from your swim and you've got a drink in your hand. Right?"

He glanced uneasily at the little Roman temple, as if it were a camera. "Just about."

She laughed happily and reported the news to someone else in her office. "And—don't tell me!—you gamble all night and have won ten thousand dollars to date."

"I'm afraid not, just about breaking even," he said untruthfully. "Listen, I . . ."

She was passing on the funny news to someone else. They'd all be rolling in the aisles soon. Mrs. Anderson had always been a talker, but this familiarity, this kidding of a senior executive, was new.

"Listen, Mrs. Anderson, I've now called my office three times and there's never any answer. And I didn't receive any mail all the time I've been here. What's happened to Dorothy?"

"Oh, Dorothy, she's been transferred to Mr. Hendricks. His own secretary left and we thought she was the best one to give him. She was only with you a few days and didn't have time yet to relate to your work."

"Well, then, who's my secretary now?"

"Just nobody at the moment. But don't worry, Mr. Oppenheimer, we're trying to find you a new one. We're hoping to interview some applicants this week or next."

"Next week?"

"We think it's really important to find just the right one for you." She added, "We thought maybe you'd prefer someone a little older this time."

Walter Oppenheimer took the point and winced. Personnel could not be expected to like executives who knocked up the girls.

Mrs. Anderson went on, "Or maybe we could defer a final decision till you get back. Whoever it is won't have much to do before then."

"Only send on my mail. Incidentally, what's happening about that?"

"I understand Mr. Norstrand's secretary is taking care of all that."

In due course he was transferred to Mr. Norstrand's secretary. He knew her well, a broad-nosed woman with glasses, married.

"Mr. Oppenheimer, well, hello! Are you calling from Las Vegas?"

"Yeah, I'm still here."

"You bet! And there you are, lying in the sun getting yourself a lovely tan, and here we are in New York in the rain. We're just so envious of you we could die." He could hear her saying to somebody, "It's Mr. Oppenheimer. He's getting a suntan in Las Vegas."

He growled. "Yeah, it's pretty hot here in the sun. Listen, Mrs. Anderson says you're handling my mail."

"Why, yes, glad to help."

"But I didn't receive any at all."

"I don't think there's been any personal mail for you, Mr. Oppenheimer. But I'll check if you'll hold the line."

"I wasn't meaning personal letters."

"Oh, I think Mr. Norstrand is taking care of all the rest for you. But, of course, anything that needs your signature I'll send to you."

"Yes, do that. Maybe I'd better have a word with Mr. Norstrand."

"I'm afraid I can't reach Mr. Norstrand just at the moment. He's in conference with Mr. Gutwilliger."

"He's always in conference when I . . ." Mr. Oppenheimer bit it back. He musn't sound petulant or anxious. It was standard procedure. How many times must Debbie have told callers that he was in conference and couldn't be reached!

"Shall I ask him to call you?"

"Yes, do that. Ask him to call me before he goes home tonight. I'd like to talk to him. Incidentally, do you know when the Finance Board meeting is to be held?"

She said simply, "Oh, that was last week. Thursday, I think."

"Last week! But I was going to fly back for that. Mr. Norstrand was going to let me know the date and I was coming back for it."

"I'm sorry, Mr. Oppenheimer, Mr. Norstrand didn't say anything about that. But I think it was only a routine meeting. I don't think anything urgent was discussed."

"All the same, I'd have liked to be there. It was my report . . ." He bit it off. "Are they going to have another meeting?"

"I don't know, Mr. Oppenheimer. I think there may be going to be one next week or the week after. But I don't think it will be anything special."

"All the same, I want to come to it. Will you let me know the moment the date is fixed?"

"Yes, I'll tell Mr. Norstrand you want to be there. And I'll ask him to call you tonight. Let me just check that we have your number."

"I'll give it to you again." He read it off the telephone. "It's Area Code 702. 734–7110. And I'm Room 1134. If I'm not in the room they'll call me wherever I am."

She repeated the number. "Well, thanks for calling us. Have a good vacation."

He put down the telephone and swore. "Vacation, hell!" Disappear for two weeks and you were lost to sight. In another four weeks they wouldn't even remember his face. They'd discussed his report without his being there, they weren't sending anything on to him, they'd transferred his secretary to old Hendricks. He didn't have a secretary at all now, just as if he were a young trainee executive. He glared at the tower in which, somewhere, the best secretary he ever had was even now having her hair done, or playing roulette.

He decided to change out of his wet trunks. He finished his drink, and went up through the cool hotel to his room. In the air-conditioned passages his trunks felt clammy. The maid was doing the room, and he changed in the bathroom. Then he went back to the pool. There was really nowhere else to go.

If he were to stop by in the casino and try his luck he might miss being called to the telephone. The girl's voice over the loud-speaker was not audible there. The management did not want anything to interrupt the gambling. And the bars were really part of the casino. He had suggested, when they came, that Debbie might listen for calls upstairs or outside while he gambled, but she had been keen to demonstrate that she was no longer his secretary.

"Cleopatra does not answer the telephone," she had announced. "Her slaves do that."

He had laughed, as he was no doubt meant to, he hadn't showed that he was annoyed. But now, out of annoyance, or perhaps a wish to test his luck, he pulled out a quarter and put it in a slot machine. Instead of having to get three oranges or lemons or whatever it was in line, he had to get the words VENI VIDI VICI to win the jackpotus. He pulled the handle, the dials spun, the quarter disappeared into the machine's inside. Just not my day, he thought.

It was very hot outside and he sat under the rotunda by the bar. The girls were still lying, broiling on their air beds, the Centurion-ette said, "Hello again, enjoy your swim?" The Muzak was playing an old favourite "Just One of Those Things," there was no sign of Debbie. He ordered another Bloody Mary.

The music broke off to call Mr. Helm, Mr. Julius Helm, to the telephone. Walter Oppenheimer checked his watch. Bill Norstrand usually left the office between four-thirty and a quarter of five. Three hours' difference here. If Bill hadn't called by one-thirty he'd fucking well call himself and never mind if he sounded too anxious.

In due course Debbie arrived. It was impossible to tell if it had been her hair or her face which had been worked over, but she looked very sweet. He told her about his call to Mrs. Anderson, how his new secretary had been transferred and she was in no hurry to find him a new one.

Debbie took his arm and smiled up at him. "I guess she hates us both. But we don't care, do we? I mean, she's only a clerk, really, isn't she?"

He had smiled at her, and put his arm round her, and tried to order her a drink. But she didn't want anything, said she was hungry and felt like lunch when he was ready. He finished his drink and they went into the Noshorium.

In the Noshorium (or coffee-shop) they ordered hot turkey sandwiches with cranberry sauce. He didn't feel like any more tomato juice, so he ordered a straight vodka martini on the rocks. Debbie asked for orange juice; she had been off alcohol since becoming pregnant. The Muzak was audible in here, the female voice asking for Mr. Julius Helm. Walter Oppenheimer checked his watch again. Better not leave it till one-thirty. It would be the end of the working day in New York, there might be a delay on the line.

At one-twenty he excused himself and went to the elevators. There was quite a delay, waiting for an elevator to come, and he became impatient waiting in the lobby along with the girls in their damp bikinis and the new arrivals with their baggage. On the way up he looked crossly at anyone who was getting out at a lower floor and consequently delaying him; his room key was already in his hand. On the eleventh floor he strode to his room, slammed the door shut behind him. Without looking round, he went straight to the telephone and called New York long-distance. Then he looked around the room. The maid had finished, the damask covers were on the bed, the curtains were partly drawn. The television was still on, however, a man giving the high temperatures over the West Coast. Walter Oppenheimer fiddled with the remote control under the telephone, but he couldn't get it to turn off, only to change channels. After trying a news flash and a commercial from someone lending money in downtown Las Vegas, he found a channel which merely flashed and buzzed. He turned the sound down and said, "Hello!"

He found he was connected to Mr. Norstrand's secretary again.

"Why, hello again, Mr. Oppenheimer. We were just trying to call you. Hold the line a moment, Mr. Norstrand is right here."

There was quite a long pause. Then he heard Bill Norstrand's voice, amazingly loud. The man must be shouting across the miles.

"Well, hello, Walter! It's great to hear you again. How are things? How's Las Vegas?"

"Oh, fine."

"And how's Frankie?"

"Frankie?"

"Sinatra."

"Oh, I don't know. I haven't seen him. I doubt he's in town."

"Well, try and get to know him. Find out how to become a millionaire. And then pass it on to me. I could use the information."

"So could I. But . . ."

"And how about the gambling? Are you winning at that? If so, remember your friends, and pass the secret on to them too."

"Only breaking even, I'm afraid."

"Well, that's better than losing. Remember, when you go broke, call us and we'll cable you your fare home."

"I hope it won't come to that. But, Bill . . ."

"And how's the suntan? I bet you're as brown as mahogany."

"Right now I'm peeling a little."

"You don't know how lucky you are. It's raining here in New York and there seems to be a strike of cab . . ."

"Yeah, I know. Listen, Bill, I hear there was a meeting of the Finance Board last week."

"Yeah. Yes, that's right. Just a routine meeting. Didn't last more than half an hour. Not worth bringing you back for."

"Was anything decided?"

"No, not really. No, I don't think so. Oh yes, John said to thank you for your report, he really appreciated that and the trouble you'd taken."

"Well, thanks. I hear there's going to be another meeting next week or the week after."

There was a brief conversation at the far end. "Well, nothing's settled at the moment, Walter. I doubt myself there will be a meeting and even if there is I don't think it'll be worth your coming back for. If anything urgent does blow up I'll certainly call you and you can fly straight back. I think John means to keep your report by him till you get back. He said—we all said—that it was important and how grateful we were to you for taking so much trouble over it."

"Well, thanks, but . . ."

"And he also said how you'd earned a really good vacation. I know it's not exactly a vacation, but there's nothing wrong with that, is there." Bill was laughing at the far end. Walter Oppenheimer tried to intervene. "Nothing wrong with that. I can't think of a better place to mix business and pleasure in than Las Vegas. No, seriously, Walter, and I mean this most sincerely, we'd all like you to have a good vacation without worrying about things here. Relax, friend, learn to unwind. We've all got to take time off to recharge our batteries some time, you know."

"Yes, I know, but . . ."

"You're a lucky devil. The rest of us have to wait till next summer. Never mind, you have fun, and make your million and get to know Frankie, and tell us all about it when you get back. We'll all still be here. Oh, and watch that peeling. Mrs. Cowan is telling me that Sea and Ski is the best. Right?"

"Maybe. The sun's pretty strong. But, Bill, listen, I'd like to come to the next Finance Board meeting, even if it's only routine. You'll let me know definitely when the next meeting is to be?"

"You bet! If the roof falls in we'll rush you back by private jet. No, seriously, Walter, just have a good stay, we'll look after things, and keep you in touch too, why not? You just watch your blackjack and find out from Frankie how to make a million and pass the news on to us when you get back and we'll just love to hear. Okay, Walter, have fun, see you soon."

Walter Oppenheimer put the receiver down slowly. Jesus, he thought, Jesus! Whatever's going on they're not saying. And I'm goddam sure something's going on. I'm right out in the desert and I've gotten to be the goddam office joke. Frankie, huh! Jesus, when I get back I'll find I'm not even on the Finance Board. Maybe I'm off it already. I'll find I'm in charge of office stationery or running the sports club or something. Just relax, he said, unwind.

He lit a cigarette and stared at the television screen, the pattern of flashing lights. Then when he had calmed down he went down again to the Noshorium. As he saw her blonde hair drooped over her plate, he thought, That's another thing. Three times I've called New York this morning, and not one of them asked after Debbie, sent her a message, even mentioned her.

"That's fine," he said, sitting down. She looked up eagerly. "I talked to Bill, and everything's fine. Things are pretty quiet there at the moment, but they'll pull me back if anything urgent breaks."

"Let's hope it doesn't."

"Yes. Yes, of course. They don't seem to be able to talk about anything except the weather. It's raining and there's some sort of cab strike, and they all sound pretty miserable. They're envious of us here."

"How right they are!" She touched him affectionately on the arm. "How right they are!"

"Right!" He smiled at her. "And they asked after you and said hello to you. Oh, and they think pretty highly of my report. John Gutwilliger's keeping it by him to discuss when I get back. It's not that urgent, of course."

"Oh, Walter, that's fine! Just what you wanted to hear, isn't it? Oh, what about your mail?"

"They're sending that on. There was a mix-up because of Dorothy being transferred. But I gather there's nothing urgent in it." He ordered yet another vodka martini. "Honey, you haven't eaten any of your turkey."

"I guess I'm not too hungry. I never seem to want to eat much in the middle of the day. I suppose it's the heat."

"But it's the same temperature all the time here. It's air-conditioned."

She smiled at him. "Well, maybe it's the time-change then. I seem to have more appetite nights. Let's go somewhere nice and have a good dinner tonight, shall we?"

Dinner was a daily problem. Walter Oppenheimer would have been glad to eat every meal in the Noshorium, a turkey sandwich for lunch, prime ribs au jus with an Idaho potato and sour cream, and a tossed green salad with Thousand Island dressing, every night. But Debbie wanted gracious dining, gourmet cuisine, bright lights, entertainment. She didn't want to spend the whole day in a coffee-shop.

They had gone first to the hotel's restaurant, the Bacchanal, which advertised gourmet cuisine. This turned out to be a seven-course dinner, the details of which were not revealed in advance. Debbie could hardly eat any of it, and he had been bored by the fact that it lasted unavoidably two hours and cost twelve dollars fifty each without drinks or tips. So now they went out on the Strip to the House of Lords or the Casino de Paris or the Painted Desert Room or Don the Beachcomber's or the Flamingo Room. Or Downtown to the Golden Nugget or the Sky Room or the Mint. Debbie liked theatre-restaurants, she seemed to eat better if there was a man in a tuxedo singing a romantic song at her through a microphone. To Walter Oppenheimer it was all rather monotonous, when you had heard one you had heard them all. Of course, it solved the problem of conversation. But when he picked up the tab at the end, saw the figure, shuddered, pulled out a credit card, and smiled back at her, he couldn't help thinking nostalgically of New York.

He had been in the habit these last two years of visiting with her twice a week. They'd make the date in his office by nodding, he would come to her tiny apartment and they'd have several strong martinis. Then they'd go out to dinner at a little Mexican place on Seventh Avenue or down to the Village to one of several Italian restaurants. Afterwards they would go back to her apartment and have a real bang. He'd get back home around midnight, just about when Joann returned from the chess club. They liked to pretend, he and Debbie, that it was a big secret, that they were safe inside their hidden world, and nobody knew about them. In the office he was careful to give no sign of their affair, to treat Debbie as just another good and hard-working secretary. And it had all gone fine until this last trip when he was drafting his report, and that dinner in Beirut, and Debbie crying in his arms in Abadan. And now here he was, night after night, eating Beef Burgundy or Filet Mignon, listening to Tony Bennett or Dean Martin or Jerry Vale. When they were back in New York next month he'd like to go back to those little Mexican and Italian places and try to recapture something which he could identify but not name, and which seemed to have slipped away from him in the Middle East.

All the same, he must give Debbie fun, show her a good time. If she wanted flashing signs and gourmet cuisine and Jerry Vale, she must have it. This was their honeymoon, even if they were not yet married. He didn't put it like that to her. She was still dropping dark hints about going on to honeymoon in Acapulco. But, of course, that was ridiculous. After six weeks in Nevada he wouldn't be able to take any more time away from New York. However, he hadn't put it to her like that. He hoped she might just take the point without it being spelt out to her.

Their wedding was also causing him some private qualms. Since reaching Las Vegas he had only been downtown once in daylight, to see the lawyer who was collecting a fee for handling the Nevada end of the divorce. He had returned in his Hertz Cadillac, mistakenly, by way of Fremont Street and Las Vegas Boulevard South. He had thus found himself passing all the wedding chapels, the Hitching Post, the Wee Kirk o' the Heather, the Silver Bells, the Candlelite. He had remembered his last conversation with Joann. The Romeo and Juliet Wedding Chapel with Buster and Pete. If there was one place in the world where he was not going to marry Debbie it was the Romeo and Juliet Wedding Chapel. Or any of them, come to that. He saw himself being married in the courthouse in the same room where he had just been divorced, probably by the same judge, probably on the same occasion, get it all over together, save time and money. And he was sure Debbie would want that too, though he hadn't yet put it in so many words.

But all the same, when driving Debbie downtown to see the lights of Fremont Street or the show at the Mint he took care not to drive along Las Vegas Boulevard South but to take the other route along Main Street. He didn't want her to see the wedding chapels. He felt sure that she wouldn't want anything like that, especially if he told her about Joann and Buster and Pete. But he wasn't completely certain. He was learning a good deal about Debbie and it wasn't quite what he had expected. A girl who could barely swallow a mouthful of Filet Mignon without Tony Bennett singing "The Shadow of Your Smile" at her through a microphone might well fancy the Candlelite Wedding Chapel. It was as well she shouldn't even know about it.

After lunch they separated. Debbie had been advised to lie down after lunch; she lay in the cool room and slept or read a magazine or watched television. Walter Oppenheimer gambled. He could do that safely now, as there was no possibility of a call from New York. In any event, there was nothing else to do; he had had enough of the pool, it was too hot for golf, and what on earth was the point of driving out into the desert and then driving back again? The afternoon shows didn't have the big names and you couldn't drink all day. Anyway, it was stupid to be in Las Vegas and not gamble.

The casino was still pretty empty and he went to a craps table with only two others playing. The man on his right was throwing; he was a thin dark man in a white shirt, who spat on the dice and shouted at them. Walter Oppenheimer changed ten dollars into one-dollar tokens, each one with its imperial inscription. The shooter made his point. Walter Oppenheimer put a dollar on the pass line, the dark man threw a seven and the dealer pushed the dollar he'd won at him. Walter Oppenheimer left it there. Then he decided that this was no way to play, in dollar bets. He put ten dollars on the pass line, and changed a hundred-dollar bill with the dealer. The thin dark man threw a five, the dealer moved the white marker to five, the shooter spat and shouted at the dice, the dealer called the throws, "Six, easy six," "eight hardways." After three throws the shooter made his point, and Walter Oppenheimer collected some more winnings. He was clearly in a winning streak. This was, after all, his day. He had a wish to roll the dice himself, he wanted the thin dark man to pass the dice. So the next throw he didn't bet on the pass line, he put five dollars on the field. "Come on," he muttered, "quit the shouting and throw craps for me." The man obligingly threw twelve, craps, losing. Walter Oppenheimer was the only one to win that throw. He collected another ten dollars. The thin man picked up the dice and swore at them.

It was now Walter Oppenheimer's turn to throw. He chose two dice, leant on the cushioned edge of the table, put ten dollars on the pass line and prepared to enjoy himself. He threw a natural seven, winning another ten dollars. He left it there and threw again. "Come on," he muttered, "another seven for me." He threw a six, and the dealer moved the marker. "Okay," he muttered, "six will do."

He threw a long, long time. Neither a six (on which he would win) or a seven (on which he would lose) came up. He went on throwing. The thin dark man had gone away, but others had come up and were winning money on the other numbers, on the field, on the big eight, on Come points. It was only he who was in the doldrums. He was getting hot from so much throwing. "Come on," he muttered, "six, six, six."

He started betting on Come too. He won five dollars on a Come point of eight, but his next Come point, five, would no more be thrown than his original shooter's point of six. He decided to bet on the field, win that way, get some action. He had now twenty dollars on the pass line, ten on a Come point of five, five on the field. He put another three on the big eight. He had now almost as much on the table against himself as with himself. If he threw a two, three, four, five, six, eight, nine, ten, eleven or twelve, he would win something somewhere. He threw a seven, losing everything. Sadly he passed the dice.

Three-quarters of an hour later he had lost the hundred and ten dollars he had changed, and he wandered away to the bar in Nero's Nook. He ordered a bourbon and club soda on the rocks and took gloomy stock. He had felt confident of winning and it had gone wrong. He hadn't later been able to recover his earlier luck. That had run out on him, he saw it now, when he began to bet against his own point, against himself. That was his mistake. Next time he would do better. He'd finish his drink slowly, change some travellers cheques, and try again. He'd win back that hundred and ten all right.

He went to the cashier and changed three hundred dollars' worth of First National City cheques. He put them in his billfold and stood surveying the casino. It was rather fuller now, more tables were in play. He watched a man betting in great stacks of chips, and apparently winning even greater stacks. Walter Oppenheimer considered his suit, his shoes, his shirt, and decided that he probably earned three or four times as much as this other man; possibly even more. That was the trouble; he thought big and acted small, while this other fellow, looking small but playing big, was raking it in. Where Walter Oppenheimer put on five dollars (or even, at the start of the day, one-dollar bets), this other man, a salesman maybe or a hotel employee, was thinking big and winning. Walter Oppenheimer returned to the tables, determined to play big and to back himself and his point.

He went back to the same table, though both the dealers and the other players had changed. But in three-quarters of an hour he had lost three hundred dollars. He was just wondering whether to change another cheque or retire to Nero's Nook and watch a show called "Bottoms Up," when a voice said "Mr. Oppenheimer, I presume." The man was vaguely familiar. Long-nosed, short, dark-suited, something about him said "Chess!" He said, "John Boghossian. I'm a friend of your wife's."

"Yes, indeed. You've come to our apartment in New York."

They shook hands coolly. Walter Oppenheimer thought, Chess, hell! As if I wasn't having a bad enough time without a chess-player turning up. He said, "Glad to see you. Are you here on vacation?"

"Let's say a working vacation."

"But it's a long way from Switzerland." Wasn't the man nominally Swiss?

"Switzerland was two years ago. Last year I lived in France. This year in New York. I am going to compete in the U.S. Championships in New York. I expect I shall see your wife."

Walter Oppenheimer said firmly, "My former wife. We're getting divorced, in case you hadn't heard."

"Yes, I had heard. I am so sorry. Your wife is a wonderful woman. She is a great chess-player. I think she is the greatest woman player in the Sicilian Defence, either in defence or in attack. She is the Tal of the Sicilian Defence of the Ladies."

"Yeah, I've heard that's so. Maybe that was the . . ." He stopped himself saying the word "trouble" and changed to "Maybe you're right."

"I heard you were in Las Vegas getting a divorce." Boghossian smiled, and Walter Oppenheimer wanted to hit him.

That goddam chess grape-vine! He was only good for laughs, and they all knew. He said, "How do you mean, working vacation?"

"Enjoying the sun and making some money. I shall not make any money in the U.S. Championships even if I beat Bobby Fischer and Carl Sandbach."

"Well, you won't make any money here." He waved at the décor. "Who do you think pays for all this? Not the management."

"Just the people who lose. The people who do not know how to win."

"Okay, you just show me a man who knows how to win." Boghossian patted his chest. "I know how to win. Would you like to follow me?" He pointed towards the blackjack tables.

"Craps," said Walter Oppenheimer, firmly. "The odds are much better at craps. Almost even. But blackjack . . ."

"Blackjack is where I win. Follow me if you like."

Reluctantly Walter Oppenheimer followed him. Sicilian Defence. Blackjack. Let the fellow make a fool of himself.

They went to a table which was deserted. Nobody was playing there, but the dealer stood there waiting, his deck spread before him like a fan. Without speaking, Boghossian and Walter Oppenheimer sat down, Boghossian sitting at the extreme left of the table. Neither spoke to the dealer, who stacked the deck, shuffled, and held it for Walter Oppenheimer to cut. The dealer put the top card into the stack and waited for them to bet.

Printed on the green cloth was DEALER MUST DRAW ON SIXTEEN AND STAND ON SEVENTEEN. Boghossian put out a dollar token. Walter Oppenheimer did likewise. Fine way to make a million, he thought.

The dealer won the first hand. Boghossian drew a card and bust on twenty-two, Walter Oppenheimer stood on eighteen, the dealer put down two court cards. Walter Oppenheimer started to say, "How do you mean, win?" but Boghossian waved him down. The dealer was waiting for them to bet. They each put up another dollar. This time Walter Oppenheimer won, the dealer and Boghossian lost.

And so it went on. Another couple, a middle-aged man and a young girl (wife? girl friend? secretary? wondered Walter Oppenheimer), joined them at the table, played for a while, and then left. Walter Oppenheimer estimated that he had lost six dollars and Boghossian eight. Some million, he thought. These chess-players never know the full score. As long as it's a great Sicilian Defence that's all that matters.

Boghossian fumbled in his pocket and pulled out a handful of coloured tokens, not the usual silver dollars. He counted out a hundred dollars and put them on the square. The dealer raised his eyes, but said nothing. Walter Oppenheimer bet his usual single silver dollar.

He drew a nine and eight, and, after a moment's doubt, stood, pushing the cards, still turned down, under his silver dollar. The dealer looked at Boghossian, who scratched on the cloth with his cards. The dealer dealt him a four, turned up. Boghossian didn't scratch again with his cards, so the dealer turned up his own pair, a five and a nine. He drew, a two, and then a ten, busting. Impassively he pushed a dollar at Walter Oppenheimer and ten tens at Boghossian, who nodded impassively and rose from the table, pocketing his winnings.

Boghossian nodded at the Centurionette who stood by. "Let's have a drink on the house. My dear, I'd like a Scotch and soda."

"Mine's bourbon, on the rocks," said Walter Oppenheimer. "How did you know? What's the secret?"

"Larry Evans told it to me last month. You know him?"

Walter Oppenheimer nodded. Another chess-player, another grandmaster. The world was a great secret society of chess-players, knowing each other, speaking and writing a secret language, not interested in anything else or anybody else. And he, Walter Oppenheimer, was always on the outside looking in.

"This is the first time I've tried it, my first visit to Las Vegas. You simply sit at the left end of a blackjack table, and watch the cards as they are played, and remember them. When the dealer comes to the end of the deck you know what's left and can calculate the odds against you."

"You can remember all the cards in the deck?"

"Of course. It's no worse than chess. Or bridge. You do that over and over again in an evening of bridge. You can make money from bridge too, but it's more difficult. You are always winning from friends. But here . . ." He shrugged, and then stroked his long nose. "You do not win every time, of course. Perhaps it is not quite the end of the deck. And there is the first card they put face down in the stack. And, of course, you do not know which way the cards will fall. But you can calculate the odds. If there are no aces left, only one court card, three others playing and the dealer, you can guess what you will draw. If the odds are bad you just bet one dollar. If they are good you bet a hundred. Even then you may lose, but you'll probably win. I aim to win seven hundred dollars a day."

"They'll run you out of town if you keep doing that."

"Not for a few hundred dollars, it wouldn't be worth it. I'm just a beginner. And I keep changing casinos. I'm only here till I've won ten thousand dollars."

"And when will that be?"

"Another nine days."

"Jesus! You've gotten it all worked out, haven't you. But aren't there easier ways of making a living?"

"Like what? Like playing chess? Like what you do?"

Walter Oppenheimer drank his highball and nodded. "Maybe

you're right about that. Are you staying here?" He gestured at the black ceiling.

"Oh no! I don't come all the way to Nevada to spend my money in places like this. I like to gamble here because it is comfortable and because of the free drinks. But I stay in a small motel down the Strip and I eat at Foxy's. I keep my money for New York."

"Very wise too."

Boghossian finished his drink and wiped his mouth on the back of his hand. "I must be going. I think I shall go across to the Flamingo. I have to make another two hundred dollars before dinner. It has been nice to meet you here. I hope you win."

"Thank you. I hope you win too."

Boghossian held out his damp hand. "And how is your beautiful daughter?"

"Moraine? Oh, she's fine. She's in New York."

"Yes, I know. I expect I shall see her at the U.S. Championships. She is still in love with young Carl Sandbach, I'm afraid."

Walter Oppenheimer laughed. "Yeah, I'm afraid too. I know what you mean. Never marry a chess-player." He shook Boghossian's hand warmly. "Glad to have seen you again."

Boghossian smiled thinly and slid away. Walter Oppenheimer watched him, thinking, Never marry a chess-player, if it's a small blue-eyed girl from Bryn Mawr called Joann Carey, or a six-foot-three beanpole from California, or a five-foot-nothing sawn-off Armenian runt. He wondered if Boghossian were trying for Moraine, and pushed away the thought. She wouldn't want a little Armenian immigrant, no class, no money, nothing except chess and a lot of languages. But girls, he knew, fell for chess and languages. They were brains-symbols, and brains were very sexy things. All the same, not Boghossian! Joann would discourage it, chill it down with some sarcastic comments. Or would she? You couldn't be sure with chess-players, they hung together like a fraternity, they spent their time admiring each other, even when they spent their time trying to knock each other down in games. They never seemed to have heard of anybody else.

However, Moraine still seemed fully tied up with the Sandbach boy. At least he was one-hundred-per-cent American, tall, lean, good-looking. But a total moron, nothing in his head except chess, no languages, hardly English even. Still Moraine was infatuated, she thought he was a genius, an egg-head (though it didn't look like an egg, even under the crew-cut fair hair). And egg-heads were very attractive to young girls.

Walter Oppenheimer finished his drink and sighed. What was wrong with his daughter? Beautiful, sexy (he was sure), educated, not too intellectual, travelled, with taste, money, a warm heart, a gentle manner. Why did she have to fall for a chess-player? Why couldn't it be a nice young Ivy League diplomat, or a clever young trainee banker just out of Harvard Business School, or even a promising advertising executive?

He disposed of his glass, and tried to switch his thoughts. Moraine was out of his care now. He just hoped it wouldn't be a chess-player. In the meantime all he could do was to win back some of the money he had lost. If a little Armenian immigrant could win seven hundred dollars a day surely he could do as well.

He went back to the blackjack table and sat on the left-hand stool. When the new deck started he bet a dollar and watched the other cards like a scientist. There were lots of cards to watch; the other seats were full and the dealing went fast. He had never been very good at memorising cards, which was one of the reasons why he was such a poor bridge-player, or, come to that, chess-player. By the time the last cards in the deck were dealt he had no more idea what they were likely to be than at the beginning. He only bet one dollar on the last hand, and lost it.

He stood up and thought, Well, we can't all do everything. I'm not a chess grandmaster, I can't remember thousands of cards, I only speak one language. But I do help finance the world marketing of oil. And isn't that more important than playing games?

Across the casino he saw a blonde head, and he went to greet Debbie. She was bright-eyed and pink-cheeked and pretty. She glowed at him.

"Honey, I've had a good sleep and I've watched an old Fred Astaire movie, which was real neat, and now I just feel ready for a big win."

"You look marvellous." She was wearing a black sleeveless dress, but a little full to hide any bulges, with a pattern of sequins round the neckline; false eyelashes, silver nails; a diamond engagement ring, a wedding ring. "Just ready for a killing."

"That's right! How have you been getting on?"

"Oh, breaking even." He added: "Almost."

She laughed. "Oh, I can do better than that. All I need is some capital."

"Don't we all!"

He found her a chair at a roulette table, changed a cheque at the cashier, and provided her with a hundred dollars. "Right!" he said. "Go in and win!"

She put five dollars each on eleven and thirty-four, which made up their room number. She lost.

"Keep trying!" he commented. "I'm going to try craps."

He went back to the craps table and played in a desultory way, not caring if he won or lost. Not knowing. Playing only for single dollars. He was thinking about Debbie and Boghossian and Bill Norstrand and Moraine. After a while he switched to blackjack, but his heart wasn't in that either. He went back to the bar in Nero's Nook, and had a bourbon and club soda on the rocks.

Here he was, going from table to table, playing around, trying to win a few dollars. Trying to win back a few hundred dollars. Peanuts, that's what it was, peanuts! And all the while his job in New York was sinking under him, and his report was being shelved, and his career was fading away. So many people hanging on him: Walt, Moraine, Debbie, and soon the new kid. Kids in college, whoever invented the system? In the good old days boys went to college and emerged four years later, and did something. Got themselves jobs, started a career, paid their way. But now they settled into college for life, one college after another. Walt, twenty-five, and still a college student. Graduate, post-graduate, advanced studies, research, theses, Ph.D.s, there was no end. And Moraine, pretending to major in art history, while she hung around the chess-playing gang. And eventually, the new one and the whole thing to go through again. Two homes to keep up, life insurance, cars. The figures on that document about Joann he had signed in Henry's office and which he didn't dare remember. And here he was, worrying about the odds at craps and whether to bet one or ten dollars and whether twelve dollars fifty was too much for a gourmet dinner. And he was going on doing this for another four weeks.

He finished his drink and went back into the casino. Across the tables he could see Debbie's blonde head, bowed over the table. She used to droop like that over her shorthand book. He found it very touching. It was that which had first prompted him to confide in her the sorrows of a chess-widower; and which had led him, by stages, all the way here.

It was a moment of recognition and he took a decision, or, at least, half a decision.

Debbie seemed to be losing too. There were only a few chips left on the table in front of her, and she was playing now in single dollars. He went to the cashier, changed yet another hundred dollars, and brought her the chips.

"Executive credit," he murmured.

She looked up and gave him a quick kiss. "Oh, honey, that's sweet of you. I didn't do too well to start with, but I'm starting to win now. I'm going to win on your birthday number."

"Why not. I'm just going upstairs to take a shower. We'll meet in Nero's Nook for a drink. Or here if you're still playing. You try and double that by the time I get back." He pointed vaguely at her chips, or was it at her lap? "Remember, you've some growth potential there."

He immediately realised he might be misunderstood, be tactless. She looked up quickly, but the lighting was overhead, and he couldn't see if she were blushing. He covered up, smiled, patted her shoulder and slipped away.

In Room 1134 the television was still on. He walked to the window and looked out through the screening. It was dark now, and the lights were flashing. Las Vegas had come to life. Across the Strip, the Flamingo was like a fountain of white circles, rippling up the walls. On the right was the huge sign of the Dunes, climbing up into the sky like a firework. Caesar's Palace too had a flashing sign on the Strip, but it was more restrained. Indeed the whole hotel was more restrained, outside. He looked down at the floodlit fountains and statues, the gallant lawns, the struggling cypresses. To the left it was the glare of the rest of the Strip, the great river of neon, the jazziest in the world. And what am I doing here, he thought.

He crossed to the beds and turned on the bedside light, turned down the television sound, and pulled out the phone book. He looked up a number, lifted the receiver and dialled 9–735–1177. A girl's voice answered immediately.

"T.W.A., the all-jet airline."

"I want a flight tomorrow to New York. I have to get there and back in the day."

"What time do you wish to leave?"

"In the morning. I'd like a non-stop."

"We have a non-stop flight at two-fifteen, getting to New York at nine-forty-three. But I doubt there's space on that. If you'll hold, I'll just check."

He held and looked at Debbie's bed. It was tumbled where she had lain and watched Fred Astaire. She had had coffee, Room Service, before coming down, and the Room Service menu was open before him. "My palace is your home," he read, "have a feast in your luxurious chambers. I, Caesar, welcome you and invite you to enjoy yourself." I thought I was meant to be Caesar, not the management.

The girl came back. "I'm sorry, that flight is full."

"Well, another non-stop then. And earlier in the day."

"I'm sorry, that is the only non-stop we have to New York tomorrow."

"Well, what about one of the other airlines?"

"United have a flight out of here at eleven-thirty at night, but I doubt there's space on that either. If you'll hold, I'll check."

"No, don't trouble. I don't want a night flight." It was going to be tricky, sorting it out with John Gutwilliger and Bill, not to mention Mrs. Anderson. He'd be in no condition for that after a night in a plane. Anyway, there was the question of checking with Beverley on the front desk. "I'd like a morning flight."

"We have one at ten-fifty-five, reaching New York at nine-thirty, with stops at Albuquerque, Kansas City, and Chicago."

"Kansas City! Jesus! But I'm in a hurry."

The girl said coldly, "I'm doing my best to help you."

"I'm sorry. Haven't you a flight earlier in the morning, with fewer stops?"

"We have a flight at six-thirty-five, with stops at Tucson and Chicago, arriving at New York at four-twenty-five."

"Yes, but four-twenty-five! Even if I take the helicopter, I won't be in the office till five, maybe five-thirty. They'll all have gone home."

"I'm sorry," said the girl, still cool. "It's a four-and-a-half-hour flight to New York even direct, and there's a three-hour time difference."

"Is that right? Maybe I'd better take the night flight. I'll be at the office in time for some work."

"We have a flight to New York at one-twenty-five a.m. There's one stop in Chicago, and it reaches New York at ten-o-two."

"Yes, maybe that's the one I ought to take. Can you get me on that?"

"Tonight? I'm not sure if there's space, but if you'll hold, I'll check."

He held the receiver to his face and thought, Would you believe it's so hard to get from Las Vegas to New York, and you can call it in a few seconds? He read, "Our lavish oasis awaits you. The artistry that suits a Caesar has been commanded to offer you new vistas of happy hours."

"Yes, there's space available on that flight."

He felt a feeling of relief. Sometimes it seemed that everything was conspiring to keep him here for ever.

"I'll take that seat, will you hold it for me, please. My name is Oppenheimer, with two p's. I'm staying at Caesar's Palace, my room number is 1134."

"1134," she repeated it back. "And when do you plan to return?"

He took a deep breath. "No, I'm not planning to return. I'll stay in New York."

"Just a one-way trip. Right, I'll hold a seat for you on flight 58, departing at one-twenty-five, for New York. Is it first class or coach class?"

"First class."

"Right. Will you collect your ticket at the airport before twelve-fifteen tonight?"

"Right. I'll charge it to Carte Blanche." He remembered his manners. "I'd like to say that I appreciate the way you've looked after this reservation for me."

The girl sounded unmollified. "You're welcome. Thank you for calling T.W.A."

He put the telephone down. I, Caesar, have commanded. He would be out of here in a few hours. He went to the window, looked out at the Flamingo lights, and lit a cigarette. Well, there it was, business was business, how would it help anyone if he loused up his career by not being on the scene at the right moment? He would tell Debbie that he'd had a call from Bill from his home, cocktail-to-shower. He'd taken it, dripping, and Bill wanted him in New York for a Finance Board meeting tomorrow. By sheer good luck he'd found a seat on the one-twenty-five. He'd take his overnight things with him, to freshen up with after the night flight. He'd be back tomorrow evening, the time difference would work his way then. She'd have to check with Beverley tomorrow morning, and cover up for him.

He turned round and looked at the rumpled bed. He sighed. Sometime tomorrow afternoon he would call Debbie long-distance, she'd be lying there watching TV, and he'd tell her the full score. It would be a difficult conversation, and in his experience these things were best done on a long-distance call. He looked at her things on the dressing-table. Poor Debbie, he thought, but in the circumstances what else was he to do? Then his eye caught the Room Service menu on the bed.

I, Caesar, having dallied long enough in Egypt, return now to Rome.

MANCHESTER

It was a grey November afternoon, dark with murk and low cloud and grimy air. A light rain, something between a drizzle and a mist, was drifting across from the west, across Stretford and Chorlton-cum-Hardy and Chorlton Park and Manchester Southern Cemetery, across Withington and Fog Lane Park and Heaton Mersey to Stockport. Each small drop of moisture carried a cargo of soot from the factories of Trafford Park. When it settled on white collars or nylon stockings or the backs of hands it left a small dark circle.

Four o'clock and the boys and girls of Lady Wynyard's were going home, turning up their collars, chattering loudly, carrying enormous and very heavy satchels full of textbooks and notebooks and pencils and protractors and compasses. Robin was one of the last to leave. The others were always in a hurry to get back to their homes in Chorltonville and Wythenshawe and Didsbury, to their tea, to cake and eggs and chips and salad, and lit rooms with flowered chintzes and brass ornaments on the mantelpiece, and television, and homework. They walked quickly away along Barlow Moor Road and Darley Avenue, they waited in the concrete bus shelters for the 104 bus to take them to Alexandra Park or, in the opposite direction, to Wythenshawe.

Robin came alone. His friends, if they could be called that, had gone on ahead. He was not often able to persuade even the members of the chess club to stay behind after work to play a few games, study the openings, practise. It required Mr. Hammond and a bit of arm-twisting to make them do that.

Robin heaved his satchel further on to his shoulder and trudged across the yard, a tall, stooping, rather comic figure. He stopped at the gates and slowly turned up his coat collar against the rain, watching the headlights on Princess Road, the wet glare of the road. He was going slower and slower. Why hurry? he asked himself yet again. What's the rush, I'm tired, anyone would be after a physics lesson like that.

Across Barlow Moor Road were Christie Playing Fields which the school was allowed to use, where some of the most humiliating hours of his life had been spent. Short-sighted, clumsy, he had been a laughable sight playing football. Being tall and slow, he was often made goalkeeper. This at least involved no running; only standing and peering myopically through the rain, and then suddenly everyone shouting and dozens of people running and a large wet heavy football kicked very hard at him. He would lunge desperately, sometimes he would connect with his hands, his stomach, his face, sometimes he would miss miserably. They would laugh at him, it all seemed to matter so much. Was there anyone else in the North of England, he used to wonder, who didn't think football was the only thing that mattered in life? Even his dad.

Things were much better in the sixth form. He could escape games to prepare for his "A" levels, and was now surrounded by people who thought that "A" levels and university entrance were all that mattered in life. His name was unlikely to appear on the school notice-board as one of those chosen to represent the school at football or cricket the following Saturday afternoon against another nearby school. There was only one game in which he was fitted to represent his school and that was played sitting down.

He dawdled across the yard, alone, the last of the four hundred to leave. His fawn raincoat was too small, and he showed two inches of bony wrist beyond the sleeve. Beneath the turn-ups of his grey flannel trousers showed another two inches of bony ankle and wrinkled grey socks. On the back of his head was a small maroon schoolboy's cap. It gave no protection against the rain, and he would have liked to cram it into his pocket, but the headmaster insisted almost daily that the cap was part of the school uniform and must be worn at all times.

At the gates he hesitated, telling himself how tired he was, how there was no need to hurry. In fact he was postponing the moment of decision: either he would cross the road and catch the bus back to Wythenshawe, tea and homework, or he would stay this side of the road and take the same bus in the opposite direction into Manchester. He knew what he wanted to do, he knew what he ought to do; whichever he decided he would regret it. Fortunately, he told himself wryly, his flag wasn't up.

A red Mini drove out of the gates, braked. Mr. Hammond's head peered out of the window.

"Coming up to the club for a game? Can I give you a lift?"

Robin stooped to answer. "Oh, thank you, sir. But I ought really to be getting home. Homework."

"Not even time for one game?"

"Well . . ."

"Have you got a lot to do? Can't you fit it all in?"

"Oh, not a lot, sir. I just felt . . ." He left the sentence unfinished as he walked round the car and got in, doubling himself up. "Perhaps one game," he mumbled.

"You've got Saturday afternoon to catch up in while the others are playing football."

"That's true." He took off his cap and stuffed it into his pocket. It was bad enough having to play chess at the club in a maroon blazer with the Wynyard crest on the breast pocket without having to appear in a small shrunk maroon cap too. He swivelled sideways to make more room for his legs. The windscreen wipers made smeary arcs on the glass in front of him.

Mr. Hammond was talking about the match he was arranging a fortnight off against Trinity Grammar, Sale. Robin, of course, would captain the Lady Wynyard team. Another boy, Wyatt, was an obvious choice. But the others were a problem. Some were not available, some would be playing football, the rest were simply not good enough.

"Still, we need match practice as a team," Mr. Hammond said.

"We've got to get in as much as we can. I'm determined to enter for the *Sunday Times* competition next year, just for the experience. But I think it'll be a pretty good wash-out. We've got a long haul before we turn in any good results. A lot'll depend on you."

Robin felt pleased and mumbled that he would do his best.

They passed from the new houses and lawns of Alexandra Park into Moss Side, the coloured quarter, the slums. Even in the rain sad Negroes were standing at the street corners.

Mr. Hammond said, "I've entered you for the Lancashire Junior, and I'd like to put you in for Liverpool at Easter. Or Bognor. You can't manage both, which d'you prefer?"

"Liverpool would be easier to manage, sir."

Mr. Hammond nodded. "And then Blackpool again next year. That should give you quite a bit of tournament practice. What's happening about this Munich business?"

"Oh, they've asked me to go. I—I've accepted."

Mr. Hammond shook his head. "I still think it's a mistake. You don't want to plunge into these international jamborees too soon. Some of these foreign juniors are practically grandmasters."

Robin knew their names and games as well as anyone, and after Blackpool he didn't feel particularly scared of grandmasters. He said, rather tactlessly, "Mr. Butler wrote to me. He said it was a big chance for me. If I turned it down I mightn't get asked again another year. He thought I ought to go."

"He would!"

"Anyway, I'd like to see Munich."

Mr. Hammond laughed. "Oh, you won't get time for any sightseeing, I promise you that. It isn't just a holiday outing to see the sights. I shouldn't think you'll ever leave the congress hall except to go home and sleep."

"I heard they sent you on a guided tour of the city on Sundays, sir."

"Beer and circuses for the foolish brethren, young Jackson. The wise ones stay at home and study their games. These Russians and Yugoslavs are not to be dismissed too lightly."

Once again the threat of Russia, and once again Robin shrugged it off. What were Russian champions to him? However, he said pacifyingly, "I don't fancy the idea of German beer much."

"Just as well. But I still think you're making a big mistake. What's the hurry, why not leave it till next year?"

"But supposing they don't ask me next year, sir?"

"If you do well in the Lancashire Junior and Liverpool, they'll ask you, all right. And if you don't, well, better not go."

Robin couldn't think of an answer to that. All these people wanting you to wait till you were middle-aged before doing anything. How long did they imagine you could go on being a junior for?

He was glad when they arrived. They turned left out of Oxford Road, and with a whinny of delight Mr. Hammond saw a car move out from the parking meter outside Williams Deacons Bank and manœuvred his Mini into the space. While he locked up, Robin uncoiled himself from the cramped seat and walked to the corner. In front of him was the black Gothic tower of the university, of Whitworth Hall. Next year, when he was a student here, he'd be here all the time, here or in the Students' Union next door in Moberly Tower. He'd be able to come to the club every night when there was play. There'd be the university chess club too. He visualised himself in the first team, playing top board against Oxford or London, captain in his second and third year.

Mr. Hammond caught up with him and they went up to the club over Smallman's Snack Bar. This was hardly a club in the strict sense. It had no formal membership, no subscription, it sent no teams to play other clubs. It was simply a small room with brown wallpaper and a gas fire and some tables and chairs and a cupboard of miscellaneous chess-sets. It was open to anyone who cared to come and play, three nights a week, and it was run by Mr. Hammond. The expenses, such as they were, were paid by him out of his pocket. Most of the players were from the university, but there was a sprinkling from other schools and colleges and libraries, and from chess-playing homes.

Tonight there were eight young men there, all from the university. Robin knew them all, and they nodded at him. He was the youngest present, though he was the tallest. He wished he were wearing ordinary clothes instead of a school blazer. Never mind, next year.

The eight were playing against each other, so Mr. Hammond got a board and pieces out and started to play against Robin. It was a strange type of chess everyone was playing, much too fast, no clocks or scorecards, even taking back moves occasionally with a laugh. There was no murmuring silence; conversation was general, flat Lancashire vowels sounded through the room. Players would converse with the next table freely, breaking off abruptly to consider the new position in front of them; or, vice versa, interrupting their train of thought to join in some distant remark. They would walk about, analyse each other's positions, theorise about the latest opening analysis, joke, and point out each other's mistakes. As conversation, it was "in" and learned, but the standard of play was in consequence moderate and relaxed.

Robin lost an erratic and fast end-game to Mr. Hammond. It might have gone otherwise if he had given more time and thought to it, but half his mind was on the chess talk. Mr. Hammond nodded at his win in great contentment. It supported all he had been saying. They then changed opponents, and Robin found himself playing a fat boy called Lewis. But the conversation was still absorbing. They were now discussing who was likely to be chosen for Munich. Robin waited excitedly for Mr. Hammond to reveal the great news, and when it became apparent that his form master was going to say nothing he let it out himself.

"You have? They've asked you?"

Robin confirmed it shyly.

"They never! What's Britain coming to?"

"Talk about a bloody massacre of the Holy Innocents."

"Nothing like getting your name in the papers."

"I played against some of those Yugoslav boys at Bognor. That Kurajica. Lad, it'll be bloody murder."

"Oh, hold on, he beat Toklovsky in fair combat just the other day."

"Toklovsky? Who's he these days?" asked Lewis, who had stopped playing chess and was busy writing something on a piece of paper.

Mr. Hammond said, "I'm with you, I think it's too soon too. One tournament doesn't make a summer."

Lewis produced his piece of paper, covered with a pattern of noughts. "There you are! The boy Jackson's score in Munich."

"Oh, I think he'll mow 'em down. What I want to know is, how'll he do in the Interzonal."

This was greeted with much laughter. Indeed, each sally had

been greeted with laughter which had buttered over the sharpness and toned down the envy. Robin laughed as much as anyone, partly out of long school training and partly because he was enjoying himself. It was nice to be envied. Here was he, arrived from nowhere, didn't play for a proper club, his school not even in the *Sunday Times* tournament, and just because of one famous game and getting his name in the papers he had leapfrogged over the lot of them and was going to Munich. You couldn't help laughing, could you?

"I'll send you a picture postcard of a beer cellar."

"Just so long as it's Worthington E. I don't want to see photos of that German muck."

There was much laughter over this.

Mr. Hammond said portentously, "All the same, young Jackson, I think you'll find there's a lot of difference between tournament games and team games."

"He's going to find out a lot."

Robin let it go and concentrated on his game with Lewis. He didn't agree about team games. Chess was chess, one man against one man, except in a simul, simple White against Black. The game was still the same whether it was one team against another or all against all. But these schoolmasters always had to make it into a team game like football, talk about doing your best for the side. Better for your *esprit de corps,* he supposed, and that was all that mattered to some of them. Old Hammond now, he'd be far prouder if his school team got through to the *Sunday Times* quarter-finals than of Robin beating Toklovsky. He swore under his breath with annoyance. He was glad he was annoying old Hammond by being invited to Munich, he was glad he had accepted, he'd show 'em all.

The gas fire went out with a plop. Mr. Hammond found another shilling in his pocket and started it again. Somebody said, "I say, we'll miss our grub if we don't buck up. The snack bar'll be shut in ten minutes. Come on, chaps, fork out your hard-earned brass."

They produced half-crowns and two of the young men went downstairs to the snack bar. This was part of the evening, part of the terms on which they were allowed to use the room. In due course they returned with two trays of ham sandwiches and cups of tea. Everyone went on playing, while they munched and sipped. There was a lull in the conversation, Munich seemed to be forgotten.

It was revived when two more players arrived. They were third-years, come across from Moberly Tower. One of them, Stan Ashcroft, was the strongest player to use the club regularly; he had won Lancashire Junior two years ago. The other was a less successful player, Jim Harris.

Ashcroft came in bawling. He had a naturally loud voice. "Where is he?" he bellowed. "Where's our hero of the month? Where's our infant prod? Is he here? Yes, of course he's here! Look at this, fellers, get a load of this."

He threw a magazine on to a table, a copy of *New Princess,* and found the place. The others crowded round, looking over his shoulder. Robin, hopping round behind them, was unable to look over their shoulders, despite his height.

Phrases came to him.

"Look at that photo, isn't that a pin-up for you?"

"Proper cunt-throb."

"Now, now, mind your language, there are infant prodigies present."

"My hero of the month is dot dot dot a young North Country lad."

"Listen to this, handsome as any film-star, with the born genius of the natural chess master."

"Tall and courteous, with the engaging shyness of the young who suddenly have greatness thrust upon them, engaging shyness, hear that?"

"And how about this? Britain should be proud of its new infant prodigy, though infant hardly describes either his height or his mature approach to the great game of chess and to that even greater game dot dot dot life."

Robin, tantalised, danced about behind them. Ashcroft pushed through the group, and shook hands with Robin.

"Infant prod," he said, "I'm proud to know you."

Robin came back bravely with "I owe it all to you."

The others were crowding round him now. Jim Harris took his chin and twisted it away till his face was in profile against the light. Out of the corner of his eye he could see them crouching, examining him.

178

"Yes, I think that's a film-star's face, now you come to mention it. He'll have to give up chess, though, if he wants to get into pictures."

"Don't tempt him. We've got to keep our infant prod on the straight and narrow."

"Would you say he had John Wayne's nose?"

"More like Twiggy's." Howls of laughter.

"And the engaging shyness? That should show in the mouth."

"C'mon, smile, baby. Doesn't he look like the singing nun?"

"More like James Bond being tortured." More howls of laughter.

Jim Harris slapped his face and let him go. "Okay, you pass your film-test. You can give up chess and go into pictures."

Robin slipped away and grabbed the magazine, the others drifted back to chess. Ashcroft began to munch a sandwich though he had not paid his half-crown.

It was, of course, Paul Butler's article on Blackpool, and Paul had done him proud. That photo was a smasher. He didn't know he looked so handsome, in profile with the light behind him. What Paul had written was a bit embarrassing, too effusive, sort of gluey, all those dots. Still it was written for women, not for lads like these. He'd show it to Val, if she hadn't seen it already, she'd love it, handsome as any film-star. He was taking her to the cinema on Saturday, he'd show it to her then, she'd be thrilled. So would his mum. Dad too, perhaps he'd begin to understand about chess. About time too. He'd show it to Mr. Hammond too, tomorrow at school. Then he remembered that Mr. Hammond was in fact in the room, concentrating on a chess position, carefully ignoring Robin and the fuss about the article.

The mean old bastard, thought Robin. He read again Paul's last sentence. "Our hearts will be with this gallant young David when he goes forth next month to Munich to do battle against the European Goliaths."

He said to Ashcroft, "Can I keep this?"

"It'd break my sister's heart. She wants your photo back."

"Why can't she buy another copy?"

"Buy another copy? Are you daft? She'd like to buy a dozen. But there isn't a copy left in Manchester. It isn't every day you get a genius who's also as handsome as any film-star."

Much laughter. The art of this sort of dialogue was in talking

179

about someone present as if he weren't there. It was very flattering.

"Why not ask him for it back? He can't want to read about himself for ever?"

"He's waiting till he's alone, and do you know what he'll do then? He'll read his horoscope on page sixty-seven. And do you know what he'll find? 'Beware the friendship of an older man.' "

There was a gasp and a moment's silence. Jim Harris had gone too far. Then they all laughed. Robin too, though he was flushed.

"Come off it, chaps, you're just jealous," he said. He added ingenuously: "Anyway, how do you know you're not going to Munich too? There are six of us going, after all."

Lewis, the practical one, said sourly, "We'd've heard by now if it had been us."

Mr. Hammond went on staring at his game, saying nothing, letting his pupil fend for himself. It was Stan Ashcroft who came to his rescue.

"Will the engagingly shy young David engage in a joust with one of his erstwhile peers? Winner to go to Munich?"

Robin, beginning to feel at bay, said, "If the B.C.F. agrees, I'm on. Even if it doesn't, I'd like a game."

"Proper game, mind you. With a clock."

Jim Harris said to Ashcroft, "Prithee, gentle knight, do not murder the boy David before he even goeth forth to battle."

They found a clock in the cupboard and set up the pieces. Ashcroft picked up two Pawns and held his fists behind his back. Robin picked the right hand, the black Pawn. Black against Stan Ashcroft who had won the Lancashire Junior. Outside Blackpool, Ashcroft was the strongest player he had ever met. Let me win, he thought, let me not lose, let me not lose too quickly.

Ashcroft opened with the King's Pawn and pressed the clock button. Robin thought quickly, with everyone else breathing down his neck. The Sicilian Dragon and go all out for a win? The French Winawer—but he wasn't up to date with the latest analysis on that. The Robatsch Defence and try to close the game down? The Ruy Lopez and counter-attack with the Marshall gambit? After Spassky, after Tal, after Wade, he knew his way through the Marshall all right, like every other chess-player in Britain. So, of course, would Ashcroft. Something unusual like Alekhine's Defence? He dithered.

"If he's got you beat, resign," said Jim Harris.

Robin looked up and grinned. Then he played his King's Pawn. The Robatsch was thought to be unsound by many players. Better the Lopez and Marshall. More exact.

The others waited till he sacrificed the Pawn which was the point of the Marshall and broke the Lopez grip. Then they drifted back to their own games.

"Bloody ridiculous starting in on the Marshall at his hour. They won't seal before midnight."

The evening seemed to peter out after that. The others went back to their games and the remains of the sandwiches. After a couple of hours they began to drift away, with quiet good nights. The time for chaff was over. Eventually only Mr. Hammond was left. He pulled up a chair and watched the game.

It was a complicated locked middle-game and both players were slow and thoughtful. Mr. Hammond said, "You haven't forgotten your last bus, have you, young Jackson?" He added unkindly, "Or your homework?"

Robin looked at him quickly. That was an unfair crack, he thought. It was Mr. Hammond who had talked him into coming up here tonight.

Ashcroft moved a Pawn and Robin considered the new threat.

Mr. Hammond said, "All right, give it another half-hour. After that I'm going home. You can lock up, and Jackson can walk back to Wythenshawe."

Robin forced his mind back from the game. Usually Mr. Hammond gave him a lift home if the last bus had gone. He couldn't be serious. It was miles back to Wythenshawe.

Half an hour later the game was still blocked. Mr. Hammond said, "Well, lads, I'm off. Turn off the lights and lock up when you go."

Ashcroft's eyes met Robin's. "Let's pack it in. I could do with some sleep."

Robin nodded. He wasn't going to suggest a draw himself, but he was glad to be out of it without failure. Before any more could be said, he pushed the pieces aside and began putting them away in the box. Abandoned without dishonour.

They put the boxes and boards back in the cupboard, collected the empty plates and cups, put on their raincoats. Robin looked round for the copy of *New Princess,* but somebody had pinched that. They turned out the fire and the lights and carried the trays and crockery downstairs, leaving them outside the passage door into Smallman's. In the morning someone would find it all and wash it up. They let themselves out into the street, and put the key back into the letter-box.

It was raining harder now. "Proper Manchester weather," said Ashcroft to Mr. Hammond.

"It makes me wonder why we don't all go and live in the South of France. Well, good night, Stan, see you on Thursday?"

"Probably."

Mr. Hammond and Robin walked round the corner to the Mini. It was the only car left in the street. Mr. Hammond unlocked the car, and Robin hauled his legs in. Mr. Hammond backed the car into Oxford Road. The windscreen wipers clicked rhythmically across the glass.

Robin began to talk about the game he had just abandoned, and which was in his mind. His weak King's Bishop's Pawn. The possibilities of a Queen's side attack with his Queen and Knight. But Mr. Hammond just grunted and let it drop. It dawned on Robin that Mr. Hammond had been unusually silent the whole evening, hardly saying more than the occasional sentence. Normally he was the life and soul of the club. Moody. Or tired. Or cross about Munich. Mean old bastard, you'd think he'd have been pleased at one of his pupils being chosen for the British students' team.

Robin relapsed into silence. The sodium street lights were reflected on the wet road, and so was the yellow headlight glare of the few passing cars. They were out on to Princess Road; on the right were playing fields, athletic grounds, cemeteries; on the left were council estates, mile after mile of small red-brick houses with damp lawns and bare lilac bushes. There were hardly any lights on; Manchester goes to bed early, soon after the pubs shut. An occasional bluish light behind chintz curtains betrayed the night-owls, those who were still glued to the telly, watching the news headlines, the weather forecast for tomorrow, the parson behind his desk, giving an epilogue.

They passed Lady Wynyard's, where he (and, of course, Mr. Hammond) would be tomorrow morning. Mr. Hammond, after dropping Robin in Wythenshawe, would have to turn round and come back this way; turning off on to Barlow Road and then on to Burton Road to his own home, supposed to be in Albert Park, though no one at school was sure about this.

It would probably be snowing in Munich. Robin imagined huge churches with snow on the roofs, and beer cellars with people coming out of them, laughing and singing. He'd be allowed to drink beer in Germany, wouldn't he? He liked beer, the little he'd had of it already. His father sometimes gave him a small glass of light ale on special occasions like Christmas.

He wondered what sort of a welcome he'd get at home. Dad would be in his big armchair, drinking tea or beer, watching telly. Mum would be doing something in the kitchen. Would there be trouble about his being out so late yet again? Probably they wouldn't even have noticed. They'd think he was upstairs doing his homework, swotting physics and geography. He could drop dead doing his homework and they wouldn't notice.

His parents, however, had noticed. Mr. Jackson usually came home from his work at the Council offices an hour and a half after his son. Today he had settled into his tea (fried egg and tomato and chips and four or five cups of tea) in the kitchen; he could see the television in the lounge through the open door, though in fact he was reading the *Daily Mirror*.

He looked up. "Robin back yet, Mum?"

She shook her head.

"S'pose he's at that chess club again. That lad's got chess on the brain."

"He's keen, all right."

He ate and read some more, and then he pushed the paper away.

"I don't like it, him spending all his evenings playing chess. What about his homework, eh? What about his 'A' levels?"

"Robin says he's up with it all."

"Aye, he would."

"And you asked Mr. Hammond about him, you remember, love? That last Parent-Teacher meeting. He said Robin was doing all right?"

"I remember. That Hammond, he's daft about chess too. The whole bloody lot of them are daft about chess."

Mrs. Jackson became unexpectedly firm. "Now you're not to use words like that in this home."

"Sorry, love, beg pardon. But it's true, isn't it? This Butler chap writes to him every week."

"Aye, there's a letter from him now on the table, big fat one. I know his writing."

"Well, there you are. And all these chess books and magazines. It's just chess he thinks about night and day. It is that," he added heavily.

"He's keen, all right."

"And another thing. These brown envelopes he keeps. getting, you know, look like bills, used over and over again till they're proper worn out. You know what they are?"

"Postal chess, he says."

"Aye, postal chess. Playing bloody games—excuse me!—against chaps he's never even seen, in London or Birmingham or somewhere. How's that for sport, eh?"

"He says it's just a hobby."

"Funny sort of hobby, playing chess by post. He never goes and watches any proper sport. How many times has he been up to Old Trafford to see United? Just the once. And he's never been to see Lancashire play. He won't even watch a Test match on the telly. He doesn't even go and watch his school side any more. Postal chess!"

"Now, love, don't fret yourself. It's just a sort of craze. I expect he'll grow out of it."

"He'd better if he's going to get to university."

Mr. Jackson helped himself to strawberry jam, and spread it thickly on his bread. He read the back page of the *Daily Mirror,* and then returned doggedly to the point.

"This Hammond chap says he's all right, but supposing he isn't. Supposing he fails his 'A' levels. Supposing he doesn't get to university."

"I'm sure he'll get it, all right."

"Aye, but supposing he doesn't. I'm ambitious for that lad, I want to see him make his mark in the world. He's got the brains, all right."

"Mr. Hammond says you've got to have brains to play chess, I mean play it properly. He says it's a sort of test of brains."

"Aye, he says this, and he says that. But how's chess going to get him into university? What's he going to do if he doesn't get

184

in? Become a pro chess-player? What sort of money do they earn?"

"I expect they earn a lot of money. Like sort of film-stars."

Mr. Jackson had to laugh at that, though he wasn't in the mood for laughing. "Our Robin a film-star! Whatever next!" He read some more of the paper and swallowed some bread and jam. His wife poured him another cup of tea, and then put the teapot back under the cosy which was intended to look like a thatched cottage. He caught her hand and pressed it affectionately.

"Love, we didn't have just the one lad for him to be a chess-player."

She paused, moved, not pushing the hand away. There was a moment's silence, an elegy for all those other boys and girls who might have been. Then she smiled and nodded. "He'll be all right, you'll see. He's a good lad, and plenty of brains with it. He'll be all right, you'll see."

"I think I'll have a talk with him."

"Fred Jackson, you'll do nothing of the sort. Talking to him will just make him stubborn. It's just a craze like stamp collecting. He'll come out of it, you'll see."

"But suppose he fails his . . . ?"

The conversation was capable of going on and on, being endlessly repeated and slightly varied. But they both heard the sad wail of the introductory music for "Coronation Street" on the telly, and they moved in to watch it. After it was over, Mrs. Jackson went back into the kitchen and washed up the tea-things. Then she came back into the lounge with her work-basket, watching the telly while she darned her husband's and her son's socks. She was used to doing more than one thing at once. Mr. Jackson, sitting under the parchment-shaded lamp, read his other newspaper, the *Daily Express,* barely noticing that its views opposed the *Mirror* on every subject. He also kept a close eye on the telly. He too could do more than one thing at once.

Mr. Hammond dropped Robin at the corner of Greenwood Road and Boothfield Road. He said briefly, "Good night, see you tomorrow."

Robin said, "Good night, sir, thanks for the lift."

The car backed round, went out into Altrincham Road, turning left towards Princess Road. The last life, it seemed to Robin, was going out of Wythenshawe. He turned up his raincoat collar against the rain, and looked round at the dark factory, the dark Esso station, the dark Royal Oak, the dark cinema, the dark Salvation Army chapel, the dark Labour Club. The poster outside advertised a visit and speech by Mr. George Brown two weeks ago. Robin's parents, loyal Labour supporters, had gone, and had been cross with Robin for playing chess instead of going too. But there was nothing going on now, no sign of life anywhere, except, he noticed suddenly, a couple kissing in the bus shelter.

He gave them a sympathetic glance. He'd cuddled with Val in a bus shelter last week-end. She was cold and he'd put his raincoat round her. Little Val, it was nice to have a girl who was keen on you; she was impressed by his brains and his being Grammar and his going to university and, of all things, his height. She laughed and she kissed ardently, but she never had much to say for herself. She still didn't understand the first thing about chess, though she must have spent hours watching it in Blackpool and sometimes even at the club in Manchester. Still, it was nice to have a regular girl, a pretty one, even if his parents didn't think much of her. He was taking her to the cinema on Saturday.

But otherwise! He walked down Boothfield Road. Honestly, you'd go barmy in a place like this if it wasn't for chess. There were hardly any lights in the houses; the road was lit only by the cold street-lights. A light was on behind the print curtains of the bedroom in No. 14. Mr. and Mrs. Jennings must be in bed, reading the papers. It was impossible to think of them making love. Impossible to think of anyone making love in Wythenshawe, except in a bus shelter.

He crossed the road to his home, the semi-detached red-brick house where he had lived for the last nine years. It was concealed from the front and side by a tall hedge for privacy; just outside the side hedge were four black pollarded trees. Inside was a rough lawn with a bare cherry tree, a few old iris leaves left over from the summer. Like the other inhabitants of Boothfield Road, Mr. Jackson was no gardening enthusiast.

The gate squeaked as he went through, alerting his parents to his arrival. He went round to the back, and walked into the kitchen, throwing his satchel down on a chair and taking off his raincoat, which he hung on the back of the door.

"That you, Robin?"

"Who else?"

"Well, at least you can answer civil."

"Sorry, Mum." He kissed her distantly.

"You're late. You been at the chess."

"Hammond drove me up there after school. He's just brought me back. Otherwise I'd have had to walk. In this Manchester weather." He could see a difficult scene coming, and was hoping to keep to the weather.

"You can't walk back from Manchester, it's a long way. You'd catch your death of cold in this weather."

"Never mind the bloody weather." Mr. Jackson had arrived in the doorway, the *Daily Express* in one hand, his pipe in the other. "It's too late for you to be out. It's quarter to twelve, and you've got to be at school in the morning. I don't say it's wrong Saturdays, lads need a night out once a week. But it's the third time this week."

"Oh, let the lad alone to eat his supper. He must be hungry." She produced a slice of veal-and-ham pie, and salad, and bread and butter. The kettle was simmering, and she made another pot of tea, and got out three cups.

Mr. Jackson still stood in the doorway; he was staring at Robin's satchel. "You must have the whole of Manchester Central Library in there. That's what I mean, lugging all that stuff about and never looking at it."

Robin, through a mouthful of pie, said, "How do you mean?"

"All right, lad, I'll be blunt. Are you doing any homework these days, or are you letting it all slide? Isn't it just chess, chess, chess every day and never mind the work?"

"Dad, let the boy eat his supper!"

Robin swallowed the piece of pie, the bit of hard-boiled egg in the middle. "I'm all right, Dad," he said. "I'm well up with it all. I catch up with it all dinner-time while the others are fooling about. All I've got to do is an essay on the fishing industry in Norway, and that's easy. I haven't got to show it up till Monday. I'll do it over the week-end."

Mr. Jackson said doubtfully, "Well, so long as you really are keeping up."

Out of the corner of his eye, Robin could see his parents waving at each other. Mum was gesticulating, telling Dad to shut up and leave the lad alone. He was waving back, explaining that he never got a chance to speak to his son. She gesticulated back, not now, not when he's tired and trying to eat. Robin ignored them. Just so long as they left him in peace they could make signs at each other all night. He was hungry, he'd had nothing except a ham sandwich since school dinner.

His father gave way and went back to his armchair in the lounge. His mother waited on him and brought him cheese and jam and apples.

He asked, "Any letters for me, Mum?"

"Oooh yes. You get more letters a day than we get in a month of Sundays. They look all about chess."

She went to fetch them for him. While she was gone, Robin felt his heart starting to pound in excitement. Tick, tick, tick, went the pulse in his head. Two of his postal opponents should have answered by now, Gibbs from Ealing and Matthews from Birmingham. He'd set a trap for Gibbs; had the man seen it? He had a positional advantage over Matthews, but Matthews could get considerable counter-play (as Robin had analysed it) with a Pawn sacrifice; had the man seen it?

He drank some tea and tried to calm himself. He smiled as his mother brought him the letters: three cheap brown envelopes, one from Ealing, one from Birmingham, one from Bristol. Two games in each; add the one from central London which had arrived that morning, and that meant eight games where he had to make difficult crucial moves. He had seventy-two hours to make the moves in, but if he got off his moves by tomorrow night they'd get them by the week-end. He might get their replies Monday evening.

Trembling, he put the postal chess envelopes in his pocket unopened. He knew better than to look at them now and get involved in an argument with his parents about the worthwhileness of postal chess. But it needed a lot of self-control. If his mother would go out of the kitchen for even one minute he'd be able to see the Gibbs game.

He looked at the other letters; the *British Chess Magazine,* and a thick envelope addressed in Paul Butler's handwriting. Robin opened it without much excitement. He was sure it would be a magazine with an article about Munich, probably about churches or art or opera. Paul was trying to get him interested in Rubens; the great chess-player, he had written last week, must have a wide culture, wider than just chess. Robin had argued back; he just wouldn't have the time in Munich to go to art galleries and operas, he'd be busy playing chess; he wouldn't win many games, would he, if he spent all his spare time looking at Rubens or listening to Wagner? And now Paul was firing back about the greatness of Rubens and Wagner and God knows who else. It was like playing yet one more game of postal chess.

One thought led to another. "Oh, by the way, Mum, I'm in the papers again. A woman's magazine called *New Princess,* yes, what a name, laugh if you like. Anyway, there's a smashing picture of me, and it says I've got the looks of a film-star, and I'm an infant prodigy and a genius and you'd never know it was me. He calls me a young David."

"Whatever for?"

"I'll get you a copy in the morning. Oh, here it is, he's sent me one." He had opened Paul's envelope and pulled out a copy of *New Princess.* He glanced briefly at the blonde cover girl with her lovely teeth; his own name wasn't on the outside. He found the article inside and showed it to his mother. She got her glasses out of the drawer of the kitchen table, and he found the place for her again.

She gave a little squeak. "Ooh, look at that. That's you! Isn't that smashing! Ooh, you do look handsome, your dad'll be really proud of you now." She began to read, while Robin gave himself yet another cup of tea. Suddenly she jumped to her feet and ran into the lounge. "Dad, Dad, look what it says here about our Robin, it says he's their hero of the month and as handsome as any film-star."

"The daft things they put in the papers."

The moment she was out of the kitchen, Robin whipped the postal-chess games out of his pocket. Gibbs hadn't fallen into the trap, he'd made a move which Robin hadn't foreseen, and which he couldn't visualise without the board. The game was getting deeper, more complicated; it had been too much to hope that a knowledgeable player, as Gibbs obviously was, would fall into a simple trap. Robin glanced briefly at his second game with

Gibbs which was much less interesting (or less hopeful, to be exact) and looked at his games with Matthews. Matthews didn't seem to be sacrificing a Pawn. Indeed, he hadn't moved a Pawn, he had moved a Knight. Again Robin couldn't visualise this without the board. He glanced briefly at his other game with Matthews, and at his two with Wilson in Bristol. Then he crammed them all back in his pocket.

In the big envelope, together with the copy of *New Princess,* was a six-page handwritten letter from Paul. Robin started to read: "My dear Robin. Such a long lovely letter, but, if I may have the temerity indeed in these days to disagree with one younger than myself, I think you are mistaken . . ." Robin skipped, reading only the words with capital letters. Rubens, I, Munich, Capablanca, I, Wagner, Mozart, Pinakothek, Leonardo, I, Bauhaus, Gropius, Klee, I, Franz Marc, Leipzig, Munich, I, New York, Robin, Manchester, Paul. Robin put it too in his pocket. As well as taking his "A" levels in geography and physics, it seemed that he was having to take them in art appreciation too. Discuss the importance of the Bauhaus Movement on the artistic life of (a) Munich and (b) Germany as a whole, giving examples. And "A"-level chess too.

He finished his supper, picked up his satchel and went into the lounge. His parents were still reading, or re-reading, the article in *New Princess,* but now that his supper and television were both over there was nothing further to stay up for. The cat had to have its scraps prepared, and be put out. Mr. Jackson unplugged the television and turned out the lights. Mrs. Jackson altered the milkman's dial on the doorstep to "2 Pints." They went upstairs, the narrow stairs with the red and green carpet fastened down with brass clips. Robin went to the bathroom first, cleaned his teeth, stared in the mirror at the film-star features, grimaced. Then, not wanting to get involved in a cosy good-night talk about his future, he went quietly past his parents' bedroom, the door of which was still ajar, to his own room.

He pulled out the postal-chess games, the worn brown envelopes, the battered score-sheets. He got out the folding cardboard chess-sets where he kept the position on each game permanently set up, and he made the new moves on each game. Gibbs, far from falling into the trap, had made an unexpected move which opened up a whole field of new threats. This was going to need careful thought or he might find himself with a suddenly lost position.

He put the cardboard folders down and covered them with his satchel. His mother sometimes came in to say a last good night, and he didn't want her to find him studying them. No point in bringing all that up again. He pulled some books out of his satchel, although he didn't want to be questioned about his homework either. Though he could get away with it, tell her he was well up, just looking over a point for the morning.

He opened his notebook and looked in a spirit of masochism at the homework which he had not yet done. Evaluate the importance of the fishing industry in the economy of Norway. Compare the present-day agriculture of Ireland and Switzerland. Using actual examples, compare the landforms characteristic of the English chalklands with other areas of limestone in Britain. And the physics. Describe how you would use a small magnetic needle, fastened horizontally in a non-magnetic heavy bob suspended by a silk fibre, to explore the distribution of magnetic-field strength, due to a current in the coil, along the axis of a flat circular coil carrying a current. Show how the results are derived from the observations and sketch the form of the curve that you would expect to obtain. A glass U-tube is inverted with the open ends of the straight limbs, of diameters respectively 0–500 mm and 1–00 mm, below the surface of water in a beaker. The air pressure in the upper part is increased until the meniscus in one limb is level with the water outside. Find the height of water in the other limb, assuming the density of water to be 1–00 gm cm^{-3}. Describe an experiment to verify that the intensity of y radiation varies inversely as the square of the distance from the source, being provided with a suitable radioactive source for the experiment chosen. Well, that was easy, but, all the same, old Crabtree set too bloody much homework.

And, of course, he hadn't done any dinner-time. That was when the chess club met, when the games for the chess-ladder were played off. Old Hammond expected him to be there, ready to play. If he stopped coming, said he had other things to do, the whole chess club would fold up in no time. He'd told old Hammond that he hadn't yet been able to draw a longitudinal profile on graph paper of Watendlath Beck from 275160 to 165193 on the Ordnance Survey Map, and he'd answered that in the circumstances Robin could have another day's grace, but be sure to have it in tomorrow morning. Robin still hadn't done it. It was the sort of thing that took hours.

Some of it was for tomorrow, but he could probably get away with it, pretend he'd left his book behind, show the whole thing up together on Monday morning. He'd have to work at it on Saturday, he'd have to wash out his date with Val. He was to meet her at the Chorlton Street bus station at half past two. He couldn't phone her, she wasn't on the phone. He'd have to write, but would she get it in time? Well, even if she didn't, there was plenty for a girl to do in Manchester on a Saturday. She could go shopping, or something.

He put these thoughts out of his mind, and undressed quickly. It didn't look as if Mum was coming to say good night tonight. He opened the door and called out, " 'Night, Mum, 'night, Dad." They called back, " 'Night, Robin." Their door was still ajar, their light was still on. They'd probably go on reading *New Princess* all bloody night.

He was safe now—she wouldn't come after he had got his light out. He set his alarm for seven o'clock and carefully placed his quilt across the bottom of the door. He had studied the door from the outside a year (or was it more?) ago. The door fitted close and showed no light round the sides. This meant that he didn't have to pin a blanket over the door. Of course, anyone across the road could see his light through the curtains, but who would be looking out at this hour?

He could never analyse on a folding cardboard set, so he got out his proper board and the wooden pieces, and set up the new position with Gibbs. The new threats, the chances of winning back the initiative. Then there was the other game with Gibbs. Difficult, complicated, positional, a struggle for the centre and the long diagonal. Perhaps he shouldn't have tried the Caro-Kann against someone like Gibbs. But then how was he to know, he'd never played Gibbs before, he was just someone from the Postal Chess Club. That was one of the snags about postal chess. It wasn't that it was slow or boring, but that you couldn't find out anything about your opponent before the game. And if you picked the wrong opening, or made some mistake, you were stuck with that for the next ten months.

After Gibbs, his two games with Matthews. Matthews hadn't noticed, or had decided against, the Pawn sacrifice, and seemed to be grouping to bring King's side pressure. Robin felt fairly happy about this game, but he was much less sure about the other one against Matthews, a potentially dangerous Nimzo-Indian.

After Matthews, Wilson. Wilson had tried the Blackmar-Diemer on him, and Robin, caught off balance, had had to do a lot of research with the book and the back numbers of *Chess* to make any sort of answer. Even now it looked a probably lost game. The other was an orthodox Queen's Gambit Declined, level, blocked and probably drawn.

And then Henderson in central London. These were probably the two most exciting and original of the twelve games he was currently playing. An irregular Catalan System, and an opening which Robin had finally identified as the Budapest Defence. He wasn't very familiar with either, and had had to do a lot of research in the opening weeks. Now the position was clearer and he was hoping for a win on both boards, eventually, in a few months' time. But he should have got his moves off today. Unless Henderson got his moves by the week-end, he might claim a win on time.

And by the week-end he'd have four more games in, two from White in Chester, and two from Bloomfield in Cambridge.

He was still sitting at his table when the first grey wet light seeped into the sky above Wythenshawe.

NEW YORK

Mrs. Oppenheimer seated herself in a Louis Quinze chair in front of a Louis Seize escritoire. She looked out of the window. Across Fifth Avenue the Central Park reservoir gleamed dully through the murk; beyond, like a spectacular stage backdrop, were the towers and battlements of Central Park West. But she didn't notice the view. She had seen it most days of the year for the past fifteen years, and anyway she was thinking.

She picked up the telephone, which was the only modern thing in the room, and dialled. A girl's voice answered.

"Hello, is that Nancy? This is Joann Oppenheimer. How are you, dear? Is your husband there? Could I speak to him for a moment?"

"He's right here. Would you hold the line?"

There was a brief conversation at the far end. Then Colonel Edmondson came on the line. He sounded wary.

"Hello, how are you?"

"Oh, I'm fine. Listen, I've something to ask you."

"I hope I can answer." He sounded very wary.

"I hear Heller's dropped out of the U.S. team for Munich."

"Who told you that?"

She laughed. "Oh, I have my ear to the ground. And I know the boy to replace him."

"Well, I've quite a number in mind. Who are you thinking of?"

"His name is Jeff Falkner. Jeffrey M. Falkner, if you want it in full."

"That name's new to me. Where is he from?"

"From right here in New York. And the name will be well known to you quite soon. I think he'll be U.S. Champion in a year or two's time. And World Champion three years after that."

Colonel Edmondson laughed. Joann Oppenheimer always went on like that. Every player she met was always on the edge of being World Champion.

"I'd heard you were training an Iranian boy to be World Champion."

"That's right! This is him."

There was a moment's silence at the far end. "What did you say his name was?"

"Jeff Falkner."

"And he's the boy from the slums of Teheran, who can't read and write?"

"He's learning to read and write. He doesn't have to write a thesis, only to play chess. And it was Isfahan, not Teheran."

"What's his real name?"

"Jeff Falkner's his real name now. It's been changed officially. In Iran he was Jaafar Mir-Fakhra'i, but he can't walk around New York with a name like that, giving it in stores and hotels. Anyway, he isn't sure that was his real name, it might have been one of his brothers'. He's not sure that he has the right birth certificate. But it doesn't matter, he's Jeff Falkner now."

Colonel Edmondson wrote it down. Jeff M. Falkner, care of Mrs. Oppenheimer. "What does the M stand for?"

"I don't know. It was Mir, I don't know what it is now." She suddenly took a decision. "It's Merton, you know, like Thomas Merton. The Trappist monk."

He laughed. "Jeffrey Merton Falkner, the boy genius from Iran."

"Yes, laugh if you like, but he is a genius. That's why he should be in the team for Munich."

"But if he's Iranian how can he play for the United States?"

"He's in process of becoming a U.S. citizen. We've taken out the first papers, I'm sponsoring him. I went to Washington and saw the State Department." (You bet! thought Colonel Edmondson.) "You can play for the U.S. while becoming a citizen. Look at John Boghossian, playing in the U.S. Championships at this very moment, and he's meant to be French or Swiss or something."

Colonel Edmondson began to feel persecuted. "Does he speak English?"

"He's learning English." She swept the point away. "Why, I had a cab-driver this morning, and he spoke only Spanish."

Colonel Edmondson thought that was irrelevant, but forbore to point it out. "Has he any qualifications, any good games? Has he played in any tournaments or clubs?"

"No." She paused, and added dramatically: "None at all."

"Well, I hardly feel I could recommend . . ."

"But he's going to. I'm bringing him down to the Manhattan Chess Club tonight for the Rapid Transit tournament. Will you be there?"

"I hope to come, certainly."

"Well, you'll see him in action, then. I bet he beats them all, Sandbach, Chaimovitz, Robert Byrne, Lombardy."

"He'll be good if he can do that. But, all the same, Rapid Transit isn't tournament chess."

"I reckon if he's good enough to beat Sandbach and Robert Byrne in Rapid Transit he's good enough for a students' team. And, Ed, you must send a good team this year. Paul Butler tells me he's found a boy genius in Manchester, England, and he's going to Munich."

Colonel Edmondson groaned. Everybody was always discovering chess geniuses. It was his job to find good players, and build them into a team.

"Listen, Ed, I'll make a bargain with you. If Jeff wins the Rapid Transit tonight will you put him on the plane to Munich? Right?"

"Right, I'll think about it," he said firmly. It was at moments like these that he wished he were back in the Air Force. There was a procedure for choosing the teams and he meant to stick to it. But he also didn't want to annoy Mrs. Oppenheimer. He had been just about to call her himself; he was hoping to get three thousand dollars from her to send Bobby Fischer to Havana. Now he could hardly do that. He couldn't trade a place in the team for three thousand dollars. He couldn't try Mrs. Piatigorsky again, he'd got the money from her last year. Maybe Mrs. Gresser would help him out. He sighed. It was a problem trying to run an organisation, on which the national reputation depended, without enough funds.

"Anyway, dear," Mrs. Oppenheimer chirped, "you'll see what I mean about him tonight. Do bring Nancy too."

He was left holding a dead telephone. A thought came into his mind. Who were the people who wanted Fischer in Cuba? The Cubans. Therefore who would be most likely to pay? The Cubans. Where was the best place to arrange this? Right here in New York at the United Nations. He'd have to go round there tonight or tomorrow, meet the right people, have a drink or two with them, and talk them into it. But it was possible.

He looked across the room at his wife. "Things were easier in the Air Force," he said.

Mrs. Oppenheimer, however, pushed the telephone away briskly, made a note on a pad, and called loudly, "Moraine!" She summoned her daughter like a secretary from another room.

Moraine, who was sitting two yards away unnoticed on a sofa, reading Tennyson, said, "Yes, Mommy?"

"Oh, there you are, dear. You quite made me jump. Well, never mind. Where's Jeff?"

"I don't know," Moraine said wearily. "I guess he's out."

"Out? You're sure he's not in his room? He's meant to be working."

"I think he's out, Mommy, but I'll check if you like."

She put down *The Idylls of the King* beside her on the sofa, stood stiffly up, and went out of the room.

Since his arrival in the States, Jeff had been lodged in Walt's old room, looking out over Ninety-Second Street. Moraine hadn't carried out her threat to move out, partly because she didn't know where to go, and partly because Jeff himself now behaved so impeccably. He had taken the point in Teheran, he wasn't hired to be the lover of either woman. What he was hired to be,

197

what he was doing here, suddenly living a luxurious though chaste life in the East Nineties, was probably still a mystery to him. Mrs. Oppenheimer had explained it all to him several times, but there was no reason to think he had understood. After the homily he would merely bow and salaam and leave the room. He made a point of bowing and salaaming every time he saw either woman. Mrs. Oppenheimer thought it an embarrassing affectation, and several times told him to cut it out. Moraine thought it enchanting. The two Negro servants who looked after the Oppenheimer household regarded him with deep suspicion, but wisely said nothing.

He was meant to work for six hours a day in his room; three hours in the morning learning English and reading and writing with a teacher; and three hours in the afternoon studying chess with Sol Chaimovitz. It was difficult to believe he was making much progress in any subject. He seemed to have learnt only a few words of English; he rarely spoke, and never wrote or read anything. His teacher complained that when she set him work to do in the evenings, reading or writing something, he never did it. But he seemed to listen attentively. Maybe it was her fault, she just wasn't relating to him.

It was much the same with his chess. Sol Chaimovitz told Carl Sandbach about it: "See, I show him an opening, the Sicilian, say, or the Caro-Kann. I explain it to him, tell him what it's all about, why you move this Pawn and not that Pawn. And he listens very politely and you just don't know if he's understood a word. God, I don't think that kid's learnt a word of English since he came here. Anyway, after a few moves I start taking back the pieces to show him a variation, and then he starts moving the pieces himself and lousing it all up. I used to say, 'Listen, this is a lesson, not a game,' but later I thought what the hell. If he wants to play a game, okay, let's play a game, more fun for me. If he doesn't want to learn the Caro-Kann, why should I push it down his throat, see. So we play a game, maybe two, every afternoon, five hundred bucks for that. Why should I care?" He suddenly remembered that Carl was close to Mrs. Oppenheimer, and he must be careful what he said. He didn't want the job to fold up yet. "Anyway, I guess he's learning as much this way as out of a book. Some folks learn better by actual playing, and maybe he's one of them."

"Is he any good? I mean, is he as good as Joann thinks he is?"

"Shit! Nobody in the world is that good! But the kid's got talent, I admit, sort of natural. He seems to play by instinct, fast too, almost Rapid Transit. And boy! are his games wild! Combinations, sacrifices, you never know what he's going to play next. Well, maybe that's a nice change after Reshevsky or Portisch. And his sacrifices! I'd like to match him against Tal. They'd both sacrifice every piece on the board. By the middle-game they'd just have the two Kings left."

"Could he beat Tal, do you mean?"

Chaimovitz had nudged Carl and laughed. "I'm just kidding. Tal would just take him to pieces."

"Joann's still talking about him and me playing a match."

"Yeah, I heard. Two weeks at Miami, all expenses paid and five grand to the winner. Some guys have all the luck, eh? I tell you what, you get sick and drop out, and I'll take your place, and I'll give you a cut of the winnings."

Carl had laughed. "These games you play every afternoon, who usually wins?"

"I usually win. Sometimes I let him win a few games just to keep him happy."

Carl had nodded, understanding.

Moraine came back into the room. "No, he's out, he isn't there."

"But he's meant to be there studying." Chaimovitz had said he couldn't coach Jeff as well as playing in the U.S. Championships. So it had been agreed that Jeff would study by himself for the moment, and watch the Championships, which would be an education in itself. "What's he do with himself when he's out? Is he buying another watch?" she asked.

"Oh, I don't think so. He has two already, the one he bought in Teheran and the Rolex skin-diving one he bought here. I mean, he only has two wrists." Moraine sat down again on the sofa and giggled. "He hasn't gotten round to wearing them on his ankles yet. He has a Ronson lighter, though he doesn't smoke. And a barometer. I think he's planning to buy a camera, one of these ones with big lenses and lots of gadgets. Mommy, why do you have to give him so much money?"

"To keep him happy. Same reason we give you plenty of money. Right, so he isn't buying a watch but he may be checking the cameras some place. You don't think he could be playing chess somewhere?" she asked hopefully.

"I doubt it. He's probably in Times Square."

"Oh no! Not Times Square again. You'd think he'd be sick of those lights by now."

"I don't think it's really the lights," Moraine said thoughtfully. "I mean, I think it's more the time. He checks the time on the Coca-Cola sign and the Accutron sign and the B.O.A.C. sign and all the others, and all the banks too, and checks it with his watches."

"Whatever for?"

"I guess he likes to be sure they all say the same. I suppose it kind of worries him if they don't all say the same thing."

"He must be pretty worried then."

"And the weather too. You know, those signs that say Tomorrow's Weather: Fair or Rain or whatever, and the light on that tower on Seventh Avenue that flashes when it's going to rain, he goes round checking them to see they all say the same."

"Well, at least that suggests that he is beginning to read something."

Moraine gave a big smile. "I think it's sweet. Oh, and do you know the latest? Would you believe the Dow Jones?"

"I never believe the Dow Jones."

"I mean, he goes around all the stockbrokers' offices uptown, you know where they put today's movements in the Dow Jones in their window, and he checks to see if they all say the same."

Mrs. Oppenheimer said, "You seem to know a great deal about his private life, considering his command of English."

Moraine flushed and picked up Tennyson again.

They both looked up at the sound of someone letting himself into the apartment. It could only be one person.

"Jeff!" Mrs. Oppenheimer called, "Jeff, come here!"

He came in, standing just inside the door, looking polite and enquiring. Mrs. Oppenheimer thought once again what an evtremely good-looking boy he was, with his straight nose and his black eyebrows. He seemed to have become paler in New York. Perhaps a lot of his earlier tan had really been suntan, from sitting all day in the Maidan-Shah. Now he might be an Italian. Good clothes had done a lot for him, and he was immaculately groomed. His Brooks Brothers suit was pressed, the heels of his Florsheim Royal Imperial shoes had not been trodden down, he was wearing socks. Only the faintest smell of Revlon's That Man came from him, though it must have been much stronger when he first went out. She didn't mind his wearing two wristwatches, but she must tell him not to wear two gold rings at the same time.

"I want to talk to you."

He came in and salaamed to her and to Moraine.

"I told you before, we don't do that in the States. Now you're an American citizen, or almost, you'd better remember that. In the States we shake hands."

She held out her hand, and he bowed and shook it. He shook hands gravely with Moraine, and started to leave the room.

"No, come back, I want to talk to you."

He went across to her and produced a small piece of paper and gave it to her. She found her reading glasses on the escritoire and studied it. It was difficult to decipher and she held it first one way up, and then the other.

"Please?" he asked.

Suddenly she got the message. She read:

Harris Upham —1.28
Walston & Co —2.35

"Never mind the Dow Jones," she said sharply. "I expect they both say the same now. What I want to know is why weren't you working at your chess this afternoon?"

He said nothing. It was impossible to tell if he was being sulkily silent or patiently uncomprehending.

She moved into gear. "You're meant to be studying chess every afternoon, but you don't. You go out, though God knows where you go or what you do. You're meant to be watching the Championships every evening, but what do you do? You sit there for half an hour, looking at your watch, and then you go to the john, and don't come back. You ought to be following every game, every move, on a pocket board, analysing in your spare time. It's not enough to be a genius, you know. You have to work at it as well, like a violinist or an opera-singer." She paused, took a deep breath, and went on again. "You've a tremendous opportunity now, and if you mess it up it won't come back. You can go all the way from nothing to being United States Champion, World Champion even. But you won't do it if you spend all your time thinking about the Dow Jones. Take Sol Chaimovitz now. He was just a poor uneducated kid from the Bronx. And look at him now, a grandmaster, one of the world's greatest players, travelling all over the world, earning a lot of money. And he didn't do it by looking at the lights in Times Square either. Do you know how you'll end up if you're not careful? You'll end up in Washington Square playing anybody around for a dollar a game. You'll be lucky if you earn ten dollars a day."

She paused again for breath. He held out his hand to say goodbye. She brushed it away.

"What I'm leading up to is that you've a great chance tonight. I'm taking you down to the Manhattan Chess Club to play in the Rapid Transit tournament. It's fast chess, lightning chess, ten seconds a move, just the sort of thing you're good at. You're not ready for the big time yet, but I think you're ready for this. It doesn't matter if you don't yet know all the openings, all the variations. Indeed, it's better if you don't. Play something unexpected, they won't have time to find the answer in ten seconds. All the big names are going to be there—almost all, that is. Sandbach, Byrne, Lombardy, Chaimovitz, Benko, Boghossian and goodness knows who else. If you can beat them, or even do well against them, Colonel Edmondson told me that you're pretty sure to make the Student Team for Munich next month. He's going to be there tonight. You'd like to play for the United States, wouldn't you, even as a student? You'd like to go to Germany, wouldn't you? Well, do your best tonight and maybe you'll make it. Something else—you win that tournament tonight and you'll be famous by morning. You'd like that, wouldn't you?"

She turned on a friendly smile and held out her hand. He took the hint, bowed and shook the hand.

"Well, go and do some study now. The tournament's at eight o'clock."

He salaamed to Moraine and went quietly out.

Moraine said, "Mommy, I think you're wasting your time giving him all that spiel. He didn't understand a word."

Mrs. Oppenheimer was making notes on a pad. "I know, dear. But I had to say it or I'd burst."

Today was an off day in the U.S. Championships. For religious reasons two of the chief competitors, Fischer and Reshevsky, were unable to play on a Saturday, and the Chess Federation had decided that it was easier for everyone to have a rest day. Taking advantage of this, and of all the leading players assembled in New York for the Championships, the Manhattan Chess Club had organised a Rapid Transit tournament in the Henry Hudson Hotel, open to all members, or visiting grandmasters, officials, guests, and pretty well everyone who liked to come.

Mrs. Oppenheimer arrived with Moraine and Jeff in good time. She wanted to see everyone, talk to everyone, before it started. She kissed Mrs. Gresser, greeted Mrs. Piatigorsky, smiled at Lisa Lane and looked to see if Colonel Edmondson had arrived. Moraine wandered over to talk to Carl, smiling as if she had just had wonderful news. Jeff stood by himself, looking rather lost. He had put on an extra amount of That Man just before coming out, and there were some raised eyebrows in his direction. It was Moraine who took pity on him, and brought him over to meet Carl. He started to salaam, caught Moraine's eye, and instead bowed and shook hands.

"I've been hearing a lot about you," Carl said, looking him over with interest. "They say you're pretty good."

Jeff answered politely, "Thank you."

"I hear Mrs. Oppenheimer wants to stage a match between us sometime."

"Please."

"I hear we're to play a match sometime."

"Thank you."

When Colonel Edmondson arrived with his wife, Mrs. Oppenheimer disengaged herself from Mrs. Piatigorsky, scooped up Jeff and, timing it nicely, introduced him to the Executive Director of the U.S. Chess Federation. Colonel Edmondson's eyes widened at the sudden fragrance of That Man. They shook hands, Mrs. Oppenheimer glaring at Jeff in case he might salaam to the Colonel.

"This is Jeff Falkner I was telling you about. You're going to need him in Munich."

"Mrs. Oppenheimer tells me you're a very strong player."

"I said genius, Ed, not just a strong player. It's all right, he doesn't speak English, not yet."

"I hear you're going to beat us all tonight."

"Please."

"I hope you enjoy the tournament this evening."

"Thank you."

Chaimovitz said to Boghossian, "There he is, the boy wonder."

"Uses quite a lot of cologne, doesn't he. Is he a homosexual?"

Chaimovitz gestured meaninglessly. "He hasn't made a pass at me, if that's what you mean. Guess he probably lays Joann every night. You know that dirty book about love in Persia or something, you bet he knows every trick in it, and gives it all to her. She's fallen for him, all right, she can't talk or think about anyone else."

"Well, I suppose it takes her mind off her troubles. How good is he? Is he as good as she says?"

"Hell no, nobody's that good. Well, he has some natural talent. No, I'll be generous, he does have a lot of talent. But he doesn't know the first thing about chess. He doesn't know the Ruy Lopez from his brown ass, and he doesn't mean to, either. He'll never make it to the top, he's too goddam lazy. Well, why should I care?"

"So it will be just one more disappointment for poor Joann." Inquisitiveness overcame him. "Is her husband around? I heard he was back in New York."

"Yeah, he's back. But he hasn't been 'round us. I just hope he doesn't move in with her again. He'd chuck that Arab bastard straight out, and bang goes my job."

"I saw him in Las Vegas."

"Right. He was trying for a Nevada divorce, but he didn't stick it out."

"He seemed pretty bored when I saw him. I saw his girl too."

"Yeah, he'd knocked up his secretary or something."

"Little blonde girl, nice-looking. She was standing at the desk saying she was Mrs. Walter Oppenheimer and asking the clerk to check the mail again and see if there was anything for her. She looked as if she'd been crying all night. So I went up and said I knew her husband—husband, mark you—and could I help. She said no, she was just expecting a letter from him to say when he was coming back. She'd tried to call him at the office, but she couldn't reach him. That sort of stuff."

"Yeah, he just walked out on her."

"Next thing, just as I was leaving, I was at the airport waiting for my flight, and I saw in the local paper that Mrs. Walter Oppenheimer had been hospitalised with a miscarriage."

Chaimovitz stared at him. "You mean she lost the kid? Well! Well, that sure lets old Walter off the hook. Maybe he *will* move back with Joann again." He stared across the room at Mrs. Oppenheimer and Jeff talking to the Gressers. "No, I don't think she'd have him back. I heard her talking to somebody on the phone—I guess it was her lawyer—and she was saying no question of a reconciliation, or something like that. I mean, if this Arab's giving it to her every night what would she want old Walter back for? Bet he couldn't do it every night, never mind all the Persian love-tricks."

Boghossian was watching them too. "It could be you're right. She is certainly obsessed with him."

Colonel Edmondson had been busy arranging the tournament, dividing the players into groups of six. The winner of each group moved on into the next round, and so on to the final and the winner. He asked everyone to make a point of moving on the bell, and not before it, and then he switched on the machine. The bell rang through the tournament room shrilly, maddeningly, every ten seconds. Everyone started to play.

Jeff did badly in his first game. He hadn't understood the Colonel's speech, he didn't understand about moving on the bell. He wasn't accustomed to the shrilling bell, to the ten-second rhythm. He was mated by an unknown player in his group. Halfway through the second game he found his touch. He smiled and nodded in quiet confidence. Mrs. Oppenheimer had been right, this was just his sort of chess, fast, complicated, unprepared. He played irregular openings, happily forgetting all the well-known openings, the over-analysed variations, the theoretical middle-games, the classic end-games. He played a series of glorious improvisations. This was how chess should be, had been before the analysts got to work on it.

He won the other four games and moved on into the next round, the leader of his group. Mrs. Oppenheimer, however, did much less well. Her mind wasn't on her game, she was looking over her shoulder. She was trying to deduce from Jeff's calm profile how he was doing, whether he was winning. She looked round the room to see how the others were doing, how strong the opposition was. Some of the expected grandmasters were missing; no doubt they were in their hotel bedrooms, analysing, preparing for tomorrow's games. But the tournament was still pretty strong, a fierce challenge to a beginner, a baptism of fire. Carl Sandbach was very strong in Rapid Transit; John Boghossian was an unknown factor, he had played so little Rapid Transit in the United States. But she would expect him to do well, and he seemed to be crushing his opponents with some ease. Only Sol Chaimovitz was doing poorly, and this was expected. He needed to take his time to think about a new situation, even if he had to rush his moves later on. But this time was denied him by the bell, an alarm clock ringing every ten seconds, every minute, every hour.

Boghossian, between rounds, commented to Chaimovitz, who had been eliminated, "The boy wonder seems to be doing well."

Chaimovitz answered, "Yeah, he's fine at this sort of thing. Kid's stuff. You know what they say about Rapid Transit? It sorts out the men from the boys. The boys win, the men lose."

Boghossian laughed. He was winning, he didn't mind being thought of as a boy. But he was eliminated in the next round by an unknown young man. There were dozens of these playing tonight, students from Columbia or New York University, immensely keen and expert, well prepared, quick thinking, tireless. They were the terror of the champions, of the tired grandmasters. Even when they were eliminated from the tournament they still went on playing each other, moving on the bell, trying as hard as they had at the start. After two hours there were almost as many boards in play as there had been at the beginning.

Mrs. Oppenheimer, however, gave up after the first round. She was in no mood to play practice games against others who had lost. Instead she hovered behind Jeff, watching every move he made, clucking like a hen, willing him, praying him to win. Jeff, fortunately, didn't seem to notice her. He was concentrating on his games, grave, silent, smiling faintly at his opponents as they resigned.

In the semi-final he defeated the unknown young man who had beaten Boghossian. In the final he found himself facing Carl

Sandbach, who was favourite to win. The game was played not on a platform, not behind ropes, but in the middle of the bare strip-lit room, across an ordinary table. There was no silence. Everybody left their own games and crowded round, breathing down the players' necks, talking. The young experts commented aloud on the game. Mrs. Oppenheimer stood and palpitated behind Jeff, Moraine hovered by Carl. The bell rang remorselessly through the room.

Chaimovitz, who couldn't see, perched on a table away from the throng and said to Boghossian, "Bet you a dollar the Arab wins."

Boghossian shook his head. "It's hard work earning a dollar. I'm not parting with it so easily."

Jeff had drawn White and opened with P–KN3. It soon became apparent that he was playing an irregular King's Indian Attack, which transposed into a Double Fianchetto Attack. Carl calmly built up a strong position in the centre, and then Jeff hit back with a series of hammer-blows. It became apparent to the experts that Carl had over-extended himself. His pieces seemed to be on the wrong squares, while Jeff's were placed more exactly. Carl began to chew the tips of his fingers.

The middle-game was involved and difficult. There was a massacre of exchanges, and when the dust had settled it was seen that Jeff was two Pawns up, one being a passed Pawn. In addition both players had a Bishop on opposite-colour squares. Carl now had his black Knight mascot out of his pocket, and was fiddling with it.

Things were momentarily calmer in the end-game. There was a manœuvring of Kings and Pawns. Suddenly Jeff took one of Carl's Pawns with his Bishop, putting the Bishop *en prise*. Carl had ten seconds to decide whether to accept the Bishop sacrifice. He accepted it, taking the Bishop with his King, moving his King in the process fatally out of position. Jeff advanced his passed Pawn.

Three moves later Carl resigned with a handshake, a nod and a smile. Jeff would Queen his Pawn in two moves and he could do nothing to prevent it. There was a loud burst of clapping as the two players stood up. Moraine clapped too. Mrs. Oppenheimer felt hot with pride.

They turned off the bell while Mrs. Edmondson presented the

trophies: a Rook on a stand to Jeff, a Knight on a stand to the lady who had got farthest through the tournament, Mrs. Gresser. Jeff accepted his award charmingly, saying, "Thank you, please, thank you," smiling shyly, shaking hands with Mrs. Edmondson, with Colonel Edmondson, with Carl, with Moraine, with Mrs. Gresser, with Mr. Gresser, with anyone else who congratulated him. He salaamed Mrs. Oppenheimer which brought a cheer. The Shah himself couldn't have done it better.

A woman beside Moraine said, "It's just not fair to be as handsome as that, and to play chess so well."

Moraine said loyally, "Carl Sandbach is pretty good-looking too."

"Yes, that's right."

Someone turned on the machine again, and the bell started to ring every ten seconds. Everyone drifted back to the tables and started playing friendly games against each other. An unknown young man challenged Jeff to a game. Mrs. Oppenheimer found herself playing Colonel Edmondson.

She lost easily. Her mind wasn't on chess tonight, at least not on her own games. She felt happy, triumphant, completely justified in everything she had done, but not able to play chess herself at the moment. The lights were too bright, the bell which had been ringing for nearly three hours was making her head ache.

She looked round for Jeff. He was still playing, while a small group stood round watching. It suddenly dawned on her that this was potentially a damaging moment. He was in danger of being spoilt, lionised, made to feel too successful. And it did a promising player no good to play too many Rapid Transit friendlies. Too many quick thoughtless games, when he ought to be preparing for serious chess at the proper speed. Awful thought, he might want to play for money; she knew him capable of it. Worse, he might lose. Nobody could win every game, and the opposition was strong. He had made his presence felt, his impact, his sensational win. She musn't let him fritter it away now.

She stood up, pleaded a headache, and said she must go home. She stopped Jeff starting another game, and pulled him away to say goodbye to her friends.

To Colonel Edmondson she said, "Well, you see what I mean.

You'll have to take him to Munich now, won't you. I'll call you in the morning. 'Bye, Ed, it's been a lovely evening; 'bye, Nancy." She towed Jeff around, saying goodbye to her friends.

"Congratulations on your win."

"Please."

Moraine stayed behind. She was sitting beside Carl, watching him play Chaimovitz. The two men had spent a great deal of time sitting across the table from each other. They had met in the Championships on last Wednesday afternoon. After three sessions, three adjournments, their game was still unfinished. It was a complicated end-game which might yet end in a draw. The next session for adjourned games was on Tuesday morning. In the meantime they were relaxing by playing each other at Rapid Transit chess. The two men were in great contrast: the stocky sweating man from New York, and the lanky finger-biting boy from Los Angeles. Both geniuses, both dedicated, but it was impossible to know if they were great friends or great enemies. Even Moraine had no idea.

Mrs. Oppenheimer sighed with relief when she got Jeff into the elevator, away from that bell and the noise and the corrupting adulation. Out on the street it was cold and cloudy, and she wrapped her mink coat closer around her. In other years Walter would have driven her home in the Lincoln, but now she had to fend for herself. Jeff just stood there beside her, holding his trophy. He didn't understand that he was meant to find her a cab.

They walked briskly down to Seventh Avenue, and found a cab setting down outside the Park Sheraton. Mrs. Oppenheimer sank back on the seat. She felt unbelievably happy, euphoric, very tired. Maybe, she thought, I'll look back later and think this was the happiest moment of my whole life. She glanced at Jeff's fine silhouette. He was peering out of the window at the signs, at one above them. Of course, she thought, he's checking the weather forecast, the star that flashes when it is going to rain.

"Is it going to be fine tomorrow?" she asked, but he didn't answer. He was looking ahead now, towards the lights of Times Square.

The cab turned left into the comparative darkness of Fifty-Fourth Street. As they crossed the Avenue of the Americas, Jeff looked out at the great glass canyon. Even in the middle of Saturday night the Sperry Rand Building was ablaze with lights. There were lights too in the Penney Building, in the Hilton. A sign gave the time as 11:17. Jeff checked it with his watches.

Mrs. Oppenheimer decided she must say something to him. She had banked so much on him, on his performance tonight, and he hadn't let her down. So she spoke, expressing her thanks, her appreciation of his win, her admiration of his games, particularly the last one against Carl. It was a fine start to an exciting career, which would bring him fame and fortune, the U.S. Championship certainly in due course, the World Championship probably in the end.

She ran down. She was tired, she hadn't expressed herself very well and anyway he didn't understand English. But he should have taken the point from her tone.

He held up his trophy for her to see. "How much?" he asked. "How much dollars?"

"Only a few. That's not the point. This is a prestige prize. You'll win the big money in Miami. You'll get five thousand dollars if you win, if you beat Carl Sandbach like tonight." She almost added, "And two thousand if you lose," but she bit it back. Jeff might understand, he might be quite happy to lose for two thousand dollars.

They crossed Fifth Avenue, which was one-way traffic going downtown, and finally turned left on Madison. Jeff peered out along Fifty-Ninth Street, past the General Motors Building, at the Plaza, the crowds lining up to get into the Playboy Club. He was getting ready for a flashing glimpse of the Dow Jones in the stockbrokers' window on the next block. This part of town was one of his haunts.

Then they were out of the area. They went north for thirty-two blocks, past the hotels with their blue awnings, and the dark art galleries, and the apartment blocks. They turned left on Ninety-First Street and turned on to Fifth Avenue. Mrs. Oppenheimer climbed out slowly. The lights of the lobby were welcoming.

"I know what we need," she said. "A celebration. I've a little surprise for you."

The servants were off duty, so she got out the champagne

herself. Mumm's Cordon Rouge, Brut. She filled the bucket with cold water and ice, found tulip glasses, and brought them into the living-room. It suddenly dawned on her that Jeff was probably a Moslem and therefore teetotal. True, she hadn't noticed him putting his forehead on the floor or facing east at sunset. Anyway, he was American now, and Americans weren't Moslems, and it was high time he learnt to hold his liquor. She opened the bottle and poured two glasses.

"To your next tournament win," she toasted him.

"Thank you."

She sank down on to the Chippendale sofa, and waved him to the Louis Quatorze armchair opposite. She drank half the glass, and Jeff did the same. She began a long monologue about chess, about the great players, about Fischer and Reshevsky and Botvinnik, about the great tournaments, Sochi, Bled, Mar del Plata, Hastings, Los Angeles, about the prospect before him, Munich, Miami, Moscow.

She poured herself a second glass, started to pour him one too, and then checked herself. If this was the first time he had ever tasted alcohol, one glass was quite enough. She mustn't let him become debauched, dissipated. She had brought him home early from the club, and now an hour later here he was sitting in a genuine antique armchair, sipping champagne, and listening politely to an incomprehensible monologue. He must go to bed.

She said abruptly, "Good night," and held out her hand. He knew the signal and reacted like one of Pavlov's dogs, shaking hands, bowing, going to his room. Mrs. Oppenheimer drank the rest of the champagne, sitting alone, dreaming of Munich and Miami and Moscow. When Moraine returned she found her mother half-drunk.

"There's a glass left. Would you like it?"

"No, thank you, Mommy. You have it."

Moraine went and fetched some Seven-Up from the kitchen.

"Well, who won?" Mrs. Oppenheimer asked. "Carl or Sol?"

"Oh, they're still playing. Carl had won two, and Sol one when I left. Oh, and Mommy, it looks as if Carl really means to come to Miami. He said he'd have his revenge on Jeff there, and Jeff would find match chess pretty different from Rapid Transit. Carl said he'd take him to pieces."

Mrs. Oppenheimer poured out the last glass and laughed. "That's great, as long as he comes. I want him to try his best. I don't want Jeff to win too easily like tonight. I want it to be in doubt till the last game."

Moraine said, "Oh, Mommy, you *are* going to have a hangover tomorrow." She came up and kissed her mother. "Still, you've worked hard for this, haven't you?"

But Mrs. Oppenheimer woke the next morning feeling fine. She had slept right through the night in the big Roi Soleil bed. She had become used to having it to herself, to Walter not being there. She hadn't once switched on the bedside light (a Ming vase with a huge pink silk shade). The things on the night-table, the copy of *Modern Chess Openings,* the pocket set, the score-pad, the latest copy of *Chess Life,* the signed copy of Paul Butler's *The Early Middle-Game,* were all untouched since Betty had dusted them the day before. She had slept right through.

She had woken clear-headed with a bright idea. Why don't I cable Paul Butler, tell him about Jeff last night, suggest he puts it in his own papers, build up the two young geniuses, Jeff and this Manchester boy Paul had discovered, work up some excitement for their meeting in Munich? And just as soon as she'd fixed it with Colonel Edmondson, she'd try to get it into the American papers. *Chess Life, The New York Times, Time* magazine, *Life.* Other centres too, Boston, Chicago, Dallas, L.A., San Francisco. Maybe she should hire a publicity agent for Jeff, for the Miami match as a whole. She'd better alert the Florida papers. But she'd better make sure of Munich first. She looked at her bedside clock. Quarter of nine. Too early to call the Edmondsons on a Sunday morning.

When Betty brought her her coffee in bed, she was propped up, drafting her cable on the score-pad.

PAUL BUTLER 12 HARRINGTON GARDENS LONDON SW7 DEAR PAUL MY DISCOVERY GENIUS JEFFREY FALKNER FROM IRAN SCORED FAMOUS WIN LAST NIGHT MANHATTAN CLUB RAPID TRANSIT STOP WON OVER NINETY SEVEN PLAYERS INCLUDING SANDBACH CHAIMOVITZ BOGHOSSIAN STOP GAME AGAINST SANDBACH TOTAL MASTERPIECE INCLUDING ROOK AND PAWN END-GAME WITH BISHOP SACRIFICE STOP PITY NOBODY WROTE IT DOWN OTHERWISE MIGHT HAVE BECOME

CLASSIC LIKE EVERGREEN STOP HOWBOUT YOUR GENIUS STOP SUGGEST YOU WRITE UP BOTH BOYS IN ALL YOUR PAPERS AND BUILD UP TO THEIR GAME IN MUNICH STOP EYELL TRY ARRANGE SAME FOR YOUR GENIUS IN PAPERS HERE IF YOU SEND DETAILS AND PERFORMANCE RECORDS STOP THINK WE MAY BE ON TO SOMETHING TREMENDOUS DO WRITE AND ANYWAY SEE YOU MUNICH HAPPY CHRISTMAS

LOVE JOANN

Satisfied, she telephoned it through to an extraordinarily stupid girl in Western Union. Then, irritated but triumphant, she leant back on the pillows and sipped her now rather tepid coffee. The telephone rang. Hoping it was one or other Edmondson, she picked it up.

"Can I speak to Mr. Walter Oppenheimer?" said a girl's voice.

"Which one?"

"The elder. The father."

"He doesn't live here any more. Come to that, neither of them do. One's at the St. Regis. The other's in Cambridge, Massachusetts."

"I've called the St. Regis, but they say he's checked out." The girl sounded forlorn.

"Who is that speaking?" asked Mrs. Oppenheimer, knowing already.

"Why, this is Debbie. I'm sorry to bother you, Mrs. Oppenheimer, I just thought maybe he . . ."

"Well, he's not," Mrs. Oppenheimer said sharply. "Right now he's probably riding in Central Park."

"Riding?"

"Yes, why not? He always rides every Sunday morning in Central Park. Didn't you know? Didn't he ever tell you that? He never misses his Sunday-morning ride, even when it's raining like today. He always says he likes it better when it's raining, makes him feel earthier."

"What?"

"Earthier, dear. More animal. You should know. Why don't you call the Tavern on the Green and ask them to give him a shout as he rides by. Or maybe you're joining him there for lunch?"

213

"Oh no! I just wondered if he was . . ."

"Your best plan, dear, is to drop by and see him at the office tomorrow morning. He won't be able to get away from you there. I expect you still remember the address," she added icily.

"I can't!" the girl wailed. "I'm in Los Angeles."

"Are you? Well, I expect you're having nice sunny weather."

"He wants me to stay here," she blurted out. "He's gotten me an apartment and a job with Webster and Fish . . ."

"You take it, dear. You stay right there on the Coast."

She put down the receiver sharply, feeling as if a debt, or a part of it, had just been repaid. Glad, annoyed, embarrassed, all at once. She looked at the clock. Ten minutes before ten. Ten minutes before seven on a Sunday morning in L.A. The girl must be desperate.

She finished her cold coffee, smiling at the very idea of Walter riding in Central Park in the rain. He had once as a boy been sent to take a vacation on a dude ranch in Arizona, and he grumbled about it still. She laughed and went to the bathroom.

Later she gathered up Moraine and Jeff and took them out to brunch at the Rainbow Room. This had been her habit with Walter. Clarence and Betty couldn't prepare lunch as they were attending some immensely long service on 112th Street, and she and Walter, often rising late, had taken to brunching out. Now that Walter was gone she went on with it. She wondered where Walter would be brunching today. Not at the Rainbow Room, obviously. Nor at the Tavern on the Green, not on a day like this. And, for that matter, where was he living, now that he had apparently left the St. Regis?

Being Sunday, Jeff had put on a large amount of Arden's Sandalwood, and there were some surprised looks in the elevator of the R.C.A. Building. But the abrupt change in altitude took their minds from their noses to their ears, and they pressed their fingers over their eardrums. On the sixty-fifth floor Mrs. Oppenheimer led the way out, checked her mink coat and entered the restaurant. The *maître d'*, who knew her well, greeted her and led her to her usual table on the north side.

The first time Jeff had seen the view he had shown some slight signs of astonishment. But the novelty had worn off some weeks ago, and anyway there was nothing to see today. Grey sleeting clouds blew past the window, hiding everything, even the next building. The *maître d'* brought the menus, but Mrs. Oppenheimer barely glanced at hers and Jeff presumably could hardly read his. She ordered, as she did every Sunday, orange juice, Eggs Benedict, coffee and iced water for herself and Jeff. Moraine, who liked to be capricious and incalculable, ordered something different every week. Today it was English kippers. Then Mrs. Oppenheimer sat back, looked round the room, and waved to the other regulars.

When the orange juice came, in the tureens of ice, she started in on Jeff. He was not, she thought, taking sufficient interest in the chess games they were going to watch that afternoon, in the U.S. Championship as a whole. The Championship, she explained, was one of the world's greatest tournaments. It was also, every third year (though not, unfortunately, this year), the Nation's Zonal Tournament where the three greatest players in the nation would be chosen to go forward into the Interzonal and, if possible, onward to the World Championship. And it wasn't true that this year's Championship would be dull and, as some journalists had suggested, a routine formality. Of course, it was obvious that Fischer would win, and Sandbach come second. But the third place was wide open: Evans, Benko, Reshevsky, Byrne, Chaimovitz, Lombardy, any of them might take it. And then there was the question of how easily Fischer would win; would he lose or draw any games, and if so how many? How far behind him would Sandbach be? Might he even tie with Fischer?

And then there was Boghossian, playing in his first U.S. Championship, the new element, the controversial figure. A nicely timed piece in *Time* had pointed out his unusual tactics, his psychological approach, his use of "gamesmanship" to unnerve his opponents; especially the manifest enmity between him and Sandbach. Three times they had now played, at Mar del Plata, Bled and Montreal, and each time Boghossian had won—"swindled the win," as Sandbach put it. Today would be their fourth meeting. Would Sandbach gain his revenge?

"And, anyway, there'll be fine chess played on every board. So I hope you'll watch it all carefully. Have you brought your pocket board with you? You'll be wanting to analyse the games as they go along."

"Oh, Mommy," said Moraine, "I don't know why you bother." Jeff gazed blankly at them both.

Mrs. Oppenheimer glanced at her watch, summoned the waiter and ordered cocktails. The waiter said it was not yet one o'clock. Mrs. Oppenheimer showed him her watch (diamonds, from Cartier). Jeff, getting the idea, showed him both his. The waiter gave way, and took the order. Mrs. Oppenheimer ordered a daiquiri, Moraine a tomato juice on the rocks.

"Champagne," said Jeff.

"Certainly not," said Mrs. Oppenheimer. She turned to the waiter. "Beer for Mr. Falkner. He likes Miller's High Life. It's called the champagne of bottled beers," she added pacifyingly to Jeff.

He pulled a postcard out of his pocket and showed it to Moraine. "What is it?" he asked.

"Why, it's a Christmas tree. It's the Christmas tree on Rockefeller Plaza, just below us here. Mommy, it's a picture of the Christmas tree here."

"So I gathered."

"What is it?"

Moraine gasped. "Of course, Mommy, he's never seen a Christmas tree."

"You explain it to him, dear. You tell him all about Christmas."

"But I can't! I don't speak Iranian."

"Well, tell him in English then. It doesn't matter if he doesn't follow you. At least you'll have tried." She added, "And while you're about it, explain to him why you have to have your cocktails after lunch instead of before it on Sundays. He may not follow that either."

Moraine scowled, and ate her lime sherbet. Mrs. Oppenheimer called for the bill, and charged it to her American Express card. Then she swept her party out into the lobby. She seized Jeff's arm and pointed at the sign leading to the men's rest-room.

"You go to the john right now," she commanded, "especially after drinking beer. I don't want to see you slipping out in the middle of the game."

He obeyed, and so did Moraine. Mrs. Oppenheimer called for the coats. Then she led them down in the ear-popping elevator, out into the sleet on Fiftieth Street. The women huddled into their furs. Mrs. Oppenheimer, checking to make sure that Jeff was still with them, led them firmly over to the avenue and round the corner to the Hilton.

Entering the Hilton, she experienced her usual feeling that she was entering Grand Central or the Airlines Terminal at rush hour. But she didn't falter. She led her small party to the right, up the escalator, along the interminable corridor, past the ballroom, to the Austin Room, where the Championship was being held.

Being Sunday afternoon there was a crowd of three or four hundred assembled to watch the afternoon play. The boards were set up on a low platform on two sides of the hall. Beside each board, operated by a keen young boy, was a form of epidiascope which threw a picture of the game on a huge white board above, for all to see. Mrs. Oppenheimer found three seats opposite the board on which Sandbach was to play Boghossian, sat Jeff down to keep them, and went off to chat with her friends. Moraine went to talk to Carl Sandbach, who was already on the platform.

Most of the other players were already present: Fischer at the snack table at the end, hastily eating a sandwich; Chaimovitz, seated at his board, his head buried in his hands, staring at the pieces as if he were already in a difficult situation; Lombardy, in his Jesuit's soutane, talking to Colonel Edmondson; Reshevsky, his head properly covered with a hair-piece, so that he might be able to drink coffee during the game, sitting quietly at his table, waiting for it all to start. Boghossian, as expected, was still missing.

At two-thirty the umpire called for silence, asked everyone to be particularly quiet during today's play, asked for photographers to use their flash-bulbs only during the first five minutes, and the spectators not to eat in the main part of the room. Then he walked along the tables, starting the White players' clocks.

Sandbach immediately pushed out his Queen's Pawn, stopped his clock, wrote down the move, glared at the empty chair opposite him, and sat back and crossed his legs. He took his black Knight out of his pocket and began to fiddle with it. He smiled at Moraine. Then, at a loose end, he stood up, uncoiled to his full height, and wandered along the other tables, seeing which openings they were all doing. A photographer flashed a picture of the empty table.

After five minutes Sandbach, still without an opponent, returned to his own table, checked to see that Boghossian's clock was ticking, examined his score-pad and pencil, smiled again at Moraine, studied the position on his own board, climbed to his feet again and strode off to see how Fischer's game was coming along. Then he went back to his own table, and started fiddling with his Knight.

"Relax, boy, relax," said Mrs. Oppenheimer aloud.

The rest of the room was humming too. The umpire shushed loudly.

Boghossian finally arrived fifteen minutes later. This was the moment the photographers were waiting for, flashing him as he entered the room. He strolled in, relaxed, unhurried, smiling at friends, pausing to say hello to Mrs. Oppenheimer, Moraine, Mrs. Gresser, the Edmondsons. Finally he reached the platform and shook hands with Carl Sandbach, who politely rose to his feet, and towered over him, fifteen inches taller.

This was the other moment for the photographers, who crouched round the table, flashing the handshake and even the clock. As it was long after the five-minute period, Fischer immediately rose from his seat to complain to the umpire. The umpire shushed vigorously and drove the photographers away. Boghossian sat down, checked his clock, slowly unscrewed his ball-point, and wrote the names and Sandbach's one move down on the pad. Then he sat back and studied the simple position so far. Finally, he moved out his King's Knight.

The game was under way. Sandbach had taken a few seconds over his first move, Boghossian twenty-two minutes. The room became very quiet.

Five minutes later it became noisy again when the expert audience realised the sensational fact that Boghossian was playing the Lugano Variation against Sandbach.

"Crazy, just plain crazy to play the Lugano against Carl Sandbach," said the man sitting immediately behind Mrs. Oppenheimer.

She turned round. "Right. But it'll give him a big pull psychologically. It may be worth the risk."

"It is not!" said the man firmly. "Psychological advantage doesn't count for much in grandmaster chess compared with in-depth analysis. Carl Sandbach has analysed this variation to Move 20."

Bobby Fischer rose wrathfully to complain about the noise, and the umpire shushed frantically.

"Oh, Mommy," Moraine whispered, "looks like Carl will win now."

The Lugano Variation had first been tried out by Bogolyubov in Lugano in 1932, hence the name; and again the following year at the Unilever Tournament in Amsterdam. But he had no great success with it, and dropped it. After the war Lilienthal and Kotov experimented with it in Moscow, but extensive analysis showed it to be unsound. Then in the sixties Carl Sandbach had taken it up, analysed it at greater length, introduced some new ideas for the King's and King's Bishop's Pawn, and had had some remarkable successes with it, the most recent being against Dietrich at Bled. In essence it was a variation of the Gruenfeld Defence, but with the black King remaining uncastled in the middle of the rank, and Black making stronger efforts not to lose control of the centre while developing his Bishops. Nimzowitsch would have hated it, but Carl Sandbach had gone on record recently that it was the finest modern defence against the Queen's Pawn opening. And now Boghossian was playing it against him.

Mrs. Oppenheimer looked round to make sure that her protégé was following the subtlety and excitement of all this, but Jeff was not following any part of it. Almost alone in the room, he was making absolutely no noise. His legs were crossed, his left hand was in his lap, and he was studying his Rolex with concentration. Mrs. Oppenheimer wondered crossly if he were timing his breathing; it wasn't possible otherwise to look so long at a watch without getting bored. She nudged him and pointed at Carl Sandbach's game.

"He's playing the Lugano against Carl," she whispered, hoping that, after all these weeks of instruction from Chaimovitz, the phrase might have some meaning for him. Otherwise, of course, it would be totally incomprehensible.

It was impossible to know if he understood or not. He half bowed, half nodded at her and glanced towards the players. Then he rose to his feet and began to edge out.

"Oh no! Not already! You can't want to go again so soon."

He was edging further away from her along the line. She called after him, "You didn't drink that much beer! You come right back after you've been."

Everybody was staring at her and shushing. Bobby Fischer turned round and glared at her. The umpire looked at her, held up both his hands, and shushed her personally. Mrs. Oppenheimer felt embarrassed and furious. The room was rather hot too, the heating perhaps too high. She eased her mink off her shoulders on to the back of the chair. How could Jeff go out at a moment like this! And after all she'd said to him. Didn't he understand anything?

Jeff, nodding graciously to the doorkeeper, went out of the room, and so he missed the sensation of the tournament. Ten minutes later Carl Sandbach suddenly held out his hand to Boghossian in resignation. He gave a bleak smile, nodded, signed the score-sheet, and rose to his feet. As he walked out of the room, he nodded to Mrs. Oppenheimer, caught Moraine's eye, and jerked his head towards the door. Moraine climbed back into her fur coat, stood up and edged after him. Mrs. Oppenheimer was left alone, an empty seat on either side of her.

The room was in uproar. Fischer stood up and strode to the umpire to complain about the noise. Even Chaimovitz looked round. The umpire shushed feverishly, even announcing that he would clear the room if there wasn't silence immediately. Only the photographers were missing. Gradually silence seeped back. Mrs. Oppenheimer looked round frantically for Jeff. Perhaps he hadn't missed it, perhaps he had returned from the john and was standing at the back. The boy marking the game put the figure 1 beside Boghossian's name on the board. The umpire hissed and shushed again. Any moment, he knew, Bobby Fischer would demand to have his game transferred to a private room.

It was a pretty sensational event. After the build-up of the Sandbach-Boghossian game, with the known enmity between the two players, it had been assumed that they would fight on till the bitter end. To resign on the thirteenth move would have been startling enough even in a provincial unimportant tournament. To do it here was almost unbelievable. It meant, amongst other things, that now Carl Sandbach would have almost no chance of catching Fischer, of becoming joint U.S. Champion. Even if he won his adjourned game against Chaimovitz, which was very doubtful, he might easily lose the second place.

The room hummed with speculation. Was it because Boghossian was playing the Lugano Defence? Was Carl Sandbach sulking? Or was there simply no answer to the Lugano, and was Carl Sandbach simply accepting the inevitable defeat? (Keen young men brought out their pocket boards to demonstrate to their neighbours or girl friends that the Lugano was by no means as marvellous as that, that there were several good lines against it, and, anyway, had not Lilienthal said it was unsound?) Or was there some deep strategic tournament plan? Was Sandbach conserving his strength, wisely avoiding what might be a long game, to keep himself fresh for certain wins later on? But in that case wouldn't he have tried for a draw around Move 30? And wasn't this *the* game in the whole tournament for him, the one that he wanted most to win? The umpire shushed and shushed. Never had he known such a terrible afternoon.

Mrs. Oppenheimer was feeling pretty gloomy too, isolated in the middle of the front row in front of an empty board. Jeff had walked out on her once again, after all she had said to him. Carl Sandbach had lost ignominiously to Boghossian. How was she ever to work up interest in a match between Jeff and Carl? Maybe she should try to match Jeff and Boghossian? Or Jeff and Fischer? Or Carl and Fischer? Or Boghossian and Fischer? Or Boghossian and Chaimovitz? Or Boghossian and Reshevsky? Or Fischer and Reshevsky, once again? She felt hopeless, she wanted to cry.

Moraine caught up with Carl in the passage outside.

"Honey, what happened?"

"Nothing happened. I just lost, that's all."

"But everyone was saying you were bound to win, with him playing your favourite defence."

"Looks like everyone was wrong. Not for the first time."

"But it was so soon. It was only Move 13."

"Why not? What's the point of going on with something once it's over?"

"You mean he was bound to win with that defence? Against you, against anybody?"

"I didn't say that. Look, let's go get ourselves a drink."

He led the way down the escalator, across the lobby to the Roman Pub. The bar was almost deserted. Carl perched on a high stool at the bar, hardly needing to take his feet off the floor. Moraine climbed up beside him. The bartender stood before them, a Negro wearing a sort of Roman tunic. She ordered a Coke, Carl a glass of Michelob beer.

She sipped it, looked across the bar. At a table against the wall, under a mural of the Campidoglio, Jeff was sitting, in front of a stein of beer. He caught her eye and salaamed across the room at her. She nodded back. Maybe she ought to go across to him, tell him to go back to her mother in the Austin Room. She thought better of it. If he didn't want to watch chess, why should she pressure him? Anyway, Jeff ought to be feeling astonished at seeing Carl sitting there drinking beer. Carl who was meant to be playing a needle game for the next four and a half hours, and was now suddenly free to sit in a bar. But Jeff showed no curiosity, or at least not enough to cross the bar and ask what had happened.

Carl gulped at his beer, let out a long breath and said, "That's better."

"Honey, I may be dumb, but I still don't get it. You threw that game, didn't you?"

"I lost."

"But why? Everyone was sure that was the one game you wanted to win. You gave up without a fight."

"Maybe I was tired after the Rapid Transit last night. Or maybe I was keeping myself fresh for tomorrow. You choose."

"You mean your adjourned game against Chaimovitz? Or your regular game? But that's supposed to be an easy one for you."

"All the more reason not to mess it up."

Moraine felt bewildered. It didn't make any sense to her. Perhaps Carl was just kidding her. But it was so unfair the way everybody kept assuming she knew all the answers without being told. She looked up at the blue ceiling above the bar, with the little lights representing the Roman night sky. She looked round at the murals behind the sham window-frames: St. Peter's, the Forum, that castle by the Tiber, another scene she couldn't recognise. Rome! She had been there for the first time this spring, she and Daddy and Mommy and Debbie on their way through to the Middle East. It was almost the last time they had all been together, and everyone had seemed to be so happy. And she had loved the city itself, the little open-air restaurants in the Piazza Navona, the fountains, the smell of the pines in the garden of their hotel. She'd like to go back sometime soon; with Carl, and they'd just think about each other and about the city. Nobody seemed interested in chess in Rome. Carl had called it disdainfully the city without chess. Paris was another. Paris was romantic too.

A leaflet about the hotel was lying on the bar beside her. She picked it up idly and read: "The Roman Pub. The spirit of Don Quixote and Mediaeval Spain surrounds you in this lovely room, where cocktails, spicy Spanish appetisers, and casual entertainment bring a welcome respite from the bustling world outside." But surely Rome was in Italy, she puzzled.

"Shit!" said Carl beside her. "That goddam Armenian swindler."

The bartender glared at him. Moraine said, "You mean it was because of Boghossian? You weren't just trying to keep yourself fresh? Was it because of that defence he played?"

"Oh, work it out for yourself." He picked up the tab. "Come on, let's get out of here. Let's go for a drive."

They waited in the lobby while the boy fetched Carl's blue Thunderbird from the parking lot under the hotel. Moraine fastened herself into her seat with her seat-belt. She knew Carl's driving. Always a fast driver, he drove specially fast when he was in a mood like this. She liked the feeling of speed herself, in a convertible with the top down, and the wind blowing her cheeks and hair. It wasn't so exciting sealed up in a car on a cold day. You couldn't feel anything physical.

He drove across town on Fifty-Fifth and turned on to Seventh Avenue, downtown, miles downtown, into the Village, past the Village Vanguard, Sheridan Square. There were warm lights in the Riviera, and she turned up the heater. Further on he turned right, towards the Holland Tunnel.

So we're going to New Jersey, she thought. Probably the New Jersey Turnpike. But he didn't take the turning for the Turnpike, he kept on through the grim factories and lots of Newark on to the Pulaski Skyway, westward towards Pennsylvania.

"Where are we going?" she asked.

He didn't answer. He didn't hear me, she thought, he's thinking about that game. If only I understood what was going on. But nobody will ever tell me anything.

She turned on the radio: the headline news from Vietnam, a

record of Jerry Vale singing "Love Is a Many-Splendoured Thing" (which she loved), a commercial about used cars, the time, the temperature, the weather report, the top story from Vietnam, a record of Sinatra singing "The Shadow of Your Smile" (which she loved), a commercial about a furniture store giving discounts, the time, the temperature, the weather report, the top story from Vietnam.

They were in open country now, and Interstate 78 uncoiled in front of them. Carl kept in the fast lane, ten or even twenty miles an hour over the speed limit, leaving the trucks, the Volkswagens, the cautious cars far behind. Dusk came on them slowly, blotting out the rolling landscape. The lit signs flashed by—Mobil, Quality Court, Becker's Old Dutch Barn. Carl switched on the lights, and Moraine stole a glance at his profile. He's still thinking about chess, she thought.

They stopped in Allentown for gas. Moraine said she was hungry, and they went into a Howard Johnson's. Moraine ordered a Seven-Up and a buttercrunch-flavour ice-cream. Carl had a corn-beef sandwich on rye, and coffee. Moraine nerved herself to pester him once more. She had to know, she couldn't stand being left any longer in the dark.

She was beside him at the counter. She gave him her prettiest smile and said, "Honey, be nice to me. I know I'm very stupid about chess, but please tell me why you threw that game." He was swallowing some bread—she had timed it badly—so she went on, "Was it because he was playing that defence? I mean, was he bound to win? Isn't there any answer to it?"

"Sure there's an answer to it. There's an answer to everything in chess, every attack, every defence. Nothing's bound to win."

"Well, then, but why . . . ?"

"You think I'm going to give that long-nosed swindler a free demonstration on how to play White against the Lugano? Let him sweat it out himself if he wants to, I'm not going to show him how to do it. It would be round the world by morning. What's the point in winning one point here if I also tell every Commie player the best line against the Lugano? Better give away a point than that."

Moraine was trying to work this out. "You mean you might have won if you'd gone on?"

"Maybe, maybe not. But what's one point against all I would lose later? Yeah, sure he knew all that too. He knew he'd gotten me on the hook. Either I throw him the game or I give him a free lesson on how to play White against the Lugano. So I threw him the game. Right?"

Moraine didn't know what to say.

"I don't go around giving lessons for free. Like Sol Chaimovitz, I want to be paid. But I know one thing. I've learnt one thing today."

"What's that?"

"I'll never open again with the Queen's Pawn against that Armenian chiseller."

To Moraine it seemed rather a small lesson to be drawn from such a sensational event. Maybe she still didn't understand it properly. She finished her Seven-Up and began to think warmly of home. It was going to be a long drive back.

"Okay, let's go."

The car was cold after the stop, and she strapped the seat-belt tight over her fur coat. Carl would drive fast back along the Interstate. But, pulling out of the lot, he turned west.

"Honey, where are we going?" The radio had come on as he switched on the ignition. She turned the volume down and tried again. "Honey, are we going right through to Chicago?"

"Not so far. Let's go and check the Turnpike."

She resigned herself to a whole lot more driving. They'd probably end spending the night in Pittsburgh or some place. The heating began to warm her feet.

Carl curled slowly down the entrance to the Pennsylvania Turnpike, collected the ticket, and accelerated on to the near lane like an aircraft taking off. In a few seconds they were up to sixty-five, and Moraine could feel the acceleration pushing her against the back of the seat. There was little other traffic and he crossed to the fast lane. He accelerated again, until the needle was on the hundred mark, thirty-five over the speed limit. Moraine turned up the radio and tried to relax.

You were close to the road in a Thunderbird, closer than in a Lincoln or even a Galaxy. She could feel Pennsylvania flying by her, the rushing night, the dark Christmassy winter. There would probably be snow on the Appalachians. She peered out, but it was too dark to see anything. She pressed the button on the panel between them and her window opened a little. She wanted to feel the winter night on her skin, and anyway she was getting too hot strapped in in her fur.

It had stopped sleeting, but the road was still wet. Cars coming the other way went by in a blaze of reflected glare. Considering the conditions, Carl was driving much too fast. She glanced at the speedometer, at the dials on the dashboard like four great protuberant eyes, at his profile. Then she was aware of the car slowing. She glanced at Carl, and saw that he was throwing her quick glances. He's stopped thinking about chess, she thought excitedly, he's thinking about me. It was moments like this that made it all worth while, the hours watching grandmasters thinking, the awful sense of stupidity when she couldn't seem to understand the strategic difference between a King's Pawn and a Queen's Pawn opening.

Then she saw they were only slowing for a tunnel, and she felt disappointed. But through the tunnel Carl still kept up his more moderate speed, about seventy, and kept glancing at her. Smiling too, it seemed. It's happening, she thought, it's happening! She felt the stab of excitement right there in her vitals. She began to breathe much faster, and she turned the radio down so that she shouldn't miss if he should say something.

They went through more tunnels, and then Carl pulled over into the slow lane. She waited, hardly breathing. Maybe he was simply going to leave the Turnpike, go over the flyover, back on to the Turnpike, back to New York.

"Why don't we turn off at the next exit? Find a parking lot and get in the back seat?"

So this was it. "Oh no, not the back seat!" she exclaimed. "I mean, there's no room in a Thunderbird, and we're both so tall." She glanced quickly at his profile. "There are some motels just ahead of us. We've just passed a Holiday Inn sign."

He nodded and she felt the stab of excitement again. It's happening, baby! She pointed out the turn to him, and they left the Turnpike, paid the due, and cruised over the hill, down into the brilliantly lit motel strip. On the left was the big green Holiday Inn sign, the flashing star, the lit sign saying "Vacancy." She stayed in the car while Carl checked in at the office. Then, in silence, he drove her to their room at the end of the block. He unlocked the door and let her in, then he went back and locked the car.

She stood for a moment alone in the familiar motel room, the twin double beds, the wall-to-wall carpeting, the yellow drapes, the switched-off television set on its bracket, the mock-impressionist pictures of Paris. This was how it should be, comfortable, almost luxurious, yet unplanned, spontaneous. To arrive with suitcases was like a salesman or a family vacationing. It was more romantic to arrive with nothing except her purse and the clothes she stood in. The motel provided soap and wash-cloths and Kleenex, and she could leave over cleaning her teeth till tomorrow. There was only one obvious thing she was missing and that, if she'd worked it out right, didn't matter today.

She drew the drapes, switched on the bedside light, low, medium, high, and then back to low, which was more romantic. She turned on the Muzak quietly, opened her coat, and sat on the bed, waiting for him to come in, tall, stooping in the doorway, grinning in anticipation.

He didn't waste any time. Since Allentown his needs had been growing increasingly urgent. But she resisted, she had needs too. She rolled away from him on the huge bed, and lay on her stomach, her cheek on the pillow.

"Stroke me, honey," she moaned, "stroke me first. Don't just do it. Stroke me a little."

He duly stroked her long beautiful body, which at any other time would have been a pleasure, but was now an annoying delay. He felt as if he had been asked to recite a love-poem, or sing a song. He felt clumsy, inexpert, though, judging from the sounds she was making, she seemed pleased. Then, having delayed long enough, he spread her on her back and mounted. He rubbed himself briefly against her moist hair, and she gave a little moan. Then he stabbed into her in one hard thrust and she gasped.

She hugged him to her, his spine under her fingertips. "Oh, heaven, honey, heaven," she mumbled, as he moved. "Oh honey, heaven!"

He paused, resting, and she waited palpitating for him to continue. Then, when nothing happened, she asked, "What's the matter? Honey, what's the matter?"

"Jesus!" He raised himself on his hands and pulled out.

"Honey, what's the matter? Go on, go on."

"I hadn't thought of that."

"Thought of what? Oh that, never mind that, that's all right. Just go on, honey, please, quickly."

He pulled away and looked at her aghast. "If he sealed K–B2, I figure he has a won game."

"Oh no! Oh no! Not that!"

"No getting away from it. I won't be able to stop him queening the Knight's Pawn."

"Oh no! Not that! Not chess again! Go on, go on, don't stop. Honey, you can't do this to me, you've just gotten me started. Go on, please."

She threw herself at him, touching him, caressing. But it was no use. She could see that it was all over. His excitement was gone, he had forgotten her, he had moved away from her into his private world. She gave a sob. "Oh no! Oh no!"

"I'm afraid so. It's a lost game. It's my move, that's the trouble. He plays K–B2, and I have to play something. Whatever I play is bound to lose."

"But you've resigned that game. It's all over. You threw it."

"Not that game, that's over. It's the Chaimovitz game I'm talking about, the adjourned game, the end-game."

"Oh, honey, forget it! Come back!"

"Or wait a minute! Maybe if I play K–K4 I've still got a chance."

He stood up and walked across the room to his coat. She watched his broad shoulders, his thin flat buttocks, miserably. She rubbed herself forlornly, but she had never been able to give herself any satisfaction that way. He took his pocket set from his pocket and sat down on the edge of the bed.

"Let's see, he plays K–B2 on the sealed move and I answer with K–K4."

Moraine wanted to scream and scream, but she managed to control herself. What was the point in making a noise and bringing in the neighbours? She stuffed the corner of the sheet into her mouth, and gripped her fingernails into the palms of her hands. She breathed deeply.

After a while, a long while, she calmed down and started to

cry, silently, drying her cheeks on the sheet. Then she stopped crying, her breathing and her pulse normal once more. She went to the bathroom and blew her nose on a Kleenex. Then she came back to the bed. He was still sitting there, bowed over the little board, thinking. He hadn't moved for an hour. He's a genius, she thought, you can't expect him to be like everybody else.

Feeling suddenly motherly and protective, she took his coat and draped it over his shoulders, in case he should feel cold in the heated room.

He looked up and smiled. "I think I've still a chance. I think I see a way. Maybe he doesn't have a win, after all."

"Oh, that's great, honey, I'm so glad." She stroked his head, and then left him to it. I need a drink, she thought, something strong, a screwdriver, a cocktail, even Scotch. She could put on her clothes again, underclothes, stockings, shoes, sweater, the brown suit, fur coat, the lot. And then what? They wouldn't serve her in the bar; she was under twenty-one and this was Pennsylvania, not New York. She didn't even look over twenty-one. Anyway, the bar was probably shut by now. She could go to the machine in the breezeway and get herself a Coke or a Seven-Up. But she didn't want that sort of drink.

"Honey, you got a flask with you?"

"Uh-huh." He shook his head.

She sat down on the other bed and pulled the cover round her. She wasn't cold, but she didn't want to remain naked any longer. She found a quarter in her purse and put it into the vibrator machine on the wall. There was a click and the bed began to tremble under her. She lay down and tried to relax; fifteen minutes of this vibration was supposed to be a fine way of relaxing. She thought, Wouldn't it be marvellous to make love on a bed like this. The machine was humming and she looked across at Carl's back, hunched over his board. But he didn't look round.

After fifteen minutes the machine clicked again and the bed became still. Moraine raised herself on an elbow. On the night-table was a Gideons Bible, the place marked by a leaflet about the motel. She opened the Bible, a dull piece of Deuteronomy, and she couldn't imagine why the place should be marked unless the marker had been put in at random by yesterday's occupants or the maid that morning. She read the leaflet.

"For your summertime pleasure a swimming pool is available to you for a refreshing dip in preparation for your enjoyment of the excellent food and beverage facilities."

She put the Bible away, picked up the telephone, studied the instructions and then dialled the long-distance operator. She asked for a call to New York. Her mother answered the first ring.

"Oh, hello, Mommy, this is Moraine."

"I'd recognise your voice anywhere, dear. Where are you?"

"I think we're at somewhere called Breezewood, Pennsylvania."

"How you move around! Are you eloping or vacationing or what?"

"Nothing really. Just out for a drive."

Mrs. Oppenheimer chuckled at the far end. "Well, take care of yourself, dear. Remember what happened to poor Debbie."

"Oh, nothing like that," Moraine said quickly. "Nothing like that at all. We'll be back tomorrow morning, I expect."

Mrs. Oppenheimer chuckled again. "Well, you missed some exciting chess while you were driving. Bobby Fischer won brilliantly, Reshevsky drew, Chaimovitz adjourned." She went on to give the full results.

Carl raised his head. "Chaimovitz adjourned again. Two adjourned games at once. That should give me the edge."

Mrs. Oppenheimer put down the telephone. She was alone in her apartment except for the servants who had gone to bed. She hadn't seen either Moraine or Jeff since early afternoon. She was reading a copy of *Chess Life,* but she was really planning what she was going to say to Jeff when he returned.

She heard the key in the door, the door shutting, the footsteps in the hall, as if it were Walter coming back from the office.

"Jeff!" she called. "Jeff, come here!"

He came into the room and stood there waving seven dollar bills like a hand of cards.

"Seven dollars," he said. "I won seven dollars."

"Seven dollars! And I'm planning for you to win five thousand at Miami. And thousands more after that, prizes, fees for simultaneous displays, appearance fees. All the big-time money. What's seven dollars? You mess the whole thing up to win seven dollars. Where did you win it? Washington Square?"

He shook his head, smiling happily. "Too cold. Figaro."

"Ah yes, the Café Figaro. There are plenty of chess clubs like that around the Village. But how did you hear about them? How did you know about Washington Square? I never took you there." She stared at him through narrowed eyes. "You know something, Jeff? I don't think you're playing straight with me. I think you understand a lot more English than you let on to. I think you've understood just about everything I've said to you for weeks now. It was I who told you about Washington Square, wasn't it, yesterday? I think you understand it all and are having fun with all of us, playing dumb."

She stood up. It was in her mind to slap him, but she thought better of it. She was small and alone.

"And I know something else about you too," she went on. "You're drunk."

MUNICH

It was snowing in Munich. From a white sky it swayed down in thick white flakes through the still air on to the white streets, the white roofs and cornices, the white domes and spires. It pencilled in gently the shapes of the Theatinerkirche domes, the Frauen-kirche, the spire of the Rathaus. One line of white drawn on a sheet of paper a slightly different shade of white. The buildings themselves had disappeared.

To Moraine, standing at the corner of Weinstrasse and Maffei-strasse, it was all unbelievably beautiful. It's like a drawing, she thought, almost a Japanese drawing. Just a few curves against the sky, white against white. And the snow itself, so beautiful, so thick, so—she hesitated for the word in her mind—so generous.

In her fur boots she swivelled round on the street corner, identifying the domes. Baroque snow, gothic snow, classical snow, mediaeval snow on the gables and chimney-stacks, modern snow on the window-sills of the new blocks. Snow de luxe on Moraine's mink shoulders, on her fur cap. She turned up her collar till only the tip of her nose and her big eyes were visible. She tilted back her head and closed her eyes, feeling the snow settling on her face, cool, soft, stroking her gently.

A man in a brown suit, thin shoes, a raincoat and a trilby hat crossed Maffeistrasse. As he passed Moraine he looked more closely. Beautiful, expensive. A film-star on location. Or a model posing in her furs. He looked round for the cameraman, the photographer. Nobody.

He said in English, "Good morning. Lousy weather, is it not?"

Moraine came out of her sensual dream and looked at him.

"Oh, go away, don't pester," she said crossly. "This isn't Rome."

Two miles away in Schwabing, Robin looked through the window of the stube in the Gasthof Clemens and said, "Bloody snow."

He was playing a friendly against Tom Reeves, the England second board, and was trying to decide whether to castle Queen's side.

The No. 3 board, Noel Hope-Warner of New College, Oxford, said in his Winchester accent, "I bet they have things better organised here. If it were at home the whole town would be flat on its back, there'd be no transport, no taxis, we'd never even get to the congress hall."

"I know, I know, all krauts are bloody marvellous." Dave Steiner, the No. 1 board, from Leeds.

"I didn't mean that, I merely meant . . ."

"Well, if the buses can't get through, that lets us out of our Waterloo. And I know someone who'd be glad of that."

He looked at Robin, who was wondering if he had done right in castling Queen's side, and didn't notice that he was being talked at. Finally he got the point, and smiled round at the others, trying to be friendly.

"Oh, that Persian wog!" he said confidently. "He's just a publicity stunt."

Ray Hookman, the reserve, looked up from his game with Hope-Warner and said, "They say he's got a personal manager and a publicity agent and a masseur and a photographer with him."

"You don't want to believe all you hear."

"Well, we don't do too badly either with publicity for our No. 4 board. Our young lion goes forth to battle."

"Goeth, not goes," said Reeves. "And our hearts goeth with him."

"Oh, dry up," said Robin, sick of the baiting and wishing he hadn't got a Knight stuck on Rook 4. "How can I think with all this nattering! Anyway, I didn't write that muck."

Two miles away Mrs. Oppenheimer sat in her bedroom in the Bayerischer Hof at a pine desk. She found the desk displeasing. Surely a hotel of this class could afford better furniture. There was a lovely antique escritoire downstairs in the lobby. No doubt the whole hotel had been furnished like that at one time, before they threw it all out and modernised.

She stared out of the window at the snow and wiped her mind clean of thoughts of furniture. She finished her letter to Image & Impact Services, Inc., 200 Madison Avenue, New York 10016. She looked in her purse and found her First National City Bank cheque-book, wrote out a cheque, sealed the envelope, and addressed it. She put the envelope on one side, to give to the concierge lunchtime. Then she looked out again at the snow, and saw palm trees and big white hotels and *Time* magazine.

Half a mile away Paul Butler glowered at the snow and wished he had brought some woolly boots with him. Of course he could buy some locally, but he wasn't that flush with currency and he had already bought himself a pocket tape recorder as a belated Christmas present to himself from himself. Perhaps he wouldn't need woolly boots. It was warm indoors in Munich, and as long as he could find taxis he wouldn't need to walk in the snow.

He oughtn't to be staying in this second-class hotel. He always stayed at the Bayerischer Hof, but this year he couldn't afford it. The *Post* was losing money and was having a drive to cut down on expenses. And so here he was, in a small bedroom and a small bed, a shower but no bath, and he had to use the public loo down the passage. The hotel had been recommended to him by Dietrich; it was where he and other players often stayed when they were in Munich. Dietrich was staying here now, but Paul had only seen him once, going out.

If he had been at the Bayerischer Hof he would have run into the Oppenheimers all the time, in the bar or the restaurant. It would have been a jolly party. But he could hardly hang round the hotel if he wasn't staying there. And it was worse still about Robin. The boys and the rest of the British team were in a gasthof near the university, students' rooms. It was miles away, halfway up the Leopoldstrasse, and having got there, how to get back? He had been up there once and had had to walk back almost to the Odeonsplatz before he got a taxi.

Even worse had been Robin's attitude to him. Paul had so looked forward to seeing him again, but the boy had been surly, positively unwelcoming. It had been a disappointment after all the nice letters he had written to Paul, and which Paul had brought with him in his suitcase. He would re-read them tonight, in bed, before he went to sleep. One should try not to read too much into Robin's churlishness. Boys often went through a difficult time at this age and he was probably worried about his games. Anyway, this was his first trip abroad. Perhaps he felt lost, not speaking the language. Paul had forgotten how Lancashire Robin's voice was, those terrible flat vowels that hit you every sentence. And he had a spot on his chin. Perhaps the boy wasn't well, that would explain why he was playing so badly.

All the same, it was a disappointment. He had so looked forward to showing Munich to Robin, introducing him to baroque churches and rococo ceilings, Nymphenburg and the Residenz, Rubens, Franz Marc, Feininger, Richard Strauss. But all the boy had said, standing in the hall of the Clemens, blocking Paul's entry into the stube, was:

"I haven't got time for any sightseeing just now. P'raps I'll be able to fit some in after the chess."

"Sightseeing!" Paul had been horrified at the word. "It isn't a question of taking a Cook's Tour round the city. It's a question of appreciating the Bavarian culture."

"Well, I don't think looking at pictures is going to help me to beat Mecking."

Beating Mecking! That was all they ever thought of. Paul explained once again that to be a great chess-player you needed to have a wider culture than simply chess. It was the same in any walk of life. Churchill needed to appreciate literature. Pierpont Morgan needed to appreciate art.

Robin fidgeted, and fingered the spot on his chin.

Anyway, Paul had told him reassuringly, it wasn't only looking at pictures. There were other things about Munich it was important to understand. Drinking beer in a keller, singing German songs, drinking wine or apfelsaft in a Schwabing *lokal,* and singing quite different songs. It wouldn't matter in the least his not speaking German.

Robin had answered firmly that perhaps there would be time for that when the tournament was over. In the meantime he was concentrating on his chess.

Paul could have cried with frustration. Worst of all had been the opera. Paul had bought two seats, and terribly expensive they were too. It was to be his Christmas present to Robin. But the boy had flatly refused to go (this time it was on the telephone). He had repeated stubbornly that listening to singing wasn't going to help him beat Kaplan. Stupid oaf! thought Paul, banging down the receiver.

What to do with the extra ticket? The opera house were very doubtful if they could re-sell it for him. Joann Oppenheimer had refused to go with him. ("It's lovely of you, Paul, but you know I don't like opera, and anyway I'm much too busy just now. Why don't you ask Moraine?")

So he had taken Moraine. Not the person he would have chosen, but at least she was docile and well-mannered. She had loved the pink and gold opera house and had been disappointed when he told her that it had only been built, or rebuilt, two years before. She had been disappointed in the opera too, it seemed so quiet, so improbable.

He explained to her about the beauty, the perfection of *Cosi Fan Tutte,* the divine *Cosi,* as he usually called it.

Moraine asked, "But why did he choose such an unromantic story? And it isn't even likely!"

He explained to her about its being formal, symmetric, like a dance. And about its delicious cynicism. And what a mistake the designer was making in dressing everyone in dark brown and olive green. ("It's a pastel-coloured opera!") And what a mistake the conductor was making in taking it all so slowly.

She told him about the *Bohème* she had seen at the new Metropolitan in New York. *Bohème!* He sighed. Hardly the same as the divine *Cosi.*

All the same, the evening had been quite a success, largely because of the interval. Moraine had obviously taken great trouble with her appearance, piling up her dark-honey hair, wearing a jade necklace and ear-rings. She looked beautiful, radiant, and in the bar many admiring envious eyes were turned on her and on her escort. It was a smart audience and Paul preened himself. Robin would have worn a tweed coat and grey flannel trousers. Or did the boy possess a blue suit?

He ordered *sekt* and smoked-salmon sandwiches for Moraine, and asked about her dress, clinging black jersey silk with a plunging neckline and a chain belt. "Is it Saint-Laurent?"

"No, we didn't go to Paris this trip. This is Miss BeeGee." Seeing him looking baffled, she added, "Bergdorf."

The man beside them looked round. Paul felt that most of the bar were eyeing them. She was looking so bright-eyed and gay that for a fraction of a second he found himself envying Carl Sandbach.

But the magic hadn't survived the second act, or the thirty-six hours since then. Moraine had telephoned him to thank him, but she hadn't been able to think of anything to say about the opera. She had sounded like a child of twelve. Robin would have done better, Paul thought unreasonably. But Robin hadn't telephoned at all, about anything.

And then there were the two letters, in his suitcase along with Robin's, though he felt no need to re-read either of them. One was from the editor of *New Princess,* telling him what a success his chess articles were, but that when the present series was finished she felt they should rest chess and widen their range to include bridge, sailing, show-jumping, skiing, rally-driving. Paul had snorted. Skiing, rally-driving! Women couldn't keep their minds on chess for more than a few minutes at a time. Or on anything except clothes and men. And *New Princess* had been paying him seventy-five guineas an article.

The other letter had been from the editor of *Chess World* suggesting that Paul devote more of his space to tournaments inside the United Kingdom. The readers wished to read about the tournaments in which they or their friends were playing and were less interested in foreign tournaments in which no British players were taking part, more especially since many of these games were grandmaster draws and were often less lively than the games played at Bognor or Blackpool.

Of course, the magazine, like the *Daily Post,* was merely trying to cut down on expenses. Paul hadn't yet answered, but phrases, sentences, drafted themselves in his mind. Provincialism! Parish-pump! How would England ever become, or perhaps regain, her status as a major chess power if her players would rather study Ilford or Liverpool instead of Zagreb or Sochi? When would any of the British clubs have a grandmaster? Not since Staunton, and that was a long time ago. Lively! Grandmaster draws! Less interested in foreign tournaments!

Anyway, what would it all do to Paul, to his image? He was a cosmopolitan, at home anywhere in the world, knowing the squares, the hotels, the restaurants, the galleries, the operas. His status depended on travelling. How would he manage if his penny-pinching papers confined him to Ilford and Coventry and Appleby-Frodingham? How would he ever write *Sixty-Four Squares?*

He stared gloomily out at the snow. Even the weather was against him. And he had so looked forward to this trip, his Christmas treat.

Two miles away in Schwabing, in a gasthof in the Maria-Josephastrasse, Jeff Falkner sat at the window, staring out at the snow. The others were downstairs playing chess in the stube, but he preferred to stay up here. He had never seen snow in a city before, and he watched its movements with interest. Sleet in New York hadn't been at all like this. He had bought himself a thermometer, and had stuck it by magnetism on to the railing outside his room. The outside temperature was −3 Centigrade. Jeff was surprised. He had expected it to be much colder.

Mrs. Oppenheimer, having dealt with her correspondence, picked up the telephone and asked for a number. The call took a few minutes to come through as the girl at the desk had to look the number up in the book. The bell rang in Paul's room. For a moment he hoped that it was Robin, but he was almost as pleased to hear Joann's voice.

"I thought it must be you."

"Who else? Moraine's voice is much deeper. Listen, I've a whole lot I want to talk to you about, to discuss with you I mean. Are you busy for lunch? Or could we eat together before the great match?"

"No, I'm quite free. Come and have lunch with me." Thoughts raced through his brain. The Ratskeller had an old picturesque atmosphere and wasn't expensive. Or Luitpolds. The place had been modernised and was hardly more than a snack-bar nowadays. But quite cheap. And he could tell her about its great days when it had been a famous literary café, the Algonquin, the Deux Magots of Munich.

"No, I'm inviting you. It's my turn. Let's have lunch here, and then we can all go down together to the chess afterwards. Moraine will be coming too. Why don't we meet downstairs in the bar for a martini at twelve-thirty?"

He accepted gladly. A date in the Bayerischer Hof bar. This was more like it, perhaps things weren't turning out so badly after all. And there were other promising signs too, he mustn't let himself get depressed and forget them. An unexpected cheque for thirty-eight pounds, additional royalties from his old book on Euwe; out of which he had bought the tape recorder and the opera tickets. And Geraint, his agent, had been quite keen about his idea for *Sixty-Four Squares,* and looked forward to seeing the complete typescript soon. And this wasn't really such a bad little hotel—warm, clean, with good service, perfectly placed in the heart of old Munich, and the Hofbräuhaus was just across the street. It was quiet too—in this weather no drunken revellers would be tempted to sing in the street outside when the Hofbräuhaus closed.

An idea came to him, and he rushed to the window. Maybe he would write his Munich chapter about this little square, the Platzl, and not about the Odeonsplatz or the Marienplatz. It was pretty enough, and more original. He'd write about it under snow, the snow which emphasised the gables and the chimneys; the snow on the Hofbräuhaus Christmas tree; the small hotel with its clientele of brilliant chess-players; the Hofbräuhaus itself with its centuries-old tradition of beer and music and *stimmung.* That chapter should be a real winner, perhaps he could sell it as a separate article to *Go* or *Holiday.* He hummed to himself "In München steht ein Hofbräuhaus."

He kissed Mrs. Oppenheimer when he met her in the Bayerischer Hof, but he only shook Moraine's hand. He sipped his martini and looked up at the ring of lit bottles in the cupola above

them, the phoney chandelier of tumblers, the dripping but un-
lit candles.

"I remember when the whole thing was eighteenth century,"
he reminisced. "Chandeliers, brocades. The things they're doing
to Munich these days. It's a crime. This new metro, messing up
all the streets."

Moraine said, "I went into the Frauenkirche. Mommy, it's terrible, all modern. You'd have hated it. I mean, there, in that
church or cathedral or whatever it is, it's all wrong."

"My dear, you're so right," said Paul. "And have you been inside the Theatinerkirche? It's quite dreadful, they've whitewashed the whole thing. The most beautiful baroque church in
Bavaria and they've whitewashed it all. And they've put up a
notice to say this is a church and not an art gallery. The van-
dals!" He wrung his hands in despair.

"If they're throwing out all the old stuff there should be lots of
lovely antiques going round. Mommy, why don't we have a look
for them?"

"You do it, dear, if you like. I simply don't have the time at
the moment."

Paul remembered something he had meant to say. "I gather
this is your first visit to Munich. I'd be delighted to show you
both round the city, if you'd allow me."

There was a moment's pause. Moraine began, "That's darling
of you, but . . ."

Mrs. Oppenheimer said, "That's nice of you, Paul, and of
course we'd love to. It's just that I don't see how to fit in anything
like that just now. Maybe when the chess is over. But, darling,
why don't you and Paul . . ."

"But, Mommy, I've done a trip round the city. My first afternoon. It was an American Express tour."

"American Express!" Paul groaned. "A guided tour!"

"Well, why not? They show you everything, tell you everything, and you don't have to walk miles."

"Did they show you the pictures, the Rubenses?"

"No, but I'm not too crazy about Rubens, to tell the truth.
I've seen so much of him in New York, and London, and Paris.
It's all so much the same. And all those naked Flemish women
with their fat behinds, they aren't romantic."

Paul looked pained. "I think perhaps you've missed something in Rubens."

"No, I haven't!" Moraine leaned forward and became, for her, surprisingly vehement. "All that flesh and everything and nobody relates at all. Nobody cares about anybody else. All they ever do is give each other apples or hold up a crown. Nobody ever *touches* anybody else."

"Those Sabine women were touched, all right," said Mrs. Oppenheimer.

"Oh, I love that! But there are so many others you have to get through. All those Graces tiptoeing around the fields."

Paul said pacifyingly, "Well, never mind Rubens, if you've got a personal antipathy towards him."

"Yes, I have! It's his attitude I don't like. A woman takes off her clothes. Right, that's natural. And then nobody does a thing about it and she has to dance around with a lot of other naked women. That's unnatural."

"Dear, I think you should lower your voice. You must be shocking the stolid Bavarians."

Paul felt hot in the face and tried again to change the subject. "As I was saying, never mind Rubens. There are lots of other treasures in the Pinakothek I'd be happy to show you. Or the Haus der Kunst, where the moderns are. Franz Marc, Feininger, Klee. You'd love those."

Moraine looked doubtfully at her mother. She had already done the divine *Cosi* with Paul. Mrs. Oppenheimer got the message.

"It's sweet of you, Paul, we'll have to see. But I think we ought to go in to lunch or we shall miss the opening of the great game."

They went into the dining-room and Paul exclaimed, "Oh, no! no! Not cosy nooks! Iron scrollwork! Red candles! And it used to be . . ."

"Don't tell me, let me guess!" Mrs. Oppenheimer interrupted, handing Paul the menu at the same time. "It was chandeliers and brocade."

"Yes, and now it's pure J. Arthur Dixon." He paused to let the name sink in, and then said it again.

Moraine looked up from her menu and asked politely, "Is he an interior decorator?"

"No, my dear, he's the man who does those Christmas cards. You know, those coloured photographs of iron lanterns and tankards and poinsettias and red candles and 'Christmas Greetings' or even 'Remembrance' in gold italics."

"They sound just darling," said Moraine, returning to the menu.

Mrs. Oppenheimer said vaguely, "Well, maybe there was once an old inn on the site." She grabbed a waiter and organised their meal: venison in cream sauce for Moraine, pheasant with bacon, cabbage and pineapple for herself and Paul. "And you'll order some wine for us, Paul, won't you. But don't make too much of a thing of it, we've a lot to discuss."

Paul subsided and tamely ordered a half-litre of Kalterersee.

"Now," said Mrs. Oppenheimer briskly, "I think it's all organised for this afternoon. I've arranged for the photographer to be there, and also the local press. Not that they matter, but it all helps. I take it that the game itself is a foregone conclusion."

Paul made a wry face. "Oh, I don't think anything is certain in chess. I know Robin's been going through a bad patch lately, but perhaps he has been holding himself back for this game."

"Almost held himself back out of the team," Mrs. Oppenheimer commented. She wasn't much impressed by Robin's performance.

The point was justified. Robin was playing fourth board for England because of his lack of team-play experience, but even here he was doing very badly. His first game, against the Bulgarian Chaudarov, was a bad loss. Robin had blundered badly on the twelfth move and again on the eighteenth, resigning soon after. Well, anyone can have first-night nerves. The second round, against Ireland, was supposed to be an easy one, but again Robin had got into a mess. He had managed to scrape out of the humiliation of a second loss, by a draw through repetition of moves. All the same, it had been an ignominious performance, which hadn't raised his prestige with his team. His third game, yesterday, against Nielsen of Denmark, had also been drawn, but again this hadn't counted to Robin's credit. The English captain, anxious to keep his team fresh for the round against the United States, had arranged with the Danish captain that all four games would be drawn by the thirtieth move at latest, irrespective of the states of the games. The Danish captain, keen to keep his team fresh for their round against the Soviet Union, had gladly agreed.

All the same, two half-points out of three games was not an impressive score. It was being recalled how few triumphs Robin had had, apart from Blackpool. People were asking, why all the fuss, the write-up. Paul felt defensive, at bay, given to repeating that anyone could go through a bad patch; the boy would strike his best form at any moment. Worse still, there had been rumours that Robin Jackson would be dropped to reserve for a few games. This would, of course, have been a tremendous blow to Paul, and would have meant that Robin would miss the round against the U.S. But fortunately nothing seemed to have come of it, and Robin was apparently being given a last chance. Paul breathed again. If Robin could only pull out his best form today, nothing else really mattered.

Jeff Falkner, in contrast, was playing brilliantly. Out of three games so far, he had got two and a half points. He should have got the other half-point yesterday against East Germany, but with a won game he had unexpectedly offered a draw which the East German fourth board had accepted gratefully. There had been talk that Jeff might be promoted, as the American second board was clearly off form, but nothing seemed to have come of it, perhaps because of the draw against Smidtz. Mrs. Oppenheimer and Paul were much relieved. The game between Jeff and Robin was finally "on."

"But I haven't forgiven that draw yesterday. I've told Jeff that if he does that again today against your boy I'll put him on the plane back to Iran the moment the tournament is over."

Moraine said, "Maybe he had a good reason, I mean something to do with the game we didn't follow."

"I followed, all right. He was three Pawns up, with a strong Bishop and a well-placed King. He just couldn't be troubled to play an end-game. He's just lazy, from his scalp to his heels. Well, that's my problem. Anyway, it's all set up for today. What I want to talk about is Miami."

She outlined the plans so far. Carl Sandbach had formally accepted, the dates of the match were fixed for June, ten games spread over two weeks. The hotel, the Fontainebleau (she pronounced it, correctly, Fountainblue), were giving special congress rates, Eastern and National Airlines were co-operating, but she hadn't yet had an answer from United about groups coming from Chicago; there'd be simuls, rapid-transit, five-minute chess, kriegspiel, lectures in the evenings and off days. And a magnificent banquet in the Fleur-de-Lys Room to end up; Ed Edmondson would preside, she would hand over the prizes. And, of course, she added casually, there'd be all the usual Miami entertainments, sunbathing, water-skiing, sail-fishing, alligator-shooting, dancing, drinking for those who liked that sort of thing.

"Like me," said Moraine.

"Now what I need is an umpire for the match. I can't ask Ed, I don't want an American citizen. Paul, would you do it for me?"

Paul felt a sudden glow like hot wine inside him. Miami! Then he demurred. "I don't think my papers would send me all the way to Miami if there wasn't a British player taking part."

"I'm sure they won't. I'll pay all your expenses, airline, hotel, meals, and a fee too. You won't lose by this."

Paul felt the hot wine turn to hot brandy. This was more like his image. Miami in June to umpire the Sandbach-Falkner match. Everyone would say, You lucky man, you just have all the luck don't you, can't you take me with you as your valet? Was there a square in Miami he could use in his book? It didn't matter, he'd have to pass through New York, he could take notes on Times Square or Washington Square. Or perhaps a smaller, more exotic square like Sheridan Square in the Village or Cooper Square in the Bowery.

He demurred again. "In principle I'd love to. But I haven't got my diary with me. I'll have to make sure I'm not meant to be covering some dreary congress in Bradford or somewhere."

Mrs. Oppenheimer nodded, understanding perfectly. She took a small gold-covered notebook from her purse, opened it and ticked off Paul's name.

She said, "Right! You'll give the match a good spread in your papers, won't you, Paul?"

"I'll do my best. I think we could work up quite a lot of interest in Britain over this. The American Sultan Khan, the natural genius who can't even read or write . . ."

". . . he can now, after a fashion . . ."

". . . and the all-American Californian, lean, tall, the New Frontier cowboy, the Gary Cooper of chess, or perhaps . . ."

Moraine gave a giggle. Mrs. Oppenheimer said, "Yes, that sort of thing. I'm not sure about Gary Cooper, it might make Carl sound too old. But you'll cover the games too, won't you, not just the personalities?"

"Oh, of course." But that would be for the chess columns, the chess-addicts. The story would be for the general reader. Perhaps *New Princess* would reconsider their decision. Or he might be able to interest *Nova* or *Honey*.

"I can only think of one thing that might go wrong," said Mrs. Oppenheimer.

Nobody coming to watch it, thought Paul, but he didn't say it aloud.

"Hurricanes!" exclaimed Moraine. "Mommy, it'll be the hurricane season."

"A hurricane would be fine. It wouldn't stop the chess and it would drive them in off the beaches. We might get a record crowd. No, what I'm scared of is draws. Remember that match right here in Germany between Unzicker and Pfleger? Every game was drawn. Remember Santa Monica in 1966? Two-thirds of the games were drawn. Remember Hastings last year? People are going to be pretty sore if they come all this way to watch a string of draws."

"Carl won't draw," said Moraine loyally. "He's like Bobby, or Larsen. He just hates grandmaster draws."

"Carl would take one quick enough if he were losing. And I don't trust Jeff, not after yesterday. A won game and he offers a draw because he's too lazy to play it through to the end."

Paul said, "Can't you talk to Jeff, explain it to him?"

"Talk to Jeff! I've talked to Jeff, I'll talk to him again, every night till June. But I'm never sure if he gets the point. I'm still not sure how much English he understands."

"Well, then," Paul went on, "raise the value of the winner's prize and lower the loser's. That'll give them something to play for."

Mrs. Oppenheimer nodded thoughtfully. "Yes, incentivise them to play for a win. But how can I know they won't do a secret deal to draw every game and share the prize money?"

Moraine said quickly, "Carl would never agree a thing like that. He isn't a cheat."

"Nor were the grandmasters at Hastings. But look what happened."

"Well, I've got another idea," said Paul, his mind stimulated to brilliance by vodka and Kalterersee. "Make a special match rule that the umpire must approve all draws before they are agreed. And I won't approve except in a totally drawn position."

Mrs. Oppenheimer shook her head. "I want the match played under normal F.I.D.E. rules. I want F.I.D.E. sponsorship."

Paul was doubtful about this, but he decided to say nothing.

"Think about it all, Paul. This is a tough problem. Let me have your ideas when you've had time to think it over seriously."

Paul got the point. He was expected to take time and trouble, and put in a thoughtful report. He couldn't see that there was much to think over; Carl Sandbach, International Grandmaster, would obviously win every game in the match, as and when he pleased.

Mrs. Oppenheimer looked at her watch. "We'll have to miss dessert or we'll be late for the opening. Waiter, coffee, please, and the check."

Paul came back abruptly to Germany from Florida. Yet another splendid idea struck him.

"Tonight one of us will have something to celebrate. One of our protégés will have won . . ."

". . . Unless they draw . . ."

"Well, anyway, why don't we all go to the Hofbräuhaus afterwards, and drink beer and eat sausages and sing songs?"

"Oh, Paul, I doubt I'll have the opport . . ."

"Oh, Mommy, let's! We never do anything like that. Don't let's just sit here and write letters all evening."

Paul smiled at her gratefully. "I'm inviting you as my guests." Beer and sausages shouldn't cost too much, and, anyway, Miami! He really owed himself a celebration party.

"That's sweet of you. Of course we'd love to. It's only that I promised to cable the annotated score to Image & Impact tonight."

"Well, I've got to telephone the results to London. But we

could go after that. I'll see if I can get Robin and the boys to come too."

"I'm not having Jeff coming," Mrs. Oppenheimer said quickly. "I don't want to start him off drinking beer again. I had trouble enough last time."

She swept out of the restaurant, a small but dominating figure. Moraine and Paul followed. Moraine said, "You will tell me what all the songs mean, won't you? Even if they're indecent."

Paul laughed. "Oh, they're just drinking songs."

In the foyer they looked through the glass doors at the snow.

Moraine said, "I'd forgotten the snow after all that talk about Miami."

It was coming down like a white veil between them and the houses across the Promenadeplatz. It lay thick and deep in the elbows of the trees. Paul plunged bravely out to look for a taxi, remembered his thin shoes and retreated. Mrs. Oppenheimer sent the boy for a taxi, and Paul fumbled for a mark.

The congress was being held in the conference room of the Deutsches Museum, on its island in the middle of the Isar. There were ice-floes on the river, under the trees, and hundreds of sea-gulls hopped unhappily about on them. The huge propeller, which stood outside like a large modern sculpture, was stranger and more beautiful under snow. In the white sky were the faintly shadowed outlines of domes.

"I'll never forget this," said Moraine. "It's so pretty!"

It was warm inside, from heating and people. The hall was sombre, with obscure murals of females and heavy wooden chandeliers and a dark ceiling with inset suns and stars. At one end was a platform normally used by musicians or politicians, but now by officials and umpires and scorers and huge charts. The hall itself was a near solid mass of tables and chairs and chess-sets and clocks and flags. Paul walked round, talking to anyone he knew, passing on quickly, too busy to stay with anyone for long.

England had not yet arrived. (Why not? he thought; a great mistake to run these things fine.) He went and talked to Scotland who were going to have a difficult afternoon against Brazil. He noted down the names and the colours of pieces, and moved on to greet the Americans. As he caught sight of Jeff he thought once again, God, what a good-looking boy! Like the young Shah. The thick eyebrows, the straight nose, the perfectly cut grey suit. The fragrance that came from him, Paul decided after reflection, was Tabac. He shook hands with Jeff. The first twice they had met Jeff had given him a little salaam, which Paul found enchanting, but today he only shook hands gravely.

"I hope you have a good game today," Paul said, going as far as he could. The boy gave a little bow, but said nothing. Mrs. Oppenheimer had routed out the photographer from somewhere at the back, and was explaining the pictures she wanted taken. Out of the corner of his eye Paul saw the England team arriving and hurried across to greet them.

He was careful to greet them in board order, first Steiner, then Reeves, then Hope-Warner, and lastly Robin. To Robin he said, "All ready for the great game?"

"It's just a game like any other," said Robin disagreeably.

Paul went on hopefully, "Good game to win."

"Every game is," said Robin, moving on.

"Oh, Robin, I'm taking a small party to the Hofbräuhaus tonight, when this is over. You know, drink beer and sing songs and forget our troubles. Why don't you and the others come and join us?" He smiled warmly, unsnubbable.

"Oh, we won't have time for that sort of fun and games. We'll be analysing all evening."

He turned and walked away towards his table. Not a word of regret or thanks. Paul stared after him, wondering. The surliness was perhaps pre-game nerves; he might be more approachable later. But, all the same, it was hard to forgive. Robin had so much to be grateful to Paul for. To be rude to him, here, in public, where several people might have overheard, was inexcusable. And his letters had been so friendly, at least until the beginning of December. His accent, too, seemed, on reacquaintance, to be more aggressively Lancashire, the vowels deliberately flatter. And why didn't his father buy him some decent clothes? To turn up at an international event like this wearing an old tweed coat with patches on the elbows, and grey flannel trousers that were much too short, was letting down Paul, and England.

Mrs. Oppenheimer, too, watched him cross the room. She had met him, shaken hands with him, before his first game two days ago, and saw no need to shake hands again. Personally she couldn't see what Paul saw in the boy—and his chess wasn't so great either. But she was watching for the moment when he and Jeff would shake hands across the board. So was the photographer who caught them with his flash-bulb. Mrs. Oppenheimer decided that Robin's face wasn't photogenic enough to help, and made the boys shake hands again, photographed this time from the side with Jeff full face and only the back of Robin's shoulder showing. They sat down and stared at the board, while they were taken again, from the same position. The other English and American players looked across from their tables, in amusement or irritation. Robin flushed scarlet and scowled.

No need to sulk, thought Paul, taking up position behind him. You need publicity as well as talent to succeed. Every famous chess-player liked to see his picture in the papers.

Robin wrote up his score-pad, fiddled with his ball-point, fidgeted on his chair, blew his nose, stared at the board, polished his glasses. Jeff, more relaxed, took two pocket thermometers out of his pocket, set them up beside the chess-clock, and studied them intently. Mrs. Oppenheimer, behind him, caught Paul's eye and smiled.

The umpire made a brief announcement from the stage and then the controllers moved round the games, starting the white clocks. Across the room Paul saw a sudden movement of white hands like birds, moving the opening Pawn.

Jeff had the white pieces, and was to move first. Paul was sorry about this. Robin needed all the help he could get. On the other hand he had won with Black at Blackpool; and if they should draw, this would be creditable for Black, given the opening disadvantage. Paul might make something of it in his articles. And, of course, if Robin should win with Black! And why not? Strong opposition had brought out the best in him at Blackpool.

Jeff opened with the Queen's Pawn, and Robin answered with his King's Knight (1. P–Q4 N–KB3). Paul nodded approvingly. Probably the King's Indian or the Modern Benoni. Very sound. But then instead of bringing out his Queen's Bishop's Pawn, the Gambit Pawn, Jeff brought out his Queen's Knight, blocking the Pawn. It was an unusual move, an irregular opening, and Robin spent ten minutes over his next move, trying to work it out, identify the opening Jeff was playing. Finally he too brought out his Queen's Pawn (2. N–QB3 P–Q4). It looked as if it were going to be the Gruenfeld Defence, Paul thought. Unusual. Probably Robin had prepared it specially for this game, in which case he would have a distinct advantage.

Jeff in one decisive movement moved his Queen's Bishop right across the board to attack the black Knight. Again very unusual. A sort of Queen's Gambit Declined, without the Gambit Pawn being moved. What sort of an opening was that, Mrs. Oppenheimer asked herself. Hadn't Jeff learnt anything from Sol during all those weeks? Or had he just forgotten the Gambit Pawn? She caught Paul's eye across the table, and grimaced.

Robin again took ten minutes over the next move. He clearly decided too that it was a sort of Queen's Gambit Declined and moved out his King's Pawn one square. The following move, Paul guessed, would be to move his black square Bishop on to the square vacated by the Pawn (3. B–KN5 P–K3).

Jeff immediately brought out his King's Pawn all the way, and Paul almost laughed aloud. A French Defence! After all that, it was an ordinary French Defence, which was a King's Pawn opening, approached round the back way. Jeff had opened with the Queen's Pawn and had now turned it into a King's Pawn opening. What a joke! Robin moved out the Bishop as forecast (4. P–K4 B–K2).

Paul wrote down "French Defence Transposed" on his pad, and felt happier. Robin presumably knew all about the French, one of the basic openings. This might give him a slight edge in theory over Jeff, whose theory, Paul gathered, was not his strong point. On the other hand, Robin having to think it out from scratch had used up twenty minutes of his clock time, while Jeff had taken barely a minute. Paul glared into the back of Robin's head and willed him to play faster or he would be in serious time trouble later.

It seemed as if Robin got the message, or else that his moves were forced, but he began to play more decisively. Jeff took his Knight with the Bishop, and Robin recaptured with his own Bishop, which had been placed there for that purpose. Jeff advanced his King's Pawn, attacking the Bishop, which Robin retreated to its original square (5. B x N B x B 6. P–K5 B–K2).

Jeff then brought out his Queen to the Knight's file. Again Mrs. Oppenheimer felt some misgivings. It was terribly early to bring out the Queen; and although she was threatening to take the black Knight's Pawn, long-term good rarely came of this move. It looked a little as if Jeff might be overreaching himself. On the other hand, it was aggressive points-hungry play. Robin, however, decided to protect his Pawn and moved it out one square (7. Q–N4 P–KN3). Continuing his King's side attack, Jeff moved out his King's Rook Pawn, and Robin countered with the same move (8. P–KR4 P–KR4).

Paul didn't feel too happy about Robin's position. He had weakened his King's side Pawns and now could scarcely castle that side. He seemed cramped, undeveloped. Indeed, he had not yet moved a single piece on the Queen's side, after eight moves. If he was going to win, or even draw, it was time he got some counter-play.

At the moment, however, Jeff's Queen was *en prise,* and he side-stepped her one square where she would still be able to defend the Rook's Pawn which was under attack. Robin, for the first time, had the initiative, and, after ten minutes' thought, moved out his Queen's Bishop's Pawn. Paul sighed. The boy was Pawn-mad today. His great need was to develop his pieces now, rather than his Pawns, and anyway the move would weaken his Queen's side Pawns and make it hard for him to castle that side too. Jeff took the Pawn instantly with his Queen's Pawn, and Robin recaptured with the Bishop (9. Q–B4 P–QB4 10. P x P B x BP).

The initiative was now back with Jeff and he castled Queen's side. This was unusual for White in any game, but then he was playing an unusual original game. Mrs. Oppenheimer watched with a thrill of pride. This was how he had played in Isfahan, in the Manhattan Chess Club, this was the natural untaught game of the original genius. But then a qualm overcame her. It was working beautifully against this English oaf from Manchester. But would it work against the real big boys, the professional grandmasters, against Carl Sandbach or Mischchov or Toklovsky? She put the thought away, looked in her purse and took out a sweet throat lozenge. Her throat felt dry, she must have been breathing through her mouth for the last half-hour without noticing it. She looked round to say something to Moraine, but the girl had wilted and gone to sit on a distant chair.

Robin replied to Jeff's move by bringing out his other Bishop (11. O-O-O B–Q2) and Paul nodded approvingly. At last! Both players then brought out their remaining Knights, and Jeff developed his Bishop to the Queen's file. Robin moved his Queen one square (12. N–B3 N–B3 13. B–Q3 Q–K2), and Jeff advanced his King's Knight to N5. His King's side attack was under way with a vengeance.

Robin was clearly in great difficulties, under heavy attack, cramped, hardly able to move. Two of his Pawns were in danger, and even his developed pieces seemed to be blocked. He looked round irritably and said to Paul, "Do you mind not standing right behind me? Do you mind!"

It was a humiliating snub, a public rebuke. Everyone looked at Paul and he flushed furiously. The cheek of it! The young lout! Chess-players were accustomed to being watched, to having people looking over their shoulders while they played. Who did this boy think he was? Fischer? Larsen?

All the same, Paul moved away and stood behind Hope-Warner, who didn't seem to mind. Indeed, who would mind being watched by the chess correspondent of the *Post?* Paul calmed himself. Robin was obviously in a state of nerves, and losing badly. Allowances must be made. At the same time he remembered that he must watch the other three games as well, and he studied the positions while watching out of the corner of his eye for Robin to move.

He waited a long time. Robin took an hour over his next move, fidgeting, crossing and recrossing his legs, fingering his spots, looking at the clock, sometimes glancing up at the murals. But mostly he sat and stared at the board, his head buried in his hands, his cheek muscles twitching, his fingers scratching his scalp. Jeff, on the contrary, sat calm and still, studying his two wristwatches, comparing a minute on each of them with a minute on Robin's clock. He also studied his thermometers. One said 68 Fahrenheit and the other 20 Centigrade. Then he went to the lavatory. Neither on his way there, nor back, did he pause to look at anyone else's game, but he stared round the room, looking for someone, presumably Moraine. But she had disappeared.

Mrs. Oppenheimer, however, was beside him at once. "You're playing just fine," she whispered. "You've a really won game there. But if you offer him a draw now I'll murder you."

Jeff gave a little bow and sat down again. Robin still hadn't moved. Twice he raised his hand as if he were going to move, and each time thought better of it. He's lost his nerve, thought Paul, he'll just sit there till his time runs out. However, Robin pulled himself together, and finally moved his Knight to the Queen's file (14. N–KN5 N–Q5). A freeing move, thought Paul; it might work yet. Jeff advanced his Bishop's Pawn which had been under attack, and Paul felt easier. If Jeff was worrying about defending his Pawns he couldn't be meaning to deliver the *coup de grâce* just yet. Robin moved his Knight again, to the King's Bishop's file (15. P–B3 N–B4).

This presumably was the point of his plan, to bring his Knight by this roundabout route to the defence of the King's side, and at the same time open up a diagonal for his white-square Bishop. It was a short-lived plan. Jeff promptly took the Knight with his Bishop, and after a few minutes' thought, Robin recaptured with the Knight's Pawn (16. B x N NP x B). Smoothly, without a second's reflection, Jeff played the spectacular move of the game, Rook takes Pawn.

Paul felt a shiver of excitement run through him. It was always an exciting moment when, after all the preliminary manœuvring, the attack went in. A Rook sacrifice! Paul studied the position to see if the sacrifice was sound, and decided with mixed feelings that it was. Perhaps Joann had been right all along about her boy, perhaps he was a genius, in which case it was no disgrace to Robin to lose to him. Perhaps he could write it like that.

Robin took ten minutes more to ponder the position, to see if he could reject the Rook sacrifice. Finally he took it with the Pawn (17. R x P P x R), pulled out a grubby handkerchief and mopped his forehead. Jeff took the Pawn with his Knight, attacking Robin's Queen, and Robin quickly retreated her to her original square (18. N x QP Q–Q1). Still without pausing, for no doubt the whole plan had been clear in his head for some time, Jeff attacked Robin's King, moving his Knight to the King's Bishop's file. Robin, after some dithering, advanced his King

(19. N–B6ch K–K2). Jeff moved his Queen across to the Queen's Bishop's file, so that she could come in on the wing.

The situation was now drastic. Jeff was threatening mate on the move in two ways: either Queen takes Bishop mate, or Queen takes Pawn mate. Mrs. Oppenheimer smiled happily and looked across at Paul, who was shaking his head sadly. Politely she made a deprecating gesture, implying what could anyone do against play like that? But Paul just turned down the corners of his mouth and shook his head again. Jeff suddenly held out a hand and something inside her turned over. He couldn't be offering a draw! Not now! With the end in sight! Then she breathed again. He was only contemplating his rings.

Robin, after more thought, did the only possible thing. He moved his Queen away to provide an escape square for the King. Jeff took the Pawn, giving check (though, of course, not actually saying it). The King moved to the vacant Queen's square. (20. Q–QB4 Q–QB1 21. Q x Pch K–Q1). Jeff brought up his other Rook, and Robin's King continued his flight (22. R–Q1 K–B2). Jeff took Robin's Bishop with his Rook, and this time it took Robin only a few seconds to decide to abandon the hopeless struggle (23. R x Bch Resigns). The two players shook hands, neither smiling.

Mrs. Oppenheimer dropped her cat-with-cream expression instantly and looked round for the photographer. By the time she had summoned him it was too late to take the moment of victory. Robin had already left the table. She told the man to take Jeff brooding over his triumph. "And get the clocks in," she added. The clocks were sensational. Jeff's showed 3:38, Robin's 5:44. Jeff had taken only eight minutes over his twenty-three moves, Robin had taken two hours and fourteen minutes. The bulb flashed, protests were made, an official rushed up to point out that photographs were forbidden after the first five minutes. Mrs. Oppenheimer expressed regret. The picture was safely in the camera, tomorrow she'd mail it to Image & Impact.

Paul caught Robin as he left the table.

"Too bad! Pity you couldn't manage to castle."

"It's always easy to be wise afterwards."

He loped off to look at the other games and Paul watched him go. This was the end. They'd be certain to drop him now from

254

the team, he'd fade out from international chess, from the big games. Just another flash in the pan, yet one more promising boy who couldn't stand the pace at the top. Still, he had been worth trying. Paul didn't regret it; if you didn't give these youngsters a break you'd never find a winner. It wasn't his fault if they couldn't always make the grade. He must just keep trying, look on the bright side. There were plenty more clever young boys coming up. He'd scout round the Easter congresses and see who he could find.

All the same, something hurt, something rankled. It wasn't so much Robin's weak play as his bad manners, his sheer ingratitude. Seventeen should have been such a charming graceful age. An ugly nature in that slim boyish body! It was so sad, Paul felt near to tears. He went to look at the other England games, and then on to Scotland, West Germany, any other nation that took his fancy.

Two hours later he was ready to go home. Reeves had won against the American second board, but Hope-Warner had lost like Robin. Steiner had drawn his game, giving the United States the best of it by two and a half points to one and a half. Scotland had done better, remarkably so, by drawing all four games against Brazil. Dour defence, he thought. Robin could have done with some of that.

He looked round for the Oppenheimers, but they had all disappeared, so he cadged a lift back to the Platzl with Dietrich in his Volkswagen. Dietrich was in a happy mood. West Germany had done well against Rumania and were now well placed for the final. Paul mentioned that he and others were going to the Hofbräuhaus later on; wouldn't the Dietrichs join them? Dietrich said he was sure they'd be glad to come, but he would ask his wife.

In the foyer of the hotel a family, wearing ski-clothes, were standing at the desk, registering.

"Himmel!" Dietrich exclaimed. "Look who's here! Hansgeorg! Ursula!"

The parents spun round and greeted him. "Franz, you old friend, what are you doing here?"

The mother added, "We have just driven from Kitzbühel, we are on our way back to Stuttgart."

Paul remembered them. Grandmaster Stuck, who had been such a great player, and had suddenly given up chess three years ago and disappeared from the scene. His beautiful and supposedly rich wife in her otter coat and yellow ski-pants, the woman who had made him give it up. Paul edged firmly forward.

Dietrich introduced him. "Herr Butler, the English writer. Herr Grossmeister Stuck. Frau Stuck."

They shook hands. Hansgeorg Stuck said, "Of course. We met in Zürich."

"And in Barcelona," said Paul. "And Moscow."

Frau Stuck gave him a wintry smile. Stuck said, "And what are you all doing here? Is there a chess congress?"

"Yes, indeed. The Students' International."

"I did not know. I had not heard. How long does it go on?"

"Ten days more."

Frau Stuck turned to her husband. *"Liebling,* we have a long drive tomorrow. Perhaps we should go on further tonight. It is still quite early."

"Ah no, Ulla, not any more tonight. I am tired with driving. The children are tired too." This was undeniable. They were grizzling round their parents' legs. "Perhaps we meet later and you tell me all about the chess. How is Germany doing?"

"Very well. We hope for a good place in the final."

Paul said, "We are all going to the Hofbräuhaus tonight to drink beer and talk. Why don't you both come too?"

"Oh, I think dinner and early to bed," said Frau Stuck firmly. "It isn't the skiing that is tiring, it's the après-ski." She laughed a brittle laugh. "Hansgeorg, we must take the children up."

The Stuck family and their luggage went up in the lift. Dietrich nudged Paul in the ribs rather hard and said, "Ah, women, women! But tonight we shall be men, eh? We shall drink a toast to men."

"Yes, indeed," said Paul, thinking anxiously of Mrs. Oppenheimer. He hoped Dietrich wouldn't be too aggressively on the sex warpath.

When the lift was free, Paul went up to the Bauernstube, and over coffee with whipped cream and cake he wrote his report for the *Post.* He praised Reeves' fine win on the second board, Steiner's careful draw, the dour draws of the Scottish players.

Robin he hardly mentioned. Then he went up to his bedroom and telephoned it through to a moronic girl in London.

He took a shower and changed his shirt. There was no doubt about it, he was putting on weight, his waistband was getting tight. Perhaps this was no moment to spend an evening drinking litres of beer. He gazed anxiously at himself in the mirror. On the other hand, didn't it really suit him not to be too skinny, to be on the plump side? Didn't it make him look younger, boyish, chubby? A little beer could do no harm.

He was downstairs in the foyer, watching television, when Mrs. Oppenheimer and Moraine arrived. They had arranged to meet in the hotel, as they didn't fancy walking by themselves into the Hofbräuhaus. Together the three of them crossed the street through the snow. Moraine paused to look up at the Christmas tree with its lights.

"Isn't that just pretty!" she exclaimed. "Oh, isn't this just the prettiest place in the world!"

They went through the swing doors into the old Schwemme. Moraine was amazed by the size of it, by the pillars and vaults, by the vistas of men drinking extending into the distance, by the noise.

"Sixteenth century," said Paul. "I don't suppose it's changed much."

The Schwemme was fairly full, but Paul found a table across from the band and only occupied by a grey-haired man in a military-type suit, and a younger dark-haired man whose head was down on the table, apparently asleep.

"This is my *stammtisch,*" said the grey-haired man. "I bid you welcome."

"What's that?" Moraine asked.

"He says this is where he always sits and says we are welcome."

"Isn't that nice of him!" They all shook hands with him and sat down.

"Beer, everybody?" said Paul, gesturing expansively. "Beer? Beer, my friend? And for your friend?"

"I guess we ought to try it," said Mrs. Oppenheimer cautiously.

Paul caught the waitress's eye. "Please, five steins. And pretzels."

The grey-haired man had green patches on his lapels and a

leather cross-brace with a badge on it. He explained that it was the badge of a rifle club. Paul passed the news on to Moraine.

"I thought maybe he was a soldier in that uniform."

"No, this is just his best suit. I think he said he worked in a post office."

The waitress brought the litre steins, holding all five in one muscular fist. They clinked steins and toasted each other, all except the sleeping man who merely groaned and turned the other cheek to the table. The women sipped cautiously, the men drank in gulps and wiped their mouths on the backs of their hands.

"I am called Sepp," said the grey-haired man.

"I'm Paul."

"And I'm Moraine."

"Please, how?"

"Moraine," Paul said. "Moräne, like a glacier."

"Why is she called that?"

"Why are you called that?"

"I don't know. I think it's after some hotel in Switzerland."

Mrs. Oppenheimer said, "A moraine is the debris a glacier leaves on the side when it moves on. Doesn't that just describe children?"

"Oh, Mommy! Anyway, Walt said you meant to call me Loraine, but you had a cold."

Sepp was pulling at Paul's sleeve, trying to attract his attention, speaking to him.

"What's he saying?" Moraine asked.

"He says you are very beautiful. He thinks you are my wife. He hopes we shall have many grandchildren."

"Grandchildren!" she exclaimed. *"Grand*children! Hey, wait a minute."

Sepp said, "A happy family is the most important of life's joys. The most important," he added, clasping Paul's hand.

Paul didn't agree, but he disengaged and drank a toast to happy family life.

The band started again, playing "In München steht ein Hofbräuhaus," and Paul and Sepp joined in singing. They linked their crossed arms and swayed to the music. Moraine linked and swayed too.

"This is the true *gemütlichkeit,*" Paul shouted in her ear.

"Yes, they have that in New York too, at Lüchow's. But it's different there, kind of gracious. This is the real thing."

Paul nodded, pleased. He felt relaxed, happier than he had for some time, a genial host entertaining his friends, able to demonstrate his command of German, his knowledge of German songs. When the band came to "Ein Prosit" he made them all rise and clink steins. Sepp put down his stein and clasped Paul's hand in both his.

"Paul," he said. "Paul, Paul, now we are true comrades. True comrades for eternity."

His eyes were swimming with tears. Paul looked deep and emotionally into them. "True comrades," he repeated, "for eternity."

They drank to each other with their arms linked. Moraine asked, "What are you saying?"

"We've just sworn life-long comradeship for ever."

"But you've only just met!"

"Yes, I know. It's pure *Götterdämmerung.*" Seeing that he was not carrying Moraine with him, he explained, "Siegfried arrives at the house of the Gibichungs. He has never met any of them before, but he immediately swears blood-brotherhood with them. It's very German, that."

"I think that's lovely."

"Yes, but it doesn't stop them all killing each other later on."

Sepp was tugging at his sleeve. "Please tell your wife that we are now true comrades for eternity."

"I will." They clinked steins again and toasted their comradeship, Moraine too. She suppressed a grimace as she swallowed. She had never learnt to like beer.

Paul looked up and saw the Dietrichs arrive, surprisingly with Frau Stuck. He waved to them, beckoning them to join him. Frau Stuck eased her shoulders out of her otter coat and looked round her. "In all the thousands of times I've been in Munich," she remarked in perfect English, "I've never been here before. Oh, it's a dreadful place, isn't it." She smoothed the hair back from her forehead.

"Where is Hansgeorg?"

"Oh, he's gone up to Schwabing to play chess with the students' team. I shan't see him again before morning. If then."

Paul felt sorry that Hansgeorg was not coming, and, secretly, that his wife had decided to come. But he was determined that nothing should spoil this evening. It was his long-promised treat. He summoned the waitress.

"Beer!" he said. "More beer. Beer for the newly arrived. Joann? Moraine?"

Mrs. Oppenheimer and Moraine hastily demurred. They had hardly started the first stein yet.

"Sepp? Yes? And for me too." He glanced at the sleeping man with his cheek on the table, but he hadn't touched his first stein. "Five beers. And we want something to eat. Sausages for everyone. Weisswurst for seven." He explained to Moraine, "They're the speciality of Munich."

"Are they the ones they have pictures of on the postcards?"

"Yes, they're white, with little flecks of green."

"Isn't that just lovely." Moraine swallowed. "I've always liked hot dogs," she added bravely.

The band was playing again. They linked arms and sang; at least Paul sang.

> *"Wer soll es bezahlen?*
> *Wer hat das bestellt?*
> *Wer hat so viel Pinka-pinka?*
> *Wer hat so viel Geld?"*

"What's it all mean?" asked Moraine.

He told her.

"That's all it's about? Grumbling about who's going to pick up the tab?"

He smiled at her. "Don't worry, I'm not grumbling. I'm picking up the tab tonight."

Sepp was plucking at Paul's sleeve. "You and your wife have many children?"

He turned to Moraine. "Have we many children?"

"Help! I thought it was grandchildren we were meant to have."

"You can't have one without the other."

She gave a grimace and leaned forward. *"Nein,"* she said to Sepp, shaking her head firmly. *"Nein, nein."*

Sepp turned to the Dietrichs on his other side. "You have many children?"

Frau Dietrich, a small blonde woman, said, "We have no children, unfortunately." She put her arm round her husband. "But perhaps soon?" she said to him softly. She stroked his cheek amorously. *"Liebling,* perhaps soon?"

Paul buried his face in his stein and tried not to listen. Sepp shook his head in a puzzled way, and then pulled out photographs of his own grandchildren and passed them round. Hoping to change the conversation, Paul produced his pocket tape recorder and passed it round for them to play with. The sleeping man suddenly awoke and grabbed the recorder, and started to take it to pieces. Paul snatched it back.

The weisswurst came and they all started to eat, Mrs. Oppenheimer a little tentatively. Frau Dietrich wolfed hers down in a few mouthfuls and followed it with big gulps of beer. Alone of the women at the table she drank her beer like a man. Paul was feeling very happy. Beer and music and sausages. The band was playing again.

"Humbta humbta humbta tätärä," he carolled away. *"Tätärä, tätärä."*

"What's all that mean?" asked Moraine.

"I don't think it means anything."

Frau Stuck's voice came across the table. "They are monsters, complete monsters. There should be a society for chess-players, like Alcoholics Anonymous. Chess-players Anonymous. I tell you it is like having an alcoholic in the house, or a drug-addict, or a compulsive gambler. They are monsters, you do not know what they are like."

"Maybe I do," Mrs. Oppenheimer commented.

"You cannot know if you have not been married to one. It is chess, chess, chess, all day, all night. They have no other thought in their heads. Just chess. They do not think about their wives, their children, their homes. We chess-wives, chess-widows, need a society to protect us."

"It sounds as if somebody needs some protection."

"I told my husband frankly he must chose between chess and me."

"I know which I'd have chosen."

"Yes, the family must come first. So he agreed no more chess. I threw out all his boards and pieces, all his books and magazines.

I cancelled his subscriptions to the magazines, to his clubs. For three years he hasn't thought once about chess, I swear. He has been a good husband. And now, we come through Munich and we walk straight into a tournament. It is like an alcoholic, you know, he doesn't touch a drop for years and then one day somebody gives him a glass of wine, and all is lost. Now my husband wants to stay in Munich till the end of the tournament, watch the games, play against the boys. He is back on the chess, what do I do? I have told him that if he does not come with us tomorrow to Stuttgart, he is not to come at all. Ever."

"Cracking the whip. Will he obey?"

"Yes, I think so. But he will be changed, I'm afraid. He will be studying chess again, following the games, wanting to play in tournaments. I shall have all to do again to break him of it." She gave a little laugh. "It is all my mistake, in a way. He wanted to stay in the hotel across the street, we were there when we were first married. And I thought why not, chess is all forgotten now. And then we run into Franz and Erna Dietrich, and he hears about the student tournament, and everything is lost. If we had stayed at the Vierjahreszeiten or the Bayerischer Hof everything would have been fine. He would never have heard about the student tournament."

"If you had stayed at the Bayerischer Hof," said Mrs. Oppenheimer coolly, "he would have heard about it. I should have told him."

Frau Stuck looked at Mrs. Oppenheimer for the first time. "You? Are you interested in chess then?"

"I was four times No. 2 in the United States Ladies' Championship."

"Oh. Oh well, you know about chess then. But, of course, it isn't the same for women. We simply can't give our whole minds to it, we have so many other things to think about—clothes, hairdos, our husbands, the children, the shopping, the servants. While the men think of nothing else. That is why we women are not as good as men, not at chess. How could we be?"

Mrs. Oppenheimer said, even more icily, "I was very good. I could hold my own against any grandmaster. I drew against your husband at Baden-Baden." She forbore to add that it had been a friendly game in the hotel. The point was still valid.

"Did you? Well, perhaps you hadn't got a family."

Mrs. Oppenheimer pointed at Moraine. "That is my daughter."

Frau Dietrich picked up the word. "Your daughter? She is your daughter?" She caressed her husband again. *"Liebling,* you would like a little daughter, our own little daughter? With blue eyes, like us. She has brown eyes, but our daughters will have blue eyes like the heaven."

Dietrich's eyes flashed, but whether it was excitement, embarrassment or beer, it was impossible to say. "How many?" he shouted. "How many daughters? Five, six?"

"Just one, *liebling,* one for now. Little Karen Erna. Perhaps tonight?" she stage-whispered.

"Erna, we have to think, we must not decide in a hurry. There is much to think about, my work, the money, your work, the home."

"Liebling!" She tweaked his nose.

Frau Stuck suddenly pointed at a fresco on the ceiling. It showed a chess-board with masks and devils. "There!" she exclaimed loudly. "That's it, the dance of death. Chess is the dance of death."

Moraine felt the need to intervene, to say something. She had prepared what she meant to say.

She leaned forward. "Sepp! Paul, please tell Sepp that my family comes from Germany. From Oppenheim on the Rhine."

Paul hastened to translate, to change the conversation. He wasn't enjoying either Frau Dietrich's or Frau Stuck's remarks very much.

Sepp was no longer able to follow about Moraine's ancestry, but he picked up the word Rhine and began to sing "O du wunderschöner Deutscher Rhein!" But he didn't last long, as the band was playing again "In München steht ein Hofbräuhaus."

Moraine sank back. Her head was beginning to ache. How long had they been here? Two, three hours? She had sung "Ein Prosit" ten or eleven times, "In München steht ein Hofbräuhaus" at least five times. The same tunes going round and round. She had only been able to swallow three or four inches of her beer, just enough to get the sausages down. The sausages, though, hadn't been bad, they hadn't really tasted of anything. And she had liked the pretzels. But what she wanted was a screwdriver on the rocks and she didn't know how to get hold of it. The men were doing all right. Paul and Herr Dietrich were both on their fourth steins—or was it their fifth? And goodness knows how many Sepp had had. Only the sleeping friend had given up, gone to the john at some stage, and never come back.

"What time does this place close?" she asked Paul.

"They start pushing us out round midnight."

Another hour! Her back was beginning to ache too.

Dietrich suddenly leaned forward, his face flushed, a blond lock falling over his eyes. "Herr Schriftsteller Butler!" he said aggressively; or was it only extreme formality? "Your boy lost today. The young English boy you said was so brilliant. He lost to the American in twenty-three moves."

Paul nodded sadly. "He did not play well."

"He lost! Why do the English always lose? Why do you never win any tournaments? Why have you no grandmasters?"

Paul sighed, and he began to make, not for the first time, the usual excuses. Not enough public interest, no official interest, not enough money, the best young players having to spend their time and energy in other jobs, earning their living.

"But it is the same in Germany. We have no official support, our chess-players have nothing except what they win in prizes. And yet we win tournaments, we have grandmasters. Why do the English always lose?"

"Not always," Paul remarked, "not at everything." Then suddenly he felt needled. The beer flushed to his face like rage. He counter-attacked. "I will tell you why. I will tell you why we have no grandmasters. It is because our best young players do not wish to be grandmasters. They do not wish to be champions. They do not wish to be you. They wish to be me!" He patted his chest. "Our young players dream of being chess correspondents, authors, earning a good living, travelling. Experts on chess, yes, but also experts on art, music, travel, food, wine. They wish to become civilised people by way of chess. And isn't that the object of life, to be a civilised person?"

Dietrich banged his stein on the table. His voice was very loud. "I will tell you why you do not win. It is because you have no will to victory. You cannot win without a will to victory. It is the same in chess as in war. The English do not win because they have no will to victory."

Paul started to remonstrate, but Dietrich banged his stein on the table again. He continued, "Listen, I will tell you a story. Five years ago Hansgeorg and I were playing in the Zürich International Tournament. Just before the third game Hansgeorg had received a telegram saying his wife has had a bad car accident and is in hospital dangerously ill. He looks sad, then he puts the telegram in his pocket and he goes into the hall to play Grandmaster Mischchov. He plays very well, he draws."

Everyone was listening now. Frau Stuck was hanging on his words.

"A week later another telegram has come and says his wife now better, out of danger. And he says to me, 'My God, my wife has been ill in hospital a week. I forgot. I must telephone.' "

"Hey, wait a minute," said Moraine, glancing at Frau Stuck, "is this her husband you are talking about?"

"Hansgeorg, yes. He said to me, 'We are tough guys. We must be, to win.' "

Frau Stuck said with narrowed eyes, "That isn't at all the story he told me. He told me the first telegram had never arrived. And he had had it all the time. There was I lying in hospital, on the danger list, having blood transfusions. My husband does not come, there is no message, nothing. Because he has forgotten, he is busy playing chess. And then later he tells me the telegram did not arrive."

Moraine said, "This is getting a bit rugged, isn't it?"

Frau Stuck said, "Hansgeorg, you just wait till I see you tonight! You just wait for it!"

Dietrich banged his stein again. "Ursula, you do not understand. Your husband was right, he had the will to victory. He won the tournament, joint first with Mischchov. You should be proud of him. He had the true will to victory. Without it he would not be victorious."

"And all the time that telegram was burning a hole in his pocket, and he just forgot it."

"He was right, that is why he was victorious. He had the will to victory." Feeling he was not getting his point across, he repeated the last sentence in German.

Sepp understood that; he had understood little for a long time. He said, "He had to do his duty. He was a soldier."

"No," said Paul, "he was a chess-player."

"A chess-player? Chess?"

"Yes. That's what we are all talking about."

Sepp gripped Paul's arm. "You are a soldier."

"No, I'm a writer."

Sepp looked at them all in bewilderment. "I am a soldier," he said at last. "Paul! Moräne! I am a soldier!" He patted the badge on his chest. "Paul! Moräne! Listen, I tell you a story. When I came home from the war, I had been a prisoner of war, all my family were waiting at the station to welcome me home." He ticked them off on his fingers. "My wife, my three children, my parents, my brother and his wife and their four children, my sister and her husband and their two children. They had to wait six hours, my train was late. They had prepared a welcome-home feast for me at home, but I said, 'No, I am a soldier, I must do my duty, I must report to the barracks.' They ate the feast without me and then they all went away. When I came home the next day, only my wife and children were there. But I was right, I had done my duty."

Paul decided not to translate the sad little story to Moraine. Sepp gripped both their hands. Tears were now trickling down his cheeks. "Paul! Moräne! A happy family is the only true happiness in life."

Paul translated this to Moraine who looked round the table and said, "Well, you'd never guess, would you?"

Out of the corner of his eye Paul saw three young men enter the Schwemme. He turned quickly; three familiar faces, Steiner, Reeves and Robin. They had come after all! A surge of excitement shook him. The boy had recovered his good humour, perhaps his chess form. All was forgiven and forgotten. He held out his arms in welcome, and then made gestures meaning Come and join us, we'll squeeze up and make room, have some beer on me.

Steiner and Reeves both gave him small bleak smiles. Robin merely nodded. They walked on, past the table, through the archway by the band and the postcard kiosk, to a table at the other end.

Paul slowly let his arms fall to his side. The band was playing "Das Humbta Tätärä" again, but he didn't feel like singing any more.

MIAMI BEACH

Moraine and Carl sat at the counter of the coffee-shop in the Fontainebleau Hotel. She was wearing a flesh-coloured bathing suit and, since she was inside the hotel, a black fish-net shirt over it, an ensemble which had all heads turning. All heads, she thought, except Carl's. She had been up for hours and had come down from the pool for a mid-morning snack, a Rose Marie banana split. Whole bananas, three different flavours of ice-cream, syrup, nuts and billows of pure whipped cream. She sucked the spoon sensually.

Carl, on the other hand, had only just got up. He was wearing a sweat-shirt, grey pants and sneakers, and he was eating two eggs, up and easy, a ham steak, pancakes and maple syrup. Both he and Moraine were still very lean. A middle-aged woman, wearing a fur stole against the air-conditioning, glanced at them enviously.

"Parrots," Moraine was saying. "We must see the parrots, there's a whole jungle of them. And the alligators in the Everglades. I saw a movie about the Everglades once. It's really romantic. And it may be too late soon. They say Diane'll be here in two or three days."

Diane was a hurricane at present devastating Cuba.

"Honey, I just don't have the time at the moment. I haven't gotten all my analysis done."

"But, darling, you don't have to work so hard all the time. This is meant to be a vacation for everybody as well as a chess match. Couldn't you take a morning off and relax?"

"Your mom doesn't see this as a vacation. And you don't win matches by relaxing. That's something they don't teach them in Iran."

Moraine sipped some coffee and stared ahead.

"You're winning this match pretty easily, aren't you?"

"Right! I plan to win all ten games. I've my reputation to think of."

"Jeff isn't playing well," she admitted. "And he did so well in Munich. And remember that night at the Henry Hudson when he beat you?"

It wasn't tactful. She wasn't feeling tactful.

"Rapid Transit! Anything can happen in that sort of game. Student chess. Listen, honey, I've nothing against the kid. He does have talent, a feeling for a combination, a sacrifice. He's a sort of minor Tal. But that's not enough. This is the big time, the first time he's met it, and he's all at sea."

"You mean he just isn't good enough?"

"I didn't say that. But he has a long way still to go." He ordered another plate of pancakes and syrup. "This ocean air sure makes me hungry. Look, these openings like the Lopez or the Dragon or the Caro-Kann, they've been analysed through the fifteenth or twentieth move. Hundreds of thousands of hours have been spent on them, all over the world, working out the best variations, the best continuations. And this kid expects to play them by ear. He expects to find the best continuations in a few minutes over the board. Of course he can't. He comes out of the opening in an inferior position, and after that it's only a question of technique. He wriggles a bit, tries a sacrifice or two, but it's all over."

Moraine finished her split and sighed. "But, if it's all sewn up, why do you have to work so hard mornings?"

"Oh, not on this cock-eyed match. I'm preparing for the Interzonal. I have to dream up some new variations that nobody's thought of before, see if they're sound and put them up my sleeve. You can't go and win against players like Larsen or Portisch without something up your sleeve. At the moment I'm trying with Bishop to Knight 2 on the ninth move of the Lopez."

Moraine said, "Mommy's going to be pretty sore if Jeff doesn't win a single game."

"Well, she picked him. He needn't worry, he'll get his two grand."

She signed her check and stood up. "I'm going back to the pool," she said bleakly. "See you lunchtime."

She walked out of the coffee-shop with her nose in the air. All eyes followed her except Carl's. Outside she turned left towards the Cabana Club and the biggest ice-skating rink in Florida, which was closed, and the ocean. At the doorway marked J. H. Kaplan, Stockbrokers, she paused and looked in. It was like a private movie show or a chapel service. About a dozen men, mostly middle-aged in gay pants, sat watching the illuminated tape which moved across the screen. A girl was stroking an I.B.M. machine. Another girl was eating ice-cream. At the back sat the manager himself, waiting for someone to buy or sell, but no one spoke to him.

Jeff was in the middle of the front row of chairs, staring at the tape. Moraine sank to a chair and studied the tape too. It was complete gibberish to her. What did all those letters and fractions mean? Was the market going up or down? She stole a glance at Jeff. Was it possible that he, of all people, understood it? Was he just fascinated by the moving lights? Or did he follow just what was going on? Maybe he wasn't going to be World Chess Champion, but he might make a million on Wall Street. The kid has talent.

"Jeff!" she whispered. "Jeff!"

Everyone turned. She stood up and made gestures implying that she was going back to the pool, and was he coming too? He signalled that he would be up in two minutes. Nobody was watching the tape any more. They were all staring at the beautiful girl, apparently naked except for a fish-net shirt. The girl with the ice-cream goggled most of all. "Brother!" she said aloud, "why didn't I think of that!"

Moraine went upstairs to the pool, to the chaise-longue, and the blue cushions, and the towels. She peeled off the fish-net shirt, and rubbed in more Sea and Ski. It was important not to get darker than the bathing suit or it would lose its point. Not that there was much danger of that today. The sky was covered with a dark oily film, thicker and deeper towards the south. The locks of the approaching storm, she thought, wondering again about the word locks. There was still no wind, and the ocean had only its usual swell. Still, this might be the last chance of lying out for several days. She felt both disappointed and excited.

She put on her dark glasses, which were still necessary for reading, and burrowed in her towel for the sonnets of Edna St. Vincent Millay. She read and felt soothed. Edna seemed to understand her so well, her heart and feelings; she could say everything that Moraine wanted said, in a language she could never have controlled. It was like hearing a lawyer put your case more eloquently than you ever could. And the beauty of the phrasing! If she could have written poetry, she would have written these sonnets.

She looked up and saw Jeff in his Sulka dressing-gown smiling down at her.

"T.W.A. is down a little," he said.

"Do you have any T.W.A. stock?"

"Not yet. But some day, I hope."

She smiled and waved him to the chaise-longue. He took off his dressing-gown, and lay down. His skin was darker than hers, his hair and his eyebrows and his trunks were black, setting off the two gold wristwatches and the three gold rings.

"Aren't you scared of being burglarised, with all that?"

He shook his head. "I always wear it. I never leave it alone in the room. What are you reading?"

"Poetry, very beautiful poetry. Love poetry."

"Please read some to me."

She glanced at him quickly, turned a few pages, and cleared her throat.

> "O ailing Love, compose your struggling wing!
> Confess you mortal; be content to die.
> How better dead, than be this awkward thing
> Dragging in dust its feathers of the sky,
> Hitching and rearing, plunging beak to loam,
> Upturned, dishevelled, utt'ring a weak sound
> Less proud than of the gull that rakes the foam,
> Less kind than of the hawk that scours the ground.

While yet your awful beauty, even at bay,
Beats off the impious eye, the outstretched hand,
And what your hue or fashion none can say,
Vanish, be fled, leave me a wingless land . . .
Save where one moment down the quiet tide,
Fades a white swan, with a black swan beside."

She glanced at him again to see if he had understood. He was staring at the sky.

"Did you write that?"

"Me? God, no! It's by a very great American poet." She didn't bother him with the name. "Did you understand it?"

"No."

Well, maybe the English was rather difficult for him. "Shall I read you another?"

"No, I shall read to you."

He had no book, but he lay back and began to speak in a strange language, a soft language rendered in a monotone.

"What's that?" she asked when he paused for a moment. "Omar Khayyám?"

"The Koran."

Of course! She remembered all those young men walking up and down the Maidan-Shah at sunset learning the Koran by heart.

"Go on." She hoped that it was all about white peacocks in the courts of the morning.

"Go on," she said when he paused again. The incomprehensible words wafted her away from the Cabana Club and Diane and the poolside Bossa Nova lesson. She was seeing blue domes floating in brilliant light, she was smelling the ancient dust of the Souk, she was hearing the distant call to prayer.

"Go on," she said, as if he were making love to her.

"Telephone call for Mr. Jeff Falkner. Mr. Jeff Falkner."

They sat up and glared at the loudspeaker. The call could only be from one person. Jeff went to take it at the bar. When he came back he said, "I have to go and study chess. She's seen us from her room."

"Isn't that too bad! Still, I guess it's what you're here for. Thanks for reciting all that to me. Maybe tomorrow?" she ventured.

"There is no chess game tomorrow."

"Well, would you recite some more Koran to me? We could go on the beach, we'd be more private there. That is, if Diane lets us."

He put on the dressing-gown. "Thank you," he said. He gave her a little salaam which delighted her and went down the staircase towards the hotel.

When he had gone, she lay back and looked at the lurid sky. No doubt about it, there was excitement in the air. The ocean rising, the sky darkening, and the boy from the East speaking to her in a strange tongue about strange gods. She felt the experience touch her like silk, and in the hot still atmosphere she shivered.

"Telephone call for Mr. Jeff Falkner. Mr. Jeff Falkner."

What, again! He must have been gone a good fifteen minutes, and he still hadn't reached his room. He must have been tempted, and turned aside on the way. She smiled. She imagined him back in the middle of the front row of chairs, staring at the illuminated tape, studying the fortunes of T.W.A. stock.

Paul stood on his balcony. He could see Moraine on her chaise-longue, and, since the hotel was curved like a quadrant, he could also see Mrs. Oppenheimer, as she went in and out from her balcony to check Jeff. Much of the social life of the Fontainebleau seemed to go on across the balconies. One girl away on his right was conversing with a boy miles away below and to his left by walkie-talkie. An older man above him was dating a girl by shouting at her.

"Hi, got a rope?"

"Make your own!"

Now that he was sure that he had digested his scrambled eggs, he was preparing to go and swim in the glamorous Floribbean. He enjoyed swimming in warm seas or lakes, and he felt less bashful about his steadily thickening figure in bathing trunks here where many others of his age had the same problem. He had bought himself a new pair of trunks in the shopping arcade; in the current fashion they were coloured like the Norwegian flag. And, anyway, just to be here, with the coconut palms and the Cadillacs, and that long line of huge white hotels, like a great irregular grin facing the ocean. At a time when his fellow-countrymen were wondering if they could afford the Costa Brava he was swimming among the millionaires, and at no expense to himself. They'd all be so envious, he'd probably be ostracised when he got home to Kensington.

After the swim, some Miller's High Life beer at the poolside bar, possibly (though probably not) chatting to Moraine; the girl seemed rather unapproachable these days. Then lunch, a rare, aged, marbled steak with a baked potato and sour cream and a tossed green salad, and more beer. And then the chess game: he enjoyed being in charge of that. He always made a speech before each game, introducing the players, paying tribute to Mrs. Oppenheimer, explaining what had happened so far for the benefit of those who weren't following too closely, and appealing for silence. After the game, a shower, a couple of martinis in the Poodle Room, stuffed royal squab with wild rice in the Fleur-de-Lys Room, bourbon.

It was at this point that the vacuum in his life became apparent. There was really nothing to do except swim, supervise chess, eat and drink. There was no opera, no art gallery, no foreign language to speak, no old historic corner on which to become expert. He disdained the performing dolphins at the Seaquarium, the young men in tuxedos singing romantic songs into microphones, the Playboy Club. He didn't see himself as a big-game fisherman, and anyway that was very expensive. He could go out to another similar hotel for identical martinis and royal squab, except that his meals were already paid for in the Fontainebleau. He wasn't honeymooning, or even courting.

Even the chess was disappointing; neither game so far was worth reporting in the *Post* or even in *Chess World*. Paul couldn't help a twinge of satisfaction. The boy who had humbled his Robin at Munich was now being humbled himself. Young Falkner was clearly right out of his depth. Well, that wasn't Paul's fault, he had always felt doubts about the boy's possibilities. But it would have been nice to have brought something home besides a suntan; the personal memory of a great game.

And now something was being provided—Diane! It might interfere with the swimming, but it would give him something to dine out on when he got home. He listened to the weather reports, he talked about the hurricane as avidly as anyone in Miami. He might write a great Conradish storm-piece, "Chess in the Hurricane," perhaps a holiday descriptive piece in *The Statistician*. Or he might work it in somehow into *Sixty-Four Squares*.

He went in from the balcony and turned on the radio beside the bed. After a brief commercial about used cars, the announcer excitedly reported winds of up to a hundred and forty miles an hour, millions of dollars' damage in Cuba, Diane heading for the Florida Keys, though the latest reports suggested that she was swinging away into the Gulf of Mexico. Paul felt a twinge of disappointment at the last words.

The telephone rang. It could only be one person.

"Hello, Paul. I saw you come in from your balcony and I wanted to catch you before you went swimming, but I gave you time to listen to the weather report first. Wasn't that kind of me!"

Paul felt as if he were performing naked in front of a plateglass window.

"Listen, I'm worried about the way Jeff's playing. He doesn't seem to have found his touch yet."

"No, he hasn't really yet, has he?" said Paul cautiously.

"I think maybe he's nervous. You know, the big hotel, the crowd, playing up on a platform with everyone watching. He's never done anything like that before."

"It might be that."

"And the crowd isn't always as quiet as it might be."

Paul, feeling rebuked, said, "It isn't always easy to keep them quiet. They're on vacation, and some of them don't understand about chess."

"I know, I'm not blaming you, Paul dear. But do try and keep them quieter this afternoon."

Paul felt she was referring to the man yesterday who had suddenly exclaimed very loudly, "Well, call this a spectator sport, twenty goddam minutes and nobody's moved a thing. Give me tennis!"

"Have you noticed how slowly Jeff is playing?"

"Well, yes."

"Normally he plays all chess as if it were Rapid Transit. But yesterday he was sitting over every move as if he were Reshevsky. That's not his style. I wondered if you could speak to him, tell him to relax, play his usual style. Let his genius sort of bubble out naturally."

"I hardly think the umpire could advise one of the players on his style of play."

"Oh, I don't think anyone would mind. I think someone should speak to him and he won't take it from me, I'm sure. It's important for the sake of the whole event that he should win a game soon, today if possible. I'm sure he can, if he would only relax. I'd really appreciate it if you would have a word with him."

Paul got the message. "All right, I'll drop him a quiet hint sometime."

"You're a sweetie, dear. I always knew you were the right person to do this match for me."

After she rang off he went on to the balcony to look for Jeff. But Moraine was alone beside the pool, reading. He called Jeff's room, but there was no answer. God alone knew what the boy did with himself all morning. He'd try to catch him at lunch. Then he went down to swim. The soft sand, the warm heaving sea, the eerie sky reassured him that he was having a suitably exotic time.

The game started at two-thirty. The attendance, about two hundred, was satisfactory, as it had been for the first two games. Not all these were dedicated chess-players. There were other congresses besides chess going on in the Fontainebleau—a congress to study religion, architecture and art, the Florida Insurance Agents' Association, and others, and these conventioners often came to watch for a while. But the hard core were chess-addicts, taking their vacations with the favourable conditions and special rates arranged. As far as Mrs. Oppenheimer could make out, the better part of two whole clubs was here, one from Chicago, one from Philadelphia.

Paul opened proceedings by explaining that it was a ten-game match between Carl Sandbach of California and Jeffrey Falkner of New York. Carl Sandbach, having won the first two games, was now two points ahead, so perhaps today was Jeff Falkner's turn. He appealed for silence from everybody—"and that goes for Diane too," he added, glancing towards the South. He liked to make little jokes, he prided himelf on his after-dinner speaking. The Fontaine Room, where the match was being held, was insulated against all storms, but there was a gratifying titter.

"I just love your British accent," a woman called out from the end of the front row.

He smiled at her and said "Ssshh!" He smiled at Mrs. Oppenheimer and Moraine, glared at two young men who were playing a game of their own, their board on an empty chair between them, and pressed the button on White's (Carl's) clock. "Ssshh!" he said again, "SSSHH!"

Moraine, in the middle of the front row, felt that they were fighting over her. She was the prize. Two knights jousting at a tournament for her favours; that had been her dream yesterday, when the chess became too difficult for her. But the setting was wrong. The Fontaine Room with its chandeliers, its rose lamps, its French statues, didn't seem right for it. A French château! Of course. Wine had been drunk at dinner, cognac had been drunk, tempers had flared, words had been spoken, the great dining-table pushed back against the wall, doublets removed, rapiers drawn, the great gasp from the other guests. And she, the Marquis's daughter, against the wall behind the candelabra, the prize for the winner. The thought sustained her throughout the opening.

Mrs. Oppenheimer beside her was following the game breathlessly on the huge demonstration board behind the platform which was being manipulated by a boy from the Miami Chess Club. In honour of the occasion she was wearing a dark-red silk dress from Bergdorf, a fur stole and a straw pill-box hat with a veil. If you didn't dress up for this, she felt, what would you dress up for? She glanced at Moraine, and wished the child wouldn't turn up in slacks.

Paul obviously had spoken to Jeff, as he was playing today at his normal Rapid Transit speed. He seemed more relaxed too, strolling up and down the platform while Carl was thinking, watching the way the pieces stuck to the demonstration board by magnetism. Carl too was more relaxed than usual. He had taken out his black Knight mascot from his pocket, but he didn't fiddle with it. He didn't bite his fingertips or re-cross his legs. This game was peanuts.

The kid—Carl thought of him as a kid—whatever his instinct for combinations, obviously didn't know the first thing about positional play, the hidden strategic threats and balances. The game was a Ruy Lopez, with Jeff playing a peculiar version of the Steinitz Defence. But had nobody ever told him that the key to the Steinitz was a strong King's Pawn on K4? What had Sol Chaimo-

276

vitz been doing all those months when he had been coaching him? Anyway, Jeff blithely exchanged his vital King's Pawn for Carl's Queen's Pawn, and Carl recaptured with his King's Knight, establishing the Knight strongly in the centre of the board.

When they emerged into the middle-game Mrs. Oppenheimer saw with dismay that Carl had complete control of the centre, had blocked the Queen's side and had his raking Bishops poised for a joint King's side attack. She told herself that Jeff had never been strong in the opening, but he was great in the middle-game, which gave scope to his special genius. Now surely there would be some brilliant counter-play.

Jeff indeed did try. He tried to break the stranglehold by sacrificing first a Knight and then a Rook, but he gained no compensating advantage. The pressure was increased against him without ever turning into an actual mating attack. Finally the fire died in Jeff and he quietly resigned. Paul caught Mrs. Oppenheimer's eye, and shook his head sadly.

One or two of the inexpert protested at the resignation. ("He hasn't been mated, has he? Why does he give up? Why doesn't he play on?") But the club members saw that it was inevitable, indeed that it would have been discourteous to play on in such a lost position. They applauded Carl, who smiled modestly; Jeff slipped away out of the room. Moraine wanted to follow him, but she was headed off by a group of keen players wanting to analyse the game with Carl, or maybe just to get his autograph. By the time she had got outside the door, Jeff had disappeared.

She took the elevator up to her room, shut the door behind her, kicked off her shoes. She felt low, depressed. She called Jeff's room, but there was no answer. The Cabana Club was closed, so was Wall Street. He must have gone for a walk or down to the coffee-shop. Idly she switched on the television. While it was warming up, she went on to the balcony. The ocean was higher than before, with a dull metallic colour, and there were unhealthy flecks of white cloud against the lowering sky. Hot puffs of wind came from the south, moving the palm fronds.

The announcer's voice came on and Moraine went in to watch. The screen showed Diane, flashing like a neon sign, moving across a map of the Caribbean. High winds were already reported in Key West, and the full force of the hurricane was likely to hit the town within the next thirty-six hours. Present indications were that Diane would move north to Miami and Palm Beach, and then, with luck, veer east into the Atlantic.

An older man with glasses then appeared to advise on hurricane precautions: laying in a stock of candles, keeping the bathtub filled with water, getting the coconuts down from the palmtrees before they blew down on your head.

"And who the hell's going to do that?" she asked aloud.

She switched off the television and turned on the radio. There might be gentle soothing music; but it was only another man, giving the latest details from Key West, extracting every possible ounce of drama from the news. There was a knock at the door.

Moraine opened it warily. It was Carl, smiling happily, confidently.

"Hi, honey!" he said, advancing into the room, driving her before him. "Well, I made it! I told you I was going to win, and I did."

"Yeah, you won."

"He's a nice kid, but he's wasting his time here. He ought to go back to New York and practise up a bit before tangling with people like us."

Moraine said nothing.

"Still, it's always nice to win. You can never be sure a game's won till the other feller offers his hand. How about a little celebration, heh?" He put his arm around her and looked down into her face. His features seemed somehow blurred with lust. With his free hand he began to unbutton her shirt. "How about it, heh?"

She wriggled free, and did the button up again.

"Honey, what's the matter?"

The blood flushed to her face. "I'll tell you what's the matter." Her voice was husky and incoherent with emotion. "You don't treat me like a human being, that's what's the matter. You think you can turn up any hour of the day or night and I'll be available. You treat me like—like"—she searched for a telling word—"like a mail-box. Every time you have something for the mail you think I'm there waiting for it."

"What's the matter? I didn't know, I thought you liked it."

"Sure I like it. I like love, I love love. I just don't like being

278

used like a bathroom. There's the bathroom there, use it, and then get out."

"What kind of talk's that?"

"Plain talk you may understand at last. A girl doesn't always want to get laid just because the man happens to have an erection."

"Honey! What kind of talk's that?" He looked at her in bewilderment. "Well, maybe it is a bit early in the day. How about some dinner and we could go dancing in the Boom-Boom Room . . ."

"Dancing! Do you know how to dance?"

"And then maybe later . . ."

"No, not later. Not at all."

He stared at her. "Why, honey, I didn't know. Why didn't you say earlier?"

"No, it's not that. It's not that at all. It's just that I don't want to do it with you again. Now or ever. Can't you get the message?"

"But we've been doing it now for two years. All but two weeks," he corrected himself.

"Well, it's over now. Can't you realise that?" She moved across the room and opened the door. "And don't go on or the whole hotel will hear you."

He looked at her incredulously for a minute or two. Then he came to her and tried to put his arm round her again. Once again she wriggled free.

"Aw, honey, I'm sorry. I didn't know. I didn't know how you felt. Forget it. But how about coming for a drive, heh?" he went on brightly. Counter-play on the King's side. "How about going to find those parrots, heh?"

"Parrots!" she exclaimed incredulously. "It'll be dark in half an hour."

"Well, how about a drive up Collins Avenue and see the lights. We could stop off somewhere for a drink."

"I'm not going anywhere. I'm staying right here—alone. Now, are you getting out or do I have to call the bell captain?"

"Okay, okay," he muttered, going out. "I know when I'm not wanted."

She pushed him out of the room and fastened the door behind

him. She felt drained, her legs weak. She tottered across and sat on the bed. Never had she refused him before. Always she had been docile, biddable, eager to please. Maybe it's the hurricane, she thought. And now he'll lose all his games, and it'll all be my fault. She knew that he often liked to make love to her—if you could call it that—after winning a game. He said that it relaxed him. And now, suddenly, she didn't want to be used as an aspirin any more.

She stretched out on the bed, wanting to cry, and yet not able to. A commercial for a money-lender in downtown Miami and then—yes!—her favourite song. The greatest of them all, the one she would have chosen above all others, for this moment: "Unchained Melody."

The deep amplified baritone soothed and comforted her.

> "Oh my love, my darling, I've hungered for your touch
> a long lonely time.
> Time goes by so slowly, and time can do so much. Are
> you still mine?"

Behind the voice was a huge symphony orchestra, with hundreds of violins, stroking her, reassuring her.

> "I need your love, I need your love, God speed your
> love to me."

There was a knock at the door. "Oh no! Not again!" she thought. When she opened the door her mother walked briskly into the room.

"Oh God, that tune again!" she exclaimed. "Everywhere you go here they're always playing that tune. It's the National Anthem of Miami. I suppose it's all the honeymooners asking for it."

"Ssshh, please," said Moraine, trying to listen.

"Next time you go to the Boom-Boom Room with Carl, why don't you ask the band to play this specially for you." She said the word "specially" very slowly. "And then you'll get teased about hungering for his touch, and that'll be fun for everybody."

"Oh, Mommy!"

The singer notched up a semitone and the violins swooped up

to the new key-note. He was repeating the original words, the original tune, louder, more meaningfully. The violins made patterns like clouds behind him.

"Is this Sinatra?"

"No, it's Jerry Vale."

"The trouble with singing as slowly as this is that you can't keep your mind on the tune. You keep forgetting which was the previous note. So much has happened since then."

"Oh, Mommy!"

She hoped he might be going to sing through once more, but the violins floated higher and faded out. Then it was merely the time and the temperature and "for the latest news of Hurricane Diane, stay tuned to this station."

"I wondered if you knew where Jeff was."

"No idea." It was the literal truth. Kaplan's office would be shut at this hour, like the whole Cabana Club. "This area is now closed for your convenience." Anyway, she wasn't going to give away his secret hiding place. "Isn't he in his room?"

"If so, he isn't answering. I'm very disappointed at the way he is playing this match."

"Maybe he is too."

"God knows what he does with himself all day when he's meant to be working. What do you and he talk about at the pool? Chess?"

"God, no! We read poetry to each other."

"Don't tell me Jeff can read poetry. Edna, I suppose. And he's meant to be studying his openings."

"I read Edna to him. He recites the Koran to me."

"The Koran?"

"Yes. Would you believe he knows it all by heart. It sounds wonderful."

"He can't know it. He couldn't read till I had him taught."

"He didn't need to read it. He learnt it from the others in the square. That's the way it's always been handed down."

"Well, anyway the Koran isn't poetry. I've always understood it's all about taking laxatives."

"Oh, Mommy!" The endless needling, coming after her fight with Carl, finally sent her over the top. She gave a few whimpers and then started to cry seriously.

"Oh no, not you too! There's a fat woman sobbing in the coffee-shop, and a child crying in the lobby, and that girl crying in the elevator—and now you! I don't know what it is about Miami that makes everyone cry all the time. Maybe it's the air stimulating the tear-ducts."

"Oh, Mommy, stop stop! Lay off, please!" Her voice came out huskily with occasional squeaks, louder than she meant. "I know I'm the world's big joke. I'm everybody's fall guy. I don't have a brain in my head. I know, I know. I can't even get off the ground at chess. But I do have a heart, and that's something nobody else seems to have around here. I care! And I wish I were dead!"

She threw herself face down on the bed and howled into the counterpane.

"Quite right, dear. Self-pity is the most consoling of all human emotions. Never choke it back." She looked down at her daughter's shuddering body. The girl had been in a funny state ever since they came down here—or was it longer? Maybe she was pregnant. Or had she just had a fight with Carl? Or possibly it was the hurricane. That was often supposed to affect people's nerves. Anyway, there was obviously nothing further to be done with her at the moment, until she had had her cry out. Mrs. Oppenheimer would have to search for Jeff alone.

"We're meeting in the Poodle Room for a cocktail at seven. Why don't you put on a dress and come and join us? We'll ask the band to play 'Happy Birthday' for you."

"It's not my birthd . . ." She choked off the word. Then she lay quite still, crying silently, till she heard the click of the door and knew she was alone. She lay and cried for a long time. A few inches from her head a man gave out thrillingly the latest news from Vietnam, Washington, Key West, the time, the temperature, the hurricane. The Beatles. Used cars. Credit facilities. And then finally, wonderfully, Tony Bennett singing "The Shadow of Your Smile." It was almost as good as "Unchained Melody." She sat up and listened carefully. "A tear-drop kissed your lips, and so did I!" She searched in her purse for a handkerchief and failed to find one. When the song was over she went to the bathroom, blew her nose on a Kleenex and washed her face. She looked a real mess, and she looked how she felt.

She had no intention of going down to the Poodle Room for a

drink. Her mother needling, Paul being superior, possibly Carl or some of the other conventioning chess-players. All those gay girls in trouser suits dancing the frug, and nobody asking her—not that she felt like dancing tonight. And, this being the State of Florida, no alcohol for her. She went to the telephone, called Room Service, and ordered orange juice and ice to be sent up. She had brought a half-bottle of vodka with her in her suitcase, so she could have a screwdriver up here without anyone stopping her. Later if she felt hungry she would send down for ham and eggs. She would just stay in her room the whole evening, and read Edna.

They left her alone. In the morning she took breakfast in her room and then, carefully avoiding anywhere her mother might be, she went down to the Cabana Club. She had slept late so that it was already mid-morning, but there were few people about because of the bad weather. She looked in at Kaplan's office, and there he was, sitting in the middle of the front row, watching the tape.

"Hi, Jeff!" she whispered. "Jeff!"

He glanced round and smiled at her. She gestured that she was going to the beach, and he came and joined her.

"How are things?" she asked, really glad to see him.

"Trading only started half an hour ago, but there is perhaps a slight rally. T.W.A. have gone up a little from yesterday."

They walked to the beach and sat on the sand and stared out at the ocean. The clouds were low today and blowing hard, the ocean pounded higher up the beach, a hot gusty wind blew the hair over her face.

"I.B.M. and Xerox have gone ahead too, a little, but not the blue chips, not American Telephone or U.S. Steel. So I think maybe the rally will not last through the afternoon."

"How sad! You really do follow it all, don't you."

"I am interested. We shall see this afternoon. Why does the hurricane not come?"

"They only move quite slowly. Ten miles an hour, or something. They say it's going to hit us tomorrow night, or the day after. It's supposed to be causing millions of dollars' damage in Key West."

"I hope it doesn't damage the tape in the office. It will cut communications with Wall Street."

"I suppose it may. But I expect they'll repair it as soon as they can."

He nodded resignedly. A sharp gust blew the hair clear of her face, like a flag, and then it flopped back, covering her like a veil.

"Now you look like a Moslem woman," he said.

She smiled. "Jeff, would you recite some more of the Koran to me?"

"You liked that? But you did not understand it."

"I liked the sound of the language, the way you said it."

He propped himself on his elbows and began to recite. At once she was back in Isfahan, and the hot wind was the desert wind in the alleys. Of course it wasn't about laxatives, and if it were she didn't want to know. It was just beautiful. Without knowing why, she began to cry. She looked round guiltily, but there was no one else on the beach, and they weren't in view of her mother's room. She found a Kleenex in her trouser pocket, turned her head away and wiped her eyes. She didn't want him to see her, one more weeping girl on Miami Beach.

He went on for a long time and then he stopped suddenly.

"Is that the end of it?"

He shook his head. Then he turned to her and said, "Moraine. For you I will give up chess."

She stared at him. It was the most moving thing anyone had ever said to her. "Oh, Jeff," she murmured, "Jeff. What will you do then?" she added, putting her hand on his.

"I'll go back to Isfahan. Will you come with me?"

It took a minute for the message to sink in. Then she jumped to her feet. "You mean, elope with you. Elope with you all the way to Isfahan. What a crazy idea! Marvellous! Crazy! Beautiful!"

He was standing too now. She took his hands, grinning at him, laughing. "Boy, are you serious?"

"Yes, we'll go tomorrow. We won't say anything to nobody, just go."

"Tomorrow? The airport will probably be closed tomorrow. It may be closed already. If we're going, let's go now."

"Now," he said, nodding. She gave him a light chaste kiss on his mouth.

"Let's meet in the lobby in twenty minutes' time. I have to change, I can't go like this. But don't let's bring any baggage. It'd look kind of suspicious. Do you have your passport?"

He nodded.

"Oh, Jeff!" she said. "Jeff! This is the craziest, marvellousest moment of my life. What a thing to think of! I'd never have thought of it in all my life. Oh, I just hope the airport's still open. We'd better hurry. Let's go separately through the hotel, in case they notice. See you in twenty minutes, okay?"

"Okay."

She went away so light-headed that she thought she might fall. Her heart was pounding. Who says romantic things only happen in books and on records? She slipped quickly past the coffee-shop door in case Carl might be there, and went up to her room.

There was no chess today, nobody would miss them till evening. She'd call Mommy this evening from New York before she put the police on to tracing them. No, better keep clear of New York, maybe the Mann Act applied to them. If they could get a plane to Bermuda or Canada that would be best. "Oh, I do hope the airport's still open."

She changed into a dark-blue suit. It was so romantic travelling without baggage. But all the same she was going to have to change planes in Montreal or London or Paris, or some other big city, and she could hardly travel in beach clothes. She looked at her clothes; maybe Mommy would bring them back to New York, but even if she didn't, there was nothing here she really minded abandoning, except perhaps the skin-coloured bathing suit, and she could hardly wear that in Isfahan. She wondered if she'd wear a black veil like the women in the Maidan-Shah.

She picked up the telephone and called the bell captain, ordering car No. 19, a white Lincoln, Oppenheimer, to be brought to the door. Then she checked her purse for her cheque-book and credit cards; she knew she was going to have to pick up the tabs the whole way. Impulsively she stuffed Edna into the purse, to read on the plane. That's all, she thought, a book of verse, some credit cards and thou; not even the unfinished half-bottle of vodka.

She went cautiously down in the elevator to the main lobby. She had no wish to run into her mother or Paul or Carl, and was prepared to dodge behind the statues. The lobby was in semi-darkness now that the storm shutters had been put over the windows. Workmen were sandbagging the wall below the windows.

Phrases came to her. "They say the rain gets into the top of the elevator shafts and puts them out of action."

"American Express aren't answering their phone."

"They say Key West is cut off."

"It is not. The hurricane still hasn't reached Key West yet, according to the news, and Key West'll only get the edge of it. It's Miami that's likely to get the full blow."

Moraine thought, Oh I do hope the airport's still open.

She hurried through the door and tipped the boy who was holding the Lincoln door for her. The engine was running, and she climbed in and fidgeted. I'll hand the car in to Hertz at the airport, she thought, and they can send it back here to Mommy. Oh, where was Jeff? Isfahan was calling, the Blue Mosque was waiting, the airport was about to close, and Jeff wasn't here. He was late. Was he still sitting in Kaplan's office, staring at the tape, having forgotten all about her? Ought she to go and see? Supposing Mommy was just inside the door?

A bell-hop arrived with a suitcase, checked the car number and put it in the trunk. She began to protest, but then she realised that it was Jeff's suitcase. Of course he wasn't going to leave his suits, his dressing-gown behind! At least it showed that he was coming. She turned on the radio. The Beatles, not what she was wanting. She looked at the palms beside the lagoon, the fronds writhing in the strong wind. She would have to get used to the oriental tempo.

He came at last, elegant, fragrant with Dunhill's cologne. He gave her a smile, said "Hello" and climbed in beside her in a leisurely manner. The car was moving before he had even shut the door. She glanced in the driving mirror; it was wrongly adjusted and she caught a glimpse of her face, the all-American girl, bareheaded with dark glasses even on a cloudy day.

"Would you believe Isfahan!" she murmured. "We're really on our way."

Twenty miles to the airport, little traffic about. She ought to do it in fifteen minutes. On the Arthur Godfrey Causeway she remembered a question she had meant to ask.

"I'm longing to meet your family. But you've never told me anything about them."

"I have a father, a mother, ten brothers, seven sisters, four

286

nephews, six nieces, lots of uncles, aunts, cousins. Do you want to know all of their names?"

She laughed. "Well maybe later. I'd like to learn Iranian so as I can talk with them."

"Maybe a little. They would like that. But we shan't stay with them, they don't have the room. We'll stay at a hotel and visit with them. The Shah Abbas is the newest hotel."

She drove in silence, digesting this. So she wasn't to be a Moslem woman in a black veil, sitting in a harem with the other women. She was to be a visiting fireman in clothes from London or Paris, making polite conversation. She felt disappointed.

"But we can't stay in a hotel for ever. It costs too much. We'll have to look for an apartment."

"Not worth it for a short stay."

"Short stay! I thought we were going for ever. How long do you aim to stay, then?"

"A few weeks, months maybe. Until you get bored."

"Bored! I'd never get bored in Isfahan. I could live there for ever."

"But not me."

She overtook a Ford and then said, "Okay, where do we go after Isfahan? Shiraz?"

"If you like. I have never been there. We could take a trip there."

"But, Jeff, we can't roam for ever. We'll have to settle down some place, find an apartment. Where do we do that? Teheran?"

"No, not Teheran either. New York."

"New York! I thought you'd had just about enough of New York to last you a lifetime."

"Wall Street."

She burst out laughing, and then choked it back, in case he might be offended. "Wall Street, of course. I should have guessed. You're just crazy about the stock market, aren't you."

"When I was in Isfahan playing chess in the square against your mother, against anybody, I knew an Armenian money-changer. His name was Ghassabiyan. He would wait in the square too, to change money. He changed some cheques for your mother."

"Yeah, I remember. She said he gave a better rate than the hotel."

"When I was not playing chess I'd talk to him about money. He knew all the currencies in the world, rials, dollars, pounds, francs, yen, escudos, bolivars, guilders." The words dropped from his lips like a song.

She took one hand off the wheel and squeezed his arm. "All right, Jeff, I get the point. We all have our dreams, don't we. Just so long as we can go to Isfahan first. Maybe Daddy could help you," she added. "He knows lots of people on Wall Street."

An Eastern Airlines DC8 roared into the sky above them and disappeared into the clouds.

"See?" she exclaimed. "See that? The airport is still open. Oh, I know this is just our lucky day. Oh, and listen! Listen to that! Don't say anything, just listen!"

From the radio came the familiar voice of Jerry Vale singing "Unchained Melody." They listened in reverent silence.

"That's a sort of *bon voyage* present from Miami," she said, when the orchestra finally faded out.

Mrs. Oppenheimer heard the news that afternoon on a long-distance call from Moraine. It astonished her. For a while afterwards she stood staring out of the window, shocked, letting it sink in. She, who prided herself on noticing everything, how could she not have noticed this? Of course they had been together at the pool a couple of times, but that didn't mean anything. Moraine hadn't liked Jeff very much, hadn't even been able to see his good points. She had been full of prejudice against him, couldn't bear the thought of him touching her. And now, this!

Maybe the girl had had a fight with Carl, and had turned to Jeff on the rebound. Oh, the silly child! A tiresome tear trickled down her cheek. She remembered her comments on tear-ducts in Miami, and wiped it away guiltily. This was a moment for decisiveness. She went to the telephone and called Paul's room.

"Listen, Paul, something's happened. Can you come round here straight away? Room 917. And I mean straight away."

Paul, terrified that his Miami holiday was about to be taken away from him, arrived panting two minutes later. Was it something to do with Diane?

"No. Jeff and Moraine have eloped. That's all."

"Eloped! Where to?"

288

"I don't know. Iran, I suppose."

"But how did you hear?"

"She's just called me."

"From Iran?"

"No, of course not. She wouldn't say where she was except that she was outside United States territory. So I suppose she's in Bermuda or the Bahamas. She couldn't be in Canada yet, unless they went very early this morning. I suppose they might have. And all the time I thought she was just sulking in her room."

"Can't you get them back? Get the police after them?"

"I don't know for sure where they are. And, anyway, if she wants to be a fool, let her be a fool. I'm sick of chasing around after her, picking up the pieces."

"Of course he is a very good-looking boy."

"Yes. And she's just crazy about the mystery of the East, all that stuff. She sees herself as a houri in a harem. She'll get tired of that pretty soon. Cooped up in the same room with all his female relations twenty hours a day! That should take her mind off Omar Khayyám. Though it would serve her right if she ended up as a white slave in some Arabian sheikh's harem. They still have them, you know. Oh, the silly child!"

Another treacherous tear escaped, and she dealt with it briskly.

Paul said, "I suppose he saw he wasn't doing any good here, and he wanted to show his family his watches and his rings and his . . ."

"And his rich girl friend. I think he'll be back pretty soon when the money runs out. He's going to find Isfahan rather dull after seeing all this. Anyway, never mind them. It's the match I'm thinking about."

Paul sat down at the table and put his fingertips together judicially. "Of course, I'd have to look up the F.I.D.E. rules, but I think if one of the players withdraws from a match after only three games, all the scores are cancelled, and I would have to rule a non-match. No prizes would be awarded."

"I don't grudge Carl his money, but Jeff isn't going to have anything. But that's not the point. I've two chess clubs and lots of others here to see a chess match. And now there's no match. We have to find a replacement for Jeff. How about you, Paul?"

Paul stopped being judicial, and panicked. "Oh, I hardly think

I could do that. I'm very short of recent practice. I think you need a more active player to take on Carl Sandbach."

Mrs. Oppenheimer smiled a secret smile and nodded. She had enjoyed that piece of dialogue. "Right, we have to rush a grand-master here as soon as possible. Now who?"

They exchanged possible names. Bobby Fischer? He probably wouldn't come at such short notice, and anyway he would be sure to want an appearance fee. Reshevsky? Probably not available, and anyway he often played a lot of draws. Chaimovitz? He had a job programming the computer at Stanford University. (He had written: "At least it doesn't keep going out and doesn't stink of cologne." Mrs. Oppenheimer had answered: "I hope you pro-gramme it better than you did Jeff.")

She said, "Wait, I have an idea. Why don't we match Carl against the computer itself. That should get the headlines."

"I doubt if you could set it up in time. And, anyway, that's the computer that played the game against the Russian computer. It plays very badly. Real children's chess. Do you remember the game?"

"I heard about it, of course, but I never saw the score. I must have missed that number of *Chess Life*."

"I'll show you," said Paul. "It's only nineteen moves."

He pulled the board on the table towards him and began to set up the pieces. He knew the game by heart; he had written articles about it for all his papers. For the readers of *Chess World,* who would all be delighted to think that they could all play better than a multi-million-dollar computer, he wrote a gleeful piece: "After the dizzy prophecies ten years ago about computer chess, the real-ity came as a sad anticlimax. Perhaps it made the point which chess-players had long ago suspected, that there was more to chess than mathematics and permutations. After all, there was no logical reason why a machine which could prepare bank accounts or book hotel rooms should also automatically be a chess genius." For the readers of *The Statistician,* who would be computer enthusiasts, he wrote more cautiously: "Perhaps the poor showing of these com-puters should not only be blamed on inferior programming but on the inability of computers to recognise and think in terms of pat-terns. Human chess-players were always thinking, sometimes con-sciously, always unconsciously, in terms of evolving patterns." The readers, to judge by subsequent correspondence, were much dismayed.

He had finished setting up the pieces and said, "The Russian computer is White, the American Black." He began to play the game through.

1. P–K4 P–K4 2. N–KB3 N–QB3 3. N–B3 B–B4 4. N x P N x N 5. P–Q4 B–Q3 6. P x N B x P 7. P–KB4 B x Nch 8. P x B N–B3 9. P–K5 N–K5 10. Q–Q3 N–B4.

"Not a very inspiring start," Mrs. Oppenheimer commented.

"Ah, wait till they really start to think."

11. Q–Q5 N–K3 12. P–B5 N–N4 13. P–KR4 P–KB3 14. P x NP x NP 15. R x P R–B1 16. R x P P–B3 17. Q–Q6 R x P 18. R–N8ch R–B1 19. Q x R mate.

"Yes, I see what you mean," she said thoughtfully. "Kids' stuff."

"I doubt if either machine would last ten moves against Carl."

"Maybe it plays better now that Sol is there."

"It's got a long way to go. I gather the M.I.T. one at Cambridge, Massachusetts, is better. It went in for a U.S. Chess Federation Class D tournament, and it actually won one game."

"Yes, h'mmm, but Carl Sandbach isn't a Class D player. He's a grandmaster. Right, we'd better forget about computers. What we need is a real live grandmaster. Who? Larry Evans? Robert Byrne? Benko?"

"Boghossian?"

"Boghossian." They looked at each other and nodded.

"He'll come for the money."

"And I could build up the rivalry between him and Carl, all those games when he beat Carl, that *Time* magazine article. I'll have to call Image & Impact. I wonder where Boghossian is right now. Ed Edmondson will know, I'll call him first. Bless you, Paul, you've been a great help." She blew a kiss at him, dismissing him.

The telephone rang, and Paul waited in case it was something he ought to know about.

"Yes? Yes, Mrs. Oppenheimer speaking. Yes, he's withdrawn from the match and left Miami. Yes, she's gone with him. Of course I'm happy about it. She's a lovely girl and he's a brilliant boy, he should go far. Yes, I know he hadn't been playing very well, but even geniuses sometimes play badly when they're in love.

Yes, I guess it's partly my fault for having my daughter around to take his mind off the games. Well, they've gone to Europe of course, where else. Yes, they'll cable me when they arrive. Yes, of course, I'm arranging for a replacement. I hope to issue a statement later tonight. Yes, certainly I'll keep you in touch. Thank you for calling."

She put down the telephone and looked up.

"They're on the track already. Now that I don't need Jeff any more it looks as if he's going to scoop all the publicity." She grimaced.

Paul said, "I ought to get a cable off to London."

"Better wait till I've fixed it with Boghossian. And, Paul, listen, don't make too much of this Jeff and Moraine business. I mean, it's the chess that's interesting, not that silly girl's love-life."

Paul, walking back to his room, did not agree. The story as he meant to write it would probably make the "People, People, People" column of the *Post*. He found a block of Western Union, and began to draft. It was the first message he had sent to his paper since reaching Miami, the first time there had been anything to say. CHESS GENIUS ELOPES WITH SPONSOR'S DAUGHTER IN HURRICANE. He tore the sheet off and started again. CHESS PRODIGY ELOPES WITH HEIRESS IN HURRICANE. That was better. And Moraine could technically be called an heiress, she would presumably inherit part of her mother's trust in due course. He began writing the full story, only leaving out the suggestion that he should replace Jeff.

Half an hour later he handed in the cable at the front desk and charged it to his room. He didn't feel guilty of a breach of confidence; his first duty was to get the story back, and in any event the whole story would be over Miami in half an hour, if it wasn't already. He went on to the Poodle Room and ordered an extra-dry martini on the rocks. He felt excited, happy, inclined to celebrate. Instead of ten dull games, all won by Carl Sandbach, things were humming. Chess-players were dashing to and fro, hurricanes were blowing, and whatever happened in the end he should get a good story for one of his papers. He looked benignly at the murals of poodles in eighteenth-century human clothes, which normally he found displeasing.

Mrs. Oppenheimer arrived and found him in a sunny mood.

"That's all right, everything's fine. I've talked to Ed, I've talked to Boghossian, he's flying down here either tonight or first thing in the morning, as soon as he can fix it. He's crazy to come. If the airport's shut he's coming by train, and Carl will have to hold things here with simultaneous displays till he gets here."

"That's splendid."

"Yes, it looks as if it's going to work out all right after all. And, to tell the truth, I think Boghossian will be a better opponent for Carl, more experienced, not so easily overawed by the setup. I've spoken to Image & Impact, and they're issuing a press release tonight. They're going to build up the rivalry between the two, you know practically a duel, chess-pieces for two, coffee for one afterwards. Oh, and I called the apartment in New York too, in case Jeff and Moraine were there, but Betty says there's nobody there. Oh yes, a margarita, please," she said to the bartender.

"You've certainly been keeping the lines busy. What have you said to Carl?"

"Carl? Oh yes, maybe it's time he was told something. Can I have the telephone, please, I want to call somebody's room."

She was given the telephone over the bar, and asked for Mr. Sandbach's room. "I don't know the number but it's on the ninth floor like the rest of us." Paul ordered another martini and leant against the cushioned edge of the bar, perched on his stool. Really, American bars were so comfortable, and this wasn't always so in European bars.

"Hello, Carl. Why, how are you?" There was a pause while she listened. "Yes, yes, that's right, they've left Miami, both of them together. Yes that's right, eloped is the word. Listen, why don't you come down and join Paul and me for a drink in the bar, and we'll tell you what's happening. Yes, a drink. What's the name of this bar, Paul? The Poodle Room. Yes, come down and we'll tell you the score."

She handed the telephone back to the bartender and sipped her margarita. "He's heard," she said briefly. "The *Miami Herald* has called him."

The three-piece band arrived and asked her if she would like to request a tune. She looked helplessly at them and gestured at Paul. He asked for "Deh Vieni" from Mozart's *Figaro*.

"I don't think we know that one," the cellist said. He caught the violinist's eye and nodded. They played "Happy Birthday," as they usually did when the customers were awkward. A couple on the other side of the bar smiled at Mrs. Oppenheimer, raising their glasses and toasting the birthday girl. Mrs. Oppenheimer raised her margarita back, and smiled graciously. Paul felt embarrassed.

Carl arrived and folded his long limbs like a deck-chair on to the stool beside them.

"The girl must've gone crazy," he said. "He was obviously doing the right thing, getting out before he was murdered completely. Though maybe he should've stayed till after the halfway mark so as to have the scores validated. But Moraine, what was she doing? She always told me she couldn't stand the feller. Why, she said to me she couldn't stand even the idea of him touching her, even with gloves on, she said."

Mrs. Oppenheimer remarked coolly, "Carl dear, you want to be very careful when girls start saying things like that. It shows which way their minds are working. It shows what they're thinking about."

Carl thought about that. "Yeah . . . yeah, could be. Maybe that's so. Yeah, but Jeff, I mean, he's not . . ." He broke off, uncertain how to put a complex and delicate matter into words which would be acceptable in all circumstances. "I mean, he isn't . . ." He stopped again.

"Oh but he is," said Mrs. Oppenheimer, still very cool. "He is right now, I bet." She looked across the bar corner at Carl without any great friendliness. Paul sipped his martini, thoroughly enjoying the situation. Carl ordered a Seven-Up.

"Tell me, Carl," she asked, "did you and Moraine have a fight recently?"

He searched his memory, and then shook his head. "No. Nothing like that at all. Well, wait a minute, maybe she was a bit irritable last night, or was it the night before. But it didn't mean anything. I mean, girls are often kind of irritable some days, it doesn't mean a thing."

"Funny day to choose to elope," Mrs. Oppenheimer said softly.

Paul chuckled to himself and wondered about a third martini. "And Boghossian," he prompted.

Carl took the news about Boghossian phlegmatically. Sure, he'd be glad to play that little Armenian swindler, anywhere, any time.

Sure, he'd play the rest of the match here against him for the original prize money. He'd a lot of old scores to pay off, though he'd have prepared differently for the match if he had known that he was playing Boghossian.

"So, no doubt, would Boghossian, if he'd known in advance." She patted his arm. "It's sweet of you, Carl, to be so co-operative. We'd have been in a difficult situation otherwise."

"Very sportsmanlike," said Paul, nodding approvingly and signalling the bartender for the third martini.

Boghossian flew in on the last flight to reach Miami before the airport was closed, and Mrs. Oppenheimer and Paul were there to meet him at the airport. It was blowing hard, and raining at intervals.

Mrs. Oppenheimer said, "It's good of you to come and help us out at such short notice."

"Very sportsmanlike," said Paul. "Did you have a good flight?"

"Well, the last part was pretty bumpy. Hurricane Diane, you know." His complexion was even greener than usual.

"Are you going to be all right to play this afternoon?" Paul asked. Mrs. Oppenheimer took her foot off the pedal and kicked him on the ankle.

"Oh yes, I think so. Mustn't disappoint my public. How's Carl Sandbach?"

"Oh, he's fine."

"That news about your daughter, that must have shaken him up."

"Yes, I think it did a bit. But he'll get over it."

"All the same, these things knock you at the time. You don't come round from them immediately."

Paul understood. The psychological approach, always the psychological approach. Carl would be knocked, upset, distracted by Moraine's departure. His heart might be broken. Or his ego wounded. This was the moment to get him to the chess-board, attack him when he would be brooding over his unfaithful girl friend. What was a little airsickness compared with that?

Mrs. Oppenheimer, unwilling to talk about Moraine, talked about Diane instead. "They say the eye of the storm is likely to pass right over us. You suddenly get five or six hours of complete calm, and then the wind starts to blow again, from the opposite direction this time. But, of course, we won't notice anything in the Fontaine Room. We should get a good attendance if nobody can go out. Though we've had pretty good attendances as it is, haven't we, Paul? And very keen, following the games on their own boards."

"Are the scores reported and published?"

"Yes, of course," said Mrs. Oppenheimer and Paul together.

The rain was driving across the road in sheets, and she drove carefully. The wind was strong enough to make the big Lincoln shudder and sway.

"Let's hope there aren't any trees down on the road."

The game started at two-thirty that afternoon. Paul stood on the platform and made a speech. He referred briefly to Jeff Falkner's withdrawal, which they would all have heard about. He went on to say how grateful they were to Grandmaster Boghossian for flying in to replace him at such short notice, and how grateful they all were to Diane for letting him land safely. There was a desultory round of applause, led by Mrs. Oppenheimer, but it petered out rapidly, as Boghossian wasn't present to take a bow. Paul went on to sketch briefly Boghossian's distinguished career, and referred tactfully to the old rivalry between him and Carl Sandbach. "I think," he ended, "we can all look forward to some exciting and memorable games."

Paul felt annoyed. When preparing his few well-chosen words over lunch he had momentarily forgotten that Boghossian would not be there, that he would be introducing a man who hadn't yet turned up. Trying to make a dramatic moment of the start, he picked up two Pawns, one white and one black, and held his fists out at full arm's length to Carl. Carl chose the right hand, the one with the white Pawn.

"Grandmaster Sandbach has the white pieces," Paul announced solemnly. "I am now starting his clock."

He pressed the button on the clock. Carl immediately moved his King's Pawn to K4 and pressed the button, stopping his clock and starting Boghossian's. He noted the move, and then swivelled sideways on his chair, crossed his legs, pulled out his black Knight, and stared into space. Paul went to his desk, and wrote down the

296

move, adding a note: "C.S. usually opens with QP. Is he opening today with KP to prevent J.B. playing the Lugano, as in New York?" Then he too stared into space.

After ten minutes or so the less-dedicated spectators began to drift away, including the local photographer who had wanted to take Carl and Boghossian shaking hands, and was now going to photograph damaged roofs and fallen trees. The man at the end said audibly, "Isn't this just the greatest! First we have two men sitting and not moving, and now we have only one sitting and not moving, and guess what's next!"

Paul and Mrs. Oppenheimer glared at him. Mrs. Oppenheimer said in a stage whisper, "Boghossian's often late for the start, but he catches up later. His clock's ticking."

Boghossian finally arrived eighteen minutes late, shook hands with Paul and Carl, sat down, unscrewed his ball-point and wrote up the score-pad, as if he had all the time in the world. Finally he considered the board and moved out his Queen's Bishop's Pawn. Paul wrote "Sicilian Defence" in his notes.

After a few more moves it became clear that this was the Dragon Variation of the Sicilian. Paul made some more notes. The Dragon was not usually associated with Carl Sandbach, which was presumably why Boghossian had chosen it. He must have been studying it recently, for nobody these days strayed into the theoretical labyrinth of the Dragon without previous preparation in depth. And this was the Dragon at its Dragonest, the massive convolutions of threats and balances coiling round and round the game till even the grandmasters quailed.

On the thirteenth move Boghossian tried the currently fashionable line (13 . . . N–B5 14. B x N R x B 15. N–N3 Q–R3), but he was on dangerous territory. The whole Dragon was dangerous, come to that. He seemed unconcerned, strolling up and down the platform between moves, looking at the game from Carl's side, pulling his nose. But Paul could sense the strain he was under, and he hadn't succeeded in making up the eighteen minutes he had lost at the beginning.

Paul felt sorry for him in a way. Probably at bottom a weaker player than Carl, thirty years older, living on his wits, without money, without a country, having to win his games by devious means and now having to play the Dragon against one of the most formidable positional players in the world. In the circumstances it was an achievement to appear calm and confident. Carl, on the other hand, seemed far from happy, biting his fingers, fiddling with his Knight, crossing and re-crossing his legs. The muscle in his cheek twitched with concentration.

On the nineteenth move Boghossian unloosed his thunderbolt, R x P, sacrificing his Rook to open up the Queen's Bishop's file. It was more usual on the nineteenth move for Black to move his white-square Bishop to B4 where it would threaten White's King. Boghossian's new move, thought Paul, was presumably the product of much midnight analysis, and the reason why he had chosen to play the Dragon today. It remained to be seen if the move was sound. Either way, it was worth discussing in an article, probably in *Chess World*.

Carl thought about the move for thirty-five minutes, and then made a temporising move, a zwischenzug, checking with his Bishop. Boghossian interposed his Knight, and Carl thought about the black Rook for another ten minutes. Finally he accepted the challenge, giving up his Queen for the Rook and the white-square Bishop. The Queen was worth nine Pawns, the Rook and the Bishop together only eight, so that in theory Boghossian had gained a slight advantage. On the other hand, wasn't a Queen less valuable in an end-game than a Rook and a Bishop which could attack from different directions?

The point, however, was only of academic interest, for on the following move Carl unloosed a crushing counter-blow. He advanced his Bishop's Pawn, trapping Boghossian's remaining Bishop in the middle of the board. Paul speculated much later, both verbally and in articles, how Boghossian could have let himself get into such a position. In the excitement of winning Carl's Queen, had he not noticed that his Bishop had no square to move to, if it should be attacked? Perhaps it was sheer fatigue after the flight and the rush from New York.

In addition to trapping the Bishop, Carl was threatening a Knight fork against Boghossian's Queen and other Rook. Boghossian abandoned the Bishop, and moved the Rook out of danger. But he was now completely on the defensive, trying to defend with Queen and Rook against a heavy attack by two Rooks and two Knights. He struggled on for another five moves, and then resigned.

298

There was a good deal of applause, for Carl was popular with the audience, and even the inexpert felt sympathy with him for the way his girl had abandoned him. Carl ignored the applause and played through the crux of the game again with Boghossian, discussing it with him; two grandmasters analysing a game which might have been played by two other players. Some of the keen young men who had been watching came up and tried to join in. One of them produced a copy of *Chess Informator* from a brief-case, and Carl slipped quietly away, leaving Boghossian at bay. These clever young men were capable of analysing the game all night.

He nodded to Paul, and went to talk to Mrs. Oppenheimer.

"Well, I made it!" he exclaimed triumphantly. "After all those games he swindled me, I beat him. Fair and square. No tricks, no swindling, just plain chess, how it should be."

"Yes, you played pretty well, Carl. Interesting game."

"And know something? I'm going to win all the other games too. However late he turns up for the start."

"You do just that." Maybe she could get *Time* magazine to write another piece on Carl and Boghossian. She would call Image & Impact right away.

Carl looked round for Moraine to accompany him to the coffee-shop, but he suddenly remembered that she had gone. He went down alone to the coffee-shop, folded himself on to a stool at the counter, and ordered coffee and a bagel with lox. He felt triumphant. After Mar del Plata, Bled, Montreal and New York, now at last that little Armenian had had his comeuppance. It had been a long time coming, but it had come at last. And I'll do it again tomorrow, he thought. He turned, smiling happily, to share the moment with Moraine on the next stool, and found she wasn't there.

Normally he would have gone to her room after this, or maybe they'd have gone for a drive together. Well, he could still go for a drive, it was one of the best ways of unwinding after a hard game. He signed his bill and went up to the lobby and ordered his Thunderbird to be brought to the door.

"You want to be careful a night like this," said the bellhop. "It's a bad night for driving. There may be some trees down."

"I'll be careful," said Carl. "I'm not going far. Just to another hotel."

He climbed in, pressing the buttons to make sure all the windows were securely shut. He turned the windshield-wipers to their fastest, and switched off the radio which Moraine had left on last time she was in the car. He eased down on to Collins Avenue.

The headlights tunnelled through the curtains of rain, and the wind buffeted and shook the car. This was no night for speeding. Last week he had done a hundred on this strip, with Moraine beside him, but today thirty or forty would be quite enough. The tyres hissed through the water.

Boghossian's nineteenth move had been interesting. Rook takes Pawn. He had refuted it, true, but that didn't necessarily mean that it was unsound. He would have to analyse it in much greater depth. If Boghossian had kept his Bishop out of trouble, kept it on N2 where it belonged, maybe the Rook move would have given him a clear advantage. But he would need to have his Queen more actively placed, to support the break-through on the Bishop's file. A Rook, Queen and Bishop attack on White's QB2 might be decisive. In that case White ought not to castle Queen's side. Unnoticed, the luminous line was creeping across the speedometer, the car was gaining speed.

Suddenly Diane unloosed a savage right hook between the Singapore and Americana hotels, spinning the Thunderbird round as if it were on ice. Still thinking about the Dragon, Carl fought with the skid, pulling the wheel round. The last thing he saw in the blur of the headlights was the concrete lamp standard, like a huge modern white King.

MOSCOW

At the back of the stage of the Estrada Variety Theatre was a shabby grey curtain, and pinned to it the blue F.I.D.E. flag. Below it, pinned to the curtain rather unevenly, were letters proclaiming in Russian MATCH FOR THE CHAMPIONSHIP OF THE WORLD. On either side of the stage were big demonstration boards, manned by enthusiastic boys. At a desk to one side, behind their national flags, were the two umpires, Hansgeorg Stuck of Germany and Harry Golombek of Britain. In the front of the stage, in the middle, was the chess-board, and on either side of it the two players, World Champion Toklovsky and ex-World Champion Mischchov.

Paul sat in the middle of the ninth row, watching, taking notes. Somewhere on the left he had caught a glimpse of his colleague, Leonard Barden of the *Guardian*. On the stage was his colleague Harry Golombek of *The Times*. Paul felt a twinge of envy every time he caught his eye. He would have liked to be an umpire as well as a correspondent. He enjoyed sitting on platforms, giving difficult rulings, granting the players permission to agree an early draw. But there it was, he was not an international master and could not hope for that. But, all the same, it was pleasant to be here in any capacity; still better to be here as the honoured correspondent of one of the world's great newspapers.

Could it really be three years since he had last been here? It seemed only last week. And nothing seemed to have changed. It was the same theatre, the same crowd, the same players, the same chilly draught blowing from the ventilators on the front of the balcony, the same masks and figures above the proscenium opening. Of course, there were slight differences. Then Mischchov had been the champion and Toklovsky the challenger. Stahlberg of Sweden had been one of the umpires instead of Hansgeorg Stuck. The openings too had changed; then it had been mostly the Queen's Gambit Accepted and the Caro-Kann; this time, so far, it seemed to be more the Ruy Lopez and the French Defence. But the differences were minor, and Paul himself didn't feel a day older. Really, it might have been last week.

And yet a lot had happened since he has last been here. Thousands of games had been played, bright young talents had flowered and faded, brilliant young players had fallen by the wayside, middle-aged players had studied and prepared and trained for one more great effort, older players had summoned their strength and courage for one last come-back. And it had all been in vain. It had all ended once more with Mischchov playing Toklovsky for the World Championship. Some day, Paul thought, it's bound to be different. There'll be an American or a German or a Yugoslav or a Brazilian, or even just conceivably an Englishman, up there on the stage playing the great match. And I, he thought, happily, will be here to report it.

Indeed, he had spotted a possible candidate this year at Bognor: Peter Granville, a Marlborough boy, with plenty of natural talent, polite, articulate, good-looking, and dedicated to chess. With more experience and encouragement he might go a long way, perhaps even to the top. Paul had given his Bognor performance a good write-up in all his papers and hoped he would get into the team for this year's Student International. The boy needed international experience. Pity he couldn't be here to watch this match and learn about the Russian character. Paul had written to him only yesterday, a nice long letter giving him the Moscow picture and answering some technical points he'd raised arising from Paul's book *The Early Middle-Game*. He'd probably get an answer next week.

However Peter Granville's possible achievements were all in the future. In the meantime he had to consider and write about the present match. Toklovsky, being a local man, had greater support in the audience than Mischchov who came from Leningrad. On the other hand most people, though they cheered and clapped him, felt that Toklovsky would soon lose his crown. The depression, the lethargy in his play, which had been so noticeable in Blackpool, was still there. It was not that he was playing badly, but that the fire, the brilliance had gone. "I do not play like Toklovsky any more," he had remarked sadly to Golombek last week. "I have forgotten how Toklovsky plays." Paul had immediately telephoned the conversation through to the sports editor in London.

Toklovsky was already one point down. Five games had been played so far. He had lost one, three were drawn, and one adjourned. The adjourned game was meant to have been played off last night at the Central Chess Club on Gogolevsky Boulevard. But when the umpires came to open the sealed move, they found that they could not read the writing. Toklovsky had moved his King—but to which square? It was impossible to tell. Obviously they could not ask him. He must not be given the opportunity of revising his overnight move in the light of further analysis. A long discussion developed. Was it the duty of the umpires to choose the move which he had probably intended, to try to find out his intention? Or to choose the best move? Or the worst? Was the match being played under special match rules or under normal F.I.D.E. rules? In the middle Mischchov put forward a new point. Since the written move was illegible, it was therefore cancelled, and the umpires were therefore entitled to choose any legal move for Toklovsky. It did not have to be a King move, it could be a Rook or a Pawn move. The point was academic and of theological subtlety, and Mischchov made it again and again and again. Finally, after two hours, it was agreed to refer the whole matter by telegram to the President of F.I.D.E. in Stockholm. Paul felt cross. He had wasted a whole evening, and he could have been at the Bolshoi watching *Swan Lake*.

He hoped that today's game would not be adjourned too, as

he wanted to go to the Bolshoi again tomorrow night. Vishnevskaya in *Aïda*! He could hardly go if there were a tense endgame in progress. At the moment the players were locked in a complicated middle-game, and it was impossible to tell the outcome, except that it was going to be either a draw or a long game, or both.

Mischchov had opened with the King's Pawn, and Toklovsky had replied with his King's Pawn. The game was a Ruy Lopez, and the spectators were very quiet. Every seat was taken and the players, almost entirely men, were following the game on pocket boards, and mumbling amongst themselves. On the ninth move Mischchov moved his King's Rook's Pawn to R3, switching the game into the Smyslov Variation. There was a hum of interest round the theatre. On the fifteenth move Toklovsky played his Queen's Pawn to Q4, and everyone became very excited. On the eighteenth move Mischchov counter-attacked with his Rook, and the tension became unendurable. Everyone was discussing the position with neighbours, with more distant friends, calling out advice, moves, variations to the players. The noise was tremendous, and the spectators were on the move now edging in and out of their seats on their way to and from the lavatories, discussing the position in the aisles, in the doorways. Mischchov glared at the spectators and said "Ssshh!" Golombek flashed the sign calling for silence.

It was all a very long way from the hush of Bognor or Blackpool or even Miami. Paul was reminded of a Spanish bullfight or of descriptions of a football match, though he had not seen one himself. His neighbour, a keen supporter of Toklovsky, was shouting out moves and variations. On his knees was a folding chess-board, with full-sized pieces set out in the current position. In his excitement he closed his knees, the board folded, and all the pieces slid on to the floor under the seats. He was temporarily silenced by having to go down on his hands and knees and pick them up. Paul forbore to help him. But the others went on talking and eventually a strange man appeared on the stage and announced that he would have to clear the theatre if there was any more noise.

After that things were quieter, especially during the fifth hour when it became clear that the game would be adjourned. Paul sighed. Goodbye, Aïda, he thought, farewell, Vishnevskaya. Still, Friday was scheduled as a free day, and he would be able to go to the Bolshoi then. After the fortieth move, when Hansgeorg Stuck produced the envelope for the sealed move, the spectators went away, pouring through the doors and down the stairs, queuing for their coats, glancing only briefly at a simultaneous display being given by some minor master in the entrance hall.

Paul went with them. He had glanced round for Barden, but there was no point in waiting for Golombek who would have to wait till the sealed move was finally sealed. Outside in the chilly Moscow night he walked briskly along the river, looking for a taxi. On the bridge a stranger stopped him and asked what had happened in the game. Paul guessed what he was being asked, and answered "Adjourned," one of his few words of Russian.

Across the river he plunged into the metro. There was no other way of getting home, except walking. The Moscow metro, for all its vaunted beauty, depressed him. There was no gaiety, no advertising, no smell of the Paris metro. It was like going through one neo-Egyptian mausoleum after another. But he felt comforted when he finally reached the Metropole Hotel. The marble pillars, the potted palms, the old-fashioned comfort reassured him. Communists and chess-players might come and go, but Metropole Hotels went on for ever.

It was after nine, and he was hungry. But he went first to the desk to see if any letters had come on the afternoon flight from London. There might be a letter from Peter. There were, in fact, three letters for him: one was from his publisher, one was an airletter in Joann Oppenheimer's handwriting, and one a packet in an unknown hand with a Manchester postmark. There was nothing from Peter. No doubt there would be next week, when he had had Paul's letter.

The dining-room was crowded, but the head waiter recognised him and led him to a small table beside a column facing the central fountain and the band. The English-speaking waitress arrived, placed a small Union Jack on his table, and took his order. He ordered a hundred (A hundred of what? Centigrams? Millilitres?) of vodka with his caviar and four hundred of Georgian wine with his chicken cutlets. Then he settled in to read his letters.

He opened the one from his publisher first. It was from the edi-

305

torial director and told him that they were publishing his new book *The Early End-Game* on the 15th July in exactly the same format and style as his earlier book *The Early Middle-Game,* which they would be republishing on the same date. He hoped that the public would consider them as a pair, and buy both at once. The way was obviously open for him to write a further book in the series, perhaps on the later end-game, and he would like Paul's comments on this.

The next paragraph was not about chess. "I am wondering how your travel book about the great squares of the world is coming on, and hope you are making good progress with it. I feel this is a book you could do very well and, as I mentioned when you first put the idea forward, it could well prove popular, attracting the travel-book public in addition to your normal chess-playing readers. I don't wish to press you, of course, but we are at the moment preparing our future publishing programme, and it would be a great help to us if you could give me some idea of when we may expect to receive the finished manuscript."

Paul sat back and sipped his vodka. He watched the dancing, the women in their dowdy dresses, the old-fashioned fox-trots, the timelessness of it all. He felt good. His publisher wanted two books from him, was almost pressing him to produce his travel book. A slight qualm punctured his happiness. It was almost two years since he had first had the idea of the book about squares, since he had suggested the book to his publishers. They were assuming that it was almost finished, and he hadn't yet written a word of it. Of course, these things couldn't be produced overnight; the book needed much background research. All the same, he must do something about it soon. Perhaps he would begin it as soon as he got home from Moscow. He might get several chapters, several squares done before the flood of summer chess congresses began to take up his time. And he would be able to report that he was making good progress with the book.

He finished his caviar and slit open Joann Oppenheimer's letter. He had heard nothing from her for a long time now, indeed nothing since their rather dismal goodbye last year in Miami. He had sent her a copy of the last article he wrote for *New Princess,* his noble elegy on Carl Sandbach ("The James Dean of American chess. Like his famous compatriot he symbolised the brilliance and the restlessness of modern youth, and he expressed their dreams and their frustrations in his art and in his genius. Like James Dean, he sought to console himself in the love of girls who brought him easement for a while and then reopened his wounds in abandoning him; and in fast cars which led him, perhaps willingly, perhaps inevitably, to a tragic youthful death.") Joann had not answered or acknowledged, but perhaps she had been away and never received it.

She was writing now from Acapulco, and sounded in excellent spirits. She had discovered a new chess genius, an illiterate Mexican called Jesus-Maria, and she foresaw a great future for him as he was brilliant in positional play as well as in combinative. She planned to bring him to New York and have him taught English and the openings by someone like Boghossian. Most of the letter was the score of a game he had won against her.

Paul didn't play through the score in his mind; it could wait till later. But he smiled. Dear Joann! Always the same. He would write and tell her about Peter. Perhaps the two boys would play each other in some future Student International.

Mrs. Oppenheimer ended with a paragraph of personal news. "Moraine has a daughter called Jasmin—I guess she'll change that when she's older. She has dark eyes and big black eyebrows like Farah or Liz Taylor, so I suppose she'll be a beauty later on. Jeff is working as a trainee in the Investment Analysis branch of the First National City Bank, so he may end up looking after my shares. Walter arranged the interview for him, but do you know what clinched it? It was when they found he had won the Manhattan Rapid Transit tournament. They decided he must have brains. Right! If only he'd devoted them to chess! Walt is engaged to a nice but rather dumb girl from Boston, and Walter is rumoured to be courting a blonde widow. So it's wedding-bells all over. I'm planning to be in London this fall, and hope to see you then. Love, Joann."

Paul thought, Is she hinting that I ought to marry her, to get things really tidy? He chuckled at the idea, since it was so obviously out of the question. Though it would be nice to have her trust fund behind him, and now that she was a grandmother . . .

He had been opening the packet from Manchester and a tape cassette, the same make as his own pocket machine, fell out on to the table. With it was a covering letter in a sloping handwriting on lined paper from 340 Boothfield Road, Wythenshawe, Lancashire. Paul sighed. Another clever young grammar schoolboy trying to catch him out in some analysis.

Dear Sir,

I hope you do not mind me writing to you, but we have been having some trouble at home lately. My son Robin tried to commit suicide last night. His mother and I were out at a Labour Club meeting and when we got home we smelt the gas at once. I went up at once to his room and found him unconscious on the bed. I immediately turned off the gas-fire and opened the windows and then telephoned for an ambulance. I saw the lad in hospital today and am glad to say he seems quite alright and the doctors say he is out of danger, but it has been a great shock to us and his mother is now under the doctor. He was dictating a message to you on his little tape recorder and he had also written a note saying it was to be sent to you, so I enclose it herewith. As the tape is his property, would you kindly send it back when you have heard it.

The trouble was the lad was very depressed at hearing he had failed his "A" levels (for the second time) and not being able to go now to University. If you ask me, the trouble was too much chess. It was just chess, chess all day and night when he ought to have been working for his exams. I often said to him, that's a silly way to spend your time, but he wouldn't listen to me. And it's not as if he was so bright at chess either. I'd say to him, what sort of a life's that? But he wouldn't listen to me, and his mother thought it was alright. If you ask me, the real people to blame are you and Hammond at his school who encouraged the lad to play chess all the time when he ought to have been studying for his exams. I think it was a sad day for us when you first met him at Blackpool and gave him big ideas about chess.

I hope you do not mind me writing to you but we Lancashire folk believe in saying what we mean plainly.

Yours very truly,

F. A. Jackson

A man was standing beside him, saying in English, "Excuse me, may I sit at your table?"

308

Paul shuffled away the letters and made a welcoming gesture. "Of course, do sit down."

The man sat down and said, "I see from the flag that you are English. I have studied English conversation and I like to talk with Englishmen whenever I can."

"I like to talk with Russians," Paul said politely. The man was ordering in Russian from the waitress. Paul thought, Why do they have to blame it all on me? What did I ever do except give the boy some encouragement and publicity when he wanted it? And I got him into the student team. It wasn't my fault if he fluffed his chances. I know he wasn't as good as we all hoped he was, but it was worth a try. And now they're blaming me. Well, I suppose they've got to find someone to blame.

"Are you an engineer?"

Paul started. "Me? No. I am a writer."

The man's eyes gleamed behind their glasses. "I am a writer too."

"What sort of things do you write?"

"I am a poet and a philosopher."

"You are at the university?"

"No, I am a poet and philosopher."

"In England we do not think that they are at all the same thing. What sort of philosophy do you write?" Paul asked, trying to remember what he had read about logical positivism.

"I write Marxist-Leninist philosophy."

"Ah yes, of course. I write travel-books about foreign cities. I am now collecting material for a chapter about Moscow."

"You are writing about Moscow? You are going to write about the Soviet triumphs in modern technology?"

"Well, no, not exactly. More about Russian history." There was a short silence. "I also write about chess. I am reporting the match between Toklovsky and Mischchov."

The man nodded. It seemed he was one of the few Muscovites uninterested in chess.

Paul thought, The boy was a born failure from the start. He did no good last year either at Blackpool or in the Lancashire Junior. He failed badly at Munich, his big chance. He failed his "A" levels twice. Even if he got to university he'd have been a failure there too. He couldn't even succeed in killing himself.

And now they all had to find someone to blame for his failures. Anybody except the boy himself.

The waitress brought Paul's four hundred of Georgian wine, a glass carafe containing a brown liquid. Paul felt that he needed a drink, poured himself half a glass and took a gulp. He choked. The thing was neat brandy.

He mopped his eyes and worked out what had happened. The poet-philosopher must have ordered four hundred of brandy, and Paul had helped himself by mistake. He apologised to the man.

"Please," the man said courteously. He picked up the carafe and filled Paul's glass to the brim. He then filled his own, raised his glass, and toasted Paul. Paul sipped cautiously back. He had not intended to drink neat brandy with his chicken cutlets, but now there seemed no getting away from it.

"What sort of poetry do you write?" he asked.

"Patriotic poetry," the man said.

"Ah yes, of course."

The waitress brought another carafe of brown liquid and put it on the table. "Is this my wine?" he asked.

She smiled and said yes. But there was now no glass to put it in, not until he had finished the brandy.

Another man was standing beside him, speaking to him in Russian. Not understanding, he looked at the philosopher-poet for help.

"He asks if he may join us at our table. He sees you are English and he is learning English. He hopes you may help him to speak the words."

Paul smiled, his heart sinking, and waved the man to a seat. The man, who was short and stocky, spoke to the philosopher-poet. He produced a Russian-English dictionary and showed it to Paul.

"He says he is learning all the words in the dictionary. Every time he has to wait for a bus or a metro train he learns some more words, but he does not know how to speak them."

"Wouldn't he do better to learn a phrase book by heart?"

The man opened the dictionary and pointed out a word to Paul.

"Alpaca," Paul pronounced. "Al-pa-ca. But it isn't a word we use very often."

The man repeated "Al-pa-ca" and turned to speak to the waitress. Paul thought, It wasn't I who introduced him to chess. I didn't teach him the moves or start his school chess club. I didn't persuade him to sit up all night playing postal chess. All I did was give him a write-up when he had his one success, and get him his trip to Munich. And now it's all my fault.

The dictionary was in front of his face again. "Alphabet," he pronounced. "Alph-a-bet."

"Alph-a-bet."

"Yes, that's right."

The waitress brought a bottle of Caucasus champagne, and three glasses. The bottle was opened, the glasses filled, and the English student raised his glass in a toast. Heavens, thought Paul, I shall be under the table soon. There was a singing in his ears already.

He looked at the dictionary held out to him. "Already," he said with conscious clarity. "All-red-y."

And as for trying to commit suicide, what a show-off, self-pitying thing to do. Just trying to make himself important. He had probably calculated that his parents would be home in time to save him. And as for recording a long dying speech—Paul glanced at the cassette in distaste.

"Also. All-so." It did not seem that the stocky man had got very far through the dictionary. Perhaps you didn't have to wait long for buses and metro trains in Moscow.

"Altar. All-ter. Please tell our friend that I am a well-known writer in England and that I am going to write about Moscow in my new book."

The message was passed on and the stocky man smiled and refilled Paul's champagne glass. Paul passed him the carafe of Georgian wine and said, "Won't you please have some of my wine?" The man gave a little bow and added some wine to his champagne. He passed the dictionary again to Paul.

"Altercation. All-ter-cay-shun."

And I am a well-known writer, and I am going to write about Moscow. And what's more, the first chapter is going to be about Moscow, Red Square. And I'll write it while I'm here, while I've still got the whole atmosphere in my mind. I'll start it tomorrow. I'll have the whole day. There's no chess tomorrow till six in the evening.

"Alternate. All-turn-et."

The singing in his ears was louder when he finally got to his room. But he was walking steadily, and he said good night clearly in Russian to the woman sitting at her desk in the passage. He felt tempted to ask her if she sat there twenty-four hours a day or if she had a twin sister who sat there the other twelve hours. But, fortunately perhaps, his Russian wasn't good enough.

In his room he suddenly felt the urge to start his new book there and then, while the mood was upon him. He sat down at the table, took the cover off his Olivetti, and looked in the drawer for typing paper. Or perhaps it would be better left till tomorrow. It was always a mistake mixing drinks like that, even if it wasn't done on purpose.

He picked up the letter from his publisher and read it through again, smiling. It was going to be a good book, a big seller, but having waited two years already, it could wait one more night. He read through Joann's letter again, smiling, but he didn't feel like playing through the Mexican boy's game tonight. That too could wait till tomorrow. He read through Mr. Jackson's letter again, smiling rather grimly. Really, it would be comic, if it wasn't so pathetic. Out of curiosity he put the tape cassette on to his own Grundig, and moved the red button to "Playback."

Nothing came out at all. Paul backtracked for half a minute and tried again. This time a voice emerged, unintelligible, un-recognisable. He backtracked to the start of the tape and started from the beginning.

This time the voice was clear and loud, though he would never have recognised it as Robin's, apart from the occasional flat vowel.

"Well, Paul, I don't expect you ever expected to hear my voice again. And after the way you cut me dead at the last Blackpool, I don't think you ever wanted to. But here I am like a bad penny, still alive and kicking, for the next few minutes at least. After that you won't hear any more from me, and you'll be able to say Thank God for that. I've shut the windows and filled in the cracks round them with cotton wool, and I've put a blanket at the bottom of the door, so everything's snug in here. Mum and Dad are out at a Labour Club meeting, and I don't think anyone'll come to disturb us.

"Well, Paul, this is it. This is where it all leads. I've failed my 'A' levels for the second time and that means I can't ever now go to university. Dad just kept on saying, Too much bloody chess, lad, it's daft to spend so much time on a bloody game, unless you're going to be bloody pro. That's the way he talks, that's how they all talk round here. But you wouldn't know, you've never seen the way we live. You've never been near a place like Wythenshawe, you and your operas and art galleries. What was I saying? Oh yes, I was spending too much bloody time on chess. And who was it who encouraged me to do that? You, and one or two others. Hammond at school. Pearson at Blackpool. And you know damn well what happened. You saw my scores at the last Blackpool and in Lancashire Junior. And when I turned out not to be so bloody marvellous after all, do you know who were the first people to drop me? You, wonderful you, and Pearson, and even Hammond. He demoted me from being captain of the school team. All the rats leaving the sinking ship. God, that gas is beginning to smell to high heaven. And that's where I shall be by the time you listen to this. There, or the other place down below. That's meant to be a joke, so have a good laugh, Paul. It's on me.

"What was I saying? Oh yes. Well, Paul, this is the end of the line. Chess has ruined my life. Do you hear that, Paul? I'll say it again loud and clear. Chess has ruined my life. God, I'm beginning to feel a bit swimmy, but I've probably got another fifteen or twenty minutes left, and I'd like to tell you something about chess. And about me, and life, and youth, and ambitions that go wrong. A few home truths for you, Paul. And I know you'll understand if my voice gets a bit funny before the end. After all, you've got this coming to you yourself some day. Never thought of that before, have you?

"What was I saying? Oh yes, Paul, about you and me, about the way you took me up . . ."

Paul switched off the recorder. That was quite enough of that. Just one long whine of self-pity. Facetious too. How could an intelligent boy be so awful! He backtracked the tape to the start, and took it out of the machine. Tomorrow he would post it back with a cool note saying he was sorry to hear that Robin had failed his exams again but was glad to hear he was now recovering from his recent illness. Or perhaps accident was the word.

In the meantime he had other things to think about. *Sixty-Four Squares*. Perhaps that wasn't the right title, but it was obviously important to keep the connection with chess, even if the book never mentioned a game or a player. That was something he could discuss with his publishers when the book was finished. In the meantime, Chapter One, here we come! Red Square!

He undressed and got into bed. The universe hardly swayed round him and he fell asleep immediately.

He awoke next morning, with the sun shining in, and he was immediately alert, confident, no trace of a hangover. This was the big day. He reread his publishers' letter once more while he dressed, said good morning in Russian to the woman at her desk in the passage, and had a big breakfast in the *kaphe* downstairs. Then he set out for a last look at Red Square, to check the details.

The air was cool and fresh, and he walked along, whistling an air from *Eugene Onegin,* up the gentle rise, into the huge square. There was the usual endless queue of people waiting to see Lenin's face. He had never had the great experience, but then he had never felt able to face the four hours' shuffling forward in a line to see someone who was possibly now only a waxwork. And there was no moment of the day or night, as far as he could discover, when the queue was not at least four hours long. Three years ago, coming out of the Kremlin at midnight after a ballet performance in the Palace of Congresses, he had thought that he would slip in quickly on his way home. But even at midnight the queue had still stretched away across Red Square, between the Kremlin walls and the museum, round the corner, out of sight, interminable, infinite.

He thought now that he ought really to make the effort, see the face, before writing his chapter on Red Square. How could one write about Red Square without having seen inside the mausoleum? Or, alternatively, couldn't one write amusingly about the impossibility of getting inside to see the famous face, the embalmed flesh? Undecided, he wandered into the Kremlin.

He had always enjoyed the Kremlin, the clusters of golden domes, the painted cathedrals, the wonderful St. Michael in the Archangel Cathedral, the icons in the Cathedral of the Annunciation, the treasure—those gold ornaments, those jewels! One of the good things about reporting a chess match in Moscow was that the mornings were free. He resolutely dodged the tours that Intourist pressed on him, the conducted visits to technological museums and parks of achievement, the tours of the Moscow metro, visiting every single station. But it was another thing to be able to wander through the Kremlin cathedrals and the treasure-house. Or to go to the Tretyakov Gallery, and look at the Rublev icons; and when icons palled, as they often did, to shiver with *schadenfreude* in front of the battle-pictures, those disembowelled horses bleeding all over the corpses. Best of all, perhaps, and most calming, was to go to the Pushkin Museum and soak in the French Impressionists, back in the comprehensible Western world of rivers and sky and people and food and wine. Perhaps he would go there again tomorrow morning.

He spent longer than he meant in the Kremlin, and it was late when he finally strolled out into Red Square. The queue for Lenin's Tomb still stretched out of sight, and he was still undecided how to handle this in his book. And the great event of Red Square, the May Day parade, he had never seen. He looked round uncertainly. Across the square was the huge unshapely mass of the GUM department store. On the right, beside the Kremlin towers, were the gaudy onion-domes of St. Basil's, looking just how they looked in every travel poster. What was he to write about this square?

Suddenly the inspiration came to him. He wouldn't write about this square at all. He would write about Sverdlov Square. Much more unusual, personal, interesting. His own hotel, the Metropole with its Edwardian comfort and its celebrated guests; the Bolshoi with its memories of Chaliapin, Diaghilev, Nijinsky, Vishnevskaya; the old walls of Moscow at the end; the modern metro station. That should make an interesting and evocative chapter.

He crossed the square warily to the GUM store and went inside. He felt in the mood to buy himself a present, to mark this auspicious day, but the inside was, as always, daunting; the huge crowds, the noise, the impossibility of finding one's way about. It was like being in an oriental market enclosed in a giant conservatory. The crowds poured up and down the iron staircases, looking at the booths and alcoves, examining those ghastly shoes, fingering those terrible flannel shirts. Paul wandered up and down unhappily, telling himself about the magic of bazaars, looking for something which he could not buy better and more cheaply in London. Finally he bought himself a pair of amber cuff-links. These at least were totally Russian, and could be worn and shown with pride in Kensington. Feeling satisfied, he worked his way through to the cool air of Red Square, and walked home. As he crossed Sverdlov Square he thought, This will make a fine Chapter One. This was the place, this was the day.

The Metropole restaurant was crowded, as always, but Paul spotted an empty chair. Golombek, Barden and Hansgeorg Stuck were lunching together, and Paul asked if he might join them. They were finishing their lunch, but Paul explained that he was often late for lunch in Moscow. Once he got inside those Kremlin cathedrals, looking at those paintings, he always forgot the time. The others nodded in polite agreement.

It was the first time he had seen Hansgeorg in Moscow, to speak to. During the past week they had only exchanged a few words about chess in the Central Chess Club. Now he felt that something more personal was called for. He reminded Hansgeorg of the last time that they had met, in Munich, the occasion of Hansgeorg's return to the world of chess.

"I remember."

Paul recalled the night in the Hofbräuhaus, when Ursula Stuck had been in the party. "Is your wife here in Moscow?" he asked.

"No."

Barden kicked him on the ankle, and when Paul caught his eye, shook his head. Paul got the message. He was not expected to talk about Ursula Stuck. Hansgeorg's marriage was clearly in a mess.

Paul rallied brightly and told them all about the letter from his publisher, the book he was just about to start about the cities and squares of the world.

He ordered a bottle of champagne from the waitress. "This calls for a celebration," he said. "We must launch the ship properly."

The others demurred, but he pressed them, and finally they each accepted a small glass. He told them about his book, about the squares and the cities he would be bringing to life. They listened politely, and finally they rose and left, wishing him good luck with his book. They had, they explained, things to do, people to see, articles to write.

Paul was left alone with two-thirds of a bottle of champagne. It was rather sweet for his taste, but he finished it without difficulty, thinking about the book and the afternoon ahead, savouring the moment. Then he finished his coffee, made sure that the bottle was really empty, and left the restaurant.

He called first at the Intourist Service Bureau to make sure that they had his ticket for the Bolshoi on Friday night. He bought a copy of the *Daily Worker* at the news-stand, wishing once again that the *Post* or any other British paper were available. Then he called at the desk to see if there was a letter from Peter, but the air-mail from England was not yet in. Finally he went to his room, giving a cheery good afternoon in Russian to the woman sitting at her desk in the passage.

This was, he calculated, his tenth book. His books so far must total about half a million words, all published between hard covers. His journalism, his articles, perhaps added up to another half-million. Perhaps less. All in all he could say that he had had a million words, or getting on for a million words, printed. And yet he felt as excited as if he were a child writing a poem, an undergraduate starting his first novel. He rolled a sheet of paper into the typewriter, and began to type.

Three hours later he abandoned the book. The waste-paper basket was full of crumpled partly typed sheets. During the past hour it had become slowly and painfully clear to him that he couldn't write a travel-book, that he couldn't write about anything except chess and chess-players.

He sat staring at the wall, not seeing it, watching the dream melt like smoke. One day when I have the time, he had told himself, I shall write travel-books, critical works, biographies, novels, perhaps even poetry, plays. And now the moment had come, and he could write nothing that measured to the required standard. He could report a game of Mischchov's, analyse it in the most expert way, he could write an emotional piece about Robin or Carl. But how to evoke Sverdlov Square to someone who had never been there? How to write something deeper than easy-to-read journalism? How to get to the heart of the matter?

Chess has ruined my life; somebody had said that to him recently. Who? It didn't matter. Why did he think that it was the others who were always the victims? Why did he imagine that he and he alone could tame and ride the dragon, and return unscathed? What, at last, of Paul Butler himself?

If I hadn't become infatuated, obsessed, he thought bitterly, if I had let my literary talents grow in normal ways, I might now be a famous writer, a great novelist. Chess has ruined my life. Tears of misery welled into his eyes, and he wiped them away with a handkerchief.

Half an hour later his self-confidence made its come-back. What was so inadequate about being a writer of chess books? What was so second-rate about writing expert books on a specialised yet universal subject? Did every writer have to be a travel-writer, a biographer, a novelist? Was there no room in literature for the specialist? Wasn't this what modern learning was all about, the in-depth thesis on a strictly limited subject? Wasn't he right in line with current university thought? Not that chess was a limited subject. In its principles and its repercussions it embraced the whole world.

And chess had not ruined his life. He had done a great deal for chess, and chess in return had done much for him. I have a splendid life, he thought. Here I am in Moscow, writing articles that will be read by hundreds of thousands of people. Do I have to be a travel-writer or a novelist as well? He looked at his amber cuff-links for reassurance.

It was time he went down to watch the adjourned game at the Central Chess Club. He put the cover on his typewriter, stood up and stretched himself. In the passage outside he smiled at the woman sitting at her desk. But as he waited for the lift, he felt the feeling of defeat, like a gallon of cold water inside him. The champagne sparkle had gone.

But down on Gogolevsky Boulevard everything was all right. The fine old house was still there with its elegant rooms and their egg-plant friezes. There were portraits of former champions on the walls, and on the tables were chess-boards, chessmen, chess-clocks. Hundreds of people were present, all drawn by the one enthralling purpose.

This is the real society of genius, Paul thought. This is the club with the highest I.Q. in the world. And this is where I am proud to belong.

He moved round the rooms greeting his friends, grandmasters, colleagues. He waved at Hansgeorg Stuck, smiled at Barden.

"How did the book go?" Golombek asked politely.

"Oh quite well, I think. Quite well."

He moved on, chatting to Grandmasters Flohr and Keres, having a word with B. H. Wood, shaking hands with ex-World Champions Mischchov and Tal. When World Champion Toklovsky arrived for his game, Paul, smiling happily, was the first to step forward and greet him.